# THE CABIN AT THE TRAIL'S END

By SHEBA HARGREAVES

*A STORY OF OREGON*

*BINFORDS & MORT, Publishers*

PORTLAND, OREGON

# ACKNOWLEDGMENT

THE assistance of Nellie B. Pipes, Librarian, Oregon Historical Society; E. Ruth Rockwood, Head of Reference Department, Library Association of Portland, Oregon; and Alfred Powers, Dean of the Extension Division, University of Oregon—is acknowledged with gratitude.

# FOREWORD

Although it has been attempted in a hundred ways by as many authors, the story of the Oregon Trail still looms as a mighty canvas upon which the individual narrative stands forth merely as a clump of sage or pillar of dust boldly etched against an immense and shadowy background.

When it is remembered that in the Great Migration of '43, for example, more than eight hundred men, women and children pushed westward across a relatively unexplored segment of the continent with their plodding wagons, and that during the next three decades upwards of thirty thousand people followed the trail thus boldly blazed, some notion of the complexity of its individual human dramas begins to take form.

Many writers have depicted the epic sweep of that westward march, but all too often, once the heroic trek was over, the curtain fell and the principals in the drama were abandoned at the very moment when the rewards of their colossal struggle were at hand. What were those rewards? What of the "free land" toward which they had fought so boldly, at the calculated risk of their lives, their loved ones and all their puny possessions.

Only a few discerning literary craftsmen have explored that dramatic terrain by beginning their story after the emigrants had finally brought their creaking wagons and weary oxen to rest in the land "where flowers bloom at Christmas and storms never blow"; the lush and beautiful Willamette Valley. Of these few none has surpassed Sheba Hargreaves' artistry in recreating the problems met and mastered, the homely, day by day trials, heartbreaks and ultimate triumphs which comprise man's eternal struggle with a new and primitive environment.

Sheba Hargreaves was eminently equipped to write this enduring book. She knows her beloved Willamette Valley and particularly the terrain around Oregon City. In her childhood, on this very stage, she talked with alert octogenarians who had themselves crossed the plains in the '40's and '50's and were thus able to impart the "feel" of those storied, fading times. Doors were open to her that will be forever closed at her passing. The lines will again appear in the portrait but the fine shading that gives depth and warmth and vitality will be gone.

Who in the next generation, for example, will write with such authority and homespun simplicity of the proper way to make the soft soap or tallow candles of a century ago? Who else could set down so unerringly the poignant grief of the Indian girl, Lassee, when she was abandoned by the crafty McDermott? This one scene of itself would have lifted the book forever from obscurity; and there are many of equal merit.

When I asked Sheba Hargreaves to name the greatest satisfaction she herself had derived from the book, she said: "It was when it was made required reading in the schools of the Oregon country. I wanted to leave something permanent for the children to grasp and remember about the history of their own region."

She had done that, and more. Among those who know and love the Willamette Valley—where flowers still bloom at Christmas and the savage storms of the plains never blow—*The Cabin at the Trail's End* will always be read with pleasure and profit by adults and children. alike.

ROBERT ORMOND CASE.

# CHAPTER I

MARTHA BAINBRIDGE rose stiffly from the camp fire after carefully raking out the live coals and setting the Dutch oven with the raised loaves on its three little legs. With a practiced hand she heaped coals on the cover and stepped back from the fire. She was alone, and for the moment her whole being sagged with the accumulated weariness of six months on the plains. Then she turned resolutely, squared the drooping shoulders, and lifting her face to the sky, drew in a long breath of the bracing air of a late Oregon fall, fast verging into winter.

With shining eyes she looked far down the valley from the little natural clearing where she stood to the placid blue of the Willamette, flowing smoothly northward, the sheer descents of its western bank a riot of scarlet and gold from the frost-touched dogwoods and vine maples, with here and there the subdued note of somber firs, almost black in the hard, clear November sunlight.

She turned slowly northward. The Clackamas, a smaller river, steely blue in the broad shallows and molten silver in its riffles, flowed into the Willamette from the east, a mile and a half below. Beyond stretched lowlands, lush with grass, hemmed in by the ragged Cascade Mountain Range shifting from north to east.

1

She drank in the beauty avidly, turning from the rivers below to the mountains and back again. The grandeur of the two snow-covered peaks against the ragged sky line was bewildering—Mount St. Helen's, smooth and unbroken in its symmetry, and to the east majestic Mount Hood, its snowy sides mottled with dark rocks all tinged rosy pink in the glow of the late afternoon sun.

With straining eyes she looked southward. Nothing was to be seen there but undulating waves of fir timber. Climbing to a sharp rise above, the panorama of the southern part of the country spread out beneath her gaze. In the distance the mighty falls of the Willamette dropped to the lower river, with Oregon City on the flat below. Silent with awe, Martha watched the spray of rainbow mist hovering above the cataract. Willamette Falls justified all the stories she had heard of its grandeur.

Oregon City's little group of houses held her, but as her gaze wandered up the hill, she noted a well-developed farm standing out, a clear-cut jewel, against the background of timber. The marvels of snowy peaks, cataract, and rivers had been uplifting, but this farm brought her swiftly back to earth with its silent promise of plenty so easily wrested from virgin soil. This was a farm beyond the wildest dreams of what awaited her in the Oregon country. Measuring with an eye unaccustomed to mountain surfaces, she judged it to be the full six hundred and forty acres—a square mile—that had been promised by the Linn bill, then before Congress, to settlers in the Oregon country.

This must be the McDermott farm of which such stories had been told. All the way across the plains those in the train who had been to Oregon and were returning with their families had sung the praises of this model farm above Oregon City, of the wonderful yield of its grain fields, the fruitfulness of its orchard, the fatness of its long-horned cattle, ready for beef in the winter-time from standing belly deep in waving grasses.

The snug double cabin seemed a bit of heaven to a tired emigrant woman. With a mind leaping ahead she saw a comfortable cabin where the wagon with its tattered dust-gray cover was drawn up under the shelter of two immense fir trees. It was a dejected-looking Conestoga wagon with the woodwork shrunken and warped by the intense heat of the alkali plains. The wheels dished outward so that the tires had to be held in place with wire put on at judicious intervals. The body was scarred and gaping at the corners; the tongue had been broken and roughly spliced with a peeled pole. Two emaciated oxen, well hobbled, grazed eagerly near. The mind must be able to dwell in the future to endure the immediate present.

The 21st of November, 1843, this was. The wagon, one of the first ten to come clear through to Oregon City from Independence, Missouri, was part of the great train of one thousand emigrants known to history as "The great emigration of Oregon home-builders."

Martha Bainbridge had little time for gazing at scenery. She came swiftly down to the camp fire, and removed the cover from the Dutch oven to inspect the browning loaves of bread, then with the pothooks lifted the oven into the wagon, placing the puffy brown loaves to cool.

She had heard stories of Oregon rains all summer on the plains. She stepped to the wagon to examine its tattered cover, though she knew very well that it would not turn water, and rain was not going to hold off many days. The western sky was a mass of clouds, and a stiff breeze from the southwest had sprung up with the turn of the afternoon.

"We'll pull through somehow," she muttered. "Too late to give up, now that we've reached our journey's end. The good Lord provides a way if we are willing to hew out our paths." She smiled whimsically to herself, still muttering, "I've noticed that all the Lord ever provides is the chance, and come to think of it, that's all we need."

But her heart almost stopped beating as she thought of their predicament. She rallied quickly and grinned, trying to make a joke out of a grim fact. Winter was fairly upon them. They were almost out of provisions. They had only the clothes they stood in and fifty cents in money to carry four hungry children, her uncle Adzi, her husband, John Bainbridge, and herself through the winter in a strange new country.

There was no help to be had in Oregon City. The houses of the few settlers were already filled to suffocation. There was no work to be secured to bring in money or supplies, and yet she reasoned it might be much worse. They were among the few who had succeeded in bringing their wagons clear through. Most of the emigrants had left all but the barest necessities at the Methodist mission in The Dalles to come down the Columbia River to Fort Vancouver in hurriedly-made skiffs, Indian canoes, or bateaux furnished by the Hudson Bay Company. At least they had a yoke of oxen, though they were so jaded they would not be fit for work until the grass grew strong in the spring.

There was nothing to do but carry on as best she might, a day at a time, and here chance offered her a few idle moments and there was healing quiet to be enjoyed to the utmost. She fairly luxuriated in the moment, slipping off the slatted cotton sunbonnet, so that the little breeze found the curly tendrils of hair that escaped in spite of vigilance from her smoothly-parted-in-the-middle-and-tightly-coiled-at-the-nape-of-the-neck brown hair.

Her brown linsey-woolsey dress with its tight-fitting many-gored waist and long full skirt was much the worse for wear, frayed to ragged fringe at the hem and very much soiled. She was painfully conscious that she was not neat and clean, and that neither were the contents of the wagon in which two thousand miles of hard, slow travel had been accomplished.

Although she was alone, she suddenly stooped so that her long skirt covered her shoes, shaking her head sadly. Those shoes were a sorry sight. Once they had been strong cowhide, securely laced, but now, what was left of the soles was tied to the uppers with strips of buckskin. Large holes revealed frayed strips of cloth about her feet. Stockings had long since given way before the alkali dust and the sharp stones of the plains and mountain passes.

"To think," she muttered, "that I should ever be dirty and ragged, with no soap to wash a change of clothing for the family, even if they had the change. I do hope John can find me a pair of Indian moccasins soon. A barefooted woman is a disgrace. We're all in the same fix, though, so perhaps 'twon't matter."

She turned abruptly to find work, always her panacea for black fears, especially hard work accompanied by a vigorous hymn tune. She began to sing resolutely, "How firm a foundation, ye saints of the Lord."

Uncle Adzi limped into the clearing just as she climbed down from the wagon after inspecting supplies. The Bainbridge family had reached its destination at two that afternoon. The first duty of a housewife is to take careful stock and lay plans for the new home.

In spite of his rheumatism Uncle Adzi moved briskly for his sixty-odd years. He was a wizened, cricket-like little man. A slow smile crinkled his tanned leathery countenance as he handed his niece two ruffed grouse that he had slung over the gun on his shoulder.

At Martha's exclamation of delight he drawled: "Yes, them birds be natives hereabouts. Never seed their kind before. They're twicet the size o' quail, an' look at the meat onto the breasts o' 'em. If yer oncle Adzi's rheumatiz jist lets him git inter the

woods a leetle, we wun't starve yit awhile.  Plumb
full o' squirrels an' grouse the nigh woods is."

Uncle Adzi lowered the "grub box" down to
Martha.  She quickly unfastened the sides and raised
them on the sliding supports to form the dinner
table.  From the shelves inside the box she began
taking their scant provisions—flour enough for one
more baking of bread, a few small pieces of jerky
(dried buffalo meat), some bacon rinds saved for
seasoning, a small bag of salt, a quart of parched
corn, and a small tin of rendered buffalo fat for frying.  Two or three of the little cakes of dried yeast
that she had made before starting were left; there
was a good drawing of Gunpowder tea and a gallon
jug, holding perhaps a teacupful of New Orleans
molasses.

Groaning in spirit, Martha averted her face in her
sunbonnet.  Food three times a day for seven was no
light matter.  Even with the most careful managing
she was at her wits' end most of the time.

"Tired, honey?"  Uncle Adzi inquired solicitously.  The orphaned niece that he had raised from
early childhood was to him the dearest thing in life.

"No time to be tired, uncle," said Martha gayly.
"I feel like shouting hymns of praise.  We're at home
after our long, hard journey.  It'll be a real home,
too, where hard-working folks can make a good living and their children have a chance to come through
the winter alive."

Uncle Adzi quickly caught the exultation in her
tone.  "No more fever an' ager an' younguns sick
with lung fever through the turrible long cold

winters, an' no more fierce hot summers lak we had in Sangamon County, Illinois."

Martha was herself again. "Aren't we the lucky ones?" she triumphed. "We've all had the fever and ague stewed out of us in the dry heat of the plains. I know in my heart that Esther Amelia couldn't have lived through another cold winter. Didn't Doctor Spears say she couldn't stand another attack of lung fever? I couldn't bear to lose another." Martha's eyes filled with tears. She was thinking of little Clarissa May, the baby who had died the winter before with the terrible lung fever, a form of pneumonia that attacked the children of the Middle-Western states winter after winter in spite of all that doctors and frantic mothers could do.

Quick to change a sorrowful subject, Uncle Adzi dug his heel deeply into the sod and, reaching down, picked up a handful of the crumbling black soil for her inspection. "Look at this here rich black sile," he demanded. "Here we kin raise real craps, an' we kin sell whut we raise, too, er trade hit fer nedcessities. There hain't no drought, ner grasshoppers, ner turrible hailstorms here. An' the panic o' thirty-seven didn't reach out here. The Pacific Ocean'll always furnish a outlet fer craps. Hain't I allus said so?"

"John is a hard worker and a good manager," said Martha, "and the boys'll soon be able to do men's work. You keep up the chores so well, and make so many things for the cabin, so we are sure to get ahead here if we can just keep our spirits up until we get a foothold."

"The fust winter is boun' ter be hard," Uncle Adzi admitted reluctantly, "specially on you, Marthie."

"I'll manage somehow, don't you worry, Uncle Adzi. We've never died yet, and we'll hang on hard this winter."

"But jist how ye aim ter manage ter set the table three times a day fer we-all, I jist naterally cain't figger out. They do say down at the settlement"— he brightened visibly at the recollection—"that Doctor McLoughlin loans each emigrant family two cows to use. If we can have milk this winter, we'll make it."

"John is going to Vancouver to see about it as soon as we can get under cover," assured Martha as she busied herself in making preparations for supper, placing the skillet properly on the bed of live coals in readiness to receive the grouse that Uncle Adzi was skinning with the unerring precision of the seasoned hunter.

"My word!" she ejaculated as she straightened up from the camp fire, "won't it seem good to cook in a fireplace again? Camp fires smoke so when there is a wind, and the crane in the fireplace certainly does save the back; stooping so much sort of tires me."

The children came trooping in from the timber behind the clearing, where they had been exploring. Martha had laughed when they declared their intention of hunting berries. The 21st of November *is* rather late, but they carried on a stick between them an Indian basket partly filled with shattered clusters of late-hanging elderberries.

Rose Ann was just turned sixteen, a slip of a girl

with blue eyes and light curly hair. She was freckled
like a turkey egg, but her forehead under her ragged
straw hat was of a milky whiteness that contrasted
pleasantly with her tan. Esther Amelia, eight, was
as dark and swarthy as a young Indian. The two
boys, Manuel and Asa, were thirteen and eleven.
Manuel at thirteen was tall and inclined to be muscu-
lar after the awkward fashion of adolescence. He
had, since starting across the plains, done a man's
work with the oxen, the wood-cutting, or any of the
various duties about the camp. He prided himself
on his ability with a rifle. Uncle Adzi believed in
boys learning the ways of men early in life, and had
tutored him carefully in hunting and trapping and
fishing. Asa, small for his years, followed carefully
in the footsteps of his elder brother; he, too, was
learning to use a gun.

All four of the children were barefooted. The
boys' homespun butternut jeans were in tatters.
Bare brown skin showed through holes in the knees,
and missing buttons, which had secured the pantaloons to the jumper, had been supplanted with pewter from an old spoon carefully molded into shape.
On their tow heads were ancient coonskin caps, badly
moth-eaten and punctured here and there with
arrows where they had been set up for target
practice.

Rose Ann and Esther Amelia fared rather better
than the boys. Both wore straight Indian dresses
of soft gray buckskin, jauntily trimmed with scarlet
flannel and beautifully beaded and fringed. These
dresses were a source of great pride. Sticcus, the

Indian guide from the Whitman Mission at Waii-
latpu, detailed by Doctor Whitman to guide the emigrant train through the mountains to the portage of
the Columbia, made them a *potlatch* (gift) of them
to show his regard for the *tillicums* (friends).

Martha and Uncle Adzi looked in amazement at
the elderberries. "Why," Martha exclaimed,
"they're like the elderberries back home, only larger
and with fuller clusters. And to think that fruit
could hang on the bushes so late."

"Yes," said Manuel, only there they grew on
bushes and here on trees. We'd never 'a' got 'em if
I hadn't been along to bend down the limbs."

"We must hurry supper," said Martha, and Rose
Ann and Esther Amelia immediately began looking
over the dark blue berries, washing them at a little
spring that trickled down into a clean rocky basin a
few yards above the camp. Martha bustled about
between camp fire and table. Once she disappeared
into the depths of the wagon and, lifting up a board
in the false bottom, came forth after a little rum-
maging with a piece of maple sugar as large as two
good-sized fists. Grudgingly she shaved off a scant
portion to sweeten the stewing berries.

"Didn't know mother had maple sugar left, did
you, Manuel?" she bantered. "Wouldn't have been
left if you children had known it. I never saw such
young ones for sweets. This is all that's left of the
hundred pounds father made the spring we left
Illinois."

Uncle Adzi spoke up quickly. "Don't ye fret,
Marthie. They say there's more sugar'n anythin'

else on the Pacific coast—comes in from the Sandwich Islands on every ship, an' hit's powerful cheap, too. Ye wun't have ter stent the younguns none on sugar. Hain't I allus said thet trade on the Pacific Ocean'd be the makin's o' the farmers?"

"Cheap sugar in a fruit country," exulted Martha. "Think, children, that means preserves for our bread in the winter."

"Yes," said Uncle Adzi. "And cheap sugar hain't the hull story; hit'll mean other nedcessities cheap in time; the ship thet carries sugar takes back whut we raise. Hain't I been lookin' all my nateral life for a frontier where there war a market for craps?"

"God help us to hold on until we can raise a crop," Martha muttered in the depths of her sunbonnet.

John Bainbridge came up the trail from Oregon City just as Martha was dishing up the steaming supper. He walked with the long stride that takes men rapidly over the road, although there was no undue haste in his movements. He carried over his shoulder a hemp sack containing about twenty pounds of wheat and in one hand half of a large salmon dried after the Indian fashion.

He was very tall, and stooped a little as if from the carrying of too heavy loads. But his shoulders were broad and his muscles bulging and hard under his butternut blouse. He had a grave, inscrutable face deeply furrowed and lined. His eyes were blue and kindly, small and deep-set, yet twinkling with interest and animation when he spoke, which he seldom did, unless he had something very definite to say. He took the hardships of Martha and the children terribly to heart and, while outwardly calm, worried and fretted at the responsibilities which the coming winter bade fair to lay upon him.

He had not the natural buoyancy of spirit of Martha and Uncle Adzi, but he was a tower of strength to both of them in times of need.

Cautious and hard-working, John Bainbridge had developed a good farm and a small herd of cattle in Sangamon County, Illinois, when the emigrating fever struck the Middle West. The panic of 1837 was still felt all over the East, so that it was almost impossible to meet taxes on land. The Mississippi Valley was a fever-and-ague country, undeveloped as to rail and wagon roads; there was no market for crops, even when they escaped drought and grasshoppers. Discouraged settlers, shaking with chills and fever six months in the year, and freezing the other six, snow-bound in small cabins, listened eagerly when returned missionaries told of the mild climate where grass was green all winter, and of broad waterways that led down to the ocean, with a prospect of developing trade with Asiatic countries, especially China, just opening its ports to world commerce.

The question of slavery and state rights was beginning to trouble; the more far-sighted saw war looming sharply on the horizon, with the Mississippi Valley the seat of conflict. John Bainbridge had heard Jason Lee, the Methodist missionary to the Indians, speak one evening in the winter of 1838 in the little schoolhouse near his farm, and had ever since been cherishing the hope of emigrating to Oregon.

Jason Lee had come to Oregon in 1834, and established his mission about fifty miles above the falls of the Willamette at the Indian village of Chemayway. He returned East to preach and raise funds for his work, also to enlist emigrants in the enterprise of establishing homes in the Oregon country. At that time, on the Pacific coast, there were only a few scattering Americans who had drifted in to trap and hunt and later to farm. These, with the missionary population, would, he told the Middle-Westerners, in time be strong enough to turn the balance of power away from England to the United States if settlers could only be induced to come as quickly as possible.

He carried with him a memorial to Congress, drawn up by American residents, complaining about the practices of the Hudson Bay Company in its high-handedness in dealing with American settlers, and asking two things for the protection and prosperity of American subjects. The first was that the jurisdiction of the laws of the United States be extended to cover them, and the other that the land they had taken up and improved be granted them with the guaranty that it could be held. He recommended that a square mile, or six hundred and forty acres, be allotted each American settler in order to stimulate emigration. Under the Treaty of Joint Occupancy between Great Britain and the United States, each nation had the right to settle in the Oregon country, and Congress, harassed with the question of state rights and slavery, slowly woke to action under the spell of Jason Lee's reasoning, and began deliberating on ways and means of securing the Oregon country for the United States.

Senator Linn of Missouri had introduced a bill in Congress in 1841 authorizing construction of a line of forts from the Missouri River to the "best pass for entering the Valley of the Oregon," and this had, in the minds of those contemplating emigrating, removed much of the danger of the journey. John Bainbridge had been following the bills and the debates on the Oregon question. When Senator Linn introduced the Donation-land bill proposing to give to each white male inhabitant over eighteen six hundred and forty acres of land—a square mile—half that number of acres to the wife, and one-fourth to each child under eighteen, he began to arrange his affairs to emigrate to Oregon.

There was little sale for farms in Sangamon County—too many farmers were preparing to emigrate—but the Bainbridge farm was well developed, and finally John sold it for five hundred dollars, stock, farm implements, and all.

A new Conestoga wagon and his two yoke of oxen cost him three hundred dollars. The supply of food and clothing left very little money, but the Bainbridges had not worried about that; they had as much as or even more than many of the others when they set out with the train from the rendezvous at St. Joseph, Missouri, the 11th of May.

More than once on that trip John had cursed himself for a fool, but, having started, there was no turning back. The peril of going on was less than that of returning after hardships and privations really began.

But on his arrival in Oregon it seemed that anxiety had only just begun. At the missionary trading-post in Oregon City he had been able to secure on credit only the small bag of wheat and the side of salmon. He had found the little settlement filled with people who were nearly naked like themselves and with no resources to buy either food or clothing.

In spite of the anxiety of the elders of the family, the first meal in the new home was a happy affair. The whole family carefully washed hands and faces at the spring, though Asa had to be sent back to wash behind his ears and a little higher up his wrists. The winter dusk was gathering when the family finally assembled at table. John asked his brief, simple blessing, and the rattle of pewter spoons, steel knives, and two-tined forks against scoured tin plates began.

Martha, true housewife, made the most of any situation. The work of scouring cutlery and tin plates and cups was faithfully done by the girls each morning under her close scrutiny. In spite of the soiled clothing and the raggedness, anything that could be cleaned or mended had been faithfully given the utmost attention.

After the first keen edge was off the appetite and John had told Asa for the hundredth time to turn the sharp edge of his knife inward before putting his food in his mouth, and Martha had chided Esther Amelia for carelessly upsetting her cup of water, John said: "Well, Martha, I've made arrangements to stake out our claim; there's plenty of room here to get six hundred and forty acres of land that lies right pretty, rolling hills and level benches, with a stream of living water running clear through it. There's no claim recorded just near except McDermott's down the trail and a little to the east."

His declaration was hailed with shouts of joy by the children. "I'm sure I can keep us in game and fish this winter," said Manuel with the air of one assuming a grave responsibility.

"And I can trap and hunt a little, too," asserted Asa. "I'm goin' to make a figure-four trap to-morrow and start right in catchin' rabbits."

"Six hundred and forty acres o' land with no taxes ter pay yet awhile," gloated Uncle Adzi. "A hull square mile rich an' deep an' black with fine livin' water and plenty o' timber, only three-quarters of a mile from the settlement as the crow flies."

"Most of the settlers went up the valley," said John. "They think the land is better up there. There's over fifty farms with fruit trees bearing and cattle and hogs and sheep and poultry up on a stretch they call French Prairie."

"I can't see no sense in leavin' the settlement. We gotter look to the easiest haul ter git our craps ter market, and thet there river"—he waved his hand with a sweeping gesture toward the Willamette— "beats all the wagon roads thet air been built yit."

"I'm glad to stay here," said Martha. "The children will be able to go to school all the time here; there'll surely be a school organized before the winter's over."

"Yer mother could larn ye children ef she had ter,"

Uncle Adzi said with a glow of pride. "I seen ter her schoolin' myself. But I 'low she'll be toler'ble busy this winter."

John paused in sopping his bread in the browned water gravy. "Down at the settlement they can't understand why we didn't want to locate on the bottom land across the Clackamas." They could see the beautiful lightly wooded river bottom to the north in the uncertain moonlight.

"I told 'em we'd had enough o' swamps in Illinois."

"High ground allus leads downhill ter the waterway, too," supplemented Uncle Adzi. "Hit's a heap sight easier ter haul craps downhill than ter git 'em outer the muddy roads on the bottom lands. All them things has ter be taken inter consideration in locatin' a farm."

"How many houses are there in Oregon City, John?" Martha asked.

John thought a minute. "Why, about six," he said. "And there's a sawmill on a rock island below the falls and two or three block storehouses with piles of pelts and sacks of grain around. There's a blacksmith shop and two trading-posts. The place is swarming with greasy Indians and smells of dried salmon and pelts, and the emigrants have camped everywhere."

"I'm a-goin' down an' look 'er over afore many days. I'd 'a' gone with you to-day only we needed meat. I allus had a hankerin' fer ports whar ships come an' go. Waterways is so much easier'n roads ter git craps ter market. No buildin' nor nothin' ter a nateral waterway. Put yer wheat on a ship an' down she floats ter the ports in Chiny," said Uncle Adzi.

The stars blinked between patchy scudding clouds before the girls finished the dishes to the liking of Martha, who was engaged in assembling the buffalo robes and blankets on the beds of fragrant fir boughs that the men and boys gathered from the near-by woods. The coyotes began their dismal howling and John stirred up the smoldering fire and gathered pitch to replenish it through the night.

"John," Martha asked her husband as they lay looking up at the sky, "are there glass windows in the settlement? I want to have white curtains in the cabin. Seems like white curtains and a rocking-chair and a few books on a shelf make a home out of any kind of a rough cabin. Of course right at first it won't matter so much; we'll be so busy we won't have time to notice. But I'm going to have white curtains. I've saved a pair of the linen sheets that Grand-mother Shields wove for my dower. You didn't know I had them, did you?"

John, between sleeping and waking, muttered something unintelligible, then roused and said; "I saw a few windows; one of the frame houses had 'em; but I'll get glass for you, honey, as soon as a ship-ment comes 'around the Horn.'" Then he lapsed again; a man who has worked hard all day is likely to fail in holding up his end of an after-retiring con-versation.

But Martha continued: "You know, John, I didn't say a word when we threw out the feather beds back on the Sweetwater, and I let my little box of keep-

sakes and all our Sunday clothes go without a murmur at Fort Boise. I felt so sorry for poor Buck and
Bright; they had more than tired oxen could pull;
but the sheets didn't weigh much. If it came to the
worst I would have thrown them out, or carried them
in my hand."

John was fast asleep, but Martha lay for a long
time building in fancy the home she would have, with
hollyhocks and June pinks and sweet Williams in the
dooryard; with ruffled white curtains fluttering in
the light breezes from the partly opened windows.
But now there was only the weird call of the coyotes
in the darkness of a night growing dense with the
portent of rain.

# CHAPTER II

BY morning the whole aspect had changed. Smooth gray clouds overcast the sky and a fine drizzling rain began with the retarded daylight. No wind; just a melancholy drip, drip. Oregon rains are seldom the violent driving tempests of the California country to the south. The Willamette Valley, with the hills scrolling back to the jagged Cascades on the east and the Coast Range on the west, is protected from winter snows and the fierce heat of summer. Warm moisture-laden winds, coming in from the Pacific Ocean, strike the low Coast Mountains and precipitate soft rains, alternating with fogs and mist equally mild.

In this luminous gem of a valley from October to May there is a week or so of incessant weeping rain, followed by a few days of soft cloudy weather or heavy fog, with a gradual breaking away, ending in three or four frosty nights with sparkling blue daytime skies and warm clean-washed air.

Cattle stand up to their knees in grass, and the rains do not interrupt the out-of-door work very much through the winter, except during an occasional gale. The rare snowstorm drives the Oregonian, native or acclimated, grumbling to his fireside.

After the dry heat of the plains, the Bainbridge family were chilled and miserable as they huddled about the fire or sought refuge from the dampness in the wagon. Breakfast was a scant meal of the remnants of last night's supper eaten with chattering teeth by the fire.

John and Uncle Adzi drew the wagon under the shelter of two large fir trees whose interlocking boughs shed most of the rain from the tattered wagon cover. But the wagon was damp and cold in spite of the big pitch-knot fire burning as close as possible to it.

In spite of rain the camp was all bustle and hurry. John and Uncle Adzi, with the help of Manuel and Asa, were looking over the tools and sharpening the broadax and the knives preparatory to working in the woods beyond the clearing, felling timber and cutting logs for the cabin.

"Thank Heaven, buildin' o' cabin hain't a hull winter's job," ejaculated Uncle Adzi as John yoked up the oxen. He ran a sympathizing hand over the thin flanks of Buck and Bright, counting each outstanding rib.

"Gad! how I hate to work the oxen!" ejaculated John in response to Uncle Adzi's understanding look. "But all they'll need to do will be to snake in a load of logs when we come to dinner and another in the evening."

"We'll spare 'em all we can, but we got ter git the wimmen under shelter ez quick ez possible. We'll be livin' at hum inside o' three or four days, with a big roarin' fire in the fireplace, an' Marthie an' the gals keepin' house accordin' to the best Illinoi' idears inside a week."

They were going through the timber, the boys

making détours to throw a stone at a squirrel or to look for signs of grouse. John was carefully selecting straight fir trees of the right size and did not answer for a few minutes, but when his mind was free he spoke of the burden on his soul. "I hope Esther Amelia stands this chilling weather. Martha'll keep her rolled in a buffalo robe in front of the fire, but she looked pinched and peaked this morning. It's hardest on Martha and the girls. Beats all the way that woman holds up her end. I believe I'd give up if she whined or complained the way some of the women did when we struck hard sledding."

"Marthie's one o' the blessed," Uncle Adzi said. "When things are goin' good she jest naterally gloats over the present, an' if the lookout gits dark she revels in the prospec's jist ahead. I never seed Marthie downed yit. She reminds me o' them willer saplin's by the branch at hum, bend ter the groun' afore a storm an' spring right up straight an' tall soon's the blow's over."

As John cut the trees with the one broadax, sharpened at the grindstone earlier in the morning, Uncle Adzi and Manuel hacked off the limbs with draw knives while Asa manfully did what he could with a keen-edged hunting knife. It was slow work for the lack of tools, but John and Uncle Adzi thanked their lucky stars over and over that they had saved the grindstone. Tools have to be kept in condition to work in the timber. Heavy as a grindstone is, it is the last thing before the actual tools that an emigrant will part with.

"If we had the tools we started with we could have this cabin up in a hurry," mourned John. "To have to throw out tools and farming implements and come into a new country with just a broadax and a couple of draw knives after we'd spent everything we had on earth for our outfit sure is hard lines," John grumbled, wiping huge drops of water that fell from the dripping limbs out of his eyes.

"Yes, 'tis," Uncle Adzi agreed, "but we got our shaky ole wagon. We'll let 'er stand out in the weather all winter ter swell the wood, an' she'll be a right smart wagon by spring. Recollec' there's only ten wagons got clear through. The oxen air well-nigh dead. It'll take 'em all winter ter put on fat, though I never seed sech grass in all my born days. Hit could be a heap sight worse, John, a heap sight worse." He grabbed his gun as a grouse drummed in the distant timber, and came back in twenty minutes with the grouse over his shoulder. "Make a right good supper, this here bird will. Hope I git another afore we go in ter dinner. Heartens Marthie up ter see meat come in.

"The way things grow here beats the oldest man alive. Jist give us a little time an' see what we do with a nateral waterway for our craps down to the ocean an' all the ports in Chiny waitin' fer our exports. It's wuth undergoin' a few inconveniences ter gitter a country with a market fer craps, with craps growin' while ye sleep," said Uncle Adzi, reverting to his favorite theme.

"Don't you think we've cut nearly enough logs for the cabin now?" asked John, running a calculat-

ing eye over the piles neatly stacked along the trail
they had cut through the timber, to be at hand for
snaking out when dinner-time came.

"Putty close ter hit," agreed Uncle Adzi. "We'd
best notch 'em down by the camp; they'll go inter
place quicker ef the notchin's done ez we set 'em up.
The battle's half over ag'in' we git the wimmin folk
under kiver." He began hacking off limbs with renewed vigor, at the same time recalling the lagging
boys to the task.

Martha had spent a busy morning about the camp
fire, wet through and numb with the cold in spite of
her activity. There must be something to feed the
hungry men when they came in at noon. She had
filled her large iron cooking-pot with wheat carefully
cleaned by hand. Rose Ann and Esther Amelia had
helped. Put on in cold water and brought slowly
to a boil, it expanded generously, but would not
be tender by noon. Wheat in any stage of cooking
is palatable and filling. Martha told the girls that
by night the wheat would be soft and good and then
she would be able to keep enough ahead. Keeping
enough ahead had been the burden of Martha's song
since she started across the plains.

The salmon was new to her. Dried it was, but
the Indian used no salt, simply splitting a salmon
down the back and hanging it in smoke until it cured
dry and hard. She prepared a generous amount by
shredding it and boiling it in salt water. There
was bread from the last night's baking—the last the
family would have for some time. She had decided
against using the remainder of the flour for bread-

making. John had said that there was no flour
ground in either Vancouver or Oregon City. The
grist mill was inadequate to keep up grist for the
fast-incoming emigrants—they would be obliged to
subsist upon boiled wheat with what coarse flour they
could grind in their small coffee mill. An occasional
tablespoonful of flour was necessary for thickening.
They could manage without bread, and be thankful
for wheat until it could be ground into flour.

Three stolid squaws paid them a visit during the
middle of the morning, one old squaw, very fat, and
two supple and young. They were all dressed in
buckskin clothes with fringed leggings and beaded
gray moccasins. The two girls had bright bandanna
handkerchiefs tied about their heads, with the four
ends caught in two knots at the back; the eldest one
wore a curious hat woven like an Indian basket, but
so tight as to shed water, and turned down like a
large flat pan over her head. Her chin was ornamented with alternating perpendicular stripes of blue
and black—a badge of mourning with Willamette
Valley Indians. She was very dirty and smoke be-
grimed, the seams of her wrinkled brown skin outlined with years of accumulated grime. The young
squaws had in a crude way a sense of personal responsibility in regard to face and hands, though all
three were overpowering in the reek of the Indian
lodge that surrounded them like an evil aura.

They came into Martha's camp and seated themselves near the fire before offering a word of greeting, exchanging views as to the status of the family
between themselves in a guttural tongue unlike the

Chinook jargon which the Indian speaks when among the whites or in trading with different tribes. Chinook jargon is in reality a trade language, a mixture of Indian, French, and English, which has developed through the intercourse of the various tribes and the white race. The real Indian language is spoken only in the tribe, each tribe having its own vernacular, so that tribes living close together do not always understand each other.

The old squaw peered into the cooking-pot and stirred its contents with a long cooking spoon that lay near, to satisfy herself of the nature of the food, probably with a view of remaining to dinner, but grunted disgustedly to the other two and seated herself by the fire again, ready to open conversation with her hostess.

Martha and the girls knew chance words of Chinook picked up on the trail. They could not understand enough to carry on a conversation, but listened respectfully.

"*Hy yu tillicums*" ("We are friends"), grunted the old squaw, including her silent, though interested companions with a comprehensive wave of the hand. "*Potlatch* [gift]?" she inquired hopefully.

Martha shook her head sadly. She had no gift, but after a moment's reflection, while the three studied her face closely, she took a loaf of bread and cut three generous slices, smearing them with molasses as it gurgled out of the jug, and with a smile handed each a slice. They accepted the potlatch in the spirit it was offered. Martha pointed to the wagon and the sodden bedding drying near the fire to show them that she had nothing. The three rose and peeped into the wagon, fingered the cover wonderingly—a covered wagon was not so common in Oregon. The previous settlers had brought their goods in canoes. They inspected the cooking utensils on the near-by table, and finally examined the small grindstone, turning the handle and laughing gleefully at its swift revolutions. To their incredulous delight, Rose Ann showed them how to sharpen a knife.

*"Tenas klooch-man et-sit-sa?"* ("little woman sick?") inquired the old squaw solicitously, pointing to Esther Amelia by the fire wrapped in a buffalo skin, with one end drawn over her head to keep off the rain. Martha nodded and the three carried on a lengthy discussion, evidently speculating as to the nature of the illness.

They sat cross-legged by the fire for an hour or so in silence after that, watching Martha's every move with bright black eyes, then rose to go, departing as unceremoniously as they had come.

Martha scarcely heeded their going, except to nod and smile; she was busy with dinner and very shortly the men came into the clearing behind the oxen, snaking along a load of logs for the cabin. There was much discussion around the dinner table about just where the cabin was to stand. "Below the spring an' in a straight line from hit," insisted Uncle Adzi. "Hain't I seed wimmen afore now a-breakin' o' pore backs a-totin' water uphill ter a cabin? Hit's tarnation careless o' men folks ter sot a cabin to suit theirselves. When I git time I aim ter holler out some split cedars and run that thar water plumb down ter the cabin door fer Marthie."

It was two days more before the logs were drawn in from the timber and notched ready to raise the cabin. During these two grilling eternities the rain fell incessantly. John and Uncle Adzi made a temporary shelter under the firs with four poles upright and poles laid in their crotches at the top to form a roof by laying fir boughs and the wagon cover over it, but the bedding was damp and cold and it was necessary for the whole family to keep constantly on the move to prevent chilling in their wet clothing.

Every one went to work joyfully to help in the cabin-building. Esther Amelia filled a big kettle with wet clay from the bank above the spring for the boys to carry down. Rose Ann carefully cleared the space inside the logs as they were put in place, so that the clay could later be trampled down to dry into a hard smooth floor.

"We'll lay a puncheon floor ez soon ez we kin," Uncle Adzi assured the woman. "A dirt floor is only fitten fer a Injun lodge."

Martha was nearly as handy about the logs as the boys; she daubed the chinks between the logs with the wet clay, smoothing it into place so that not a crack of daylight showed between. John Bainbridge was an expert with the broadax, notching the ends so that the logs fitted closely together, making the chinking with clay much easier than where there was slack workmanship in the joining.

Uncle Adzi was master of ceremonies. The work progressed amazingly. This was by no means the

first cabin he had built. He was born to the frontier; pioneering was but the exchanging of frontier
Illinois, partially subdued, for the wilder, more remote Oregon frontier.

The cabin was fourteen by sixteen feet—the customary size of cabins. The bark was left on the logs
inside and out. In one end was the huge fireplace
that Uncle Adzi always built himself, with everyone carrying material so as to fit the splints in place
before the clay had time to dry and crack. It requires knack to build a clay fireplace.

Manuel and Asa carefully split the sticks an inch
square and eighteen inches long. Uncle Adzi scolded
and scornfully threw out any that were crooked or
that did not measure up to specifications. "How kin
I squar hit with the world ef the splints hain't even
ter begin with?" he asked with fine scorn. "I 'low
ter larn ye boys ter be good workmen, like your
father. Ye kin tell a slack, shiftless farmer by the
way his buildin's stand up, an' they won't stand
plumb onless ye cut yer wood true."

He considered Rose Ann and Esther Amelia better
at placing the splints than the clumsy-fingered boys,
though he thrust them aside impatiently and did the
work himself after sighting the row of splints with
his eye. "Hit must be laid precise, childern," he
cautioned again and again, "or hit may tip over
afore the clay sets."

The splints were built up in a double row just
like two Virginia worm fences, Uncle Adzi tamping
the moist clay carefully in place. The whole family
viewed it with admiration when it stood completed.

Each found a spot that could be smoothed a little firmer as they gathered lovingly about it.

It took just three days to raise the walls of the cabin and put on the pole rafters that would for the present carry a cedar-bark roof; the clouds were breaking as in the middle of the afternoon the men went to the timber to peel the cedar bark so that they would have a moisture-proof roof by nightfall.

Martha and Rose Ann were moving their goods into the roofless cabin so as to get under shelter at the earliest possible moment, when Esther Amelia said that a man on a funny horse was coming up the trail through the timber.

He rode slowly into view, his pony picking his way daintily over the rough trail. He was a large man and the pony rather small, giving an incongruous top-heavy appearance. The horse was curious, a calico Indian cayuse, pied and splotched with bay and white, with an anxious piebald white face, and ears carried back in the attitude indicating horse disgust and anger with the world, ready to take a nip of anybody who came in range. The Indian *kuitan* (horse), once he knows his master, is a trustworthy cattle horse, quick and sure and alert, tough beyond belief, but never entirely outgrowing the original sin in his nature, whites of his eyes showing overmuch, and ears always laid back.

The man rode up to the cabin and alighted, hat in hand, as Martha turned to greet him. With the gallantry of the old South he bowed low over the outstretched hands of Martha and Rose Ann, who had suddenly turned very conscious of her bare feet.

"Welcome, neighbors," he said heartily. "I'm William McDermott. I am delighted to see you have staked out your donation claim adjoining my farm. It certainly is a pleasure to see white women in the settlement."

Martha warmed to his friendly greeting. "You're no gladder than we are to settle ourselves in a warm cabin and keep house again, even if we haven't much. We lost nearly everything we had coming across the plains," explained Martha simply, offering her guest a seat which he took after throwing his horse's hair bridle rein over his head, at which movement the horse froze into a statue, to wait until his master took up the rein before moving a muscle. This is one of the great advantages of the Indian pony; he is trained to need no hitching.

"It's just within the last year that we have had women about—that is, white women," he corrected hastily. "But Oregon City is a regular town now from this on, and we'll have the charming society of ladies." He was speaking to Martha, but running an appraising corner of the eye over Rose Ann, well in the background, with her dress pulled down to cover her bare feet as she sat on a log drawn up before the fire, her wet clinging buckskin dress showing every line of a developing young girlhood.

"I am looking for my white-faced longhorn cow. She must have jumped the fence last night. She didn't come up to be milked this morning. Breechy, these longhorn cattle are; horn down a worm fence or jump anything," he explained.

McDermott rose to inspect the cabin, running a

hand over the well-pegged joints at the corners and admiring the fireplace. "Your men folks are good in the timber, and that fireplace beats anything of its kind in the Oregon country," he said finally. "I'm needing rails split for my fences and I would pay well for a fireplace like that. Do you suppose your husband would take his pay in supplies? Or"—he paused a moment and smiled—"I'll part with that breechy longhorn cow pretty cheap. She was fresh in June. Yes, I'll trade her with her heifer calf by her side for rails and some work about the farm buildings. The pesky Indians are not good at repairing."

Incredulous delight lit Martha's face. "I know they'll be glad to split rails. My husband *is* good in the timber, and my uncle, Adzi Clarke, was rated a master hand at fireplace and cabin building in Illinois."

So this was their next neighbor, owner of the farm she had seen from the rise above their camp. She was filled with joy to find him such a gentleman and so kind and neighborly. They visited together for half an hour, Martha asking numerous questions and McDermott busy answering them and telling the story of his settling the farm and how he came into possession of his band of longhorn cattle.

McDermott was a large man, rather given to corpulency from easy living, his florid face framed with a fringe of curling sandy hair, dividing it from his pink bald head. He wore a full beard and mustache which concealed his mouth and chin, but his mild blue eyes, while friendly and affable enough in lighting up when he talked, had a hint of hard steel in them which puzzled Martha, they were so out of keeping with his apparent character. She found herself wishing she could see his chin and mouth in order to judge him more accurately, but she reproached herself for any misgivings she felt.

McDermott explained that he had come to the Oregon country in 1834 with Ewing Young. Had she heard of Ewing Young? No, Martha hadn't. Well, Ewing Young had driven up a band of horses from California.

Ewing Young had not been so well received by Doctor McLoughlin, according to McDermott. The Governor of California had sent word ahead by boat that Ewing Young and his band were horse thieves and were not to be tolerated in the Oregon country. He laughed a little bitterly at the recollection.

"Ewing Young sent to California for long-horned Spanish cattle, in 1837. I bought one hundred head. I was tired of roving and decided to locate in this country where there was grass all winter for grazing stock. There was no town at the falls then. Doctor McLoughlin built a blockhouse with a stockade around it to protect it from the Indians, so he could store furs and grain there. And Jason Lee came in and established his mission the year we came."

"You've been here nine years," said Martha, calculating from 1834. "You have the oldest farm in the whole country, then, outside of Doctor McLoughlin's at Vancouver?"

"Oh no!" he corrected. "The French Canadians up on French Prairie, thirty miles south and west,

had well-developed farms when I came.  There are
fifty fine farms up there.  It was looking over their
growing crops that decided me to take up farming.
Doctor McLoughlin is a queer old man, with notions
clear ahead of his time.  He encouraged those French
Canadians, when their terms of service with the Hudson Bay Company were over, to stay and raise wheat.
His dream is exporting wheat to Russia and the
Orient.  He broke the Company's rules with those
farmers—they should have been returned to the place
they came from—but he let them take out their passage money in farm implements.  They have Indian
wives and broods of half-breed children, so didn't
want to take them back home and didn't like to send
the women back to their tribes.  Bad predicament!"
He laughed a hard little ironical laugh, and changed
the subject abruptly.

"My farm flourished from the start," he continued.
"I sent to the California missions for peach trees
and grapes and berries, and then traded roots and
cuttings with William Bruce, McLoughlin's Scotch
gardener.  I never saw orchards come into bearing
quicker or more prolific.  A whip off an apple tree
stuck in the ground in the fall will sometimes take
root and bear the third year."

"We're so anxious to set out trees and vines as
soon as possible," said Martha.  "Perhaps we can
arrange to get cuttings from you."

"Certainly you may," promised McDermott graciously, "and slips of flowers and garden seeds.  We
let nothing go to waste out here."  He turned and
looked at the neatly framed door in the cabin with

its smoothly split puncheon for holding the wooden hinges. "I'll bring over a long cutting of my pink rose to plant by your door next time I ride by," he promised. "We call it the Mission rose because the padres in California raise it, though some call it the Hudson Bay rose. There's bloom on it now; it blooms all the year around except in the early spring when it's putting out new leaves."

Martha had difficulty in believing this statement, and he noticed her incredulity.

"Yes, things grow all the winter through, here," he told her, "but our flowers have been neglected since Mary died." His face clouded. "Mary was my wife. She came on with our two little girls after I got the cabin built and the farm going well. It was too lonely for a delicate white woman. I think she died more from loneliness than from disease. There were two or three women at Jason Lee's mission and a few at Vancouver, but she couldn't see them once a year. A terrible life for a woman," he ejaculated sadly.

"Where are the little girls?" piped up Esther Amelia. "Will you let them come over to play?"

"Child, they are in a convent in New Orleans. There are no schools out here, but there will be soon now, and perhaps they can come home. Mahala is twelve and Mary Agnes is ten."

He rose to go, saying that he must find his cow before dark, but that he would come over in a few days to see about splitting rails and fireplace-making. He shook hands with all three, and, bowing low, put the bridle rein over his horse's head. After the usual difficulty in mounting his calico pony—Indian ponies, most of them, object on general principles to being mounted—he rode on up a steep trail beyond the cabin to round up his renegade longhorn.

The business of putting on the cedar-bark roof took only about an hour when the men came back, each dragging a load of bark tied with a braided buckskin rope. The pole rafters were already in place, and by laying the long strips of cedar bark so that the upper course overlapped the lower just like shingles, and holding the bark in place with slender poles fastened to the rafters at the ends with buckskin thongs to keep it from blowing off, a roof that would turn water was insured.

"Wal," drawled Uncle Adzi, squinting and sighting to be sure the thing was plumb, as he proudly surveyed their handiwork, "this'll turn the water till John an' me kin git inter the woods an' make cedar shakes. A cedar roof is jist a shiftless Injun makeshift, but anything ter turn this here moisture."

"I never saw such good cedar timber," said John.

"No, hit's straight an' tall, jist naterally askin' ter be made inter shakes an' pickets, an' hit's easy ter git outen the woods, too. Recollect how we traveled miles back into the interior o' Illinoi' ter find good shake timber? This here's a plumb wonderful country, with nateral waterways ter the ocean. I 'low the time'll come when we'll be sendin' off lumber ter Chiny." He paused impatiently when the rest laughed, and finished his work in stony silence.

"Gad! how I hate the rain!" complained John. "But I suppose it's the rain that makes the grass and the living water and the fine stands of timber. We'll have plenty of oak for firewood, and fir and cedar for fence rails and cabin and barn raisings."

A clay fireplace dries very slowly, and a hot fire is apt to crack it. A very low fire that had been burning in it since its erection began to hasten the drying, but the Bainbridges enjoyed the tiny blaze on their hearth that first evening in their new home.

Martha chanted one hymn tune after another as she worked in the dusk, moving and arranging their pitifully few belongings in the cabin. She was riotously happy to be under shelter, and then, too, there was Mr. McDermott's visit and the promise of a cow and supplies. She meant to spring this little surprise at the supper table and had cautioned the girls not to mention it.

"Martha," John called softly to her when the children and Uncle Adzi were outside in the wagon, "hang a couple of blankets over those two window openings, honey, until I can get the frames whittled out to cover with buckskin. It won't be long," he consoled, "until we'll have glass and you can put up your white curtains."

In her mind's eye the spotless white curtains replaced the dingy blankets she was hanging over the window openings, their graceful folds drawn back to disclose glass panes as clear and bright as glass could be polished. Her air castles helped to lighten the almost intolerable load under which she struggled.

She got out their little lamp and set it on the table, putting a couple of tablespoonfuls of buffalo grease in it and pulling up the wick made of a small piece of cotton rag braided and run through a small opening, so that the tiny flame would light the supper table. It was too soon to light the cabin with a fire of pitch knots, but in a few days it would glow with heat and rosy light.

Once the goods were safe under cover, Uncle Adzi, whose rheumatism tortured him more than he liked to admit, sat by the handful of fire and began putting the finishing touches to the new home. He was in his element engaged in whittling and tinkering. Whistling softly, he began making hinges for the door while waiting for Martha and the girls to put supper on the table. John was already making the door of split slabs cleated with two small cross slabs held in place with hardwood pegs driven into the soft wood. There was not a nail in the cabin—there were none to be had even if there had been money to pay for them. A small peg was carefully whittled from hard wood—oak or ash—Manuel and Asa were adept at peg-making, spending many a long winter evening at this simple task. The wood in which the peg was to be driven was bored a quarter of an inch or so with a gimlet, or sometimes a small starting opening was made with a chisel, and the peg was then driven into the soft wood with the flat side of the broadax.

In a few evenings John and Uncle Adzi fashioned window frames by whittling them down carefully with their jack-knives; Uncle Adzi took particular pride in his skill in mitering and pegging. He talked to the boys as he whittled and bent the pliant withes of hazel and joined them carefully so that the door would swing easily with no sagging.

"Ye see, Manuel," he counciled, "hit allus pays ter take time ter do yer work right. Now ef I git all hasted up, like ez not I'll spile this here hinge and have ter do the hull thing over. We need ter be in haste ter git the door shet, too. Jist hear them coyotes a-howlin'. Harmless, they be, though, even if they do skeer a body with their onearthly noise."

There was really very little furniture in the cabin, but there was very little room for it, so its lack was not felt. The grub box with its sides lifted formed a dining table. There were two puncheon shelves for the scant supply of food, and a block of wood for each member of the family to serve as chairs until Uncle Adzi got about to make serviceable chairs out of hazel withes.

There were two of the famous beds with one leg— made of puncheon—small firs split evenly and used split side up. Each bed was equipped with the customary trundle-bed for the children, sliding under out of the way in the daytime. Uncle Adzi constantly moaned over the clay floor. "No woman kin git any joy outen a clay floor; afore the winter's over you'll have a puncheon floor, Marthie," he promised.

John had wet buckskin and stretched it taut over the window frames he whittled out, and by forcing them into the window opening had a fairly translucent pair of windows when the buckskin dried taut in place. The door had a latch with the string hanging out, and a strong whittled board that dropped into a piece of forked wood on each side of the frame to fasten it against intruders at night. And within a week from coming into the little natural clearing the Bainbridges were all settled in their snug little cabin.

There was no bread, but the sack of wheat held out and wheat is filling and nourishing when boiled until soft. Uncle Adzi managed to hunt a little on clear days when his rheumatism permitted, and Manuel often caught a few trout in the stream that hurried down the north side of the bluff to empty into the stream in the little V-shaped valley below. But the problem of finding enough to eat kept Martha constantly anxious.

# CHAPTER III

AUNT MORNING ANN SIMMONS came
down the steep Indian path as fast as her
bulk and rheumatism would allow. Her
breath came in hard pants and the sharp rocks on
the trail hurt her wet moccasined feet, entirely innocent of stockings. She leaned heavily on her long
hazel staff, placing it firmly in front of her before
she made each careful step.

Her dress of faded brown butternut jeans was
frayed at the hem and heavily patched with blue
drilling in the places where the worst wear came.
Aunt Morning Ann was a billowy, shapeless woman,
not more than thirty-five years old, though the hard
life of the Missouri frontier had given her the appearance of at least fifty years. Her blue slatted
sunbonnet fell back, showing her thin hair skewered
with a single large pin on the back of her head, faded
to a dingy yellow with strong sunshine and heavily
streaked with gray. Her naturally florid face was
tanned a dull brick red, and her full lips, parting
with the effort of her descent, disclosed a desolate gap
where four front teeth were missing, like four pickets
off a whitewashed fence.

A huge woman was Aunt Morning Ann, with a
form very much like a plump feather pillow tied in
the middle, yet the universal madonna looked out of
her small rheumy blue eyes, and the strong, capable

42

work-twisted hands were those of the "mother in Israel."

She had heard just this morning that there were settlers about a mile and a half below and to the north of their claim. They were part of the wagon-train that had started from Missouri that spring. She knew nearly all of the thousand emigrants and was anxious to renew the acquaintance made on the plains earlier in the summer, before the train had broken up and separated to provide better grazing for the cattle and to permit of easier traveling by closer organization.

The Simmons family, including the seven children, had proudly started out with six cows besides their two yokes of oxen. They had traveled with Jesse Applegate's "cow column," the children walking ahead, driving the cattle clear through to Fort Walla Walla.

The emigration of 1843 was the first to make the attempt to come clear through with their wagons. Before that time the wagons had been left at Fort Hall on the Snake River and the rest of the trip made by packing over rough mountain trails. But Dr. Marcus Whitman, returning from Boston, where he had gone the year before on business for his mission at Waiilatpu, near Fort Walla Walla, had agreed to guide the train to Waiilatpu. He had brought his wagon through to his mission in 1836 by making a cart with two of the wheels, and since that time, he told them, an Indian guide with the Catholic missionaries had discovered a pass through the mountains.  He was sure that wagons could be brought clear through to the Willamette Valley.

Doctor Whitman had intended guiding the train through, but at Fort Hall a messenger from Waii-latpu met him with the news that the Indians had burned his barns and grist mill and that there was serious illness at the mission.  Mrs. Whitman was very uneasy and desired him to come home at once. So Sticcus, a trusty Indian, had brought the train to Fort Walla Walla.

It was late October by the time the "cow column" reached Fort Walla Walla.  An early snow had blocked the trail around the base of Mount Hood, so that the leaders felt it was not safe to attempt driving the cattle through, and the discouraged leaders had camped for two weeks on the sand flats outside the fort while the men fashioned large boats—skiffs, they called them—from the pine timber that had been washed high on the banks of the Columbia by the freshet of the spring before.

These skiffs, large enough to carry a family of eight or ten with their goods, were made of lumber sawed by hand with a whip saw.  The wagons were reluctantly left in charge of the commander of the fort, and the cattle branded with the Hudson Bay Company's iron and turned out to range on bunch grass until spring, when they could be driven down to the Willamette Valley.

The Indians understood negotiating the treach-erous rapids of the Columbia and making portages around the unnavigable falls.  With Indian pilots engaged by payment of clothing—mostly shirts—

and the courage of desperation and a stoic disregard of danger born of intimacy with all sorts of peril since making the start across the plains, this small detachment had set forth down the Columbia.

The Simmons family had reached the settlement at Oregon City fully two weeks ahead of the Bainbridges, who had journeyed with the main body of the wagon-train. Aunt Morning Ann gasped with surprise when she saw the wagon. She hadn't heard that anyone had succeeded in bringing wagons through. She stood a moment surveying with satisfaction the snug little cabin with the smoke curling from it. By all indications the newcomers, whoever they were, were thrifty, forehanded folks.

"Mornin'," she called, rapping vigorously on the door with one end of the hazel staff.

Martha Bainbridge sprang to the door at the sound of the cheery feminine voice.

"As I live, if hit hain't Miz' Bainbridge!" shrilled Aunt Morning Ann. "Lawsakes! how glad I am ter see you-all alive an' well."

Wordless for the instant and with sudden tears in her eyes, Martha Bainbridge rushed into the wide outstretched arms of motherly Aunt Morning Ann. "Where do you live, and how did you get here?" Martha asked as soon as she could speak.

"Why, we-all staked out our claim nigh onto a mile an' a half, or mebbe two mile, above you. Hit's level up thar, but a powerful hard climb up an' down. Our cabin is done built, fireplace an' all, the hull thing, but Pop never could build a fireplace thet 'u'd draw; she smokes like tarnation."

"We have been in our cabin just a week and are beginning to get warm. We've been chilled to the bone. Everything got soaking wet before we could get under shelter," said Martha.

"Miz' Bainbridge, did you-all get through alive?" Aunt Morning Ann asked quaveringly. "How you-all ever got thet wagon down har beats all recollection."

"Yes, we are here, alive and well," exulted Martha. "It's certainly a wonder that we did come through alive, taking that wagon down to Vancouver from The Dalles. Sixteen families of us came through to The Dalles. Only ten families decided to take the chance on rafting the rest of the way. John and I decided, after we'd shot rapids from Fort Walla Walla to The Dalles and carried over the portages, that the rest of the river couldn't be worse. There were plenty of dead pine trees, and the men made two large rafts that each held five wagons."

"Wal, do tell!" ejaculated Aunt Morning Ann. "They done said at the fort thet hit couldn't be done, an' we war thankful ter git here alive, after whut we'd been through, but we'll shorely need our wagon an' oxen afore the winter's over."

"We'd lost all we had but the wagon and oxen and a few tools, and John and Uncle Adzi decided that we had best take one more chance. We knew the oxen were so poor that they'd never come through a cold winter on the open range. We had everything to gain and nothing to lose," said Martha.

"Yas, I 'low we'll never see our cattle or wagon ag'in. They say the Injuns steal the cattle, er drive

'em off an' charge a orful price to find 'em fer ye.
So ez I see it, we've got nothin' but whut we make
here," rejoined Aunt Morning Ann mournfully.
"Still," she brightened, "I'm glad we came; we 'low
we're goin' ter like hit here."

"Yes, we like it, too," agreed Martha.

"How did you-all git the oxen down?" queried
Aunt Morning Ann, returning to the absorbing inci-
dents of the trip.

"Why, John and the boys drove them down the
north bank of the Columbia and swam them across
the river at Vancouver and came up the east side
of the Willamette. It was risky, but they swam
pretty well. Making the rafts and driving the oxen
delayed us. The trip from The Dalles was harder
than any other stretch. An Indian ferried us over
the Clackamas for a dollar, and showed us the trail
up the hill. We haven't been to Oregon City yet.
I'm curious to see the town."

"Hit's a right smart o' a town. Pretty nigh ez
fine an' large ez Novelty, Missouri, right now, with
emigrants jist pourin' inter hit every day," Aunt
Morning Ann announced proudly.

Martha hesitated to ask about Aunt Morning
Ann's folks, there were so many who had not reached
the trail's end. She knew instinctively that Aunt
Morning Ann was in sorrow and longed to tell her
about it, yet found it difficult.

"And how was it with your family?" she asked
after a sorrowful little lapse in the conversation.

Overcome, Aunt Morning Ann suddenly threw the
tattered blue sunbonnet that she had been swinging

by its frayed string over her head, and gave way to convulsive sobbing. Martha waited in silence, knowing that crying eases an aching heart, and that the telling of her story to a sympathizing listener was the balm Aunt Morning Ann needed.

Aunt Morning Ann dried her eyes on her sunbonnet and gained composure to tell her story. "Granny died of mounting fever early in the summer and we buried her in the middle o' the trail and built a fire on her grave, an' then when the ashes war cool they drove the hull wagon-train through hit, so the Injuns wouldn't find hit." Overcome, she waited again for composure. When she could speak again, she added thoughtfully: "I missed granny. For days, ez we traveled along, hit jest seemed more than I could bear to think o' her there alone. But granny war so ole an' so tired, so tired. In one way hit war a relief to fol' her pore ole han's to rest."

"Yes," comforted Martha, "life is hard on women. But they carry on until the end."

"But Jed, oh, my boy Jed!" Aunt Morning Ann's sobs broke out afresh in spite of her valiant efforts at control. "Pop an' me sold out ever'thin' and came to Oregon so's our childern 'u'd have their chancet, an' now Jed's gone."

There was a stillness in the cabin as Aunt Morning Ann told her story with pauses while she struggled with her sobs. The four children stood about with tears quietly falling, and Martha's eyes filled and her lips quivered as she listened, but no one interrupted while Aunt Morning Ann eased her grief by giving away to the luxury of tears.

"Jed war drownded in the Columbia. I knowed thet mornin' thar'd be a death afore many days. I seed a raven circlin' above our camp, an' I war oneasy when we got inter the boat, but whut kin a body do? No use frightenin' the rest with a ole woman's forebodin's. I allus git a death warnin'. Hit runs in our family ter know aforehan'. Granny could tell things afore they happened, an' so kin I. Hit's the gift o' God to soften grief by preparin' us fer hit."

"Yes," assented Martha.

"Ye mind the Devil's Gullet thet they call the narrer pass whar the Columbia jest naterally stands on edge? The water foams up so fearful aroun' the big rocks. Nights when I cain't sleep I go back over the hull thing an' live hit ag'in. I keep seein' thet Injun pilot with his greasy red hanky tied roun' his head an' his ugly pock-marked face an' his black har flying out behin'. Three families o' us war in the large forward skiff an' Jed an' the two Wilkins boys an' Grandpap Wilkins war paddlin' the small boat 'ith our goods an' pervisions jist behin' us. Our pilot dodged the big rock, but the Injun with the red bandanner didn't foller us. The boat got away from him, somehow, and struck the rock sideways and capsized. Jed must 'a' hit his head; he never came up.

"You know how men is," she continued. "They came nigh capsizin' our boat, tryin' ter save the boys an' grandpap, an' gettin' all excited 'lowin' ter shoot the Injun. Aunt Cynthia Applegate saved our lives. She kep' her head an' made 'em sit down an' tend the oars arter they'd pulled one o' the Wilkins boys inter our boat. Grandpap an' t'other Wilkins boy couldn't swim much, an' hit war so long afore we could make a landin', the bank's so slick an' steep an' the current so strong."

"What became of the Indian, Aunt Morning Ann?" asked Asa, breathless with interest.

"Chile, he either drownded er got away in the commotion o' makin' a landin'. We never seed him ag'in. Perhaps twar jist ez well. I 'low ef them mad men had 'a' kilt him, ez they'd 'a' done ef they'd 'a' found him, we'd 'a' had Injun war long o' the rest o' our hardships. The men blamed him an' suspicioned him, but I dunno. I dunno. One o' the Wilkins boys said he lost his cap and riz up ter git hit, and jist then the boat war out o' hand."

"No," reasoned Martha. "It's hardly fair to blame him when the Devil's Gullet is so dangerous. I remember how frightened we were when we went round by a hair's turn."

Aunt Morning Ann was thoughtful for a moment before she resumed her story. "I dunno. I have the feelin' thet thet Injun's not dead, an' I'm oneasy at night. I feel somehow as ef I'll see him ag'in. I've kept watchin' every Injun I see down here. He war a canoe Injun an' belonged down here to the Injun lodge. They said ez how he war a kind o' a chief. I disremember his name. Pop knows hit, though." She brightened as the name suddenly came to her. "Quimmo thet Injun's name war. He war a Clatsop chief, so they said. The Clatsops air powerful good on the river. They come up ter the Columbia every fall. Injuns never live ter one place like white folks.

"We-all war afeered o' trouble with the Cayuse Injuns jist afore we left Fort Walla Walla. Hit mout 'a' been thet thet made the pilot mad at us. An' seein' hit from his side, I cain't say ez he kin be blamed, an' in course he'd git even in the savage Injun way."

"I never could blame them," said Martha thoughtfully. "They saw us coming to take their land away from them. They said on the plains that they never made trouble until they saw ploughs in the settlers' wagons, and that meant fields of grain growing and their hunting-grounds gone."

"Yes," assented Aunt Morning Ann, "an' the way the whites treat 'em, pore ignorant savages. Our younguns near got us into war. Hit's hard enough ter keep outen a furse when yer grown an' kin keep yer tongue between yer teeth, but thar jist hain't no tellin' whut younguns'll say er do. Our li'l' rascal Silas war mixed up in hit, in course. Our boys had a fight with the Injun boys. I drug the hull story outen him by littles. Ye mind the sand flat near the big tater house jest outside the fort? Did you-all camp thar while ye made yer rafts?"

"Yes," Martha answered. "We must have come alone a few days after you left. We heard about an accident, but didn't learn who it was. Mr. McKinley at the fort warned us that the Indians were sullen and uneasy and said that we had best sleep inside the fort and have as little as possible to do with them."

"Wal," Aunt Morning Ann continued her story, "ye know how much some folks talk afore their

younguns. Hit's this tarnation hatin' Injuns an'
'lowin' whut they'd do ef sech an' sech happened
thet puts toplofty notions inter fool boys' heads.
Tradin' the Injun boys outer yampa war a good
pastime fer our boys."

"What is yampa, Aunt Morning Ann?" asked Asa,
listening in breathless expectancy to her story.

"Why, hain't you children ever tasted yampa?"
she inquired incredulously. "Yampa is thet li'l'
dried wild parsnip root, 'bout ez thick ez my li'l'
finger and twicet ez long ez hit's wide. Kind o' sweet
an' chalky-like. The Injuns dry hit somehow in the
sun er over a slow fire. Our pore younguns was well-
nigh starved fer somethin' sweet, an' their swappin'
ole nails an' tiny pieces o' iron war peaceful enough
ontil the Harrison boys began ter drop their yampa."

She turned to Martha, "Ye know, Miz' Bainbridge, how some wimmen hate ter sew pockets onto
their boys' britches. Hit air a mean, tedious li'l' job.
Miz' Harrison never'd put nary a pocket on—said
her boys'd jist carry fish worms an' sech in 'em an'
load 'em up with what not ontil the weight done broke
down their galluses, but I allus concluded thet hit
war jist naterel laziness on her part thet war the
real reason."

Martha smiled assent.

"Wal, one o' our boys ketched a Injun boy slyly
pickin' up the yampa thet pore li'l' Jason Harrison
had dropped. He war a-holdin' hit in his two han's
ag'in' his stommick an' hit kep a-droppin'. Silas
admitted ter me free enough thet him an' the other
boys had b'en a-pickin' hit up an' puttin' hit in their

pockets, but when they ketched a Injun boy tryin'
ter trade hit over, thet war different. Our boys air
all too tarnation handy with rocks, an' they'd larned
so much about the wuthlessness o' Injuns thet they
jist spited 'em on gineral principles. The Injun boys
returned their rocks with arrers, but our boys saw
'em coming an' dodged 'em easy. They took sure
aim with rocks. One Injun boy had his head laid
plumb open. They said 'twar Quimmo's boy, him ez
upset the boat. I dunno. Nobuddy knows what
would 'a' happened if Dick Skelton hadn't o' come
along an' collared two o' our young varmints and
stopped the fight."

"Just to think," exclaimed Martha to her absorbed
children, "that half a dozen thoughtless boys might
have brought down a thousand Indians on the wagon-
train inside of a few hours."

"Yes," Aunt Morning Ann supplemented, "only
the marcy o' God saved us. Dick Skelton shook those
two boys he had a hold on ontil their teeth chattered.
Some o' the squaws seen him a-punishin' o' them. I
allus wonder ef Dick didn't save us, arter all. Some
said as how hit war thet fight thet made the pilot try
ter git even with us. I dunno. I dunno."

"I can't just place Dick Skelton," pondered
Martha.

"Dick Skelton is thet bound boy thet came along
with Lafe Tompkins," Aunt Morning Ann explained. "He hain't bound no more—no one seems
ter claim him. Lafe an' Miz Tompkins both died on
the trail. Lafe war jist mean an' wuthless by nater.
They claimed he war mixed up in some dirty stealin'

business. I dunno. Ennyway, somebody done shot him. We never knowed who done hit; jist foun' him dead a few rods from his wagon one mornin'. Pore jaded Miz' Tompkins gin out afore we reached the Sweetwater."

"Poor tired little girl!" ejaculated Martha. "They camped near us often the first month, and then we lost sight of them."

"Ye mind she war only sixteen. She war his secont wife. Her baby war borned along early in the summer, an' she didn't git much keer. Meaner'n dog broth thet man war to his oxen, an' ter Miz' Tompkins an' ter Dick Skelton, too. She complained o' a misery in her back from walkin' an' carryin' the baby. Us older women helped her all we could, but she jist wore out. The baby pindled along an' died, too, in a few weeks, fust one an' then t'other o' us mindin' hit."

"A young baby doesn't stand much show on the plains unless it's strong and healthy," commented Martha. "But tell us about Dick."

"Dick cartainly war kind ter pore Miz' Tompkins, an' Miz' Tompkins war ez good ter him ez she durst be, pore cowed critter. Lafe hardly 'lowed 'em 'nuff ter eat, an' he beat Dick nigh ter death an' worked him ontil he nearly drapped in his tracks. Hit's a hard life on wimmen an' orphan children— hard 'nuff 'twar in Missouri, but meanness jest oozes out o' folks on the plains, ef they're constituted mean. Crossin' the plains sure do weed out the pindlin' ones, too," she concluded.

"What did Dick do after Tompkins died?" queried

Martha, drawing Aunt Morning Ann back to the subject.

"Why, he drove Tompkins's wagon an' jist simply adopted the hul passle o' orphan childern thet no one could take. Seemed lak our wagons war all so full an' the oxen so weak toward the last. In course we helped pore Dick all we could, but pervisions war low, an' a lot o' them pore younguns didn't rightfully have enough ter eat. Most o' 'em walked, except when the wagons war goin' down trails whar us wimmen folks war afeerd ter ride; then they climbed into our wagons an' rode down the grade ter rest theirselves."

"I remember Dick Skelton," ventured Rose Ann, a little shamefacedly. "I felt sorry for him. All the boys and girls laughed at him; he was so gawky and awkward and his sleeves were so short his hands dangled out of them. The boys called him 'Gangleshanks.' He never played games of evenings with us; he always had to chop wood or do camp chores. Once or twice I saw him watching us playing 'duck-on-the-rock,' but the boys never offered to choose him when we took sides."

"Why air younguns so cruel-hearted?" asked Aunt Morning Ann. "Thet pore boy, I knowed his mother an' father back in Novelty, Missouri. Both on 'em died with the fever an' ager when Dick war seven year ole er thereabouts. Mary Skelton war a right sweet gal, an' eddicated at the academy at Liberty, Missouri, an' Dick Skelton war a young schoolmaster when he married her; but, lawsakes! they war jist two babies when hit came ter gittin' on in the

world, an' young Dick war left onto the county an'
jest boun' out with never no chancet at all but to
be worked nigh to death by folks ez scanted his vittles
an' gin him their wornout clothes. Dick's nineteen
now, an' a man in spite o' hit all.

"Thet pore boy, I love him like my own Jed, an'
sence Jed's gone"—she turned chokingly away—
"Dick somehow seems ter take his place ter me. We
feed him every chancet we git. There hain't room
ter take him in ter live. Our six younguns air fair
bustin' outen our cabin now. He's been up ter see
us twicet since we got ter the settlement, but war he
sleeps er how he live I dunno." She shook her head
sadly.

"They say there isn't standing room in the houses
down at Oregon City and the emigrants are sleeping
in any shelter they can find. That's why we came
up to locate our claim and build our cabin at once,"
said Martha. "Of course, Dick didn't bring his
wagon or oxen down. Did he have anything with
him?" asked Martha.

"No, jist the clothes he stood in; but he struck up
a friendship with a quar Injun thet we-all met up
with at Fort Boise—crazy, some said thet thar Siah-
hen air, but I dunno. Struck me lak he war allus
makin' a joke onto us. He allus spoke Chinook
wa-wa ter us, an' when we didn't understan' he talked
jist ez good ez we do an' then laughed fit ter kill.
He war allus prowlin' roun', but he war friendly
enough. He took ter sleepin' in Dick's wagon an'
come on down with we-all. He war the first right
clean Injun I ever seed. He wore a blue drillin' shirt

an' buckskin britches, an' had his har cut jist lak a white man. Dick is with him down ter the Injun village a lot, but, pore boy, he hain't got no other place ter go."

She brightened and chuckled over some cherished recollection. "Dick be l'arnin' hisself ter read an' write," she announced proudly. "Hit do beat time how thet boy hankers fer l'arnin'. He kin read right smart, an' he didn't know one letter from t'other, no more'n I do, when we started across the plains. Lafe Tompkins 'lowed hit made younguns wuthless ter eddicate 'em, but soon's Lafe war gone clear outen reach, Dick sot erbout ter larn in arnest. I ketched him one day a-readin' somethin' ter thet fool Siah-hen, an' both a-laughin' fit ter kill. Thet war nigh onter the fust time I ever hearn Dick Skelton laugh. Pore boy, he hadn't no call ter laugh before."

She chuckled again before she went on with the story she took such delight in telling. The children in their eagerness formed a small circle about her, with hands behind their backs and wide eyes glued to her face. She paused to enjoy the situation, but the children's cries of "Tell us the rest, Aunt Morning Ann," were not to be denied.

"I done pore Dick a good turn when we sorted out our stuff ter pack inter the skiff. Pop an' t'other men war fer throwin' out everything but jist the bare nedcessities. We had a ole Webster's Spellin' Book thet Dick war a l'arnin' outer, an' a McGuffy's Fifth Reader that war too hard fer him them. I fixed the speller under his wamus an' fastened hit secure with his belt, an' put the readin' book inter the busum o' my dress, an' we fotched 'em through an' no one the wiser. I 'lowed ez how books mout be powerful scarce in the settlement, an' ef Dick l'arned ter read, mebbe he could l'arn our younguns. Pop an' me never had a chancet, but thet hain't no reason our younguns should come up ignorent."

"How did you manage to get provisions enough to last you until you got to Oregon City?" asked Martha. The subject of provisioning was uppermost in her mind most of the time.

"Why, Robert Shortis, him ez used ter live with the Applegates back in Missouri, met us at The Dalles with enough ter carry us through. He done no more'n he outer, though we're grateful ter him. 'Twar Robert Shortis got us ter come in the fust place. He wrote letters ter the papers back in Missouri an' told all erbout the Oregon country, how rich the sile war, an ez how we wouldn't have no taxes ter pay, an' all. Pop couldn't hardly wait ter sell the farm an' git out here. Robert Shortis war a-lookin' fer us. He had a canoe an' two Injuns with him. He had brung flour an' sugar an' jerky beef an' a sack o' pemmican."

"We were nearly starving when we reached that desolate stretch of wilderness below The Dalles," said Martha. "It was snowing when we made camp, and we waded through a nasty wet slush. There was a baby born on the raft, and three nursing babies besides, and we were cold and hungry. The children were crying and clinging to the skirts of their tired mothers. That long day in the wilderness was the hardest time we endured on the whole trip. The

men had to go hunting and didn't get back at nightfall, and we were all fearful uneasy, just ready to die
with discouragement. It just seemed to us that
human beings couldn't endure any more. The
coyotes howled to make the blood run cold that night
when we made a fire and tried to dry out our wet
clothing. We gave the children some dried fish skins
to chew on, and portioned out the very last of the
jerky."

"Ye pore things, don't I know that ready-ter-give-
up-an'-die feelin'? Hain't we-all been through hit,
though?" sympathized Aunt Morning Ann. "Go on.
What did ye do, Miz' Bainbridge?"

"Just as the poor babies were settled to sleep, we
heard voices and the paddling of a canoe up the
river, and we were terrified again. We were sure
they were hostile Indians, and when we heard them
preparing to make a landing, panic broke out. But
a white man spoke to us, saying that Doctor Mc-
Loughlin had just heard that there were women and
children starving in the wilderness and had sent his
men out with provisions for us."

"Thet good ole man," exclaimed Aunt Morning
Ann fervently. "We seen him at Fort Vancouver.
Thar war a long line o' emigrants afore a li'l' winder,
an' his clerks war a-sellin' goods on credit to 'em. I
'low he'll wait a spell fer his pay. Some o' the emigrants war kind o' onery-actin', blamin' him fer sellin' pervisions so high, an' them buyin' them on credit
an' a lot o' 'em awful pore pay. Thet man's a prac-
ticin' Christian ef I know one when I see him."

"He was heavenly kind to us," said Martha fervently. "He sent each family of us fifty pounds of flour and ten pounds of bacon; there was a gallon jug of molasses, and a whole pound of tea. We made up cooking fires that night and had pancakes and bacon and molasses and strong tea. We'd never tasted anything so good, had we, children?"

"Nothin' like a good strong brew o' tea ter hearten ye," observed Aunt Morning Ann. "Hit probably saved those pore nursin' mothers, li'l' slimpsy gals, most on 'em. I did pity wimmen with babies on the plains; twar hard enough when younguns kin walk, a-holdin' onto their pore mother's skirts, but ter lug a heavy baby over them mounting trails! God A'mighty knows what they went through! They didn't complain much neither."

"It's a shame the Indians burned Doctor Whitman's grist mill and his barn. Some people said they didn't do it on purpose. He was depending on the mill to grind flour for the settlers. They said at Vancouver that the news disturbed Doctor McLoughlin. He has been afraid that food will be scarce, with so many coming this fall. But there is plenty of wheat and we'll make it through the winter somehow."

"Yes," assented Aunt Morning Ann cheerfully, "b'iled wheat ain't so bad ef there hain't nothin' else an' a body works hard ter keep up a appetite."

"How are the Indians here? Do you think they are threatening?" Martha asked, as her visitor rose reluctantly to go. "We've been rather uneasy since we left Walla Walla. The Cauyses were muttering and threatening all along the Columbia."

"Oh, these here canoe Injuns air peaceful enough, dirty, slouching, bow-legged wretches!" ejaculated Aunt Morning Ann disgustedly. "There hain't so powerful many Injuns in these parts; mostly the Clackamas an' Yamhill tribes, with a sprinklin' o' all the other tribes thet air mostly died off, so Pop says. They'll pilfer ennything they kin git their dirty han's onto, an' pester a body nigh to death ter swap with 'em, but I 'low we kin stand their ornery-ness better'n livin' in terror o' bein' massacred in our beds."

There was evidently something on Aunt Morning Ann's mind. She lingered at the cabin door, hesitated, and finally turned to Martha with a little show of embarrassment. "How're you-all off fer per-visions?" she asked. "Pop done traded his draw knife ter the Injuns ez soon ez ever he finished the cabin. He 'lowed he could do without the knife better'n grub, with eight mouths ter feed. Made a good swap, too. The Injuns gin him a hemp sack o' wheat, an' a sack o' lepwah, them hard white peas they air so powerful fond of, an' four big smoked salmon an' a sack o' pemmican. We been livin' high the las' few days. God A'mighty knows we-all went ter bed hungry afore thet. I 'lowed ter loan ye-all enough ter tide ye over fer a few days ef you're runnin' low."

Quick tears of gratitude sprang to Martha's eyes. The children, too, brightened visibly. There was nothing in the house for the noon meal but a small dish of wheat boiled with a little salt, and at best it would be three days before John and Uncle Adzi would return from Vancouver. She had been uneasily turning over and over in her mind whether to ask Aunt Morning Ann to remain to dinner to share the morsel of boiled wheat with them, or to explain their plight to her.

"We have very little to eat in the house," explained Martha simply. "We'd certainly appreciate your loan. I miscalculated the amount of wheat left, and John was delayed a day in engaging the Indian with the canoe. We'd have been pretty hungry by the time they return. I can stand it myself, but I hate to have the children do without food. Not saying that we haven't gone hungry to bed before, this summer."

"Asa an' Manuel had best come along home with me an' tote you-all back a li'l' sack o' dried peas an' some wheat an' pemmican so's you-all kin hold on a few days longer. The Injuns make a soup o' dried peas; lip-lip, they call hit, an' hit's right good an' fillin'. Pemmican is tasty, too—beats all time how the squaws kin dry salmon and skin hit an' take out the bones and pound it up fine."

Alert at the prospect of lip-lip and pemmican, Asa and Manuel took their places one on either side of Aunt Morning Ann as she straightened her stiff knees after sitting so long and began the laborious ascent to her cabin.

# CHAPTER IV

**M**ANUEL and Asa returned triumphantly in the early evening, having had dinner with Aunt Morning Ann and renewing acquaintance with the Simmons family. They carried a generous portion of dried white peas, hard as flint, as well as wheat and pemmican. With relief Martha placed the cooking-pots over the fire at once, that part of the long boiling might be accomplished that evening, and lip-lip, the Indian soup Aunt Morning Ann had told her how to make, would be ready for breakfast.

She drew the bolt across the door when the children were in bed and tucked in well at the back, then covered the bed of live coals and the backlog in the fireplace carefully with ashes so that it would hold fire until morning, and placed the iron pots over it to keep their contents just below the boiling point through the night.

It was her placid custom, after going to bed, to mull over the happenings of the day, to take note of her mistakes, her lack of foresight in planning her work, the wavering of her faith in God, and her little losses of temper with the children. She made her nightly resolves to make the day to come an improvement over the day just past, wondering between sleeping and waking why the coyotes howled

63

so much louder when John and Uncle Adzi were away.

She reproached herself for her lack of trust in Divine care during the morning when there was no food in the house, and thanked God over and over for sending His messenger in the person of Aunt Morning Ann to supply the lack; she resolved to harbor no more dark fears for the future in her heart. Simple trusting souls like Martha Bainbridge discern the Guiding Hand in all their doings. She said over and over verses of Scripture, "Yet have I not seen the righteous forsaken, nor his seed begging bread," and, "In all thy ways acknowledge Him and He shall direct thy paths." Martha was what Aunt Morning Ann had aptly termed a practicing Christian.

Morning broke with a heavy frost. The children breakfasted to repletion on lip-lip, thick and hot and nourishing. Manuel and Asa repaired rather precipitately to the timber to work on the stint their father had laid out for them to finish by his return. Unpleasant consequences always followed an unfinished stint with the return of father. To-day Manuel must split the wood that had been cut and Asa was to pile it. After that there were certain little diversions loudly claiming their attention, such as making bird snares and setting figure-four traps.

Martha went about the routine work, opening the cabin door to let in light as she set the girls to scouring tin plates and cups and knives and forks with sand.

Rose Ann screamed. Framed in the low doorway

stood a very tall Indian, brandishing a long knife, grinning horribly, and speaking unintelligibly in rapid Chinook. Behind him, crowding to enter, were four others, all carrying similar knives.

Esther Amelia ran to hide her face in her mother's lap, and Rose Ann cowered and trembled beside her. Tales of wild scalping parties, and of outrages to women in lonely cabins, went through Martha's mind. She realized that she was completely at their mercy. The boys had, with their father's permission, taken the gun with them, and, anyway, the Indians were in the cabin and resistance would be futile. Realizing that there was nothing to be said or done, she did nothing, just sat quietly with her two girls beside her, waiting prayerfully for the end.

The leader advanced and waved the knife, the others did the same, still laughing and talking in their jargon. He stopped a moment and conferred with the others, then ran his finger appraisingly over the edge of the knife. His companions followed his example. The cabin was filled with the volleys of Chinook wa-wa aimed at her, then a short withdrawal while they counciled among themselves in low gutturals.

After the discussion they filed out of the cabin and stood in the dooryard before the grindstone. She could watch them without rising. They were grinding their murderous knives. Fascinated, all three watched the process, waiting, numb with terror, for the blow to fall. It took an eternity, with much testing of the edges and conversation carried on in laughing tones among them, until the work was done to their satisfaction. Then the spokesman, grinning horribly, advanced again with a flourish of his knife and more jargon. Martha faced him bravely. But when he finished his speech he turned and led the others out of the cabin, and Martha and the girls watched them going single file down the path until they disappeared in the timber. Martha, scarcely breathing, watched the path for their return, but when she was satisfied that they were out of sight and hearing of the cabin, she rose and with a trembling hand drew the bar across the door, turning to quiet the two terrified girls. Rose Ann was crying hysterically and she chided her sharply, telling her to take herself in hand, that hysterics were just lack of self-control, and a woman must, above all, possess self-control.

But she admitted to herself that she was thoroughly frightened and did not know what to do. Perhaps the Indians had gone for reinforcements, or it might be that they had been afraid to carry out their diabolical plans. The three waited in breathless expectancy all the morning, afraid to go for the boys, fearing they had been killed, wondering if there was an Indian uprising in the settlement and if for some unaccountable reason they were the sole survivors.

They started at the barking of a dog and the unmistakable sound of hoofs striking the loose stones on the trail. Some one was coming. Perhaps the war party had gathered power to themselves and were finishing up their gruesome task of killing the settlers. But it was not an Indian's voice that called the dog from annoying the hobbled oxen grazing below the cabin.

Tensely the three listened as the sound of the hoof-beats grew clearer; but Martha did not move; terror was upon her. She could not be sure. But at length her straining ears caught the muffled sounds of dismounting near the door, and then a rap with the end of a riding-whip.

"Who's there?" called Martha.

"It's Mr. McDermott," a hearty voice answered.

And Martha, pale and shaken, drew the bolt on the door and opened it wide to her guest.

"Why, Mrs. Bainbridge," he exclaimed in alarm, "are you sick?"

"No," faltered Martha, shaking like a leaf, yet struggling for composure. "The Indians," she finally gasped. "They came with knives and shook them in our faces, and sharpened them at the grindstone, and then went off down the trail. Has there been an uprising?"

McDermott's voice reassured her. "No, Mrs. Bainbridge. The Indians here are friendly. Tell me just how they acted. I'll see that they're punished for annoying you. We can't have white women frightened out of their senses by the actions of fool Indians."

Trying to treat the matter lightly, now that she knew there had been no danger, Martha told the story simply, the girls helping to piece out the details.

"So all they did was sharpen their knives," said McDermott finally. "They meant no harm to you;

they were just trying to tell you that they wanted to use your grindstone. They're probably going hunting."

He paused a moment, apparently busy with some disturbing thought, frowning and chewing the straw-colored ends of his mustache. "This is not the hunting season; a hunt means lack of food in the lodge. The Indians have traded off their supplies too liberally to the settlers; they can't resist the trading fever.

"What sort of an Indian was that leader?" he asked her uneasily. "Would you know him if you ever saw him again?"

Martha shuddered. "I would know him any place; his evil face was pitted with smallpox, and he was tall but round shouldered."

"Quimmo!" McDermott exclaimed, evidently in spite of himself, then made an effort to cover his confusion by searching his pockets and bringing to light a string of blue beads which he smilingly handed to Esther Amelia. The child, turned suddenly shy, took them wonderingly.

"Thank Mr. McDermott," Martha reminded her.

"Thank you, sir," Esther Amelia timidly obeyed.

But the subject was not so easily turned. Rose Ann was all excitement at the mention of the name Quimmo. "Why, Quimmo's that Indian that upset the boat and drowned Jed Simmons and those other two men in the Devil's Gullet, isn't he, mother? I thought Aunt Morning Ann said he was drowned."

"We heard down here about his running the boat on the rocks and the emigrants' conjecture that he was drowned because they didn't see him again, but I thought at the time that it was not likely that he had an accident with that boat. One of those canoe Indians doesn't drown any more than a water rat drowns. They belong in the water; they've handled canoes ever since they can remember," said McDermott."

"Then he's a bad character, just as Aunt Morning Ann felt he might be?" asked Martha.

"Oh no!" defended McDermott, "Quimmo might be a little revengeful, but, like all other Indians, he's a stanch loyal friend to his friends. Didn't a white boy nearly kill his boy with a rock in some boyish squabble at Fort Walla Walla? That's the story that came down here."

"Yes, there was trouble among the boys just before they left, and, according to Aunt Morning Ann Simmons—they have settled about a mile above us—" she explained, "the white boys were largely in the wrong."

"When the hunting party returns, I'll take Quimmo to task for frightening you," promised McDermott. "I'll admit I can't understand his coming here to use your grindstone; they've always used mine before." He frowned and his face darkened at some thought that apparently troubled him deeply in spite of his efforts to dismiss it.

"Where are the men?" he asked. "I rode over to see about those rails. Takes half my time riding the fences and hunting longhorns. I could use fifty thousand rails to-morrow."

"They went to Vancouver after supplies," an-

swered Martha. "We hope they'll be back to-morrow evening, but they may be detained until the day
after. We've learned to look for our men folks when
we see them coming."

"You won't be uneasy alone another night?" he
inquired solicitously. The sight of Martha's drawn
face when she opened the door had moved him
strangely.

But Martha's laugh was reassuring. "Oh no!"
she exclaimed. "The boys are here, and now that
we are not afraid of being scalped by Indians, there
is no cause for uneasiness."

"Can you spin, Mrs. Bainbridge?" McDermott
asked suddenly.

"Can I spin?" echoed Martha. "Why, of course
I can spin! Every woman can spin."

His face brightened, then saddened again. "Since
my wife died her spinning-wheel has been idle. I
have plenty of wool ready to wash and card. I need
warm wool socks. You might take the spinning-
wheel and the wool and pay me by knitting socks.
There'd be plenty of wool left to knit for your family,
and to sell. Good heavy wool socks bring fifty cents
a pair, and there's never enough in the settlement.
The hunters and trappers buy them all."

Here was an unbelievable piece of good fortune.
Wool and a spinning-wheel. Delight fairly radiated
from Martha's countenance, and a smile lit Rose
Ann's pinched little face. "We'll be so glad to spin
and knit for you, Mr. McDermott," Martha exclaimed joyfully. "'Twill help us through the winter
to be able to provide socks for the family, and if we

can sell them the money will help more than you have any idea. We are forced to buy on credit, and you know that's bad business."

McDermott rose to leave, taking occasion to scrutinize Rose Ann without seeming to do so, as she sat with her bare feet carefully tucked under her buckskin dress. She colored angrily under his glance, but her mother was too happy to notice that she did not rise to bid the guest good-by.

He took from behind his saddle, before mounting, a long rose brier which he had tied up in a coil. "Here, Mrs. Bainbridge," he said, bowing, "is a cutting from my Mission rose. If you get me a shovel I'll set it by the door." He was breaking off the leaves, still fresh and green, as he spoke, and showing her how to place a rose shoot three or four eyes below the surface just where it was to grow.

He lifted a few deep shovelfuls of the rich loam and set the cutting, tamping the soil down firmly with his foot. "This'll bloom next summer," he assured her. "You'll be sorry you own such a pest when you begin cutting it away to open the door. That's the way things grow in this country. Can't keep 'em in their place. Oh, I forgot." He was fumbling in his saddle bag. "Here are some lusty young hollyhocks that seeded themselves; they'll bloom next year, too. I thought you might like them; it takes them two years to bloom from seed, and two years is so long to wait."

Martha could only murmur her thanks. She had brought along posy seeds, but it was unexpected good fortune to have them ready to bloom in the spring, just like one had always lived in the cabin. Surely here was the home of opportunity, the Oregon country, where one casually set out rose slips in December and made a posy garden for next spring's blooming.

"I'll see that you have the spinning-wheel right away, Mrs. Bainbridge, and make my bargain with your husband for the rail-splitting. Perhaps I'd best come over to-morrow to be sure you're safe and that the Indians do not trouble again. Do not have the least uneasiness; they had no idea of frightening you; they were explaining their errand in Chinook."

He lifted the hair bridle rein, and after two or three unsuccessful attempts to mount his horse and dodging an ugly nip from the sharp teeth, finally mounted and rode off down the trail, pausing at the edge of the timber to turn and raise his broad-brimmed beaver hat.

After the business of the day was over, Martha lay quietly in her safe warm bed, listening to the howl of the coyotes. A sense of peace and well-being stole over her as she reviewed the eventful day just passed. She had had a bad fright, but, she reasoned, it was by no means her first one, and probably wouldn't be the last one. As she saw it in the stillness of the cabin, there was a ridiculous aspect to her terror, now that it was past. She laughed softly in the darkness, telling herself that even a bad fright was not without its compensation—never again need she fear Indians. She qualified this a little, though; she need never be really afraid unless there should be an Indian uprising. The mortal did not live who could withstand the abject horror of Indians on the warpath.

And if the passing day had brought its period of acute suffering and left the nerves a bit shaken, it had also brought joy in greater measure than she had even dared hope. A spinning-wheel and wool! How she had hated to throw out the spinning-wheel. She remembered looking back to where it lay beside the tortuous trail that led up over a steep mountain. John had feared for the oxen, straining forward on their yokes, and as he braked the hind wheels with a "toggle" thrust through the spokes, and Uncle Adzi threw a heavy stick of wood under the wheels to keep the wagon from rolling back downhill while they rested, she had scanned their faces anxiously. She knew without being told that the load must be lightened again.

But here were the things she needed most—a spinning-wheel and plenty of wool, with a ready sale for knit stockings—the great hand of God had opened to shower His gifts upon her. Why didn't she trust herself more fully to the care of a loving Father?

And a rose growing by the cabin door with spicy pink blooms swaying in the summer breezes. How she would enjoy looking at them when she went about her work, and hollyhocks, stately and tall, to bloom in her dooryard in the spring. Drowsily she searched her mind for one of her "promises," as she called comforting verses of Scripture which she had been taught in her girlhood. Yes, she had the right one: "Then I will give you rain in due season, and the

land shall yield her increase, and the trees of the
field shall yield their fruit. And your threshing shall
reach unto the vintage, and the vintage shall reach
unto the sewing-time; and ye shall eat your bread to
the full, and dwell in your land safely." Yes, that
was it. "Eat your bread to the full, and dwell in
your land safely." How like taking hold of a strong
hand to stumble over a hard, rough place in the trail
were Scripture verses stored in the mind. She must
see that the children learned more of them; she would
teach them one each day; she would surely begin to-
morrow. But Martha had stolen through the gracious borderland and entered deep, dreamless sleep.

Esther Amelia screamed in childish terror toward
gray morning—her fright of the day before over-
shadowed her sleep. Martha took the trembling child
into her bed, soothing her with soft reassurings that
she was safe in mother's arms and that nothing could
possibly harm her here, until she slept again.

Wide awake now, Martha puzzled over some inscrutable things that she had noticed but had not
given thought to in the daytime. Mr. McDermott
was the very embodiment of neighborly kindness; he
was such a gentleman. Why had she secret misgivings about him? There was a fascinating mystery
about him, a vague something that troubled her.
Why had he been so perturbed at the mention of
Quimmo? He had something on his mind, something
that worried him terribly in spite of his efforts to
conceal it.

He was a widower, and yet he didn't look like a
man who cared for himself, and there were very few

women in the country. He was too clean for a bachelor; there was every evidence of his being looked after by a very careful woman. There were neat patches on his riding-breeches, and where in all Christendom was the man who could put on a neat patch, mitering the edges with firm small stitches that scarcely showed? His blue broadcloth coat was faded, but had been carefully cleaned and pressed. His shirt was beautifully ironed and his beaver hat had always been brushed with the nap. He had a well-fed appearance that goes with a woman's ministrations, and yet he had never mentioned a woman. Well, it was probably all right. The intriguing mystery would be revealed soon; she would find out in good time if she just kept still and listened.

She somehow felt a deep pity for him, just why she could not say. His wife was dead, but that was not it—a something deeper stirred her compassion. A loss by death was not a present worry. Death was only a sacred sorrow and this was a living anxiety that stalked at his side.

Well, according to the adage, curiosity had once killed a cat. Why weren't adages more explicit? What had the cat been curious about? But it was rising-time and she dismissed the subject entirely from her mind, to take up the day's pressing duties.

John and Uncle Adzi returned at early candle-lighting with a sack of wheat and dried salmon. They were both silent and a little anxious at first, but cheered up over the pot of lip-lip Martha had ready for them. There is nothing like hot pea soup to hearten tired, discouraged men folks.

Uncle Adzi filled in John's silence with his favorite topic—a waterway to the sea. "Why, Marthie," he exulted, "exportin' is already begun. Thar war a brig in the river down nigh Vancouver a-loadin' on wheat. She war boun' fer Honolulu. Had brung in a cargo o' sugar. Too bad they didn't know in time ter load on hit a few other nedcessities fer the settlement, but," he excused, "come ter think on hit, they hain't got much but sugar in them islands ter swap with us."

"I'd give up the sugar to get a pair of shoes for Martha," said John mournfully. "There's not a shoe to be bought in the whole Oregon country, and all the settlers were barefooted, or thereabout, when they got here. I'll try to make those soles hold to the uppers with some buckskin, Martha. Can't have you going barefooted, and moccasins are a last resort; they'd hurt your feet when you get them wet. You can't step outside with 'em on."

Rose Ann suddenly left the table to hide her tears. She had hoped that father would bring her a pair of shoes, too, but there was nothing for it but to conceal her disappointment. Here she was sixteen and a young lady, going about before strange men barefooted like a mere child. Father would get her moccasins, if she asked him for them, perhaps, but moccasins and bare legs were just as ridiculous as bare feet. Well, anyway, they would soon have stockings if Mr. McDermott let them have wool and the spinning-wheel, and in the meantime she'd try not to worry father and mother about shoes.

Martha made a huge joke of the visit of the Indians, but neither John nor Uncle Adzi found her story in the least amusing. "One of us will stay home with you after this," said John decisively. "We can manage our hauling in by letting both the boys go along to help."

But both were immensely pleased at the prospect of wool and a spinning-wheel and promised to go over in the morning to arrange with Mr. McDermott about splitting rails for him. "This is an unexpected piece of good fortune," exulted John. "There's so little work in the settlement."

"He half promised to trade a fresh longhorn cow and her heifer calf for the rails the first time he came," said Martha. "I do hope he lets us have her. Milk will help out so with the table."

"We'll see," promised John. "There's nothing much in the settlement to eat until next year's crops are in but wheat and salmon, unless we can trade a little with the Indians and hunt, but ammunition's pretty scarce. Doctor McLoughlin has done all he can, but supplies are practically exhausted at the Post. It's God's blessing that he was foresighted enough to induce those French-Canadians on French Prairie to put in extra wheat last spring. Starvation would have stared the whole country in the face before the first harvest, with eight hundred new settlers coming in hungry late in the fall."

# CHAPTER V

McDERMOTT dropped the mask of suavity that he had been holding before him during his visit to the Bainbridges, as soon as the sheltering timber shut him from view. He sought relief to his overcharged feelings in curses and imprecations. He struck one clenched fist in the palm of the other hand, and with the sudden slacking of the bridle rein the pony stumbled, whereupon he cursed Indian kuitans in general and this piebald piece of horse degeneracy in particular. Having finished this, he cursed Indians—buck Indians, with Quimmo coming in for first consideration. Then his attention turned to squaws and he voiced his detestation of dirty, fat, wrinkled old hags, and of young ones so soon to grow old and fat and horrid. He hurled specially vitriolic maledictions at smug long-faced missionaries whose business it was to regulate the morals of everyone.

McDermott had had news to-day which disturbed him. Of late things angered him strangely, anyway, and Quimmo's coming to life after he had thought him safely drowned complicated his affairs terribly. Quimmo and his twelve-year-old son, Sootka, had been his haunting ghosts at night ever since he had sent his daughters to the convent in New Orleans to be educated. He freely admitted to himself that his little agreement with Quimmo might

78

cost him dearly, though there had seemed no danger
in it at the time. But Quimmo, like every other
dirty, skulking Indian, kept his word in all matters
and visited his vengeance in subtle underground ways
on those who broke faith with him. An Indian had
rather die than break his word, and he holds in most
withering contempt a man who gives a promise
lightly. Herein lay many of the differences between
the Indian and the white man.

McDermott, coming into the country when white
settlers were few and scattering, had developed his
farm by work he had been able to induce the Indians
to do. Until the last few years he had had a peculiar
hold upon the Indians, but he knew that this hold was
slipping precariously. There were many evidences
of their loss of confidence in him.

A small vial of strychnine which he had brought
into the country had given him his power. The timber wolves were a terrible menace to cattle. He had
put out poisoned bait about his cabin at night and
each bit of bait had killed its wolf, sometimes six or
eight of them. It chanced that the Indians had not
known of the bait with the white powder upon it;
they had just seen the dead wolves about in the morning, and with their innate superstition had immediately jumped at the conclusion that here was a
great *tah-wat-tee* (a conjurer, or one having supernatural power).

McDermott had been quick to seize his opportunity, playing up in every way to the Indians' belief
in his ability to make magic. From the first he had
been on friendly terms with them, visiting in their

lodges and pow-wowing in their village councils. It was the only safe procedure in a wild new country.

When they stood about in open-mouthed wonder and admiration at his power to kill wolves without a gun, he had straightened to his full height and dignity and explained his position to them: "Mc-Dermott, *tyee* [great] medicine-man. *Tyee tillicum* [great friend]." Like delighted children, the Indians had accepted him and showered their simple favors, such as foods and assistance, upon him.

"We'll always be *tillicums*," explained McDermott suavely, "unless you displease me, but remember, I'm *tyee keel-al-ly* [big medicine-man]. I can make you lie stiff and cold about my cabin just like those wolves." In awe his lightest wish had been a command with his Indian neighbors. His advice during those first years was to them a direct revelation from the *Sah-halee Tyee* (the Great Spirit, or, literally translated, the Great Chief above). The chiefs fraternized with him and brought their problems to be solved. And to his credit, be it said, his advice was sound and good; the chiefs were quick to recognize and take advantage of it.

Quimmo was in those days one of the chiefs of the Clatsops, a tribe of the lower Willamette Valley, who roamed up and down the Columbia and Willamette Rivers in their canoes, fishing and hunting. A strong friendship had sprung up between the two. Quimmo was in many ways a remarkable Indian. His quick native wit delighted McDermott and they passed many a lonely winter evening in his cabin. Quimmo was a *rara avis* among Indians, a survivor of the smallpox. In his early childhood this terrible scourge had swept the lodges of his people.

Sootka, Quimmo's twelve-year old son, was his father's idol; his other children, to his great disgust, had been girls. He never tired of recounting the deeds which showed very plainly the precocity of his boy. He could shoot an arrow straight; he compelled obedience from the other children in the winter lodge. Quimmo looked forward to the time when Sootka would be a great chief and bring back their lost power to the Clatsops. McDermott, secretly amused at Quimmo's boasting—he could see nothing in the *ten'-as kas-kass* (boy)—told of the remarkable beauty of his two little daughters, enlarging especially upon the charms of Mahala, who was about Sootka's age.

A few years later, when Mary McDermott came from New Orleans on a trading-vessel, Quimmo called at once, making no secret of the fact that he wished to see little Mahala. Thinking to confer a great honor upon his white friend and cement a lasting tie between them, he announced that he wished to betroth Sootka to Mahala. McDermott, aghast, but not daring to show his feeling, asked for time to consider, which the Indian graciously granted, thinking that it was the price he asked for his daughter that must be determined.

McDermott turned the subject over in his mind through two sleepless nights, discussing it with his tearful, protesting wife. She begged him to refuse or to send them back to the States on some pretext, though she knew that this meant years of separation

—McDermott, for reasons that she knew well and sorrowed over, could not return to civilization. A woman who had tasted the "acrid salt of disillusion" was Mary McDermott. She was frantic with fear of the dire consequences to come later if McDermott agreed to Quimmo's proposal and later broke his word, as she knew he was thinking of doing.

In vain McDermott had explained his point of view. There was no immediate danger in humoring the Indians, and he would get greater power over them. It would be a long time before the children were old enough to marry. Many things could happen in the interval. He argued, correctly enough, that it would be very dangerous to antagonize Quimmo, who was a powerful chief, when there were so few white settlers in the country. He could hope for little or no protection from Doctor McLoughlin in his differences with the Indians. He had never been in favor with him since his unfortunate advent into the Oregon country with Ewing Young's party. In his heart he hated duplicity, though he frequently employed it to gain his ends. Loath as he was to consent to Quimmo's proposal, he felt that here the end justified the means.

But Mary McDermott had constantly brooded and grieved over the situation, and since her death he had come to feel that this among other things was the cause of her gradual fading away, though outwardly he laid her illness to the intolerable loneliness of a woman living where she seldom saw a white woman.

The betrothal had been a source of irritation, too.

The Indians took so much for granted. The betrothed pair had by friction between themselves once come near making serious trouble. There are many points of Indian etiquette to be observed.

Sootka, a smug, overbearing young Indian of eight years, had arrived early to spend the day playing with his betrothed. A playmate was a playmate, and the children welcomed him joyfuly in spite of his filthy blanket and his bear grease and dirt-incrusted face and hands. Mary had given each of the children a piece of pie and sent them to play in the dooryard, where she could keep an eye on them as she went about her work.

Sootka, with the Indian's inherent greed for food, bolted his pie with the peculiar feeding habit common to his race—shoving most of it into his mouth and with a circular motion of his hand keeping it in place until he had hastily masticated it. He had finished his pie before the fastidious Mahala had more than started on hers. Eyeing her pie speculatively, he suggested that he hold it for her while she went to ask her mother for another piece of pie for him. Mahala obediently handed him her pie and went on the errand, returning in a moment to tell him mother said there was no more pie. Sootka was just polishing his face with his pie-sticky hands as Mahala came with the disappointing news.

She took in the situation at a glance, and her Creole blood boiled in her small veins. Sootka had eaten her pie! Like an enraged tigress, she flew at him, scratching his face, boxing his ears, and kicking his shins with her copper-toed shoes. Sootka was vanquished before he had time to recover from his surprise. A squaw never struck a buck, much less the son of a chief.

Without waiting to make formal adieus, he fled howling to the Indian lodge, nearly two miles down the hill. Mary, hearing the commotion, had arrived on the scene just in time to see him in mad flight, but he paid no attention to her calls to return, so there was nothing to do but chide Mahala and let the matter go.

The afternoon brought a delegation of very serious-faced Indians to confer with McDermott. He took them to the barn and held a long pow-wow with them. They had come to demand that he surrender Mahala to them; she had struck a chief's son, and for a squaw to strike a buck was a deed punishable by death; that the chief's only son was the victim made the offense doubly heinous. She must die. How else could order be maintained among the squaws in the lodge?

McDermott had argued with them, telling that white squaws were fools; they knew nothing; that he'd teach the white squaw. It had taken all his powers of persuasion and covert threats to work bad medicine on them to bring them around, but finally they agreed to drop the matter providing he gave them a fat steer to hold a feast in the lodge. He gladly surrendered his best steer. The incident left a disagreeable doubt in his mind; sometime something might happen that could not be adjusted. But the former friendly relations were resumed and things went smoothly enough until Mary died. He knew then that he must send the girls away to school.

Once they were out of the way, he need have no anxiety for their safety, and peace of mind was something to be considered. It seemed to him that he had lived the most of his life with large and small nagging fears tagging always at his elbow.

Quimmo had demurred at the girl's departure, shaking a sullen head and pretending that he was evading the terms of their early agreement. In vain McDermott explained that he was only sending Mahala away to be educated so that she would be a fit wife for the son of a great chief.

Little Quimmo cared about education for his son's wife. There was nothing to do but accept the situation, but he could extort a good-sized *potlatch* from McDermott. He demanded three steers and a pony, and they were reluctantly given.

By unmistakable tokens McDermott knew that the Indians were slowly, or perhaps not so slowly—he could not be sure—losing faith in him. For one thing, the missionaries were doing active work among them and they were much wiser in the ways of the white men than when he first came into the country. He suspected that they were now familiar with the use of strychnine for killing wolves, and knew that he had duped them into believing that he was a *tyee keel-al-ly*. They had a distressing way of disposing of a medicine-man in whom they had lost faith.

Instead of an eagerness to till his fields and work in the timber under his direction, he had difficulty now in securing Indians to work, no matter what inducements he offered. They had a sneering, derisive way of muttering among themselves when his back was turned, sullenly resuming leisurely work when he was in their presence. This disturbed him more than he liked to admit, though he carried off the situation with his old smiling good nature.

He had rejoiced when the party of emigrants headed by Jesse Applegate reached Oregon City late that fall with the news of Quimmo's drowning in the Devil's Gullet (Grand Dalles) of the Columbia. He would have borne up nobly if the white boys had killed Sootka, instead of merely grazing his scalp with a rock, though with Quimmo safely out of the way there was little likelihood of Sootka's ever pressing his suit for Mahala. The settlers, arriving in such great numbers, had very materially changed the Indian situation in the Oregon country, so that there was now very little to fear from them—that is, at least openly.

A large ragged load of worry was taken off his mind. He had one serious problem pressing for almost immediate solution. It had come upon him with the arrival of white women and girls in the settlement. There were still other smaller perplexities like persistent mosquitoes, stinging and disturbing his peace of mind, but he gratefully "took the good the gods provided," and hoped that somehow his greatest difficulty would automatically adjust itself, if he could but master patience to bide its time.

The news he had received in the Bainbridge cabin that morning was like a thunderbolt from the blue. He might have known that a canoe Indian did not drown, but he had so wanted to be rid of Quimmo that he had accepted the story. His seeking such terrible vengeance on innocent whites whom he blamed for the injury to his idol, Sootka, when in all probability the great, skulking, evil-countenanced lad had provoked the trouble himself, just as he had with Mahala, was a terrible warning to him. In the incident he read "the handwriting on the wall." He cautioned himself, between his curses, that he must keep up an eternal vigilance and be prepared to quit the country quickly and quietly if worse came to the worst.

His angry musing, coupled with mutterings and punctuated by lurid curses, came to an end as he emerged from the timber into the edge of his own clearing. From the top of the hill where he stood his farm swept into breath-taking view. The sun was an hour high in a clear opaline sky. There would be another killing frost to-night; the tang of it was in the still air. The glow from the western horizon illumined his fields and orchards, reminding him of the halo around the head of a saint. Clear cut and swimming in light was the farm when he came out of the cathedral-like gloom of the deep timber. To McDermott this home in the wilderness was like the fulfillment of a long-cherished dream. Here he had found the solitude he so sadly needed when he came up from the turbulent settlements of California, leaving behind him some scores whose payment would in a short time have made life there dangerous.

The nine years he had lived in Oregon had been a peaceful oasis in the treacherous desert of his life.

From the days of his first lavish sowing of wild oats in his boyhood home in the South, desolation and trouble for those he loved had followed like whirlwinds in his wake. But there had been peace and healing close to the soil, and safety from the consequences of his indiscretions in the remoteness of a new country.

The thought of being obliged to leave, perhaps between two days, never to return, bore in upon his heavily-laden consciousness. The violence of his mood had passed and he gazed long and lovingly. It was like looking for the last time upon the face of some one whom he had loved very dearly in life, like Mary's still face with the holy calm of death upon it. But he pulled himself together shortly— no use in brooding or indulging in prophetic forebodings. Perhaps things would work out all right. He was a fool to let a greasy Indian drive him out of the country. In all probability when the settlers found that Quimmo had come to life they would take care of him for their own safety. An Indian bent upon revenge for small wrongs, real or fancied, would not be tolerated long in a community of peace-loving men and women. Law and order were going to be very shortly established.

From present indications, Oregon would soon have an independent government, making and enforcing its own laws. Ewing Young's death, and the promptness and justice with which his estate had been settled, showed very clearly the mettle of the men locating in the Willamette Valley. This was two years ago, when there had been but two hundred and fifty Americans in the whole country. He recalled the meeting of the settlers on that first Monday in last March. Those "wolf meetings," with their thinly veiled object of setting a bounty on predatory animals had in reality been a cautious effort on the part of shrewd Americans to establish a government and to wrest the balance of power from the Hudson Bay Company, who represented the British claim to the Oregon country. Mass meetings had followed the emigration of 1842, when the American population had been augmented by one hundred and thirty-seven. What these hundred and thirty-seven Americans had meant he suddenly realized. Mainly professional men with their families, doctors and lawyers and men skilled in trades, they were prepared to practice the arts of peace. He felt safe again as his mind cleared. He called himself a hysterical old woman, and went on reviewing the political situation.

Hadn't he attended the meeting of citizens at Champoeg last May, when the foundations of government were so carefully laid? Hadn't Oregon a regular constitution and carefully drawn-up laws with public sentiment to enforce them? Hadn't eight hundred immigrants arrived late this fall, merely forerunners of the trains that would come each year from the States, now that wagons had come clear through and opened the trail?

Oregon would never be a lawless series of shifting settlements like the California country where every man went armed to the teeth, to make and enforce his own law. No, Oregon held the richest farming

land in the world. It would be a pastoral region.
Broad farms with homes in the center—homes pre-
sided over by soft-voiced women, tenderly mothering
joyous broods of children.

He laughed aloud at his fears. Easy enough to
adjust his little difficulties with the missionaries if
he acted quickly and decisively. A change of heart
known as experiencing religion and the turning from
what they called his evil ways; he would join the
Methodist Church and in time become a pillar in it.
Thank goodness, he had the means to contribute
liberally to its upbuilding, and that would speedily
establish him in the good graces of the community.
"A sinner that repenteth," he quoted laughingly to
himself. Yes, that's what he would be. He would
take a wife from among the young girls who were
coming into the country. He was only forty and
really in the prime of life. 'Twould be easy to pick
and choose among the available women with what he
had to offer in the way of a home and worldly goods.

He would be a planter, as his father had been in
the South, bringing up a family of children in right
ways of living. He had hated the thought of "dying
with his boots on," as outlaws did. No, he would
sit under the grateful shade of his own "vine and
fig tree" in the evening of his placid life and die like
his fathers—peacefully in his bed.

Easy enough to set the wheels of the law to grinding in the case of Quimmo, or to see that he was
turned over to Doctor McLoughlin, who had a stern
way of dealing with Indian culprits, especially in
matters of offenses against the life and property of

the white settlers. " 'Tis the eye of childhood that
fears a painted devil," he quoted with the full return
of assurance.

He told himself that he had been too much alone;
he had studiously avoided the missionaries and the
settlers of the year before, but now he would quickly
rid himself of the skeleton in his closet and take his
rightful place among them. Once convince a missionary of full and complete repentance and the erst-
while sinner is received into the full communion of
the saints. True, there were some other matters that
would have to be adjusted *sub rosa*, so to speak, but
he would manage; he would manage.

He picked up the slack rein on his pony's neck and
turned his head down the hill toward home. He was
appraising his grain field, fully twenty acres, with
three smaller inclosures, all symmetrically fenced and
cross-fenced with rails set in the Virginia worm
fashion, but secured in each angle with two strong
stakes driven each side as a precaution against the
longhorn habit of lifting off the rails with their horns.
A good full fifty acres yielding gladly to the plough!
From one of these smaller fields he had taken two.
hundred bushels of large smooth potatoes that fall
—nothing like black virgin soil for raising potatoes.
The other fields still held his root crops, that he
gathered as he needed them, to keep the milk cows
up to their full flow during the winter. There were
long green plumy rows of carrots and huge winter
turnips, their fat bodies half out of the loose soil,
and below, a small patch of corn showed stubble

checked off in square precise patterns where the
stalks had been cut for fodder.

The prodigious work of these first years had been
performed by Indians and paid for with cheap
blankets, beads, and gaudy trinkets that he had purchased in the States for a song, a regular supply
reaching him each year when the ships came in. Indian labor could not be secured like that nowadays.
The Indians were refusing to work, declaring that
since the white men came into the country they were
becoming a nation of squaws.

He rode through his five acres of well-kept orchard
set among stumps just beginning to show signs of
rotting away. He could not bear to think of alien
hands gathering fruit from the trees that he loved.
There was a fortune in apples shipped to California.
He had had a splendid crop of apples last fall, but
this was just a prophecy of what his trees would
do when they came into full maturity. One of his
greatest pleasures in life was his pruning and grafting and general experimenting with seedlings of
different varieties of fruit to find those best suited to
the climate and to develop methods of bringing out
the best in them.

He dismounted and led his horse to inspect a long
row of thrifty peach trees that had been carefully
placed where the timber would shelter them from the
east wind. These trees were the pride of his heart.
They were grafted seedlings, and the grafting shoots
he had secured from Doctor McLoughlin's Scotch
gardener, William Bruce. They were from the first
peach trees to come into Oregon. Captain Dominis,

of the brig *Owyhee*, the first independent trading-vessel to enter the Columbia River since 1814, had brought the trees from Juan Fernandez Island in 1829. Most of his trees had some bit of interesting history. He passed from tree to tree, stopping to tie up some grape vines that the wind had loosed from their moorings, thinking, as he worked, that it would soon be time to prune the orchard.

He enjoyed pruning and grafting time; trees were so like children in their need of training and stern discipline. He bent over a row of lusty seedlings, apples, peaches, and pears, elbowing each other for room. He would do a lot of whip grafting this year when the sap was right; fruit trees would bring a fabulous price now that farms were being opened up.

He was in a genial frame of mind when he returned to the pony and went to the pasture to drive up the cows before going in to supper. Quit the country? Not he; he would repent fully, largely, and publicly, so to speak, and become its richest and most respected citizen.

He stopped on his way to the house to look into the cabin where the two Indians who did his farm work lived; they were both sitting comfortably by the fire, had evidently been there all the afternoon. He called them to attend to the chores, his anger rising again at their laziness. "Stop work and lay with their heads to the fire, unless they're watched every minute," he muttered.

Then he turned resolutely to the cabin to confront a situation that must be remedied very shortly

and very thoroughly if he were to become a solid,
substantial citizen of the Oregon commonwealth,
leaving all sentiment and the play of finer feeling
clear out of reckoning.  He would be thorough in
his repentance.

# CHAPTER VI

M cDERMOTT, through a wakeful night, mapped out his plan. He would play up the rôle of repentant sinner. He realized that he must proceed slowly and carefully. He must swallow his pride. Having, through the years, held himself haughtily aloof from the long-faced missionaries, humbling himself before them was well-nigh unbearable, but not so unbearable as suffering ostracism by going on as he was, or being obliged to leave the country.

He would feel his way cautiously; first have a heart-to-heart talk with Elder Waller, the missionary in charge at Oregon City, and ingratiate himself with the Methodists by allowing them to point out the error of his ways. By this procedure the missionaries would claim the credit for his conversion. Once convinced that he was under conviction of sin, and they would very shortly garner him in. Snatching a brand from the burning would be a triumph, especially a brand in a position to contribute substantially to the building of the new church for which Elder Waller was so assiduously gathering funds.

In the meantime he could practice the Christian-gentleman rôle by being neighborly with the Bainbridges. This was no burden. After living the last few years scarcely seeing a white woman, it was a pleasure to associate with them. He felt a genuine

liking and admiration for plucky little Martha, and
Rose Ann promised to develop into a very charming
young woman. Eligible young women were not as
yet too plentiful in Oregon City. Martha, in spite
of the cruel circumstances in which life had temporarily placed her, had the speech and manner of
a gentlewoman, and of course Rose Ann would develop her mother's pose and charm when she emerged
out of the shy little-girl stage. He had scrutinized
the women coming in with the last two immigrations
and had not, so far, seen a young one who measured
up to his requirements. He would take a wife as
soon as possible, and preferably a young one—sixteen was old enough—easier molded to his liking than
the older ones.

After breakfast McDermott called one of the Indians to assist him, and began packing the awkward
spinning-wheel on an Indian travois. Transporting
bulky pieces of furniture over a steep rocky trail
is best accomplished Indian fashion. A travois is
made generally from the poles of the teepee when
Indians are on the move—two long poles placed one
each side of the pony and held in place by buckskin
straps over the back, with smaller poles laid across
behind to make a platform. When securely lashed
together a travois is a very convenient carrier for
rough roads; the load can be lifted easily and taken
by hand over bad places by picking it up by the
poles and placing it on the shoulders of two bearers.

The spinning-wheel was a treasure not to be
roughly handled. McDermott wrapped it tenderly
in a blanket before lashing it in place. A small

wheel of mahogany designed for the use of ladies
who spun and knit as a drawing-room diversion, it
had come around the Horn with the rest of the mahogany which he had sent for to make the home
comfortable for his wife.  She had been accustomed
to pleasant surroundings and he had done his best
to provide little niceties for her in the lonely home.
Parting with the spinning-wheel had cost him a pang
—it held so many tender memories of Mary—but
there were not more than two or three spinning-
wheels in the whole country and sentimentality should
not enter where crude necessity ruled.

He dismissed the Indian at the cabin door, sending the pony and travois back with him.  Indians
are a curious lot; what one Indian knows all the
others know, too.  They have a way of taking in a
situation and understanding motives when not a word
is spoken, that is almost supernatural.

Telling the reluctant Indian that he would walk
home, McDermott rapped lightly on the cabin door.
Martha opened it at once, and her face lit up with
joy as she saw the spinning-wheel. "Mahogany," she
cried, "all rubbed and polished!  Don't you hate to
sell it, Mr. McDermott?  I would hate to mar it, and
this is a crowded cabin, but I'll try my best to take
care of it."

"It's a real pleasure to know that you can make
use of it, Mrs. Bainbridge," said McDermott graciously.  "Especially when I hope to have a supply
of good warm socks before very long."  He was opening the sacks of wool to show her the quality of the
clip.  A fine long fleece, just as it came from the

sheep's back. Martha admired it, taking up a handful and picking it apart, marveling at the length and silkiness.

"Wool like this is very easy to spin," she exulted. "Easy to wash and card, too." She hesitated a moment, turning the wool thoughtfully over and over in her hands before she spoke again. "It will have to be washed, Mr. McDermott, and I have no soap, nor fat to make it. Getting along without soap has been very hard. We've been managing the best we could, scouring our dishes with sharp sand and washing our clothing in hot water, but it takes soap to cut the grease in virgin wool. We women folks gathered all the fat off the entrails of dead cattle along the trail, to make it up into soap as soon as we reached the settlement, but I had to leave mine the last time we lightened the load."

"Oh, I'll send over soap right away," promised McDermott. "And there's about ten gallons of tallow from the last butchering in the smoke-house. You shall have it."

"I'll pay for it with stockings or make it on shares for you," said Martha eagerly. "The hardwood ashes make wonderful lye. Uncle Adzi must set up a leach as soon as he comes in to-day. The men have gone to hunt our ox, Buck. He broke his hobble during the night and strayed off. He is so weak that John was afraid he might mire down. They'll be back to dinner. You'll stay, won't you, Mr. McDermott? John and Uncle Adzi were coming over to see about cutting rails for you as soon as they found

Buck, so you can make your bargain with them here, instead."

"I'll be delighted to have dinner with you," exclaimed McDermott, seating himself near the fire on the block of wood that did duty for a chair, and spreading his hands, palms outward, to the genial blaze, covertly scrutinizing Rose Ann while he engaged in conversation with Martha, busied with preparations for dinner.

Rose Ann's bare feet were her searing humiliation. She kept as much in the background as possible miserably aware of McDermott's appraisal, though he did not appear to be conscious of her existence. This close scrutiny irritated and somehow angered her almost beyond endurance. She longed to cry and she wanted to run and hide, but could do neither until the morning work was done, and after that she knew she must help mother with dinner.

Esther Amelia was whole-heartedly delighted with their guest. She seated herself beside him shyly and began questioning him about his little girls. The dark little oval of her face glowed with interest as he told her how the two children had gone off on a big ship in care of the captain's wife. He promised to show her the letters they wrote him once a year when the ship came in with the supplies for the Post at Vancouver. He would look about the house and see if they hadn't left a doll or two around, and if he could find one she should have it for her own.

Martha was just a bit anxious about the dinner, there was so little to offer company. But she would set the best she had before him and make no apology.

Wheat boiled until soft and seasoned with salt took the place of bread. She did wish they could have bacon for seasoning, but there was no bacon to be had; no fat except the little that she could save from about the gizzards of the grouse and pheasants Uncle Adzi killed. Birds were remarkably plump and fat here in the winter—the wild grasses held their seeds so long—but this fat was scarcely enough for frying them, let alone seasoning other food.

Fortunately the last of the dried peas Aunt Morning Ann had sent down had made a big pot of lip-lip; it was simmering slowly over the fire to bring out the full rich flavor of the peas, and John had brought dried salmon from Vancouver. She could set out a filling meal, even if it were just a bit monotonous. After all, mere monotony didn't count for so much when it was nip and tuck to keep six stomachs from aching with emptiness. There was one good drawing of tea left from the pound Doctor McLoughlin had sent. She had been saving it for an emergency —a strong cup of tea cheered one up so in sickness— but after taking stock of her dinner resources, she decided to have good strong tea with plenty of sugar to give a festive air to the meal.

There was commotion outside. Buck had evidently been found. Martha opened the door, and there they were. John and Uncle Adzi and two men, whom they had asked to share the dinner. Open-handed hospitality, scant fare or plenty, was the Bainbridge rule.

Martha did a swift sum in mental arithmetic and got a fairly satisfactory answer while the boys were hobbling Buck and turning him out near placidly-grazing Bright. She stepped outside to greet the guests, whom John and Uncle Adzi were cordially urging forward.

"Rose Ann and Esther Amelia, come here and see who we brung in," shouted Uncle Adzi with joy as he pushed the hugely embarrassed Dick Skelton and a tall Indian ahead of him into the cabin. Dick Skelton was the bound boy who had come along with Aunt Morning Ann and the Applegate party. He was a sorry specimen, so browbeaten and shy that meeting folks was an acute misery. His growth during his tender years had been retarded by his poor food and too much hard work. Now at nineteen he had taken a sudden terrible spurt of growing, a spurt of shooting up into a bean-pole slenderness accompanied by an elephantine enlargement of the hands and feet. Nondescript clothing accentuated his awkwardness. The buckskin breeches were too short— they had been cut off sometime when they lengthened from being wet, and now they struck him midway between the knee and the ankle, revealing reed-like bare shanks ending in huge moccasin-incased feet. The sleeves of his leather hunting jacket were three inches too short, making his large-knuckled hands seem incongruous.

No one but a tender woman would see the makings of a splendid man in Dick Skelton, but Martha, looking in his large wistful brown eyes as she put her hands on his shoulders and kissed him, standing on tiptoe, saw and understood the real Dick, who just needed mothering. The tears were very near the surface as she smoothed back his curling brown hair.

"Aunt Morning Ann Simmons told us you were here, Dick. Why haven't you been to see us?" she asked as she turned to greet her other guest.

"Mother, this is Siah-hen," said John by way of introduction, and Siah-hen ceremoniously shook the hand she offered him, holding something bulky under his blanket with his left. Siah-hen, after the manner of the friendly Indian, had brought along a *potlatch*. He handed it to Martha with a bow—a good-sized block of wild blackberries pressed into a cake by drying over a low fire. Martha received the gift delightedly.

"*Hi-yu tillicums*" ("We are great friends"), grunted Siah-hen in the Chinook jargon.

Martha hastened to introduce McDermott, who shook hands with Dick cordially, explaining that he had known Siah-hen ever since he arrived in Oregon. Siah-hen, Martha noticed, drew himself up a little stiffly, but shook the hand McDermott offered him after the barest instant of reluctance.

Siah-hen was an enigma to the emigrants; most of them thought he was crazy, and he had done nothing so far to change their opinion. He had met the train on the way down the Columbia and traveled with it. He was friendly enough and had formed an attachment for Dick Skelton, which the lonely Dick appreciated to the full. Siah-hen appeared to be about thirty, straight and tall and finely formed. He carried his shoulders well back, so he was not a canoe Indian, neither was he a horse Indian from east of the Cascades; they were tall but their legs were bowed from constant riding of their cayuse ponies.

Siah-hen's face was lined with thought, indicating maturity of intellect. The ordinary Indian is a child where thought powers are concerned, but Siah-hen was a man. His hair was cut and, with the exception of a blanket, he wore the white man's garb. His blue flannel shirt, such as the Hudson Bay Company provides for its employees, was clean. His buckskin breeches, fringed at the sides, had been carefully chalked, and his moccasins were whole. And, curiously enough, although he and Dick were living at the Indian village, neither carried the horrid smell that accompanies the Indian domiciled in winter quarters.

Martha began bustling about the dinner, moving swiftly from the puncheon shelf which served for a work-table to the pots simmering near the fire. She turned to tell Rose Ann to lay the dinner table, but Rose Ann was not in the cabin. Going to the door, she called, but there was no answer. Annoyed, she hurried to the small log shed where the oxen were sheltered at night. She called again.

A tearful voice answered from the darkness of the shed's interior.

"Come, Rose Ann, you'll have to help mother put the dinner on the table," urged Martha.

"Oh, mother, I just can't. Please don't make me. I'll die if I have to go walking around barefooted before all those strange men. Mr. McDermott was watching me, I know he was, and Dick Skelton and that Indian will keep looking at me. Please, mother."

Martha paused a moment in sympathy for suffering girlhood, agonizing over trifles. But dinner must be gotten on to the table quickly. Hungry men hate to wait for a meal. She could not possibly manage to serve nine in that crowded space alone, and, besides, John would miss Rose Ann and insist that she come and help, and that would be worse than bringing her in now.

"Nonsense, child!" she said sharply. "No one is paying the least attention to you. You're too self-conscious. You'll have to come. I can't manage alone."

"All right," agreed Rose Ann in a small, tearful voice, getting up and wiping her eyes with the back of her hand.

"I wish you had shoes and stockings, dear," soothed Martha, "but we'll just have to make the best of it. Look at mother's shoes all tied up with buckskin, and strips of cloth showing through the holes to let everyone know she has no stockings. We'll just go about as if we were clean and dressed for the occasion. Nearly all the women who came here this fall are barefooted, or wearing moccasins without stockings. Remember Aunt Morning Ann said she went to church barefooted before she got those moccasins and that there were half a dozen other women there without shoes, and they didn't allow it to spoil the sermon for them, either."

"Yes, but—" faltered Rose Ann, struggling to get herself in hand.

"There isn't a new shoe in the whole Oregon country, and no cobblers. Child, that's a right good joke on the women folks. Laugh about it and come on. A lady is a lady, no matter where she is placed. Hold your head up and your chin out and come and help me with dinner." Martha was mercifully giving Rose Ann time to overcome her tears.

"I'll run on in. You wash your face at the spring and then slip in and go about your work just as if you had been there all the time. 'Twill be easier that way." And Martha flew in to her dinner.

Rose Ann, with traces of tears showing in spite of the cold water she had so assiduously applied, came in very shortly. She haughtily acknowledged the presence of Dick and Siah-hen with the merest inclination of the head in their direction. Dick, bogged down in embarrassment, was grateful for her scant recognition, and yet he had hoped she would speak to him. Siah-hen seemed to be enjoying the situation. He went off in gales of laughter, an Indian habit in a strained situation, gaining composure with difficulty and breaking out again, until poor Dick writhed inwardly with the torture of it and temporarily hated Indians with the unreasonable fervor of youth.

Martha shooed the men outside so that she could get to the fire, and Rose Ann, relieved, pattered about preparing the table for the guests and John and Uncle Adzi. Children always waited until the second table. The men did not wash until Martha called them to dinner. That's masculine psychology— angrily impatient until a meal is announced, but taking their time over their ablutions while it cools on the table.

There was much splashing of the hot water Martha provided, and a waving about of hands and rubbing

of faces to dry them—towels were not, in the cabin—
before the men filed in and awkwardly moved up the
heavy blocks of wood for seats at the table.

John said grace, and Rose Ann swiftly carried the
plates to the pot to fill them with lip-lip. She pattered superciliously about, bending over the pots
or lifting them out of the heat of the fire with the
pothooks, her freckled nose in the air and the proud
and haughty mien of a duchess in her erect little
figure. Her manner fairly abased Dick and McDermott, so paralyzingly chilling, so indifferent, so un-
aware of their presence was Rose Ann. Martha
glanced at her from time to time with an eye that
illy concealed amusement shaded sharply with an-
noyance. She tried again and again to catch her
eye, signaling, motherwise, but impervious to glances,
even from her mother, Rose Ann pattered loftily
about her serving.

John and Uncle Adzi enjoyed themselves immensely, and the boys and Esther Amelia, hovering
in the background, were intensely, breathlessly, interested, but to Martha and McDermott and Dick
Skelton it was "the ordeal by fire." Dick was too
wretchedly embarrassed to eat. His hands were so
hopelessly useless and in the way; he was in living
terror that Rose Ann would trip over his feet as
she filled the plates—a block of wood gives no space
for tucking feet away. And Siah-hen's untimely
laughter caused cold sweat to break out on him. He
resolved to tell Siah-hen, when they were alone, that
he would not stand such conduct from him. No
wonder folks thought he was crazy.

McDermott, too, was on the rack.  Siah-hen, he felt, was probing his very soul, though he had not so much as glanced his way.  He regretted having an Indian see him in the Bainbridge cabin.  Before night the Indian lodge would be buzzing with the news that he was more than casually interested in Rose Ann.  He writhed under Siah-hen's unspoken contempt, and yet why had the dignified Indian a contempt that filled the air?  His alternating silence and laughter filled a man's heart with murder.  He hoped that the other guests would leave before he came to bargaining with John and Uncle Adzi.  One could not be too careful about talking before Indians, and Siah-hen was a powerful personage down at the lodge.

Dinner was finally finished, with the cake of dried blackberries as an unexpected treat.  The hungry children scrambled to their places and the men seated themselves by the fire to talk.

Uncle Adzi could hardly wait to question McDermott about the yield of wheat and potatoes on his farm.  Wild stories had circulated among the emigrants about the fertility of the soil in the Willamette Valley, and he was eager to have the reports confirmed.

"Mr. McDermott, how many bushels o' wheat did you-all git ter the acre last year?" he inquired, his wrinkled old face aglow.

McDermott beamed.  Here was a kindred soul, a man who loved the soil and petted it and coaxed it into yielding its best for him.  He knew by the tones of Uncle Adzi's voice that he spoke his language in the matter of growing things and shared the bond of fellowship of that gracious cult whose object was to "make two blades of grass grow where only one grew before."

"It's hard to believe," said McDermott, "but I took seventy bushels an acre from my twenty-acre field this last fall. That's fourteen hundred bushels. Of course," he amended, "that was exceptional. We had rains last year until well up in July. Some years the fall wheat dries out too much. It's the rain that makes this country. Now take the last three years. Summer before last was rather dry. I got only fifty-five bushels to the acre. But the average for the last three years is, let's see"—he made a swift mental calculation—"thirty-seven thousand bushels for the three years is well over one thousand two hundred bushels to the twenty acres."

"By gravy!" exclaimed Uncle Adzi, "then hit's the truth. I reckoned thet jest likely the emigrants war a-cheerin' theirselves along because the trail war so rough. I snum we shore have made our fortunes by emigratin' ter a kentry with a waterway ter the ports in Chiny. Jest load 'er on the boats in the river an' let 'er slide. Gimme a country with a outlet ter the sea. Beats all the wagon roads an' railroads thet kin be built."

"Yes," agreed McDermott enthusiastically. "There'll always be a market for wheat. But speaking of yields, my potato crop this year broke all records. Of course it's new ground, just broken to the plough and drains just right; there's fifteen acres in that field and I dug a hundred and fifty bushels to the acre. The last ship that went to Honolulu took them out. The wheat's all here, though; it'll bring a good price at the door when next year's emigration comes in."

Siah-hen wearied of conversation and rose to take his leave, followed by Dick, mute, but rather wishing to remain longer. Martha asked them to come again and patted Dick on the back, thanking Siah-hen again for his *potlatch*.

John opened the subject at once, expressing his appreciation of the spinning-wheel and the wool. "We can all help evenings at the wool," he explained. "The boys and I will pick it over after Martha gets it washed and Uncle Adzi is a master hand at carding it into rolls. Martha can knit a sock an evening, and after the yarn is spun Rose Ann and Esther Amelia will knit all the time just as they did in Illinois. Fifty cents for a pair of socks means that we come through the winter without going into debt. Doctor McLoughlin will give us credit at the trading-post, but we have no money and that makes us cautious about buying anything but the barest necessities."

"I spoke to Mrs. Bainbridge about your splitting rails for me," said McDermott. "I can use at least fifty thousand and have the fences put up as they are hauled from the timber. I will trade you a long-horn cow with her heifer calf by her side. She's breachy, but so are all longhorns."

"Oh," piped up Uncle Adzi, "I kin git the best o' a breachy cow any time. Jest tie her horns to her forelegs right under her shoulders so's she cain't trip

herself and yit cain't git her head up too fur; hit'll
break 'em o' jumpin' or aliftin' off the rails in no
time."

McDermott laughed. "That's a new scheme.
Might try it. But longhorns are laws unto themselves—they're all mean in their dispositions."

"We have neither sledges nor wedges, and just
one broadax. Manuel can do a man's work in the
timber, and Asa helps clear up the limbs. The four
of us could turn out a pile of rails in double-quick
time if we had the tools. I never saw such fine
straight timber. I've split three hundred rails in a
day. The three of us could easily average one hundred and fifty apiece," said John.

"I'll let you use my sledges and a couple of broad-
axes and the wedges, so you can all work," promised
McDermott. "You can cut what you need for your
own fencing at the same time. And"—he turned to
Uncle Adzi—"I need a new fireplace. You can take
that job by day's work, and there's always shakes
to be rived and crops to be put in early in the spring.
You needn't be idle, and with the three of you working, you'll be well established by spring. Take your
pay in seed wheat and potatoes, and this cow and
calf, and supplies for your table such as they are.
Wheat is about all there is besides salmon. I'll see
if I can spare a little dried fruit and a few apples,
but things are sold off rather close—so many came in
without supplies, and the trading-posts took everything I had on hand and gave me credit for it. You
might take part of your pay in orders on the post,
though. They pass for money out here."

"Hain't I tol' you, John an' Marthie, thet we'd come out all right?" shrilled Uncle Adzi. "Hit hain't so easy gittin' a foothold in a new settlement, but them as works makes a go o' hit. We're tarnation lucky ter have a chancet ter work this winter. There hain't enough work fer everyone here yit."

Martha paused in her work to tell them about Mr. McDermott's promise of soft soap to wash the wool and of the tallow to make up into soap on shares. "Soap's the thing we need worst," she said. "John, I wish you and Uncle Adzi and the boys could go over and get it this evening so's I can begin washing wool to-morrow."

"Yes, come on over with me now," invited McDermott, "and you can bring back the tools at the same time and get into the timber right away."

Martha sighed a little when they had gone. "No amount of planning and looking ahead will keep this family eating. Here I thought there was enough boiled wheat to carry us through breakfast to-morrow and we'll have a very scant supper. Oh, well," she consoled herself, "the men haven't been working very hard this afternoon and we will have a kettleful nearly soft by morning, but wheat needs a good twelve hours' simmering to be soft enough to eat. Hurry, children, so we can put it over the fire right away. As soon as you finish you may go and play until supper-time."

Esther Amelia ran to the dooryard to follow her favorite diversion of building chip houses as soon as her task was over. She had a miniature farm which she improved day by day; she was inclosing the little

splint cabin with a rail fence made with twigs from
the fir boughs. It was nearly complete, with little
green fir trees growing at proper intervals. Uncle
Adzi had whittled out two little wooden dolls for her,
and some chips did for cattle. It was a most absorbing play. She looked up to see Indians filing up the
trail, and fled in terror to hide her face in her
mother's lap.

Martha reassured her gently, telling her over and
over that the Indians were friends and she must not
hurt their feelings by appearing to be afraid of them.
Martha opened the door for them as they rapped
upon it, rattling the latch impatiently. Quimmo led
the returning hunting party. Deer were easily and
quickly taken close to the settlement. They had
three between them. Quimmo signaled to one who
had the largest over his shoulders, and he lowered it
to the floor. Taking his knife, he cut off the hind
quarters, placing the meat on Martha's table with a
smile and a wave of the hand. His pock-marked face
was alight with pleasure and he began to laugh
loudly, his companions joining him, when Martha
tried to express her thanks in Chinook. *"Tillicums,"*
was all she could manage.

And the Indians understood perfectly. *"Ni-ka
mam-ook chah-ko mow-ich ilt-wil-lee"* ("I bring deer
meat"), said Quimmo. *"Potlatch chick-a-min mam-
ook tsish"* ("Pay for sharpening knife"). He ran
his finger over the edge of the knife he held in his
hand to make his meaning clear, and when he saw
that she understood he led his companions out of the
cabin.

"Quimmo doesn't look to me like a mean Indian," said Rose Ann thoughtfully. "Perhaps he couldn't help capsizing the boat. He's friendly to us, and we'll have venison for supper, won't we, mother? See, there's plenty of fat to fry it and make gravy. How pleased father and Uncle Adzi will be!"

Martha was thoughtful for a moment before she answered. "Yes, we'll have a good supper, children; there's meat enough there to last a week if I am careful in cutting it. Do you remember the story of the widow's cruse? This having faith to share our scanty fare somehow reminds me of the prophet Elijah and the widow who fed him. Wait, I'll get the Bible and find it for you." She took down a much-thumbed Bible and turned at once to the story. The girls seated themselves to listen—their mother's Bible stories were so to the point and so interesting.

"And the word of the Lord came unto him, saying,

"Arise, get thee to Zarephath, which belongeth to Zidon, and dwell there: behold, I have commanded a widow woman there to sustain thee.

"So he arose and went to Zarephath. And when he came to the gate of the city, behold, the widow woman was there gathering of sticks: and he called to her, and said, Fetch me, I pray thee, a little water in a vessel, that I may drink.

"And as she was going to fetch it, he called to her and said, Bring me, I pray thee, a morsel of bread in thine hand.

"And she said, As the Lord, thy God, liveth, I have not a cake, but an handful of meal in a barrel, and a little oil in a cruse; and, behold, I am gathering two sticks, that I may go in and dress it for me and my son, that we may eat it, and die.

"And Elijah said unto her, Fear not: go and do as thou hast said: but make me thereof a little cake first, and after make for thee and for thy son.

"For thus sayeth the Lord God of Israel, The barrel of meal shall not waste, neither shall the cruse of oil fail, until the day that the Lord sendeth rain upon the earth.

"And she went and did according to the saying of Elijah: and she, and he, and her house, did eat many days.

"And the barrel of meal wasted not, neither did the cruse of oil fail, according to the word of the Lord, which he spake by Elijah."

Martha closed her Bible and sat thinking. "Seems to me that I am just like that poor widow—down almost to the last mouthful and ready to eat it and die, and then along comes plenty again. It takes faith, children, it takes faith."

# CHAPTER VII

ON LEAVING the Bainbridge cabin, Siah-hen paused in the muddy path a few yards above the barnyard and pointed down. The perfect imprint of a small slender foot showed in the mud. Dick Skelton gazed at the imprint thoughtfully for a moment, then took a piece of hempen cord, such as the Indian women make, out of his pocket, and began carefully measuring the footprint, from heel to toe first; he tied a knot to mark its length. Then across the instep and another knot, with another gauging the width of the heel.

In silence the two went down the path to the north, traveling along through the dripping underbrush toward the Clackamas flat. "You must locate on land, Dick," announced Siah-hen as they threaded back and forth down a steep trail skirting the sheer edge of the bluff. "Or are you thinking of going into the cobbling business?" At Dick's furious blush he went off into gales of aggravating laughter.

Dick disregarded his tormentor. "I intend to do both," he announced. "If the Linn bill has passed Congress I can take up land; I'm nineteen years old. I know a little about making shoes, too. Lafe Tompkins was a cobbler by trade, and I pegged shoes and helped him all the time." His face brightened. "There isn't a cobbler in the Oregon country, and no shoes, either."

"And no leather except elk skin and green cattle hides," supplemented Siah-hen, "and no cobbler's tools, and nobody with money to pay for shoes if you had them made."

Dick, accustomed to browbeatings all his life, shrank within himself at Siah-hen's tormenting, and climbed down the bluff in silence, but when, at last, they reached the bottom land where the Clackamas riffled and hurried just before broadening out to join the Willamette with a smooth dignity, he turned and looked back at the sheer bluff they had descended. His beauty-loving soul was strangely stirred by the nobly wooded hills rising in rough tiers to the south and east.

He gazed awhile, then, without a word, started back up the path. Siah-hen, also turned quiet and impassive, followed. Passing Dick where the trail widened a bit, he led the way by a branching path, around the brow of the precipice, just missing the Bainbridge cabin. Half a mile above, in the next bench-like plateau, he turned south until he found the object of his search. A tiny spring bubbled up at the base of a towering rock, and trickling down into a minute brook, joined the cheerful company of other brooks, and fell with joyful music over the precipice. He led Dick into a small opening in the timber much the same as that holding the Bainbridge cabin. This was the third of a series of level plateaus and sharp ascents. Beyond was slightly rolling country blending gradually into foothills where the Cascades narrowed in toward the river. The dull drizzle was breaking away with the turn of the wind eastward. Scurrying clouds suddenly lifted their leaden gray curtain from the eastern sky line, revealing against the horizon the snowy outlines of Mount Hood with a trailing creamy chiffon veil of mist partly concealing its crest.

"Why, this is the best location above the river!" exclaimed Dick. "There's fine timber, but it's in clumps—no work at all to plough the rolling land." They walked up the last ledge to see the open stretches with waving wild grass and the magnificent stand of oak timber to the south and small groves of large firs concealing it from the northern view. "Why didn't you tell me about this place before, Siah-hen?" Dick asked reproachfully, digging his heel into the springy black loam. "I've hunted all over the hills and never saw this sweep of country before."

"I know," said Siah-hen sagely. "I just let you hunt. If you had asked me I'd have brought you up here. There's no trail except around the north side of the bluff and the settlers all tried to come in from the south. Can't see this open space until you come into it. I'll build a cabin up here, too, some day. We'll cut a path down past Rose Ann's house—shortest way down to Oregon City to sell your shoes." He rocked back and forth in uncontrollable laughter, but this time the mirth did not irritate Dick. He laughed, too.

"I'll build my cabin here," planned Dick, as they descended to the bench below the spring. He was stepping off the level spot to form a rough idea of its size. "The Indian lodge is so noisy, and, ugh! how it smells!"

"The Indian lodge is no place for a white man," said Siah-hen. "I don't want white folks to think you're getting to be a 'squaw-man.' We'll build your cabin first and I'll live with you; too lonesome for a boy alone in the woods, but it'll be quiet for you to study this winter."

He sat down on a log under a fir tree and drew from the inner recesses of his blanket a tattered, much-thumbed book and, opening at a turned-down page, handed it to Dick, who, seating himself beside him, began to read laboriously with much halting and spelling out of words. The book was Pope's immortal translation of the Iliad:

"Then thus the god: O restless fate of pride,
    That strives to learn what heav'n resolves to hide;
    Vain is the search, presumptuous and abhorr'd,
    Anxious to thee, and odious to thy lord,
    Let this suffice; th' immutable decree
    No force can shake: What is, that *ought* to be."

"You're learning, boy," said Siah-hen with pride as Dick closed the book on the council of the gods on Mount Olympus. "You might have an easier book to read, but this'll give you something to think about as you read it. Let's see if we can get down the hill past Rose Ann's cabin. There'll be a sunset to-night and we'll see Tumchuck in its light, and then take the *kinnum* [canoe] that we left moored in the river the last time we were down there."

With the accuracy of a lifetime of practice in finding the easiest grade, he led Dick through a tangle

of hazel brush and vine maples, skirting perpendicular rocks and jumping from others, catching limbs of
trees to ease his leap, and showing Dick how to let
himself down at difficult points.

"Ugh!" he grunted as a limb struck him in the
face. "Trail hard and sharp to Rose Ann's, but it'll
wear down; it'll wear down!" Dick with straining
eyes caught a flickering glimpse of Rose Ann between the trees as they descended the hill, and Siah-
hen laughed insanely. "McDermott intends to marry
Rose Ann," he announced. "He's planning. I could
see inside his head. No like, no like, and yet—" He
broke off and resumed his thoughts.

"He'll not marry Rose Ann, either," Dick shouted
angrily.

"Well, well," laughed his tormentor, "perhaps he
won't, but no need to send thunder from the voice and
lightning from the eye and make hard fists at me,
Dick Skelton."

Siah-hen paused with a rapt glow on his coppery
face as they sighted the falls of the Willamette with
its shimmering nebula of mist trembling above, tinted
to the irradiant sheen of the rainbow from the glow
of the sun setting in masses of fleecy cumulous clouds.
The heavenly beauty of cataract, serried sky line,
and smooth expanse of upper and lower river, all
bathed in rosy light, lifted them out of the realm of
physical things. The roar of the mighty volume of
water, nearly a quarter of a mile wide, falling thirty-
three sheer feet over the precipice of basaltic rock,
gives a sense of the futility and impotence of man
that abases and at the same time exalts.

Sharp bluffs guard the falls on the western bank and the eastern hills shoulder each other in here until the valley narrows to a pass six hundred feet wide between walls of rock one hundred and fifty feet high. The pass extends several hundred yards below the falls and then the smooth valley floor spreads out fanwise, broadening generously until the Willamette merges into the Columbia twenty miles to the north.

Two basaltic islands divide the river below the falls into three mighty channels. Above and below the cataract the Willamette has, through æons, cut its course in solid rock, making a descent of forty-five feet from the upper to the lower river.

*Hyas Tyee Tumchuck* (the Place of Great Falling Water) was the hereditary fishing-ground of the Clackamas Indians. Salmon, ascending the river in the fishing season, are easily taken below the falls with hook, seine, or spear. This coveted fishing-place made the owners rich in worldly goods. Tumchuck was a spot endeared to the canoe Indians by generations of tender associations.

Long before emigration was thought of Dr. John McLoughlin, chief factor of the Hudson Bay Company's trading-post at Vancouver, had visioned a city at the falls. In imagination he had seen the mighty water-power harnessed to run the grist mills and cut the lumber for the thousands of people who would sometime cultivate the fertile Willamette Valley. He, too, loved the wild grandeur of the falls and in his heart planned to end his days there when he could no longer fill his post with the Hudson Bay Company.

The Indians were always friendly to the Hudson Bay Company. They exchanged their furs and salmon for guns and ammunition. Fur-traders did not interfere with their fishing and hunting grounds. The trappers married their women and were at home in their lodges, considered members of their families, but they resented occupation of the site of Tumchuck, and when Doctor McLoughlin built a block-house a few hundred feet below the falls to deposit furs and wheat secured in trade from the trappers and the French-Canadian farmers up the valley, the Indians promptly tore it down.

Siah-hen gazed in silence, his impassive face lit only by a luminous sadness in his black eyes, until the sun dropped below the horizon and the glory gradually faded from the sky. Dick was used to his long silences and he had his own thoughts.

But after a time the Indian aroused himself and sought to find relief for his sore heart in words. "Long ago," he said in a toneless matter-of-fact voice—"long ago my people were strong and rich. They roamed all over the country just as happy children go about in their play, but now they are fading off the hunting-grounds and the Sniapus [Americans] are flocking to take their place. They cannot understand, but I know, I know. Soon farms and great cities will fill the hunting-grounds; the scattering tribes will be gone, the lodges and teepees forgotten."

"Oh no!" exclaimed Dick. "There's room enough for both."

"Let this suffice; th' immutable decree
No force can shake: What is, that *ought* to be,"

quoted Siah-hen. "It takes courage, boy, to be sub-missive—to understand and to do nothing. It's weak and cowardly to fight sometimes. If my people resist they will vanish all the more quickly. The wise ones among them know it, but the simple are hopeful like children. The hardest thing of all to bear has been to see a town near beloved Tumchuck, Keenema, my people call the site near the great falling water; there will be a town here soon that will be a center for grinding wheat and making lumber for the houses that will be built all over the valley; it is always so near falling water. The valley will be settled thickly just as it is on the Atlantic coast. I have been there and I know. All things change. I can see ahead. I have my dreams and visions."

"It'll not be in your time or mine," said Dick with the assurance of ignorant unthinking boyhood.

"Perhaps not," said Siah-hen. "But our children will see it, and what is a generation or so in the great westward march of the white race? Since history be-gan to be recorded the white man has always moved toward the setting sun, trampling weaker races under his feet. I have read and I know. It is destiny, not to be railed or stormed at, but to be accepted."

The sun was gone and the swift winter darkness warned of its approach by the lengthening of the shadows as they started down the hill. Siah-hen was by turns thoughtful and talkative. Dick had learned to wait patiently for the change of mood that would give speech. No Indian can be induced to talk. The lonely boy, never having had a friend with whom he could exchange his innermost thoughts, was eager to hear Siah-hen's views and philosophy of life. It was like seeing the world through Indian eyes. The heights and depths of his friend's nature were a revelation to the evolving Dick, whose mental processes formed a churning mass of ideas that in his immaturity he could not segregate.

With the fall of night, lights along the river pricked out like stars as they came down the path to Oregon City—the fires of the Indian villages. "There is muttering in the main lodge, and the villages where the broken tribes huddle in their misery are full of old squaws' talk," said Siah-hen. "There is an old Indian adage, that a woman should never cause war, but in their weakness and degradation the old men are silently shaking their heads and the young men are listening intently. The town on the site of Keenema is the hardest blow of all for the Indians to bear; it means the loss of their right to fish at Tumchuck. Wars have been fought among the tribes in ancient days over the fishing rights, and now the Sniapus are beginning to wrangle and quarrel over the land near the falls."

"Yes," said Dick. "Doctor McLoughlin had it first, but the missionaries want to take it away from him. The emigrants are already taking sides."

"My father, White-headed Eagle [the Indian name for Doctor McLoughlin] will lose his claim to the Sniapus, even though he located on it and built a house before the missionaries came or emigration was thought of. What the white man wants he takes if he has the strength.  In 1818 there was a treaty between the Kin-Chautchs [King Georges, British] and the Sniapus, but the white race only holds to honor when there are no property issues involved. They prate loudly of their ideals, but they live up to them only when it is expedient."

"But you like the Sniapus—that is, some of them —don't you?" asked Dick, rather puzzled.  "The Bainbridges are friends; they would not wrong the Indians.  You sat at their table to-day."

"Not all of any race are good, nor all bad," said Siah-hen.  "I neither love nor hate when I wish to decide what is the just thing to do.  But my people must not rebel against the whites.  White-headed Eagle knows it and I know it—to resist means annihilation.  Mighty westward surges of emigration cannot be stemmed or turned back; never has it been in the history of the world.  The weak have been absorbed by the white race, if they were of Aryan origin, or crushed and in time destroyed if they were of another color."

Siah-hen lapsed into silence and Dick feared that he would talk no more, but he felt the need of expressing his thoughts to the friend who understood.

"The Indian is lower in the race scale, and he is no fool; he knows it.  The white man would not for a moment allow him to forget, and the Indian cannot even if he would.  He hates the white man and feels contempt for his treachery in dealing with him.  An Indian will not break his word and his scorn is unmeasurable for a liar, but even hating and scorning, he emulates a recognized superior. It is thus that races develop and rise."

"What tribe is yours?" asked Dick to prolong the conversation.

Siah-hen spoke up proudly: "I'm the hereditary chief of the Klamath tribe, the son of Chief Welap, but there are few of my tribe left now. Years ago the mighty tribes of the Clackamas, the Cowleskies, the Kathlamets, and the Callipooias—all the canoe Indians—made war on the Klamaths because they were few and weak. They plundered their lodges and killed most of the men. The women and children were taken for slaves. My brother Wis-la-how-it-ka and I were brought to Vancouver; he was ten summers and I was eight."

Dick shuddered. He had seen Indian slaves at the lodge.

"There is only one other Klamath Indian in the valley; that's the girl Lassee. Her family escaped when we were taken, but she was captured on a raid down on the Klamath lakes when she was about twelve."

"Does she live at the lodge?" asked Dick. "I don't remember hearing that name before."

"No," answered Siah-hen shortly, and dismissed the subject.

"How did you get away from the Indians?" Dick was all eager interest.

"They brought us to Fort Vancouver, and the great White-headed Eagle saw us shivering and cowering in terror and bought us. My brother died the next year with the measles, but I have lived at the Post nearly all my life. I have always been free. White-headed Eagle bought us to set us free. He knew what Indian slavery is. He has done all he could to stamp it out."

"How did you learn to read? It seems to me you know more than any white man I ever saw," said Dick.

"White-headed-Eagle sent me to school with the children at the Post when he saw I wanted to learn. Ever since I learned to read I have had access to good books. There are many scholarly Englishmen among the Hudson Bay men, and life is leisurely there. We read and think and talk things over. An educated Englishman taught me, and our joy has been in our studies. Of course we have to read and speak French. I have carried messages back and forth from York Factory, the headquarters of the company in the East."

"Does Doctor McLoughlin send you out to live among the tribes to spy on them and bring him in news?" Dick asked. "The settlers say he does."

"White-headed Eagle is my father," Siah-hen said simply. "I go among the tribes where there is un-easiness and muttering to counsel with them. I do anything he wishes to keep peace between my people and the whites. Soon he'll need his friends. Many of the Sniapus hate him now and plan to rob him while they sit by the cabin firesides he keeps safe for them and eat the food he provides for them. Ugh! Sniapus!" He made a gesture of disgust and settled into silence.

For a time they stood watching a lone Indian

fisherman, naked to the waist, standing like a bronze statue with his spear poised, on the scaffold below the falls, watching keen-eyed in the failing light for the chance salmon attempting to ascend the falls. It was dark before Siah-hen roused himself reluctantly from his reveries and they passed through Oregon City and found their *kinnum*, hid by a low-hanging willow. He waxed communicative again as he took his place in the stern of the boat to float leisurely with the current down to the main lodge.

"I'm a lonely man, Dick," he said. "It has been a joy to teach you and talk to you. I was drawn to you when I first saw you at the fort and heard from the other Indians that you were a slave just as I was in my little-boyhood."

"I was not a slave. I was a bound boy," said Dick indignantly. "Lafe Tompkins did beat me nearly to death sometimes, and he didn't feed me very well, but I would have been free when I was twenty-one."

"What was that but slavery? He didn't let you go to school, did he?" asked Siah-hen. "Sniapus have pretty ways of stating ugly facts."

Dick changed the disagreeable subject abruptly. "How did the Indians know my story?"

"Indians know everything," declared Siah-hen cryptically.

"Why did you laugh and refuse to speak our language among the emigrants? First you spoke Chinnok, and when they didn't understand you explained to them and laughed. The settlers say you are crazy. Why do you make them think that?" asked Dick.

"What matter what Sniapus think?" grunted Siah-hen contemptuously. "The Kin-Chautchs [British] understand, but to Sniapus Indians are just Indians. I had work to do. White-headed Eagle sent me to talk with the Horse Indians while the train was coming through their country. The Cayuse love war, they planned to kill the Bostons. A plough showing in the back of a horse canoe [wagon] meant that their hunting-grounds would go. My people all hate the plough."

"I see now," said Dick. "The land is really theirs, and we are taking it away from them without paying for it. No wonder the Indians want to fight. I'd fight if I had land and some one took it and made promises they didn't mean to keep."

"You're very young, Dick. You probably would fight, but you'll know better when you're mature. If 'twould save my people I'd try to drive out the whites, Sniapus and Kin-Chautchs alike, from our country to-morrow, but that would mean death to all Indians. 'Twill bring only evil to incite war. Those of us who know must hold our people in check."

"Cowards," said Dick scornfully.

"It takes real courage to allow others to think you are a coward. Sometimes it is weak and cowardly to resist," Siah-hen answered tonelessly. "There are educated Indians in the country, but they conceal the fact from the Sniapus. They are leaders among our people, but woe to them if they incite war against the whites, knowing as they do that it is useless. I have been on the Atlantic seaboard and I know. I know. No use. No use."

"There's Tom Brown," said Dick.

"Yes, Tom Brown, the Shawnee," agreed Siah-hen, "with a degree from Dartmouth, yet blind to the wrong he is doing in inciting war. The weak must fall before the strong, and we were weak when Lewis and Clarke came into the country. It would be making war on the forces of destiny; the whites are only destiny's instruments. Tom Brown knows as well as I do, but blood calls to blood. He is an Indian first and a reasoning man afterward."

"I don't blame Tom Brown," Dick exclaimed hotly.

"Neither do I blame him," said Siah-hen. "An educated Indian is an anomaly. He belongs nowhere. He loves his people, yet knows they are but children. He is not at home in the lodge and yet the lodge draws him like a magnet. It's the blood-call. There is no escape. Whites are suspicious of him, and yet he hungers for their companionship. He fears to take an Indian wife. The tie of blood is stronger in woman than in man; she will return to the Indian ways. Only a degenerate white woman will marry him, so learning is in some ways a misfortune to its Indian possessor. He goes through life a lonely soul, and yet, and yet, knowledge is my priceless possession. I buy it with a price, but it is worth the price. Get knowledge, boy. 'Twill be different with you, though don't expect understanding to make you happy."

Siah-hen had finished. He made for the middle

of the river to evade the treacherous Clackamas rapids just above the Indian lodge.

All at once long-drawn wail after long-drawn wail
tore at the still night.  They came first from the
lodge near at hand, then from the villages on both
sides of the river the cry was taken up until the din
sent thrills of pure horror down Dick's spine; but
Siah-hen took little notice of the wailing. "Sickness
at the lodge," he announced briefly. "The death wail
will float on the air before many days."

# CHAPTER VIII

R EPENTING was not so easy as McDermott
had imagined; he kept putting off his visit
to Elder Waller as the week wore away. He
had made three or four daytime calls on the Bainbridges. He was sure that they knew nothing of his
affairs. Martha Bainbridge had not left the cabin,
on account of the lack of shoes, and John and Uncle
Adzi had little time or inclination to gossip. The
Bainbridges were friendly people, but not free and
easy as many of the emigrants from Missouri and
Illinois were. He noticed a certain reserve, a tend-
ency to mind their own affairs and to refrain from
discussing personalities, that gave him a sense of security for the time being.

He noticed the miserable little lamp with its wick
of braided rag floating in a tablespoonful of buffalo
grease on the puncheon shelf. When he sent over his
tallow to be made into soap he included the candle
molds and a supply of cotton wick. The cabin would
be light enough for reading evenings now; pitch
knots in the fireplace are too fitful to be depended
upon. Carding and knitting could go on while some
one read aloud. He told Martha that he had one
thought for them and two for himself in seeing that
they had candles. He would bring over a book and
spend evenings with them occasionally.

Aunt Morning Ann Simmons was visiting at the

Bainbridges on one of his calls. It was agreed that she should help Martha for a share of the soap.

Aunt Morning Ann glowed and expanded at the joyous prospect of demonstrating to Martha the superior Missouri method of making soft soap. "I sure take pride in my soft soap, lak molasses, hit war, in Missouri, wher we had sech good hardwood ashes. Hit's the knack o' mixin' the lye with the fat an' gittin' hit the right stren'th, an' b'ilin' hit jest right. Mine never itched the baby's skin lak some wimmen's soap done."

"There's fine hardwood here," said Martha. "We have been burning nothing but oak in the fireplace so as to use the ashes for lye."

"Yes," said Aunt Morning Ann, "oak ashes here air prime fer soap-makin'. I shore do have a time with Pop, though, keepin' him from kindlin' the fire with pine knots and a ruinin' o' the ashes for lye. Onless I tend ter hit myself, he fergits ter kiver the coals o' nights an' then kindlin' hez ter be used. Hit 'pears lak men air ornery 'bout sp'ilin' ashes. I hain't never knowed a woman yit 'at didn't have the same bother with 'em," she laughed.

"The leach drips all the time, too," said Martha. The rain was coming down in torrents. "We will never have to carry water to pour over it as we did back home. Uncle Adzi made us a large leach with split cedars last night, and we filled it with ashes right away; there's a tub of lye strong enough for soap run through it already; the rain water is so soft it filters quickly."

McDermott sat long in the cabin, taking sheer

delight in the workaday conversation of the two women. Aunt Morning Ann was a good simple soul with the most lively interest in the affairs of the settlement. If she had not already learned of his past affairs, she would shortly, and of course retail the gossip to the Bainbridges. It didn't matter so much after he had repented, but his whole plan might go awry if prejudices were formed beforehand. He told her he would furnish wool for her, too. There was plenty. She should have tallow for candles and the little things that he could provide. He reasoned to himself that, once placed under obligation to him, Aunt Morning Ann would uphold him nobly, and he might need feminine defenders badly before he squared himself in the settlement.

"I shore will admire ter have a chancet ter work up wool on sheers, an' you-all don' know what hit'll mean to me ter have soap and candles."

"Come to think of it," said McDermott, expanding under the glow in Aunt Morning Ann's face, "you should both of you have a pounding-barrel to make the washing easier. There's a couple in my smoke-house. You shall have them at once. I'll send the Indians over as soon as I reach home."

Now a pounding-barrel is an absolute necessity in a household where cleanliness rules. Uncle Adzi, overhearing the conversation as he came in from the timber, said he would make them each a pounder. A pounder is made of a block of wood about eight inches square, grooved on all its surfaces like a washboard, and fitted with a long handle. A barrel of soapy hot water with a pounder plunged violently up and down in it will remove the grime very effectively from clothing. Wristbands and badly soiled spots can be rubbed clean between the hands after a pounding barrel has gotten in its good work. For washing wool nothing takes the place of this device.

"We thank you kindly, Mr. McDermott," said the radiant Aunt Morning Ann. "I 'lowed we'd git along jist like folks did afore poundin'-bar'ls wuz invented, but it's powerful hard ter wash fur a big family without conveniences."

"The pounding-barrel will certainly help; we appreciate your thoughtfulness," Martha said simply, as he rose, lingering, hat in hand, at the door. He was hoping that he might catch a glimpse of Rose Ann, but she had a habit of disappearing as soon as she could after he came, or not being in sight at all.

"Did you-all hear about the new-fangled washing contraption thet they have in Novelty, Missouri, where we-all came from?" asked Aunt Morning Ann. "They call hit a washboard. Most o' the wimmen-folks war dead sot ag'in' hit. Our elder done preached a sermon a-denouncin' o' the sinful ways o' wimmen who followed after the devil's contraptions, a-tryin' ter git outen work. I allus wondered how Sister Rimer—thet's the elder's wife—felt about hit, but o' course wimmen kept silence in the churches an' so we never knowed. Pore woman, she had twelve children an' died when the last one war borned. She war worked ter death, thet woman war, but the elder 'lowed 'twar the hand o' God Almighty a chastenin' him, an' took a sixteen-year-ole gal fer a wife inside o' three months. I dunno. I dunno. Ef the deacons knew what I think inside o' me, they'd call a meetin' an' church me."

Next day the wool was washed and a small portion dried before the fire so that spinning could begin. John and the boys picked wool by hand and then Uncle Adzi carded it into long rolls half an inch in diameter, ready to spin. After that the spinning-wheel was seldom idle through the day. Back and forth, back and forth, giving the wheel the right turn and pacing backward to make the strong firm thread from the nicely carded roll of wool, went tireless Martha. Nothing but the skill of long practice enabled the spinner to make yarn without shallow places or knots. If she paused to attend the household duties. Rose Ann took her place. She was almost as deft as her mother and fully as swift.

As soon as there was a ball of yarn finished, knitting began, and by the third evening the first pair of socks was finished. With good candle-light to work by, Martha could easily knit a sock an evening, and of course Rose Ann and Esther Amelia each had their sock to pick up in every odd moment.

The tallow candles were a Godsend; a candle makes a winter evening so pleasant. McDermott spent two evenings with them that first week; he insisted that they burn two candles instead of one, an unheard-of extravagance, but since he gave them the tallow and promised more when those were burned, it was no more than right to please him. The second evening he brought over a book to read to them.

The cabin was a homey place, with the candles throwing beams on the rafters and a roaring fire of oak knots giving warmth and good cheer. The soft whir of the wheel made music to the accompaniment of the drip, drip of the rain from the low eaves. Carding and wool-picking went steadily on. Martha and Rose Ann knit, with Martha pausing now and again to show Esther Amelia how to purl the ribbed top of her stocking, or to chide her gently for a dropped stitch, carefully knitting it up, close to the candle meanwhile.

The first evening McDermott was sure that the Bainbridges did not suspect that he had anything but a casual interest in Rose Ann, but he was vaguely uneasy about Rose Ann's attitude toward him. He must win her approval. But how? She held herself proudly aloof, never speaking to him unless he addressed her directly, when she smiled and answered courteously enough. How that girl charmed him! He told himself that he liked them proud and aloof. A woman too easily won was seldom worth the possessing.

But the next evening he was not sure of anything. He fancied there was a slight chill in the air, but it might have been just his nervous apprehension. He feared that John Bainbridge had noticed his eyes following Rose Ann at her spinning. Who could help riveting fascinated eyes on a graceful young girl spinning by the light of a fitful fire? Back and forth, back and forth, tripped Rose Ann, with arms uplifted like a wood nymph dancing, as she turned the wheel and raised the yarn to wind it smoothly on the distaff. Rose Ann spinning in the firelight! Her small bare high-arched feet and slender ankles twinkled to the rhythm of the wheel. Firelight on her yellow hair turned the braid to a rope of spun gold and tinged her upturned face a rosy pink as she emerged and retreated into the shadow. Tantalizing beauty and poetry of motion—a young girl spinning in the firelight!

It was the picture of Rose Ann spinning that decided him that night. He would make his arrangements with Lassee in the morning and henceforth be free from embarrassing entanglements with the Indians. "I hate like sin to do it," he muttered. "I wish I never had seen Lassee, but what was a man to do? It was so plagued lonely with Mary gone. And there had to be a woman to keep the house. And Mary had taught Lassee and made such a companion of her and she loved her so. I should have sent her straight back to the tribe when Mary died and the girls went to New Orleans. But, blame it all, any other man would have done the same."

He mused on and on, sometimes breaking into muttered speech and again lapsing into silence, mulling his problem over and over. The white man's relations with the Indian woman had seemed right and proper when there were no white women in the country. At first the Indians, wishing to show favor to the whites, had pressed their women upon them. The Indian's idea of the relation of the sexes differs from that of civilized peoples. A woman is simply a woman, existing solely for the convenience and pleasure of man, to be cast aside at his lightest whim. In the eyes of the Indians, the women from their tribes were wives of the Bostons, to be kept so long as the husband saw fit. They took no offense when a wife was discarded and sent back to the tribe. They did the same or worse themselves.

With the coming of the missionaries conditions had changed. Few of the Bostons regarded their marital arrangements as permanent. But the missionaries insisted that the Indian women be either sent back to their tribes at once or married according to their binding ritual. It had not been so easy to send the wives away. Some men had tried it and found that the marriage ceremony does not make a marriage— they had forged a bond that could not be broken. Indian women, given the slightest opportunity, are gentle and tractable, devoted to their white husbands, loving them with an idolatrous love, true to them, willing to serve untiringly with no thought of reward, to lay down their lives for them. Not given to demonstrations of affection, a caress was never offered, but white men had taught them to kiss and had shown them as well as they could the little mannerisms of white women.

An Indian woman's idea of paradise is to marry a white man. He may be a drunken, worthless sot, beating and abusing her, still life with him is heavenly compared with being subject to an Indian husband. But no matter what consternation she felt at being cast off, she made no outward demonstration. If the white man told her to go, she left without a whimper, first cleaning the cabin and doing all she could to make him comfortable for as long a time as possible. For days she lingered a little distance from the cabin, hoping to catch a glimpse of him. Sometimes in the

morning he found a little basket of berries at the door
or fish or game left on the table during his absence.
This might go on for weeks. If he left the cabin for
a few hours it might be thoroughly cleaned and food
prepared when he returned, but never a sight of the
woman he had cast aside, unless it were her fleeting
shadow across his path. A week or so of this and a
very stony masculine heart melted, especially as the
cabin was lonely and arms empty. Many a squaw-
man learned that marriage is marriage, either with or
without benefit of clergy, that unions are, after all,
made in heaven, and that bell and candle are only the
outward symbols of the tenderest, most intimate of
human relationships.

Many marriages followed the coming of the missionaries. McDermott had watched and sneered to
himself at the blind submission to custom. But when
confronted with the same problem, he realized that it
had not been so easy to dispose of an Indian woman.
There is a stigma attached to a man with an Indian
wife that he felt he could not bear, and yet, he told
himself over and over, it had been a very different
matter in Lassee's case. She had been in his home
since she was twelve, had been taught to read and
write. Under Mary McDermott's gentle tuition she
had developed as any young girl would. Her English was as faultless as Mary's own; her taste in dress
as good, her skill in housewifery equal to that of any
well-trained young woman.

He had admired Lassee until the emigration in the
fall before. There had been several young girls
among the one hundred and thirty seven; but now,

with the streets of Oregon City thronged with women,
young and old, she had seemed by comparison just
a crude savage with the dark beauty of the primitive
woman that fades and grows repulsive so quickly.

What in human form is more hideous than an old
squaw who has taken on flesh enormously? She finds
plenty to eat in the white man's home, and with the
savage's grossness in feeding, gorges herself. And
an old squaw's habit of wrapping up in her heaviest
blankets and squatting where the sun is hottest,
panting miserably with the heat through a summer
afternoon, ugh! He called to mind some of the aging
Indian wives of the French-Canadian colony on
French Prairie.

From fifteen to twenty, the Indian girl is warm-
blooded and merry, many times beautiful with her
fine black eyes, rich coppery skin, and thick glossy
braids, but from twenty on she ages with terrible
rapidity. It would seem as if with maturity she
broke suddenly under the realization of her fate.
Her status in the Indian lodge is but little above
that of the slave, though she does have the entire
management of the household affairs upon her
shoulders, without masculine interference. From the
time she begins as a small child to learn burden-bear-
ing, until death mercifully claims her at about fifty,
she knows nothing but never-ending drudgery, carried each day to the point of physical exhaustion,
beatings sometimes ending in insensibility and any
degradation that masculinity with the whip-hand
over her chooses to inflict. She is a wrinkled old
woman at thirty, and at forty a repulsive hag fit only

to tan the buckskins and perform the menial labor shunned by the younger squaws.

Judging from those he knew, life with the white man had not improved the appearance of the middle-aged squaw. One generation of the comparatively easy life of civilization cannot counteract racial tendencies developing from untold years of the bestial oppression of savagery. No, there was nothing to be gained by hesitating. Lassee must go back to the tribe at once. He must not waver or allow soft sentimentality to sway him; Lassee and the papoose would never fit in with the scheme of things, now that white women had come to Oregon. Besides, he must have Rose Ann; the sight of her fresh young girlhood was enough to turn any man's fancy away from the handsomest Indian girl who ever lived.

Perhaps, after all, it would be better to dispose of Lassee before he paid his penitent's visit to Elder Waller. The elder might be arbitrary and insist that he perform the marriage ceremony, though the church had heretofore frowned on Indian marriages. He had lived openly with Lassee in spite of the disapproval of the elder, and perhaps he would take pleasure in humiliating him publicly. It is so easy and pleasant to hew out a line of conduct for some one else, and there is a certain joy in insisting that he hold to it. Always nosing in the affairs of others, that was a missionary for you. Gad! how he hated them! It might be very hard to become one of them, but they had succeeded in making life hard for him, living as he was. And then there was Rose Ann; she was worth considerable sacrifice.

He recalled the case of William Shortall, who during the 'thirties had settled ten miles south of Oregon City. A fine upstanding young Englishman he was, living with a handsome young Indian woman. Elder Waller had given him no peace until he finally sent her away, but in the night there was smothered sobbing under his cabin window. Kathla had crept there to be near him, and in spite of her stoicism, her heart-break had given way to tears, a rare occurrence with an Indian woman. Kathla had not meant for Shortall to hear, but he was sleepless, too, with suffering, and the tiny muted sound had swept away the last vestige of his pride. He took Kathla into the cabin and in the morning Elder Waller married them.

McDermott recalled seeing Shortall driving into Oregon City only a week or so ago with Kathla beside him in a shiny new Conestoga wagon—a clean, tidy Kathla—with three alert black-eyed children on the straw in the wagon-bed. They were clean, well-cared-for children, too, and if Shortall felt the stigma of being a squaw-man there was nothing in his placid face to show it. Like all Indian women, Kathla had been eager to learn white ways, to rear her children well, and to keep a spotless home for her husband. Sister Waller had taught her, going the ten miles on horseback every few weeks to the Shortall home. William Shortall was a man of affairs in the settlement now, a trustee of the Methodist Church, and one of the signers of the constitution at Champoeg last May.

Seeing him with his contented little family had

made McDermott wonder if he might not face his own situation, but that was before he had seen Rose Ann! and anyway, he told himself, he had that Southern pride of blood. He could not own half-breed children. No, it was sheer silly weakness for a man to tolerate a wife of whom he must always be ashamed. He would marry no Indian woman, and that settled it.

He pondered most of the night over the situation. If 'twere summer he would send Lassee and the papoose back into the Klamath country. There were still a few scattered remnants of the tribe there, he supposed. At any rate, she would soon take up with an Indian who was in search of a comely young wife. She would thus be out of the way and no one the wiser. But she could not make her way alone through the mountains in the winter-time. A few years ago the Indians would have recognized his right to dispose of her as he saw fit. She was a slave twelve years old when he had bought her at the slave mart down at the main lodge six years ago, for ten rounds of ammunition and a bright blanket. But conditions had changed, and with Quimmo abroad and suspicious of his good faith in the betrothal of his daughter, the Indians might see evidence of his desire to repudiate his Indian alliances in his casting out of Lassee.

He decided toward morning to let the thing work itself out—just make his bargain with Lassee and allow her to go where she pleased; she would go to the lodge or perhaps to Wanaxka's village on the west side of the river. Chief Wanaxka would be glad to take another wife; he had five or six, but some of them were getting old.

He quailed at the cruelty, wondering if he loved the girl, after all. She would be subjected to all the spiteful indignities that a lodge of jealous Indian women could devise, and they are ingenious in humiliating a woman who has once lived with a white man —the height of a squaw's ambition. One who has fallen from that proud estate must be set in her place when she creeps cowering back to her people.

But Indians never refused to provide for the woman who was cast off; the lodge is open to any of their race and food shared so long as a morsel remains.

Hollow-eyed but determined, McDermott took his place at the breakfast table. Lassee had been up for some time; the kitchen was spotless and breakfast ready for him. Lassee was about eighteen, straight and slender, with the Indian suppleness and lightness of foot. Her abundant black hair had been brushed until it shone, not a hair out of place from the straight part in the middle to the coil low on her neck, just as Mary McDermott had taught her to care for it. Her immaculate linsey-woolsey dress fitted her well. There were gentleness and a naïve quaintness about the girl that had endeared her to the McDermott family. She had become one of them during the six years she had lived in their home.

To cover his confusion, McDermott made an elaborate matter of seating himself, while Lassee, not appearing to notice, moved swiftly about the kitchen, pouring his coffee, made of parched ground peas—

no coffee could be had in Oregon City—and setting
a generous pitcher of thick cream beside it, fussing
over his bacon and eggs to be sure that they were
done to his liking, and then taking her place beside
his chair to serve him on the instant. An Indian
woman can seldom be induced to sit at table with her
husband. She waits until he finishes and takes the
food that is left.

McDermott ate in silence, watched anxiously by
Lassee, who intuitively felt his change of mood. For
weeks she had been waiting for the blow to fall, with
an agony that she could scarcely keep from reflecting
in her eyes. She was braced to meet it, yet hoped
against hope that intuition was for once wrong, that
Master loved her. Yet she knew he was interested in
the white girls in Oregon City and that the spinning-
wheel had gone to a cabin where there was a very at-
tractive young girl. The Indians, grinning wickedly
with the knowledge of the torture they were inflict-
ing, had told her so on their return from taking the
wheel over.

"Lassee," McDermott called. She had stepped to
the door as he finished breakfast. Just out of the
range of his eye, she quivered at the unmistakable
quality in his voice. The blow was to fall this
morning.

"Yes, Master," Lassee came to his side and waited
for him to speak.

"Do you know that it is not right for us to be living together?" he asked, ending a long strained silence. He floundered for words to convey his meaning

to the silently waiting Lassee. "There is reproach on us."

Lassee did not by as much as the quiver of an eyelid reveal the surges of emotion that were rolling over her. "Reproach?" she questioned as if she did not get his meaning. The stoic Indian was meeting agony with outward calmness. Pride prevented quailing or blanching under torture.

"Curse the girl!" said McDermott savagely to himself. "Why doesn't she say something?" But Lassee, the impassive, the unmoved, stood waiting for him to continue, just as if she were taking his casual directions about some simple household matter. He hadn't imagined it would be like this; he had prepared for Lassee's clinging arms about his neck and tears and heart-broken pleading. A Lassee he did not know stood waiting quietly for him to announce his decision, ready to accept it without questioning.

"What shall I do with you, Lassee?" he asked brutally, when he could stand the silence no longer. "Sell you to one of the chiefs at the Indian village? He'll give me ten antelope skins and five or six ponies for you; there's always a good market for a pretty young wife." He knew he was being inhumanly cruel, but, hang it all! why didn't she say something? "I won't keep you under my roof another night, Lassee," he continued, stung to rage by her unflinching silence.

When Lassee did not answer, he asked, in a voice acrid with sarcasm; "You are not expecting me to marry you, are you? You can't stay here unless I do. I'm a respectable man, and living with a woman

without being married to her is against the white
man's law," he added virtuously.

"Are you just learning white man's law?" asked
Lassee in a colorless voice, gentle and devoid of reproach. "I thought we were married; in the eyes of
my people I am your wife; you bought me when I
was a slave six summers ago. Where has the wrong
been? Mistress didn't teach me about such things
while she lived."

McDermott, seeing he was getting nowhere, sought
to end the painful interview by rising brusquely.
"You may go where you like, but go quietly this evening. I'll not sell you," he announced in a burst of
generosity, "and I'll see that old Queen Lucy Quillis
down at the lodge looks after you and the papoose
until you choose to take a husband. When the papoose is old enough I'll put him in school at the mission. When you marry I'll give you blankets and
ammunition to make you rich. Now take anything
from the house that you want for yourself and the
papoose, and be ready to go as soon as it is dark.
This is a shameful way for me to live." He was the
high-minded virtuous gentleman again, and Lassee
the abandoned woman dragging his honor in the dust.

"I'll go," announced Lassee simply, and turned to
her household duties.

McDermott stood watching her out of the corner
of his eye, and then, unable to fathom her, strode to
the barn, ever a masculine refuge from domestic tor-
nadoes. In its cool shadows he could pull himself
together and think coherently, he hoped. He felt
immensely relieved and yet there was self-reproach

that amounted almost to a sharp physical pain, and through it all a tinge of uneasiness. It had been too simple—perhaps Lassee was planning revenge. He felt grieved at her; he had meant to kiss her and tell the papoose, John William, good-by, make sort of a sorrowful ceremony of the leave-taking. John William was nearly a year old, just beginning to walk and speak a few words like "kitty" and "bow-wow," and for all he was dark he didn't look so very much like an Indian baby. Cute little beggar, how he would have loved to watch him develop. Somehow he never thought of himself as John William's father. The papoose had just happened. He was Lassee's papoose and that was all there was to it.

With a pang he remembered Lassee's love for him —the love of an Indian woman for a white man and the love of a devoted daughter for a father; he had been like a father to her until Mary died. All day he wavered between two agonizing emotions. He was both glad and sorry to be free from a very embarrassing entanglement. He longed to resume his old tender relations with Lassee now that he realized that he had cast her off. Once he started toward the house to take her in his arms and beg her not to leave him, but just inside the barn door he cursed himself for a fool as in imagination he felt the covert sneers of white men when the squaw-man passed. Then the picture of Rose Ann spinning with the firelight on her hair rose before him.

He did not go in to dinner; it would have meant certain defeat; and yet staying away was even harder. He stood his ground, and the long day wore

itself away a minute at a time and darkness divided
it from the day to come.

As soon as McDermott left the house Lassee
dressed the papoose and, putting him in his *te-cash*
(cradle-board), hung it on a nail in the kitchen.
This was one Indian habit that she had kept; she
carried John William's *te-cash* about on her back or
hung it on the limb of a tree while she worked. Mary
McDermott had not been there to show her how white
women cared for their babies.

She went about the day's work, preparing quantities of food, cleaning the cabin thoroughly, scrub-
bing the hearth, and placing fresh salal and Oregon
grape boughs in large beautifully woven Indian
baskets, until the place had an air of almost holiday
festivity. She gathered knots to replenish the evening fire, and placed a fresh supply of candles where
they would be at hand. She mended McDermott's
clothing and laid it away in perfect order.

As the night drew in, all too swiftly, and she could
find no more to do, she gathered her belongings together, the straight buckskin dress ornamented with
the emblems of her tribe that she had worn when she
entered the McDermott household, her generous supply of clothing. How proud she had been of the
shoes and stockings, the dresses and underwear, that
had been provided for her. Little John William's
elaborate wardrobe, a singular mixture of buckskins
and white baby garments, joined the pile on the
spread-out blanket. She took food enough to last a
week and a few little necessities, making a compact
roll of her luggage.

Then looking about the home where she had spent six happy years, she adjusted the pack and the *te-cash* to her back and stole like a shadow from the house. Her destination was clearly in view; she made her way north and east, finally striking a ledge of rock overlooking the Clackamas. After a short search in the darkness she picked up an Indian trail hugging the bluff for about two miles. She worked slowly and carefully upward, pausing once to open her pack and replace her heavy cowhide shoes with worn moccasins, as the trail grew too narrow and steep to afford a safe footing in the darkness with her clumsy shoes. At last she reached her objective, a huge rock overhanging the ledge, with safe shelter and space enough in its recess to stand upright and move about easily.

She hung the *te-cash* on an overhanging limb while she gathered twigs, and then taking the flint and tinder box from the blankets, quickly kindled a small fire such as the Indian makes for cooking. When it was blazing well she undressed and put on the buckskin dress and leggings, let down her smooth coil of hair, and braided it in two long plaits, one over each ear, putting a gay bandanna on her head. Then she turned her attention to the wondering papoose, dressing him in buckskin garments. "You are little Sintwa now," she explained, as, baby fashion, he protested against the change.

She put him to sleep on the blanket, and stood looking down at her little heap of clothing as if tempted to burn it, but evidently thought better of it, for she gathered it in a compact roll and sat down

by the dwindling fire.  With her hands clasped about
her knees and her head on her breast, she crouched
through the early hours of the evening until the light
fire smoldered and died out, leaving a little circle of
cooling ashes.  She aroused herself from her lethargy
for a moment, then lay face downward in the ashes,
and through the silent woods there arose until morning the wail of the Indian woman, its wild notes bur-
dened with unutterable anguish, with all the heart-
break and sorrow that wells up in the heart of the
Indian woman schooled never to search for words to
express her agony.  The piercing long-drawn wail
of the Indian woman for her dead.

It was gray morning when the hungry cry of her
papoose aroused Lassee.  She ceased her wailing and
bared her breast to his eager little lips, rocking back
and forth and crooning to him in the soft gutturals
of her native tongue.

When it was light enough to see where she was going, Lassee worked her way carefully around the face
of the rock with the cradle-board and her pack and
disappeared from view.

# CHAPTER IX

THE commotion in the Indian villages increased as Dick and Siah-hen neared the main lodge. The wailing was intermittent, a prolonged wail from one lodge taken up and answered by another a mile or so away. Mingled with camp noises, barking dogs, crying babies, was the laughter and talk of the Indians on the banks making preparation to put out in their *kinnums*. Apparently the objective of all was the main lodge.

Most sizable Indian villages are located on high ground at the confluence of streams. This was on a promontory at the junction of the Clackamas and Willamette and had become, with the dissemination of the tribes, a gathering-place for all the remnants, a place of barter. There were a slave mart kept skillfully under cover, a gambling-place with a large track for racing horses on the level Clackamas flat to the east.

After mooring the *kinnum* they climbed up the steep bank to look into the main lodge on their way to their teepee, elbowing their way through the crowd around the door. Yelping dogs, tails between legs, protesting at the kicks of impatient braves, small children underfoot, calico ponies with braided hackamores hanging, a seething mass filled the village, with reinforcements constantly arriving.

The village was made up of houses, most of them

about thirty or forty feet long and from fifteen to
twenty feet in width.  Made of cedar planks, often
thirty feet long, two or three inches thick, and three
or four feet wide, an Indian lodge stands for centuries.   Such houses made up villages when white
men first visited the Pacific coast and had been in existence so long then that even the oldest Indians
could not remember when they were built.

A great mystery to white men is how the Indians
ever built these substantial lodges with the crude
tools they had at hand.  A few rods up the Clackamas
was the ancient flint factory where obsideon, a volcanic glass, was made into implements of warfare
and the chase as well as tools for domestic use.
Knives of all sizes with the groove for the thumb,
arrows, spear heads, and the small cruelly barbed
salmon spears were all patiently chipped out by striking the obsideon with another piece until the imple-
ment gradually took shape.  Obsideon such as used
by the Indians is found in only one place in the
country; there is a volcanic mountain on the Des
Chutes River in eastern Oregon.  The horse Indians
east of the Cascades carried flint on their travois
nearly two hundred miles to barter with the canoe
Indians in the Willamette Valley for their berries
and salmon concessions.

Indian braves were busy before the white men
came and destroyed their ancient crafts by intro-
ducing steel tools and *pil-pil* muskets.  Chisels of
beaver teeth, wedges of elk horn, and large flint
knives were employed in felling and splitting the trees
with the aid of fire carefully set in notches to save

laborious hand work. These lodges represented patient labor beyond belief. They were firmly put together with water-tight roofs of cedar bark held in position by cedar poles. The main lodge in this village was nearly a hundred feet long, accommodating a number of families. Indians live together in winter quarters, having food and household belongings in common. Even the smaller houses were intended to domicile five or six families.

Along the river bank were the sweat-houses, curious little huts shaped like the old-fashioned beehive, about four feet in height and five in diameter, made of tightly woven willow daubed with clay to make them impervious. The sweat-house was the Indian cure-all. Many a brave suffering with measles or smallpox had gone precipitately to other spheres by heating large stones nearly red hot and taking them with a vessel of water into the inclosure. Shutting the door tightly, he poured the water over the stones until the steam became too much for flesh and blood to bear; then he emerged and plunged into the cold running stream. Sometimes his lifeless body floated down the stream, or if his malady were a slight one and his constitution strong, he lived to tell the tale, but the sweat-house was one reason why sickness in an Indian lodge made such havoc. This method of doctoring and the unbelievably filthy living conditions of the winter quarters were responsible for the appalling death rate.

In 1843 there were probably not more than eight hundred Indians in the whole Willamette Valley. They were a dying race when Lewis and Clarke saw

them in 1806. In 1829 Captain Dominis sailed into
the Columbia in the brig *Owyhee,* a Boston-owned
vessel with supplies to trade with the Indians. The
Indians blamed Captain Dominis for an epidemic
that broke out during the winter of his stay with
them, obliterating whole villages and spreading so
rapidly that it shortly reached clear to the California
missions. They called it "cole sick." It may have
been a form of influenza or perhaps measles. Starting with an intermittent fever, the sufferer grew
gradually worse, until death or the quicker sweat-
house mercifully ended his sufferings. An Indian
never has but one serious illness. He falls rapidly
before any childish white man's disease.

This terrible epidemic kept up unabated until well
into the winter of 1831-32, taking off nearly thirty
thousand Indians. There was great bitterness and
muttering against the Bostons and Kin-Chautchs on
account of this plague, but it left them so broken and
weakened that there was no resisting. The crew of
the *Owyhee* were only saved from violence by the
interference of Doctor McLoughlin.

Muttering old squaws bent half double over the
lodge fires were still recalling the time, nearly twenty
years before, when McDougal, Astor's factor, had
told them he would uncork a bottle that he said contained the smallpox plague if they did not accede to
his peremptory demands when he traded with them.
After mulling over their wrongs through the years,
the Indians were fully convinced that Captain Dominis had emptied his jug of "bad medicine" into the
river and that the white men had used means to de-

stroy them in order to take their land. Bitter as gall were the hearts of the Indians toward white men.

As Siah-hen and Dick approached the village the noise was deafening. There was the continuous wailing of the women, the beating of Indian drums, and shrieks and shouts coming from the main lodge. Everywhere wild commotion.

"Chief Cleek-a-tuck is probably much worse," said Siah-hen sadly. "Poor old man, once he was mighty in the councils and the hunt and he feels the loss of his power."

His musings were apparently mournful, and it was some time before he spoke again. "White-headed Eagle knows best," he admitted at last reluctantly. "He has deliberately broken the power of the chiefs and kept my people from forming alliances, so that they are scattered and completely in the power of the Kin-Chautchs and the Bostons. Once a chief was in authority over his tribe. His people looked up to him as a father, but now we have just a few sub-chiefs who are weak and vacillating. No one listens when they speak in council under the pow-wow tree, or obeys their commands in the hunt. Every man is for himself. Cleek-a-tuck's spirit is broken—he has brooded long over the sorrows of his people. He will die tonight," he announced fatalistically.

The sick chief lay in the main lodge. An opening had been left along the ridge pole to allow the smoke to escape. There were huge cracks where the cedar planks had shrunk in curing, but aside from these the door was the only opening. The walls were eight feet high, and built into the rear wall were bunks, one above the other, steamboat fashion, for sleeping quarters.

Half-naked, unspeakably filthy children, their bodies covered with sores, tumbled about in the beds with their coverings of mangy, moth-eaten furs, their slender bowed legs and huge protruding bellies giving them an uncanny elfin appearance.

From the bunks the floor extended in an earthen platform for four or five feet to a depression two feet deep running full length along the middle of the lodge. Here cooking fires were kept constantly burning. Hanging from the rafters were huge salmon, long strings of clams, and the various roots gathered in summer. Deer and elk meat, what was left from the recent *battue* (round-up or great fall hunt) was curing in the acrid curls of smoke from the fires which eddied with the gusts of wind through the lodge, before reaching the aperture in the roof.

Men and women sprawled on the earthen platform, the women busied at intervals with the cooking, which was still accomplished after the ancient fashion of heating rocks and dropping them into the cooking pots. The water-tight cooking baskets had given way to iron pots secured from the trading-post. There were dogs, dogs everywhere, romping in the beds with the children, emitting sharp yelps of pain from thrusting experimental noses in the cooking pots. Indians never train their dogs to be of service to them, unless it be to warn of the stranger's approach, but they allow their camps to be overrun with all sizes, shapes, and ages of mongrels.

Mingled with the thick smoke and permeating all

like a powerful evil entity was a smell so solid that it could almost be felt and tasted, the awful stench of an Indian lodge. A white man in full possession of his senses would not attempt to endure the atmosphere there for long at a time, and even the hardy Indians lived in them only for the few months in the dead of winter when shelter was an absolute necessity. Frequently they were forced to burn them down to escape the vermin that infested them. *E-na-poos* (lice) are the Indian's constant companions and his villages simply swarm with *sopen enapoos* (jump lice, or fleas).

Siah-hen led the reluctant Dick inside the lodge. He made his way to the open space in the middle that had been hastily cleared for the sick chief, with two large end fires carefully tended. The emaciated features of the sick old man were just visible above the furs. Siah-hen gazed at him long and sorrowfully, but Cleek-a-tuck did not notice him. He was fast slipping beyond the concerns of mortals.

Dick was impatient to leave, but Siah-hen came away reluctantly. "There'll be a big medicine dance to-night and by morning my old friend will be gone," he announced in a matter-of-fact tone. "I have business at the medicine dance; we'll eat our supper and come back at once."

Their camp was the ordinary smoke-blackened tee-pee made of deer skin stretched around poles, meeting in a common center, with an opening in the top for the escape of smoke from the fire. On a limb safely out of the dogs' way was a pot of cold soup with its little cakes of savory kouse, or biscuit root, a species of wild celery which the squaws dry and grind to make into little balls for broth of deer or elk meat. Siah-hen heated this over a handful of fire and with jerked venison and dried camas they made a satisfying meal. Before its conclusion the din at the lodge increased in volume until the night was fairly hideous with wild discord. The medicine dance was beginning.

The medicine dance was always a last resort, only performed for a big chief or some one held in respect or dearly loved by the Indians. The whole carefully planned affair was the supreme test of human endurance, both of the sick man, who usually succumbed, and for those who participated in its wild gyrations. But the efficacy of this form of treatment was never doubted by the Indians. Should the patient die, he was fated to die, would have died anyway. They went on stolidly believing in their witchcraft.

Dick was averse to attending this function, yet curiosity mingled with a sort of hypnotic influence drew him into the outer circle near the door of the lodge. It seemed as if every Indian in the whole country was present with his wives, children, dogs, and horses. Those late comers who could not by any possibility gain entrance to the lodge milled around on the outside, adding to the bedlam by shouting in unison with the dancers on the inside. Siah-hen moved about among the dancers, who respectfully made way for him. He spoke sometimes to one and then another of the braves as he recognized friends from the different villages.

Every available inch of standing room in the lodge

was occupied. Each dancer held a long pole in his hand as they lined up in a triple rank with the master of ceremonies in the center near the sick chief, where his gestures of command could be seen by all. The dance commenced, slowly at first, but gaining terrific momentum as it proceeded. The step was simply a jumping up and down in one spot accompanied by a loud chant—two long drawn out and one sharp explosive shout—yo-o-o, yo-o-o, yo. The pole, firmly held in both hands in front of the dancer, came in sharp contact with the roof, beating a rhythmic tatto as the dancers bounded upward. The sharp explosive "yo" and the blow on the roof shook the very foundations of the lodge. The purpose of this was to prepare the patient for the departure of the evil spirit and also to frighten and intimidate the spirit so that he was willing to leave.

The medicine dance was in reality a form of religious rite, if the hazy notions of the Pacific slope Indians could be termed a religion. Unlike the tribes east of the Rockies, the concept of the Great Spirit who was good was not entertained by them, neither did they dwell much on the thought of the "happy hunting-ground," though they proved their anticipation of some sort of a future life by the preparation of tools and supplies which they invariably placed with their dead in the burial canoes, or in the shallow graves where ordinary men and women rested after the trials of this world. They were not much concerned with the after life, though they spoke largely of rewards for good deeds, entirely overlooking punishment for evil.

The Oregon Indian believed that all nature was pervaded by a force which he called *tomaniwus*. Animals and inanimate objects contained this subtle force in greater or less amounts. A man was successful in life according to the degree in which he possessed *tomaniwus*. The *shaman* (medicine-man) was set apart by the tribe so that through prolonged fasting and other rigid ascetic rites and practices he acquired this force to a degree that gave him power over nature, enabling him to look into the future, heal disease, and above all, to drive out the evil spirits which the Indians were constantly fighting with all the means in their power. Religious rites took the form of demonolatry—not devil worship, exactly, but the breaking of obsessions and the propitiation or exorcising of evil spirits. The belief in an occult power that enables the possessor to hold sway over things spiritual as well as material is innate in all Indians. Even after they come in contact with the white man they revert to it.

In days before the coming of the hunters and trappers who demoralized the Indians they claimed that the *shaman* had great power. His life study was roots and herbs for curing the sick and for working spells. By his occultism he could control evil spirits. He had the gift of prophecy and, who knows, perhaps he did perform miracles of healing when faith was simple and child-like and the race was young and vigorous? But the medicine-man was human, and power is dangerous in unscrupulous hands. With decadence and the lack of faith in the old beliefs, he used his power in low intrigues and crafty planning to gain selfish ends.

Still, he was held in a sort of superstitious respect amounting to reverence among the older men and women who recounted stories of miraculous cures and the warding off of terrible disasters to the tribes by the *shaman's* incantations. These stories invariably began with, "My grandfather had it from his grandfather, who was so old that no one could reckon his summers, etc.," at which recital the iconoclastic younger generation sneered more or less openly; but, though they had lost faith, superstitious fear constantly fostered by their elders kept them in line. Breaking away from established tradition, especially in religion, is difficult even after the belief fostering the practice is long since outgrown and discarded.

It required long years to become proficient in the arts of medicine. As a young man the would-be *shaman* went apart from the tribe to some place where spirits were known to have their dark abode. A blue, blue lake held in the cup of a mountain that once belched forth smoke and fire far to the south and east was the retreat of youths from the valley tribes who aspired to this high office, and a being who had courage to go to such a place alone to fast and run in circles for days to seek out the evil spirits and learn their ways so as to be able to exorcise them was entitled to a certain respect tinged with awe even if the later generation did not believe in the power of his medicine.

A medicine dance such as this one had not been held in the valley for years, and in the opinion of

the Indians if this one was not efficacious it would
be the last in which they ever participated.  But all
fell at once under its hypnotic sway as soon as the
performance was under way, though at first the
doubters stood muttering on the fringe of the
crowd.

The wild gyrating in the lodge kept up for hours
unending, so it seemed to the weary Dick, who was
curiously awaiting the coming of the medicine-man.
The terrific din and the nauseating stench of perspiring Indians were a severe test of physical endurance, but the dance would go on until complete
collapse of the participants.  The din outside increased, heralding the approach of the *shaman* and
his attendants, five of them, who, with hair-raising
shrieks and yells and growls, bounded into the midst
of the dancers.  Fiends from the pit were the medicine-man and his aides.  Their bodies were naked
to the waist, their faces covered with hideous masks,
resembling the demoniac faces on totem poles, the
whole get-up topped off with a hideous head-dress.
The costumes were designed to terrorize the evil spirit
who was working his witchcraft on the sufferer, and
to force him to loosen his hold so that the driving
out could be accomplished.

In their hands they held huge rattles with which
they beat an uncanny accompaniment to their measured shrieks and growls.  The sacred rattles are
awe-inspiring objects made of bladders filled with
holy relics such as the teeth of enemies, pebbles, and
what not gathered in certain auspicious times and

signs of the moon, and fringed round and decorated with feathers and porcupine quills.

The dancing and pounding did not relax for a moment as the medicine-man circled round and round the sick chief, creeping on all fours and peering beyond the range of human sight for a glimpse of the evil spirit. The circle narrowed as he crept cautiously round and round, until a blood-curdling shriek announced that he saw the evil entity invisible to the others. Then the real tussle began. No Indian devil quits his victim without a grim struggle. The *shaman* finally gave a great bound and leaped upon Cleek-a-tuck, making futile endeavors to seize the spirit in his hands. Failing time after time in this, he threw back the skins covering him and took up the slack skin on the emaciated chest with his teeth, shaking him as a terrior shakes a rat. This treatment went on for an hour or so, but the sick man was unconscious of the rough handling. He had lapsed into insensibility early in the evening and never emerged from his coma.

The medicine dance lasted all night, ceasing with the first streaks of light in the east, when the frenzy of the dancers gave way to the sleep of exhaustion; Cleek-a-tuck died in the early morning. As Dick and Siah-hen left the lodge there arose, as from an agreed-upon signal, the wail of the women for the dead. The relays of wailers had somehow been appointed in an incredibly short time. Wailing would not cease until the obsequies were performed ten days hence. Each village would keep up its answering wail during the time the chief lay in state, until the whole countryside was a shrieking hell.

"My work in the village is over for a time, now," Siah-hen said as they spread their skins to sleep an hour or two. "With Cleek-a-tuck dead, no chief has the power or the will to incite my people to war. They know that they cannot hope to gain back Tum-chuck, as Cleek-a-tuck had so often promised them before he became decrepit with age."

Siah-hen began packing his camp equipment as soon as breakfast was over. "The village will be a noisy place for the next ten days," he explained to Dick. "I must go to Vancouver soon, anyway. There is no further need for me to live in the vil-lage. My poor old friend is dead, and there will be no more talk of rising against the Sniapus. Kil-a-poos will be chief in his father's place, but he has no influence among my people. The young chiefs know that there is no hope and will submit with-out a struggle, shutting their bitterness and hatred for white men in their hearts.

"We'll leave our stuff in the end of the lodge for safe keeping, and take back our supplies and put them with the winter stores. Food will be very scarce in the village before the winter's over. The deer and elk meat from the fall hunt will be gone in a month. My people give with an open hand to anyone who is hungry. They cannot understand the white man's hoarding of food while there is want among them. We all suffer when food is gone, but no Indian goes without while there is a morsel of food left in the lodge."

Dick was eager to be off after the terrible night, and on breaking camp they set out at once down the river.

"Let's move our camp up to my claim when we come back," said Dick, already proud in his possession of land. "We can live in the teepee until we build the cabin."

"We will," agreed Siah-hen. "We're going for the things we will need now. I have plenty of credit at the Post. If there are cobbler's tools there, my father, White-headed Eagle, will let me have them. We'll find sole leather, I hope, and you will cobble shoes for all the settlement."

Hope ran high in Dick Skelton's heart as they paddled along down the placid river. Siah-hen was a friend such as he had never known before in his warped little-boy existence. He was no longer a bound boy. He was a man and free to make his fortune in a wonderful new country. He was grateful to Siah-hen, but incoherent in expressing himself, yet he knew that Siah-hen understood.

# CHAPTER X

UNCLE ADZI had risen early to walk down to Oregon City to trade three pairs of wool socks for sugar and a few little necessities at the mission Post. His greatest joy was to limp slowly down to "the settlement," as he always called Oregon City, do the family shopping, and then while away an hour or so taking in the sights, perhaps watching the Indians gambling, always a fascinating diversion, or walking about the boat landing to marvel at the loads of freight coming and going on the river. There was always color and movement to delight the eye after the level, monotonous, though withal pleasant life of the isolated settler.

This was the busiest season of the year in Oregon City. The town was full of Indians drawn there by the death of Chief Cleek-a-tuck. The great fall hunt (*battue*) was over and the Indian villages were near enough to allow all the idle braves to congregate there to gamble or to loiter about the docks, now and then doing a little lading or some other work in exchange for a few inches of the long twisted ropes of Brazilian tobacco sweetened heavily with molasses hanging conspicuously in the trading-posts.

Uncle Adzi loved to watch the gambling. The Indian did not have to learn gaming from white men. It was a terrible fever in his blood long before their coming. It was their custom to bring in all their goods and remain until everything was gone. Sometimes a particularly opulent brave came in with his entire retinue of wives, slaves, and ponies, not to mention his *ictas* (things in the shape of personal effects), and departed minus even his blanket. Whole droves of ponies that had perhaps been stolen or captured, might change hands on the mere catching of a tossed stick. Their gambling games are very simple, such as the guessing in which hand the operator held the "little joker," a small bone or a piece of polished wood, or the childish "odd or even" accompanied by the monotonous "stick-bone" song—"he-ha-ha—he-ha-ha"—accentuated by striking a stick on some hard object at regular intervals. Uncle Adzi never tired of listening to the ever-present Indian drum whose raucous beating punctuated the air, or to the shouts of derisive laughter at the expense of the loser, ringing out with every play.

But above all else in Oregon City he marveled at the shipping; it was the coming true of his long-cherished dream. Since first hearing of Oregon in landlocked Illinois, Uncle Adzi had visioned a brisk trade with China and other Asiatic countries. To see the barges loading bales of smoked salmon that represented the season's Indian fishing, and the wheat all stacked on the docks, was prophetic of the nearness of the day when the fleets of the world would anchor in the lower river to carry away the farm products that this rich country would grow lavishly when soil-hungry farmers from the Middle West came to "till the land and dress it."

Then there was his pungent delight in the moun-

tain men, who gathered in small knots on the
corners or in the trading posts.  Their red sashes
furnished a piquant note of color in the somber gathering of buckskins and butternut jeans.  The hunters
and trappers recounting deeds of valor in which the
narrator was always the hero held him spellbound.
Their modest admission that they were "the very
devil" with the Indian belles, that they could trap
more beaver, had more credit at the company's trading-post, could consume more hard liquor and were
generally better all-around "bad men" than mountain men to be found anywhere in America, for that
matter, in the world, furnished him with the where-
withal for delicious conversation to regale the family
as they carded wool in the evenings.

Uncle Adzi was accustomed to enjoy life to the
full, and life in Oregon was a sweeter, richer life
than he had dared dream of even in his younger
days when he felt that he was something of an ad-
venturer and a mighty hunter himself.  Illinois fron-
tiers were tame affairs compared with the vivid, col-
orful polyglot Pacific-coast settlement, where a stable
government was in process of formation, with all its
heated political discussions.  Three active parties in
the field, the missionaries, the settlers, and the British
factions, represented by the Hudson Bay men, furnished rich material for argument.  There were
heated expositions of the tenets of this and that religious faith set forth by adherents of rival hair-
splitting denominations in the blacksmith shop and
trading-posts.  Spirited discussions of the liquor
question were always to be encountered, with both

sides ready to stake their very lives to uphold their
sides of the argument. Some one had been giving
whisky to the Indians only last week, Uncle Adzi
learned while listening to a small group.

In frontier living there is always time to visit a
bit while waiting for a small job of blacksmithing to
be done. And just now the grist mill was so crowded
with work that a farmer thought nothing of waiting
two or three delicious days in the hope—he knew it
was only a hope—of having the two bags of wheat
ground, that he had so carefully balanced on his
calico pony and brought over fifteen, twenty, or even
forty miles of tortuous trail. A day means but little
to those who travel with ox-teams or walk beside
heavily-laden pack-horses.

Uncle Adzi learned of marvelous new and easy
methods of farming from the older settlers. Missouri
and Illinois fashions in tillage did not serve so well
in a "grass country" where there was not frost
enough in the winter to annihilate the weeds and
where root crops were planted in the late summer
and kept growing through the winter. He marveled
at the ease of farming and was eager to try out
the methods of the farmers on French Prairie,
slovenly and careless as he had thought them at first.

This morning he would have delighted to linger
for another hour before making the steep climb home,
but he hurried off, partly because he had heard a
wonderful piece of news and partly because John
and the boys were depending upon him to carry a
warm dinner to them at noon. They were riving
shakes a short distance above the house, hoping to

finish enough that day to pay for the cow and calf and the provisions they had secured from William McDermott.

Martha opened the door for him and inquired anxiously: "Did you find what the commotion the last week among the Indians was about, Uncle Adzi? Perhaps the wind has shifted so that the sound carries, but there is noise all around. There has been shrieking all the morning that seemed to come clear from Wanaxka's village across the river, and from this village above us the Indians have been coming and going all the morning. They say they are peaceful. They couldn't be planning to attack us, could they? I've been a little uneasy."

Uncle Adzi recovered his breath with difficulty, after his hurried walking. "Don't ye fret, honey," he soothed. " 'Tain't nothin' but thet Chief Cleek-a-tuck died about ten days ago and the Injuns air a-plannin' ter hold his funeral this arternoon. We stick so close hum we never git no news ontil hit's a week or so old. They say at the settlement thet hit'll make us safe. The young chiefs know thet thar hain't no use tryin' ter resist the settlers. They naterally feel bad about losin' their old chief; he was the last o' the old guard an' hit sorter leaves 'em withouten a leader." He was all eager excitement to tell his great piece of news. "What you think they done at the settlement, Marthie?" he inquired.

Martha shook her head.

"They's a school down thar, with a hull roomful o' scholards. Starts up two weeks come Monday.

I snum! the younguns 'll have a better chancet ter take a edication here than they'd 'a' stood in Sangamon County. 'Most ever'buddy har 'lows ter edicate their younguns."

"I'm so glad," exulted Martha. "I'll start right in patching their clothes."

"Ye recollec' hearin' me tell o' Sidney Moss, him as come in with las' year's emigration and laid out the town o' Oregon City for Doctor McLoughlin with the pocket compass he fotched across the plains? Ye mind he had a sorter hotel down thar this fall ter feed folks thet war jist a-gittin' inter the settlement with our emigration, an' how he went up an' down the street ringing' o' hand-bell when dinner war ready? A right public-sperrited citizen is this-ahere Sidney Moss, an' kind ter everyone. He done found a pore widder an' five li'l' childern nigh onto starved an' cold an' wet, livin' in a tent down the river. Her man died on the plains, an' God A'mighty only knowed how she managed ter reach the settlement."

He paused at Martha's exclamation of pity, but resumed at once. "Sidney Moss said he'd been 'lowin' all fall thet the younguns shouldn't be runnin' loose, an' when he foun' them pore li'l' childern an' the widder, he took the two oldest boys by the han's an' set out ter find a deestrict-school teacher an' ter round up the younguns and see how many thar war. He found a young man named John Brooks who had been a school-master in the states an' hired him on the spot, an' he's a-riggin' up a room in his hotel ontil they kin git a school-house built."

"We'll send the children," Martha paused and knit her brows as she suddenly thought of shoes. "The boys and Esther Amelia can go barefooted. They are as well off barefooted, anyway, as with those miserable Indian moccasins that keep the feet wet all the time. It seems cruel to see barefooted children in the dead of winter, but not one of them has had a cold yet, not even Esther Amelia, and they don't seem to mind it much, except for the chapping from wading in the water when they had no call to."

A sudden disturbing thought struck Uncle Adzi. He scratched the bald spot on his puzzled head. "But Rose Ann—I hadn't thought o' shoes fer her."

"And she is so sensitive about being seen barefooted," supplemented Martha. "A sixteen-year-old girl is counted a young woman. We think she's just a child because she's so small for her age. It's not right to see a barefooted woman. Whatever we'll do for shoes puzzles me. John keeps fastening the soles to the uppers of mine with new buckskin. Much as I want to go down to see the settlement, I can't leave the place until I manage to get a pair of stockings knit for myself. Seems as if we must sell what we knit for a while yet to keep the table going."

But seeing the distress in Uncle Adzi's face, she laughed off the situation. "We'll tell our shoe troubles for a good joke this time next year," she smiled. "The ship'll be in with plenty of shoes and dress goods and we'll all put on style."

Uncle Adzi laughed suddenly at some recollection. "Thet reminds me o' a good yarn I hearn

down at the settlement.  John Baxby done made hisself a pair o' brogans outen a green cowhide with
the har turned in.  They say they weighed nigh onto
seven pounds, an' when he done tuk 'em off at night
he had ter leave 'em soakin' in a pan o' water, er
he couldn't git 'em on in the mornin'.  The talk o'
the settlement them brogans war."  They both forgot
their perplexities in their gales of merriment.

"I got somethin' else on my mind, too, Marthie,"
he said slowly, pausing awkwardly in his search for
words to express himself.  "Do ye sense thet peart,
pretty gals air not so common in the settlement, an'
thet Rose Ann air plumb old enough ter marry accordin' ter most folks.  Thar be nigh onter ten lonesome men ter one gal situated ter marry."

Martha laughed indulgently.  "Rose Ann's just a
little girl yet, according to my way of thinking.
She'll not marry yet awhile.  The idea has never entered her head."

"I hearn roundabout lak this mornin' thet the
reason McDermott war so oncommon frien'ly an' ac-
commodatin' ter us war thet he had his eye on Rose
Ann.  They say thet he has sent his squaw back
ter the tribe an' thet he 'lows ter take a white wife.
In course this mout jist be idle gossip, but all the
same hit sot me ter cogitatin'.  I saw Pop Simmons
down ter the settlement an' he said they ain't seed
thet Injun gal an' her papoose fer quite a few days,
but, law! McDermott hain't one ter talk his affairs
out common lak, an' folks is always quick ter sus-
picion an' talk."

Martha turned on him indignantly.  "How you

talk, Uncle Adzi! I have never heard anything about his having an Indian wife or a papoose. And, anyway, he is old enough to be Rose Ann's father." But she paused, and a puzzled frown knit her smooth forehead as she remembered the little mysterious things that had puzzled her so. This verified her intuition that there was something in Mr. McDermott's life that he was carefully concealing from her. Never had this sixth sense failed her. She recalled her resolution to wait for time to clear up the mystery of the carefully kept clothing and the mitered patches that no one but a good needlewoman could set into the seat of a pair of trousers. Well, it had taken less time than she had expected to clear it up.

Uncle Adzi made an effort to be just to McDermott. "Wal, Marthie, I hope I'm wrong, but John an' me bin a-keepin' a eye out fer quite a spell, an' we don't 'low ter be beholden ter him from now on. We acted in good faith; we never suspicioned him at the start; but the work is all done now ter pay him cl'ar off, an' we'll have no more dealin's with him. He jist married thet squaw, so they say, accordin' ter the way her tribe marries, which ter honest white men hain't no marriage at all; but the pore Injun gal don't know no better."

But it was noon and John and the boys would be waiting for their dinner, so Martha summarily dismissed the troublesome subject of squaw-men and middle-age widowers in search of young white wives and began filling a small iron pot with hot boiled wheat, and handed Uncle Adzi an Indian basket with a generous piece of dried salmon and a jug of sweet milk.

"Ye're all alone again to-day, Marthie. Where be the gals?" he asked as he started up the path.

"They went up to spend the day with Aunt Morning Ann," answered Martha. "I was a little uneasy for them to start off, with so much commotion among the Indians, but John said it was all right when he was halfway between the two cabins, working in the timber. I hate to be nervous and full of apprehension all the time; it's best just to go about ordinary affairs and not worry over noisy Indians or anything else."

"Yes," Uncle Adzi called back. "Yer safe ez a church in this here kentry. Once ye l'arn Injun ways ye git ter like 'em. Did ye mind the gals ter gather a sack o' Oregon tea on the way hum, Marthie?" he called just before he was out of hearing.

"Yes," she answered, and went inside. "One of the nicest things about this country is Oregon tea," she was thinking. "Good for medicine and tea, too. I was afraid that we'd miss our tea and coffee, but ground parched peas make a good morning drink, especially since we have the cow and cream for it. And I do believe that the good herb has kept us all well and helped to drive the malaria out of our systems."

Most of the emigrants felt this way about *yerba buena*, the good herb of the Spaniards. Mountain tea, they generally called it here—a small trailing evergreen vine with a pungent aromatic odor that flung its rough green leaves with their rich purple

underlining so lavishly over every steep shady hill-
side. Mountain tea brewed strong and hot had saved
many a life when doctors and medicine were not to
be had.

Martha took a spoonful of boiled wheat from the
iron pot near the fire and poured herself a tin cup
of milk, eating her hasty luncheon looking out the
cabin door. She had a quantity of wool to spin to-
day. The girls should have the balls of yarn they
took on their visit all knit up by the time they
reached home. Every girl and woman knit steadily
as she walked along the road, if she was fortunate
enough to have yarn on hand to make up into stockings. No light task to provide winter stockings for
a whole family who had none at all to fall back upon
and at the same time have two or three pairs to sell
every few weeks to eke out the family credit at the
trading-post.

She began her spinning to the accompaniment of
a rather troubled line of thought. So McDermott
had an Indian wife. The pity of it! She sensed
the conditions that had forced him to consort with
an Indian woman, the gnawing loneliness of a cabin
without a woman in it, but she suddenly saw the
other side and fiery anger blazed forth at his cruelty
of a white man to a woman of an inferior race. Poor
defenseless little Indian girl with a half-breed papoose strapped to the cradle-board on her back,
making her sorrowful way back to the misery and
degradation of the lodge when the white man had
tired of her. The disgrace of the Oregon country,
so everyone said, was the treatment Indian women

had received at the hands of unscrupulous men. Men who had honor where women of their own race were concerned showed themselves absolutely devoid of human feeling in their treatment of trusting Indian girls. But, she concluded, there was no use in brooding over a condition she could not help. She would ask John if he could find the poor girl and perhaps do something for her, or it might be that the men, the upright ones in the settlement, would bring McDermott to time.

But there were happy things to think about, too. To know that a school was to open so soon was joyful news. She wondered if Rose Ann could make out with new warm stockings and a pair of Indian moccasins. John could easily secure a pair by barter with the Indians, but she decided that sitting all day with wet feet might bring on lung fever. Why was it that the Indians went everywhere in wet weather and their moccasins never appeared to be wet or to have shrunk on their feet? She reflected that those they wore were a different color, sort of a dull gray, while those they traded to the settlers were made of new yellow buckskin that wet as soon as it touched the damp earth and had an agonizing way of drawing up and hurting the feet when it began to dry.

Taken all around, buckskins were not very satisfactory for either footwear or garments in a damp climate. But buckskin would do; yes, it would do. The girls had worn their soft warm dresses all winter and the boys each had buckskin suits that saved a great deal of washing and patching of worn-out garments. They would be coming in next summer with yardage goods—wools and calico for women's clothing.

She thought of how lovely a sprigged calico would be for best, so she could go to church or visiting. She did hope she could scrape together butter money when the cow was fresh again, or that the stockings and socks they knit would somehow buy new dresses for her and the girls. She would make lovely slatted sunbonnets with a tiny ruffle around the face and ruffles on the ends of the strings of the dress material. She could almost see those beautiful dresses in her mind. There would be a soft wool delain with ruffles on the long skirt for Rose Ann. How sweet a young girl looked in her first long dress with her hair demurely parted in the middle and gathered in a knot at the nape of her neck. Rose Ann's hair would curl so charmingly about her temples.

In her mind's eye she could see the whole family setting forth to church on a sunny Sunday morning, John and Uncle Adzi brave in black broadcloth like the cherished suits they had been obliged to throw out to lighten the load, and the boys in wool pantaloons securely buttoned to butternut shirts. But dark little Esther Amelia stood out in the group; she had a high-waisted dress of pink calico with short puffed sleeves and low neck, and a long narrow skirt that reached to her ankles. She assured herself over and over that it was all possible—because folks were destitute on reaching a new country did not signify that they would always be destitute. No, indeed, not when they worked as John and Uncle Adzi did, and she was there to make the most of their resources and to help along with the knitting. And they were bringing up their children to know the value of time and to do honest work.

But her joyful musings as she paced back and forth at her spinning were rudely interrupted by the furious barking of the two dogs that John had recently acquired for a protection when the men were working in the near-by timber. They were kept chained near the stable daytimes to keep them from roaming about and to warn of the approach of strangers.

Martha stepped to the door to find out the cause of the disturbance, and saw a slight Indian girl fairly flying up the path toward her. Her wet buckskin skirt clung to her, and the tattered blanket flew out behind her as she ran. Abject terror was in the strained face of the young squaw as she forced her way past Martha and cowered in the darkest corner of the cabin, where a bed hid her from view of the doorway.

Martha knew at once that she had been swimming the Clackamas and that for some reason she must have been trying to escape from the lodge. She attempted to question her, but the girl was completely out of breath and so exhausted that she could not answer, but she made frantic gestures for her to close the door.

Too late it dawned on Martha what had happened, as the girl said something in English. She caught the words only "bury," and then "Cleek-a-tuck." They were going to bury this girl alive with the dead chief. She had heard one of the missionaries at The Dalles tell of going out to Memaloose Island, the great Indian burial-place in the Columbia River, to liberate a slave who had been tied face down in a wooden box and the dead body placed upon him. She shut and bolted the cabin door, shuddering with horror as she noticed for the first time the blood running down the girl's face from a jagged cut on her head, either a blow from a blunt instrument or a fall on a sharp rock.

She turned to reassure the trembling girl, when fresh commotion broke out; the dogs barked furiously as wild, blood-curdling yells sounded along the path. If Martha had stopped to reason she might have felt fear, but anger took its place—a fierce, overpowering anger. She flung the door open and stood drawn up to the full height of her five feet two inches, with her arms stretched to bar out the Indians, should they dare to intrude. She did some quick thinking. The loaded gun was hanging on its two forked sticks over the mantel. Was it wise to turn and leave the door to get it? No, she could manage the Indians better if she gave them no chance to enter the cabin. They'd take the girl by force. They came swiftly forward, making wild gestures and whooping to frighten her. She wished she could reach the dogs, but that, too, was out of the question. She must keep them out of the cabin. In a split second she determined fully that no matter what they said or did, twenty thwarted angry Indians should not take that cowering girl from the cabin—no, nor forty of the filthy wretches. Martha Bainbridge was powerful in her righteous indignation and fully equal to any emergency at the moment. She would drive them off somehow. Bury a young girl alive with a dead chief, would they? Not if her name was Martha Bainbridge and there was breath left in her body.

The spokesman of the party advanced, shaking his fist in her face, and yelled at her, "*Pot-latch ten-as kloock-man*" ("Give us the little squaw"). She looked him full in the face for a moment before she spoke, and the Indians fell back a step before her stern gaze.

"No, I'll not give you the young squaw," she announced in a tone that left no doubt of her meaning.

The twenty withdrew and discussed the situation for a minute or two, while Martha, never taking her eyes off them, stood with outstretched arms, firmly barring the door. Finally they came up, and the spokesman made a move as if to thrust her aside and enter the cabin.

"Come inside my cabin when I tell you to stay out, will you?" she inquired, her eyes blazing with wrath.

The brave backed off a little.

"You dirty wretches!" she went on. "Just as much as lay a finger on me and see what happens. You know very well that if you come into this cabin you'll have every white man in the settlement down on your village before night."

There was force in her argument and the leader was no fool; he motioned to the others and again they held a hasty conference. They recognized the fact that there would be some difficult explaining to do,

and then, too, slave burials were against the orders
of the great "White-headed Eagle," and should this
happening reach his ears he would punish the of-
fenders severely. White-headed Eagle was just; he
did not punish the whole tribe for offenses in which
a few were involved, but demanded the culprits and
dealt summarily with them. Besides, there was no
telling what an angry white *kloochman* would do if
they forced their way into her cabin. It was one
thing to abuse a squaw, but no one, not even a white
man, ever offended a white *kloochman* if he could
possibly avoid it. A silly tribe of squaw-worshipers
were the Sniapus and the Kin-Chautchs.

Discretion is the better part of valor even among
braves. In defeat they turned and went reluctantly
down the path, the leader muttering disgustedly to
the agreement of the others: "Ten-as t kope klooch-
man heap plenty hy-as. Heap plenty wake ten-as"
("Little white woman heap plenty big. Heap plenty
not small.")

When they were out of sight Martha turned and
calmly barred the door, took the rifle down from its
place over the mantel, and tested it carefully to be
sure it was loaded before she turned her attention
to the shivering girl crouched in the corner.

She spoke reassuringly to her and, bringing hot
water and a small jar of soft soap, began carefully
washing the long ugly wound that slanted diagonally
across her forehead. She decided that the cut was
not deep as she pressed the jagged edges together
to stanch the flow of blood; but this proved unavail-
ing, so she went to a recess behind a puncheon shelf

in the log wall and took out a sizable bundle of white stuff—Grandmother Shields' linen sheets that had been woven for her dower and that she was saving to use for ruffled curtains for the windows as soon as glass came into the settlement.

Carefully unrolling them, she took the end of one and began scraping lint with the back of a knife, applying it to the cut when she thought she had enough to stanch the blood. She measured off enough linen for a bandage with her sharp eye, cut it accurately, and sewed it firmly in place about the girl's head with a raveling drawn from the cut edge.

"Good thing I had linen to scrape lint from," she said to the girl, who seemed to understand her but did not speak. "There'll be plenty for curtains, anyway," she assured herself; "these are good-sized sheets and the windows are small."

She heated milk quickly in a tin cup over the coals and offered it to the girl, who tried bravely, but could not drink it. She drew her up before the fire and was preparing to remove her clinging wet buckskin, but was interrupted by the dogs barking again. Panic seized her this time. Perhaps the Indians were returning to break into the cabin and take the squaw by force. She picked up the rifle and stood waiting. She would shoot them in the legs, that's what she would do, if they broke into the cabin. The shot would bring the men from the timber and she could stand them off, she hoped, until they reached home. They should not have that girl without a fight.

But finally there was a knock at the door, and

Dick Skelton's cheerful voice called to her. "Let us in, Mrs. Bainbridge. It's Dick and Siah-hen."

Martha sprang joyfully to open it and the pair came into the cabin, their presence wrapping her in safety like a warm comforting garment. Siah-hen did not laugh as he had always done before when among the whites, neither did he speak Chinook; his English was as good as hers when he said simply, "You have saved a poor Indian slave girl from a horrible death, Mrs. Bainbridge, and we will always be *tillicums*."

"I am so glad I was able to keep them from taking her," said Martha. "I was so angry I was fairly beside myself. I could have stood off a hundred of them, the way I felt about it, but later I was terribly afraid. It's like that when I get right good and mad."

"I take it an Indian slave will never again be buried alive with a dead chief," promised Siah-hen. "I could have prevented this, but we went to Vancouver the morning after Cleek-a-tuck died. We came back sooner than they expected; they thought no one outside their little group would know of it. Lassee is a slave girl and the chief's son wished to bury him according to the ancient Indian custom. My people are bewildered and miserable, and only tried to go back to the habits of the day before white men came among them. They are simple, like children, in many things," he said in extenuation.

He went over and spoke to Lassee, who sat in utter dejection by the fire, the cup of hot milk still held in her listless hand. "I must take Lassee back to the village and bring the culprits to time. White-headed Eagle will deal severely with them," he told Martha.

Martha started to protest, but he was firm. "No harm will come to Lassee, and the leaders who planned this awful thing will be severely punished." He motioned to Lassee, speaking to her in a strange guttural tongue. She answered with a monosyllable and arose and followed him. Her sad black eyes followed Martha in rapt gratitude, but she did not speak as she left the cabin with Siah-hen.

Dick sat down before the fire and, after Siah-hen and his charge were out of hearing, voiced his disgust of Indians. "I suppose we must stay in the village to-night, but this'll be the last one," he announced positively. "Siah-hen has been a real friend to me, though," he conceded gratefully. "He has found a good claim for me up above you about a mile, and we are moving up there to-morrow. He's taught me to read and write and cipher, and got leather and cobbler's tools at Vancouver. They treat him 'most like a white man at the Post."

Martha's eyes filled with sudden blinding tears. The nerve strain of the afternoon had told on her. She could not have said exactly why she cried, but probably it was for the desolation and sorrow of the downtrodden, for the misery of Indian slaves and of white bound boys with none of their race to offer them shelter.

"I'll always love that Indian, Siah-hen," she said, "for the thing he has done for you and for his kindness to that poor Indian girl."

Dick was overwhelmed by the sight of Martha's

tears, and reduced to a miserable silence where he longed to say something to comfort her, but was dumb.

Finally, with a manful effort, he stammered, "Mrs. Bainbridge, I-er-we got cobbler's tools at Vancouver like I told you, and-er-Doctor McLoughlin gave us a side of sole leather, and Siah-hen says as soon as we get our cabin up we'll cut the teepee up into shoe uppers." He was trying desperately, just like a small boy, to take Martha's mind off a sorrowful subject and stop her tears.

She understood him and smiled to herself, drying her eyes as she listened.

"The Indians," Dick went on breathlessly, "always make their moccasins out of the buckskin from their old teepees—the smoke cures the buckskin so that it's nearly water-proof and does not shrink at all. I'm going to be a cobbler. And—er—Mrs. Bainbridge, would you let me make a pair of shoes for Rose Ann so she can go to school, and a pair for you?" he finished lamely. Blushing furiously, Dick awaited Martha's answer.

"Why, Dick, could you?" she exclaimed. "You're a direct answer to prayer. Of course we want shoes, and we'll pay you in warm wool socks for you and Siah-hen."

But apparently she had forgotten something. She sprang up as if her idleness reproached her and began setting out boiled wheat and salmon for Dick and heating milk for him, mothering him in a way that was strange and sweet to the awkward boy.

# CHAPTER XI

LASSEE followed Siah-hen down to the foot of the
trail before either spoke. Turning, he noticed, apparently for the first time, that she
was lagging with exhaustion. He paused and found
a seat for her on a log, and after making her as
comfortable as possible with her back against a tree,
seated himself beside her just as a white man would
have done, a little attention that Lassee was not slow
to notice.

He turned her head toward him and scrutinized
the white bandage intently, satisfying himself that
the bleeding had stopped before he spoke. Her lips
were blue and her teeth chattering with the cold.
Siah-hen took off his voluminous blanket and, wrapping it around her, began chafing her hands to start
the circulation.

"So you had to go back to the lodge, Lassee,"
he said slowly. "Tell me how it happened. I knew
quite a while ago that McDermott was planning to
take a white wife, but he sent you away sooner than
I expected."

"I went first to the Buzzard's Cave. I hoped I
could live there all winter, but the papoose was sick.
He had never been out in the cold before; he's been
raised in the house like a white baby," she said with
a faint touch of pride. "I was afraid he would die,

so I had to go to the lodge," Lassee explained emotionlessly.

"How long had you been at the village?" Siah-hen questioned.

"I think about a week," faltered Lassee between chattering teeth. "The squaws laughed and jeered at me when I first came. I expected that, but they took my papoose away. I saw them take off his little buckskin shirt and moccasins and put dirty old skins on him and turn him out with the other papooses. They play around the horses and on the bank of the river, and I have been so afraid. He has never been neglected and dirty, and he's so little; he can't walk very well. And he isn't weaned yet." Cowering in her misery, Lassee covered her face with two trembling hands, but made no sound.

Siah-hen grunted explosively and then lapsed into silence, looking straight ahead.

"I am afraid to go back to the lodge," said Lassee finally. "But you'll get my papoose for me, if I go, won't you, Siah-hen?"

"There is nothing to fear, *tal-is ats o-qua-tum* [dear little sister]," Siah-hen said gently. "We are nearly the last of our tribe; it is only natural that I should protect you. I intended to watch and take you to White-headed Eagle when McDermott sent you away, but he struck before I expected. Good Mother McLoughlin will give you and the papoose shelter. Come with me to the lodge, I'll face them with this piece of wickedness."

"I'll go," agreed Lassee. "But I'm afraid. They shut me up in one of the sweat-houses the day after

I came, and I knew then what they were going to do. I heard the *shaman* talking to the chiefs under the pow-wow tree. He told Kil-a-poos that he was to be a great chief, since his father was dead. He had a vision and had been off making medicine, as his *tomaniwus* (spirit) told him, and *tomaniwus* said that if the tribes would go back to the customs of their fathers they could get back their power and drive the Sniapus clear out of the country and gain back Tumchuck."

"It's ten years or more since White-headed Eagle forbade slave burial," mused Siah-hen. "Who would have expected them to go back to it? But Cleek-a-tuck was the last of the powerful chiefs, and they are only simple, perplexed children, Lassee, blinded with their grief."

"The old squaws jeered and told Kil-a-poos to be a great chief like his father and kill the Bostons. The *shaman* said that the signs were right and that the master had cast me off and no one would ever know what became of me. He was afraid, but the squaws taunted him until he consented.

"Quimmo warned them and tried once to get me away in the night, but they caught him and told him that they would turn him over to the Sniapus at Oregon City if he interfered. The Sniapus say they will hang Quimmo if they can find him; he upset a boatload of emigrants coming down the Columbia last fall and some of them were drowned." Lassee was calm again.

Both sat looking down over the river for a little time, busy with thoughts that could not be uttered.

At length Siah-hen rose and lifted Lassee to her feet, steadying her when she would have fallen. He waited a moment to be sure she could walk, then, as she pulled herself together with a tremendous effort, he held the branches aside and, half supporting her, they descended the trail to his *kinnum*.

It was late afternoon when they reached the lodge, but the funeral services had been delayed by the untoward happenings of the earlier part of the day. They would begin very shortly—the whole village was in a ferment of preparation.

Siah-hen strode into the main lodge, with Lassee walking fearlessly beside him. Her coppery skin had faded to olive, but she wore a mask of indifference. He went straight up to Queen Lucy Quillis, one of the many Indian women who had borne that name since the coming of the white men. To all intents and purposes Lucy was queen of the village, all the other squaws coming under her tyrannical sway. She was a fat wrinkled old beldame, toothless and with thin straggling gray hair showing beneath her dirty red bandanna. She sat nearly double over one of the cooking fires, smoking kinnikinnick, the leaves of a trailing shrubby vine that grew freely in the mountains. Occasionally she grunted a peremptory order to one of the younger squaws busy about the cooking-pots, then subsided into silence, though her rheumy old eyes belied their apparent dullness. She missed no detail of the affairs of her household.

Siah-hen spoke sharply to her in her own tongue, emphasizing his statement with a gesture in the direction of Lassee, who, showing no signs of perturbation, stood a little in the background. The effect of his speech on old Queen Lucy Quillis was startling in its instantaneity. She turned to Lassee and began to remove her wet clothing and administer a hot drink of some dark-looking liquid that one of the squaws handed her. The attitude of all the squaws became one of considerate attention toward Lassee and a cringing deference to Siah-hen, whose words evidently bore weight in the lodge. He waited a moment and then without word or glance strode off swiftly in the direction of his teepee.

His face was awful in its forbidding power as he passed a group of rather dejected braves under the pow-wow tree. There was an uneasy stir among them, that growing to consternation as he passed, followed by volleys of grunts and low agitated conversation as soon as they were sure he was out of earshot. There was dark apprehension among those braves, try as they might to pass it off with a bravado which sat but illy upon them.

Preparations were nearly completed for bearing the body of Cleek-a-tuck to his resting-place down at the confluence of the Willamette and Columbia Rivers. It was fitting that the last mighty chief should find sepulcher in a spot sanctified as the burial-place of the great ones of the valley tribes since time immemorial. *Shoc-at-til-cum* (water friend) the canoe Indians called the broad expanse of the lower Columbia, and the burial canoe of Cleek-a-tuck would float on its broad bosom with the first freshet.

Ten days of wailing instead of the seven ordinarily allowed to lesser personages had been accomplished by the relays of women appointed for the purpose. There had not been such a ceremony for years. It seemed to the Indians that in spite of their miscarried plan they were in some inexplicable way returning to their former power, though there were grave mutterings on the fringe of the circle against the *shaman*. These insurgents even advocated in whispers that the ancient custom of killing a medicine-man when he led his tribe into disaster be followed out, or that the perpetrators of this audacious piece of mischief be turned over to "White-headed Eagle" without further ado.

Even during the solemn council which had been held just before Siah-hen reached the village with Lassee there had been vague uneasiness, though each speaker had outdone himself in recounting the deeds of valor of the chief who lay in state upon an improvised scaffold a little apart from the main lodge.

Serene in death lay Cleek-a-tuck in his burial canoe. Friends had made the very best gifts to the relatives that their poverty would allow. They were beside the canoe, waiting to be divided among the surviving relatives with scrupulous accuracy. The friends surveyed them enviously—here a heap of bright new blankets, a little beyond muskets and a motley array of new woven mats, buckskins, and cooking-pots. The beads and trinkets were alluringly displayed. There was no withholding of gifts at such a time.

Queen Lucy Quillis had painstakingly performed

the rites of washing the chief. This was no light task with the means at hand. An Indian never bathes of his own accord, depending upon his swimming in the summer and the walking about in the winter rains for his sketchy cleansing. An old chief naturally gathers to himself much grime, for he does not swim or go about in the rain, but sits through the long days meditating in the thick smoke of the lodge fires.

But every Indian is thoroughly clean when he goes to his new place of abode, shaking as it were the dust of the earth from his feet. Cleek-a-tuck's placid face had been painted in the traditional mourning colors of his tribe, alternating streaks of blue and black; the women of his household could be picked out of the group below the scaffold by the same distinguishing badge of mourning, three streaks of blue and five of black upon the chin. Cleek-a-tuck was clothed in fresh new buckskins and the finest new blanket to be had at Vancouver was wrapped about him and his body then incased in new mats of the softest texture and the most intricate patterns that the skilled weavers of the tribe could produce.

Ordinary Indians were buried simply enough in the cemetery to the east of the village, but Cleek-a-tuck's burial canoe was a thing of beauty. It was his war canoe, three feet wide and two feet deep, its prow ornamented with a pattern of sea shells. The outside had been shaped with a tomahawk, both ends sharp, designed to be propelled by paddles.

A huge gaping hole had been broken in the bottom of the *kinnum* before placing the body in it, as a precaution against desecration by white men. An Indian canoe is a thing of value and the white man holds nothing sacred that belongs to an inferior race, not even the dead. This was another drop of gall in Indian hearts already overflowing with the resentment and bitterness of injustice.

The canoe Indians excelled in the art of making water craft. Their *kinnums* were made of the first cut of a huge cedar tree felled and split in quarters with the flint knives fitted with wooden handles held in place by thongs of elk skin.

The skillful use of fire was an aid in felling and splitting the log. The building of a canoe represented the patient labor of years; the bewitching curves and straight lines made them much sought after by white men as well as by the tribes beyond the mountains to the east.

This is another of the Indian mysteries, how they hollowed them out with their flint knives and beaver-teeth chisels and steamed them within with red-hot rocks and water to just the right proportions to give the balance that made them entirely seaworthy. The only weakness of these craft was at the bow and stern, where the wood was cut across the grain. They had been known to split in rough water. Canoes were of all sizes, from the light one-man hunting craft that could be carried on the shoulder, to great cruisers forty and fifty feet long and from five to six feet wide that easily accommodated thirty or forty travelers and all their baggage. Most of the freighting between Oregon City and Vancouver was done with these huge craft. Some of them were reckoned to be worth a thousand dollars and even more.

It might be thought curious that Indians are willing to sacrifice *kinnums* that represent such great value to their vague belief in an after life, but they gave ungrudgingly not only the best *kinnum*, but cooking-pots which they placed beside Cleek-a-tuck, all with cracks or holes in the bottom to make them valueless to pilferers. His pil-pil musket, carefully broken, lay beside him. A pil-pil musket is the supreme possession of an Indian, its stock is so beautifully red. The pil-pils were the first guns that the Hudson Bay Company distributed among the Indians, and never after, in the Indian's opinion, did they have guns to equal these.

Harking back to their ancient tribal custom, it had been the intention to bind the slave girl hand and foot and truss her up securely in new mats, fastening her face downward in the bottom of the *kinnum*, then the dead body was to be placed over her and all securely fastened in place by lashing. All the accouterments, together with a generous supply of ammunition—ammunition was scarce and hard to secure and would be desperately needed for the fall hunt, but a chief could not go unprepared to his mysterious new hunting-ground. Should the tribe suffer dire want, even starvation, well and good, the proprieties must be observed.

Cleek-a-tuck's funeral would have done honor to a great chief even in their golden days of opulence, long since passed. His last rites were entirely befitting his rank and the esteem in which he was held.

Perhaps, when the mourning paint wore off the faces of the women of his household and they returned again to the alluring blandishments of salmon oil and red clay for adornment, it would be possible to strangle a young slave boy and send him on with word of the doings of his cherished people. This would be in the late spring or early summer. Mourning paint is durable and a squaw will on no account allow water to touch her skin while the faintest vestige of her badge of mourning adheres to it.

The *shaman* told them that his *tomaniwus* had said that killing a slave for this purpose could easily be done without detection—slaves are denied burial and for one to come up missing would attract little notice outside the tribe. He would make medicine to prevent detection until the hated Sniapus and the Kin-Chautchs were finally driven from the country.

In the week preceding the last ceremonies there had been great hope and pride in the simple child-like Indian hearts. Even the young skeptics appeared for the moment to be won over. Surely *tomaniwus* was returning again in a superlative degree to a desolate forsaken people. The *shaman* strutted visibly, taking credit to himself. He pointed out to them certain auspicious signs of the return of the old halcyon days.

Was not a slave provided in just the proper way at just the opportune minute, owing to his medicine? Lassee had slipped into the lodge in dense darkness, no one outside the village knowing of her coming, so her end would never be known. McDermott had cast her off. She was his property, but, now that he wanted a white wife, he would be more than glad to have her out of the way. Should the Sniapus even inquire at the lodge for her, which was not at all likely, the simple thing would be to deny all knowledge of her and the papoose—one papoose looked just like another in the lodge—but to surmise that a *hy-as puss-puss* (cougar) must have gotten the pair of them. There was known to be a *hy-as puss-puss* up in the mountains back of Tumchuck.

Hope requires but little nourishment, and the young men were half inclined to believe the *shaman.* He was crafty in his planning, promising to carry out the ancient custom to the letter by visiting the canoe down on the lowlands of the Columbia at the expiration of three days to strangle Lassee with a hempen cord if he found her alive.

But subsequent events had caused misgivings among even the squaws and those braves who had been strongest in sanctioning the return to the ancient ways of their fathers. They stood about in little groups, watching the final preparations for the ceremony of embarking on the river. Except for the wailing of the women at set intervals a strange hush had descended upon the assemblage. Conversation must be carried on in whispers until the departure of the mortal remains of Cleek-a-tuck and the final arrangement of the canoe upon its scaffold among the cottonwood trees. From the time of placing the canoe on *te-wa-kan* (holy wood) (an Indian will never use the wood of a mortuary scaffold for any other purpose) until the rising floods of beloved *shoc-at-til-kum* (friendly water) lifted it gently and bore it away on its broad bosom, the name of Cleek-a-tuck must not be spoken.

All had gone well until the unfortunate escape of Lassee when the medicine-man attempted to tie her with hempen cords. Either his hand had lost its cunning through lack of practice, or he was a trifle inclined to nervousness, for in some inexplicable manner she had gotten away from him and, running like a deer, had reached the river bank before braves could lay hands on her, though once it seemed as if her capture was certain, one Indian striking a glancing blow as he came up even with her. But she was swimming across the Clackamas before they had launched their *kinnums* with the idea of rowing out and taking her before she reached the opposite side. Lassee had been too quick for them; she was flying up the steep trail before they had moored their *kinnums*.

The braves were very crestfallen indeed when they returned from their futile encounter with Martha Bainbridge, but that was not the worst. Siah-hen returned from Vancouver just in time to witness the flight, when he had expected to be away at least two weeks. Even the older ones could not be so sure that the signs were auspicious. It looked as if the *shaman* had duped them or at least read the signs incorrectly. When Siah-hen returned in a short time and led Lassee boldly and defiantly into the lodge, there was consternation, carefully suppressed in the heart of every inhabitant of the village. This meant that the news of the escapade would shortly reach

the ears of White-headed Eagle and there would be
dire consequences to follow.

But there was nothing to do but go on with the
ceremonies as if nothing had happened to mar the
splendid occasion, and afterward devise ways and
means for a working out of a very awkward situation.  Bleak, utter despair cast its sinister blight
over every simple heart where high hope had so
shortly been enthroned.  Their cause was lost; woe
and wretchedness such as they had never known when
they, at least, had hoped, evanescent though it might
be, that power and liberty would henceforth be their
portion.

There was no outward sign of perturbation,
though, in the concourse that gathered on the river
bank to witness the embarking of Chief Cleek-a-tuck
on his last sad journey, to a hunting-ground, no one
knew where.  At the exact moment of putting out the
largest of their *kinnums* containing immediate relatives and the burial canoe, a large white sea gull that
had been held captive under the blankets on the dead
man's breast was released and flew in wide circles
about the sad procession.

Gulls came up to the flats on the east bank of the
Willamette to feed when there was a storm on the
Pacific Ocean.  This one had been snared and held
captive.  His circling flight symbolized the spirit of
Cleek-a-tuck departing on its long journey, whither
no one of them troubled to so much as conjecture.
They stood silently on the high bank, watching with
straining eyes as the cortège passed out of sight,

taking with it all their hopes of gaining back their
lost power.

The factions were very clearly divided when the
braves gathered under the pow-wow tree at dusk to
devise ways and means for extricating themselves
from their predicament. The faction headed by the
younger sub-chieftains took on an accusing "I told
you so" attitude toward those who had aided and
abetted the *shaman* in his diabolical scheme. It was
hard to place the guilt; every one was inclined to lay
the blame at the door of some one else, but the poor
wavering son of Cleek-a-tuck, Kil-a-poos, came in for
severe condemnation. The young men accused the
older ones of being swayed and influenced by a lot
of jealous old squaws who wished to vent their spite
on an Indian girl who had been chosen by a white
man. The thrust struck home, being recognized as
a painful truth, though no one had mentioned it in
the pow-wows that had previously been held.

But no use bandying accusations back and forth;
a concerted line of action must be mapped out and
adhered to before White-headed Eagle took the
matter in hand. Some thought that the *shaman* and
his five assistants should be handed over to him before
he made his demand. Others were for exercising the
ancient prerogative of killing a medicine-man who
had led the tribe into trouble with his medicine or
who had failed in his predictions.

The fact that Siah-hen had not appeared at the
council boded no good. The Indians tacitly recognized the fact that Siah-hen held some authority
over them which White-headed Eagle had bestowed

upon him, but they looked up to him as a sort of
elder brother, and listened respectfully when he
straightened out their difficulties with the Sniapus.
Some thought that he should be called into council,
that he could in all likelihood placate Doctor Mc-
Loughlin or at least mitigate the punishment, but
most were against admitting him, reasoning that if
he were in the mood to be of service to them he would
have attended the pow-wow without waiting for an
invitation.

Then the question of Quimmo came up.　Quimmo
had been for a few weeks, more or less, in hiding,
taking care that no white man saw him at the lodge
or going about the country.　There was a price on
Quimmo's head in Oregon City.　McDermott was
suspected of putting up the money, but no one knew
for a certainty who had.　They reasoned that perhaps if they gave Quimmo up their chances of squar-
ing this other thing would be better.

The Sniapus accused Quimmo of purposely capsizing the *kinnum* and drowning some of its occupants in coming through the Devil's Gullet on the
Columbia; this Quimmo strenuously denied, declaring
that some one had risen up in the canoe and rocked it
so that for a moment he lost control and struck the
great rock.　He had been forced to make his escape
because the emigrants threatened to kill him.　This
the Indians believed implicitly.　An Indian does not
lie, except perhaps to Sniapus, who taught him the
arts of deceit.　To give Quimmo up seemed to them
the darkest treachery.　He would certainly be hanged
in Oregon City, and the stigma of hanging rests

on a whole tribe; there is no disgrace in the Indian
estimation to equal it.

Then, too, if they had once listened, Quimmo would
have saved them. In vain he had argued against
burying Lassee with the dead chief. Didn't he try
to release her in the night? Quimmo was also the
best hunter among them, never wasting a charge of
ammunition in bringing down a deer, and his services
were going to be badly needed at the lodge before
the winter was over and the spring run of salmon
began.

With true Indian improvidence they had given
their elk and deer meat freely to the Sniapus who
had anything to trade for it, and often they had
nothing. The fall *battue* had been a good one, but
there was but little meat left hanging from the
rafters of the lodge to cure, and the winter had not
well begun. Their stock of camas and wappatoes and
dried berries had gone the same way. No, for this
reason alone, if there were no other considerations,
Quimmo must be kept out of sight and so spared to
help his people.

They pow-wowed back and forth the better part
of the night, finally dividing into two factions by the
younger element refusing to parley longer with them
and withdrawing to one of the small lodges, where
they held a secret council. What happened there
the older braves never knew, but in the morning the
lifeless body of the *shaman* and his five aides floated
calmly down the Willamette in plain sight of the
river traffic.

The scattered remnants of the once mighty tribes had turned from the belief of their fathers and would henceforth follow as best they might, though with rebellion and bitterness against injustice in their hearts, the ways of the Sniapus.

# CHAPTER XII

MARTHA BAINBRIDGE sat talking with Dick while he ate his belated dinner. She was full of interest in his plans to take up a donation land claim and to build a cabin. "We'll have a bee and put up your cabin right away," she promised. "I know John and Uncle Adzi and Pop Simmons will want to help."

Dick stammered his gratitude. Martha looked at him in sudden wonder as if seeing him for the first time. How he was coming out since he was no longer a bound boy! He was growing to his hands and feet and filling out generously, so that he was no longer of the ungainly appearance that had gained for him the name of "Gangle-shanks." He looked at Martha out of straightforward brown eyes as he spoke. With his new-found freedom the quailing and shrinking within himself, as if fearing a blow when spoken to, was leaving him.

She laid a motherly hand on his shoulder as she gave him another cup of milk. "I'm glad that you'll be able to get an education here," she said. "Siahhen has been so kind to you. I'm beginning to believe that there are good Indians and bad Indians. Perhaps, after all, they wouldn't be so lazy and dirty if they had a chance to learn better."

But Dick shook a doubtful head and laughed. "Most of 'em are just simply no good, Mrs. Bainbridge. Don't I know 'em? I've been living in their village."

Martha thought for a moment. "What was the Indian girl's name, Dick? I was so angry and confused I fairly lost my wits. I should have kept her here and taken care of her," she reproached herself. "But Siah-hen took her away so quickly. You don't suppose they'll try to bury her alive again, do you?" She shuddered at the thought.

"No, indeed they won't, now that Siah-hen is down there," Dick reassured her. "That's Lassee. Siahhen'll take care of her; she belongs to his tribe and they're about the only ones left."

"Does Lassee belong down at the main lodge?" asked Martha. "She must be a slave girl, or they wouldn't have tried to bury her alive with the chief."

"No," faltered Dick, suddenly coloring violently. "Lassee is the squaw that McDermott had been living with since his wife died. McDermott sent her back to the tribe." He paused, looked about evasively, and cleared his throat.

"Why, for mercy's sake!" ejaculated Martha. "Didn't she have a papoose?"

"Yes, just walking," Dick admitted with some embarrassment. He changed the subject when Martha would have heard more. "Siah-hen'll take care of her and see that those low-lifed wretches are punished. I've thought sometimes that he stays here more to see that no harm comes to Lassee than for anything else, though Doctor McLoughlin trusts him to keep the Indians quiet so they'll not make trouble among the emigrants."

Martha made up her mind quickly. "Dick," she said, "you go straight back to the lodge and tell Siah-hen to bring Lassee and the papoose here to me. It's simply inhuman for a man to turn a poor girl out like that in the winter. We'll keep her until some provision is made for her, and McDermott shall suffer for this if there is such a thing as justice, and I rather think there is."

"McDermott is a dirty dog," said Dick hotly.

"He seemed such a gentleman and he was so kind to us. I can hardly believe it," said Martha. "The poor little girl; she'll need to have that cut on her head dressed in the morning. To think of a white man doing such a low, cowardly thing!" Martha's eyes flashed with anger.

"I feel like thrashing McDermott myself," Dick ejaculated. "I believe I could do it, too." He inspected the flexed muscles of his arm with boyish pride. "He's done a lot of low-down things in this country. Somebody'll take care of him, though. Siah-hen says the Indians have turned against him. He's deceived them and lied to them. If a man lies to the Indians they never trust him again, and they wait for their chance to get even with him."

"Tell Siah-hen to bring that poor girl and the papoose here either to-night or the first thing in the morning," Martha admonished Dick.

She watched him from her low doorway as he strode off. He's a man, not a boy any longer, she thought. Seemed to me he changed almost overnight, and it's mostly due to kindness, and that kindness and help came from an Indian—not a white man in the country with so much as a kind word for a lonely boy. Her musings were tinged with bitterness as she turned at last to her neglected work.

"I have been taking such joy in this spinning-wheel," she muttered to herself. "But it's kind of spoiled for me by McDermott's being such a cad. Still, we took it in good faith and I might as well go on enjoying it, so long as it'll be all paid for to-day. We can't be fussy over things like that when we're nearly naked."

There was indignation in the cabin that evening when Martha rehearsed the happenings of the day.

"Hit 'pears lak ever' time ye're alone for an' hour or so, them pesky Injuns come roun' here makin' trouble," grumbled Uncle Adzi.

"You'd best not be left alone any more, Marthie," said John, "even when we're hardly out of earshot. We're getting tired of having our women folks frightened half to death."

"Nonsense!" laughed Martha. "I'm not afraid of the filthy wretches; I was just mad at them. Besides, you'll see that this little trouble will settle them for some time to come. There'll never be another slave buried alive in Oregon, now that white women have come to put a stop to it. Poor hunted little girl! I'll see her in my sleep, cowering in that corner over there by the bed." She shuddered.

"Did you tell them to send her here to us, Marthie?" John asked.

"Yes," answered Martha, pleased that John was glad to take her in. "We'll be able to keep her for a while, won't we, John? Dick says she's just like a white girl."

"Of course we'll shelter her until something is done for her and the papoose," agreed John. "And something *will* be done shortly, take my word for it. We're not going to have any such goings-on in this settlement even if we haven't regular courts and laws yet. There are plenty of men here who'll help me settle his case for him, if I need help. He can count himself lucky if he gets out of this mess alive. The dirty cur," he ejaculated, the dark red of a man slow to wrath rising to his face. "Thank goodness, we cut the last of his shakes this afternoon and hauled them down to him."

"Hit's a good job we don't owe him airy cent fer anythin'," added Uncle Adzi fervently. "To think o' us spendin evenin's with a varmint like thet, right in our cabin 'mongst our innercent childern, us not knowin' ennyone nigh here an' havin' nobuddy ter tell us."

He rose and hobbled slowly to the stable to swear, as was his wont when he felt the need of an emotional outlet which could be had in lurid language. Martha would not for a moment have allowed rough talking in her presence, and of course the boys must not hear profanity; but there were, in his opinion, times when profanity was justified, even in a professed believer.

John Bainbridge was moody after supper, sitting for a long time looking into the fire, his horny work-gnarled hands idle on his knees, a rare occurrence for him. At last he rose slowly and took down a large piece of elk skin that he had gotten in trade from an Indian and began cutting it accurately into narrow strips with his jack-knife. Asa and Marvel followed his every movement with their eyes, and he began instructing them in the art of making a lariat. Elk-skin ropes are strong and durable when carefully braided, and there were no hempen ropes to be had, so lariat-making was likely to occupy the evenings, unless there was wool to card.

Soothed and comforted by twenty minutes of acute profanity in the stable, Uncle Adzi returned at length, carrying in his hand a straight hazel sapling over four feet long and about an inch thick. He took his accustomed seat at the fireplace and with his jack-knife began making a hazel broom.

"Now thet the shakes air all rived an' our debts paid, an' the oxen under cover, John an' me 'lows ter put down a puncheon floor right soon, Marthie," he announced. "I never seed sech timber. Hit's a downright pleasure to work in hit. Splits smooth ez if 'twar planed. We aim ter git yellow fir fer puncheons, an' ther won't be a better floor in the whole scttlement. I calculated I mout ez well whittle out a besom so ez ter have hit in readiness—a good floor hez ter be taken care on right from the start."

Martha paused in her knitting, her face flushing with delight, and the girls left their dish-washing and came to listen for a moment. "I wasn't expecting a floor so soon," she said. "There is so much work to be done outside, are you sure you can spare the time, Uncle Adzi?"

"Dirt floors air cold ter the feet, an' make a cabin look lak a Injun camp. Plenty time ter git rails

split an' fences set up afore plowin'-time. Hit hain't
January yit." He was carefully laying off the hazel
for his broom as he spoke. The boys left their
father's side and crowded close to watch him.

"See, Asa," he showed them. "An inch nub hez
ter be 'lowed." He made a careful line about the
sapling, then measured up nine inches and made
another. "Now I'll whittle down the handle," he
explained, making long careful strokes with his jack-
knife, so that in a very short time he had a smooth
white handle just the right size to be grasped easily.
It was closer work making the nine-inch shreds to
pull down and tie over the nub on the other end.
He sent the boys to help their father for fear one
of them would strike his elbow, and gave his whole
attention to shaving down to the nub marked off by
the line. Each shred must come clear down if the
broom was to be even and if any were cut off the
brush would be sparse and thin. When he finished
shredding he took the piece of elk skin that John
cut exactly the right width, and turning the shavings
carefully down over the nub, tied them securely in
place, holding the finished broom up for the proud
inspection of the family.

Martha lifted it in her hand, carefully judging
its weight, then gave it back to Uncle Adzi. "Cut
a groove in the end of the handle and put on a loop
of elk skin to hang it up by, please, Uncle Adzi," she
begged. "A good housekeeper never leaves her broom
down; it gets out of shape."

John grunted his assent from the fireplace where

he was raking up the coals and covering the back-log with ashes to hold the fire over until morning.

"Girls," she said proudly, "we'll soon have a tidy cabin. It'll seem like living when I can get down on my knees and scour a floor with a wisp of straw and sand and cold water. You boys'll have to clean your feet when you come in, I'll tell you. I'll not have a beautiful white floor ruined by the trackings-in of careless men folks," she warned severely.

After the candle was snuffed out and John had threatened to trounce both boys unless they quit scuffling in their trundle-bed, or if he heard another sound out of them until morning, one of his routine threats, he lay down to rest. Martha waited until she shortly heard the measured breathing of the children and the snoring of Uncle Adzi before she reached for her husband's hand in the darkness.

"John," she whispered softly, "do you think Mc-Dermott has been boasting openly among the settlers that he intends to marry Rose Ann? Uncle Adzi heard them talking about it down to Oregon City to-day. Do you suppose that was his real reason for turning that poor Indian girl out of his house?"

"I'll settle with McDermott," John promised her in a metallic whisper. "But I don't think he really said anything about it; he's not one to talk much about his affairs. I don't propose to have the name of my daughter bandied around linked with the likes of him. There are white women here, and this is going to be kept a fit place for them to live, if it takes every decent man in the country."

"I don't think Rose Ann suspects anything, and

we'll just not mention it to her," cautioned Martha. "I don't want any notions of marrying put in her head for a long time yet." But John was asleep.

"I just wonder where I'll put that girl to sleep," Martha puzzled before she finally dropped off. She rose up on her elbow and looked about at the two beds each with its trundle-bed drawn out from beneath so that the cabin was nearly filled. But suddenly she had an inspiration—a bed for the boys in the stable!

Breakfast was in progress the next morning when Siah-hen and Dick came up the trail bearing most of their worldly goods on an Indian travois drawn by an ugly little cayuse pony. Siah-hen had borrowed the contrivance from one of his friends just after he crossed the river in his *kinnum*.

Lassee, tired and listless after her adventure of the day before, was with them, but the burden of carrying the papoose on her back had been too much for her. He rode in state in his *te-cash*, securely lashed to the top of the load. Martha paused in dishing up the boiled cracked wheat that they used as a breakfast cereal. There were sugar and cream for the porridge, and with pea coffee it made a filling breakfast.

She brought the timid girl into the house, seating her at the table and pouring a cup of the ground-pea coffee. Esther Amelia danced wildly about as her mother lifted the solemn-eyed papoose off the load, demanding that he be taken out of his basket at once so she could see how big he was. To have a real baby to play with was the most wonderful thing that had happened in her whole life, she declared.

"Mother, see the cunning thing!" she shrilled with delight. A flicker of interest showed in Lassee's tired eyes at the notice her papoose attracted. She took him out of the *te-cash* and set him on his unsteady little feet before the fire, then returned to her coffee and cracked wheat that she tried bravely to eat, but without much success.

Esther Amelia immediately installed herself as nurse to little Sintwa, offering the nonchalant baby her cherished doll, which he observed with complete indifference and made his uncertain way to his mother's knee. Rose Ann stopped in her dishing up breakfast to admire him, but her mother urged her to hurry back to her task so as to get the men off to work.

Little Sintwa was again in possession of all his baby finery. His round little face was very clean and his straight silky black hair carefully cut. An elaborately beaded round new buckskin cap was on his head, with a dress to match, also beautifully beaded and fringed.

Siah-hen and Dick were busy unpacking the load. The boys and Esther Amelia shrieked and danced with joy when they peeked into the hempen sack that Siah-hen put down inside the door. Siah-hen had gifts for the family. One bag contained dried olallies, the luscious blue-black huckleberries. With washing, very careful washing, indeed, and then soaking in water overnight, they would eke out the monotonously bare winter table deliciously.

He had three large smoked salmon and a sack of fish pemmican. Fish pemmican is made of dried salmon carefully divested of the skin and bones and then pounded in a stone mortar to a fine paste. This was a gift indeed. The Indians counted a sack of pemmican worth as much as one of their calico ponies. There was a large piece of jerked venison and dried camas, for the children to gnaw on with their strong little teeth. Sweet and of a peculiar nutty flavor is this onion-like bulb that the squaws dig from the marsh lands and dry and grind for their winter bread.

Indian foods have a piquancy all their own, and the appetites of those who have lived for a few months on boiled wheat and salmon are not apt to be at all finical.

The whole family were fervent in their expressions of gratitude. This splendid unexpected *potlatch* would tide them well over the winter. Siah-hen grinned broadly with embarrassment, but said nothing. He and Dick were reorganizing their load with a view to taking it up the trail they intended to cut to Dick's claim.

Martha, of course, asked them to have breakfast, and both came willingly enough. Rose Ann refilled the cream pitcher and placed a generous plate of cracked wheat before each of them, sidling off to prevent their noticing her bare feet.

"Are you going to school?" Dick asked her by way of making conversation and, best of all, compelling her to look straight at him when she answered.

Rose Ann blushed furiously, and made first an

unconscious effort to hide her bare feet, then straightened up and said with dignity, "I am if father can find a pair of shoes for me; but there are none in Oregon City."

"Your mother says I may make you a pair of shoes. I'm going to be a cobbler right away as soon as our cabin is built. Lassee has promised to bead them for you." He glanced at Lassee for confirmation of his statement. She nodded and smiled, showing even white teeth, but immediately relapsed into apathy again, as if the light of her soul had flickered up for a moment and suddenly gone out again.

Rose Ann was all eager animation. "Will you really, Dick? I'll knit stockings for you and Siah-hen to pay for them."

Siah-hen laughed and said. "You'll have your shoes before the week is out. Dick'll work evenings on them." He paused as if wondering whether to give away the secret, glancing teasingly at Dick. "He's got the shoes made already," he chuckled. "Good strong soles, and deer skin from an old tee-pee. Lassee is planning to put on a pattern of blue and white beads. Go get them, Dick."

Dick, in huge embarrassment, the blood mounting in a great wave clear to his curly hair, pulled the shoes from the pocket of his leather coat and handed them to the incredulous Rose Ann for inspection. She hesitated a moment, catching Dick's embarrassment as she turned the little shoes over and over in her hands. Then she ran outdoors with them and, once around the corner of the cabin, put them on, marveling at the way they fit.

"How did you guess my size, Dick?" she asked as she burst into the cabin wearing the shoes.

They fit perfectly. Buckskin uppers had been deftly sewed to strong leather soles; they laced in front with buckskin thongs curiously cut and braided and the uppers finished at the top with an elaborate buckskin fringe.

Siah-hen went off in one of his gales of laughter and seemed about to impart the cause of his mirth, but desisted at a frown and an imperative gesture from Dick.

"Now we can all go to school, can't we, mother?" exulted Esther Amelia. But she paused thoughtfully. "I hate to go, though, when there's a baby in the cabin to play with."

"He'll be here evenings when you come home, child," Martha said, glancing at the papoose holding fast to his mother's buckskin knee.

She looked sharply at him again after working about for a few moments, then came over and felt his little wrists, to see if he were warm. If a young child's wrists are comfortably warm his whole body is at a normal temperature. She passed a motherly hand over his forehead and a look of consternation crossed her face. She said nothing but picked him up and carried him out of sight at the back of the cabin, before placing an experienced ear to his chest. Returning him to his mother while she busied herself about the fire with bear's grease in a tin cup, she heated it and then poured turpentine into it from a large bottle.

Lassee watched her in silence. When Martha

tore a square out of a piece of ragged old blanket, and cut a hole for the baby's head and shaped armholes, she understood. Fear crossed her face. She began undressing little Sintwa before the fire. Martha took him across her knees and applied the bear's grease and turpentine freely over his lungs both front and back, putting it on the soles of his feet and in the palms of his indifferent little hands, then held him up to the heat of the fire to drive the turpentine inward, before adjusting the blanket over his head and sewing it under the arms to hold it in place. He whimpered a little as his mother held him to put him to sleep, but finally dozed off peacefully enough, and Lassee laid him carefully on one of the beds.

"You've kept Sintwa in the house all winter," Martha said.

"Yes, Mrs. Bainbridge," Lassee answered. "But he was out in the rain all day while we were down at the village; that's the way he caught that terrible cold. I'm so glad to come into a cabin again." She paused, searching awkwardly for words to express her gratitude, then said simply: "My people never forget a kindness. Siah-hen will repay you if I never can." She crept to the bed to listen to the labored breathing of the baby as he tossed restlessly in his sleep. Esther Amelia followed her on tiptoe, gazing raptly at the little round face above the blankets.

Dick and Siah-hen had gone up the trail and the men and boys left for the timber before Martha had

time to think of her own breakfast. Getting breakfast over with the meager facilities of the cabin was
strenuous work for an hour or two. Rose Ann,
proudly arrayed in the new shoes, came to the table,
and they hurriedly ate a bite before beginning the
real work of the morning.

"Mother, wasn't Dick kind to make that lovely
pair of shoes?" said Rose Ann between spoonfuls of
porridge. "Please, mother, let me wear them all the
time," she coaxed.

"Why, yes, child," Martha consented. "But first
put on your new stockings. How glad I am that
we have so much knitting done. It pays to drive the
work, doesn't it?"

But Rose Ann was absorbed in putting on her
stockings and replacing the splendid shoes, and did
not even hear her mother's moralizing. She had
no thought of breakfast or of anything else in the
joy Dick's gift had brought her. "I just wonder
how he knew the size," she kept repeating to herself.

Lassee smiled as she turned from bending over her
papoose and came to see how she could help Martha
with the morning's work.

She still had the soiled white bandage about her
head, and Martha brought the jar of soft soap and
a basin of hot water and prepared to dress the
wound. First she washed the bandage very thoroughly and hung it before the fire to dry. White
linen was too precious to be careless with. She would
dry it and replace it. The cut was healing to her
satisfaction. After a gentle cleansing by dripping

warm water over it, she applied turpentine and then a thick coating of bear's grease for rapid healing.

Having replaced the bandage, Martha turned to her spinning, leaving Rose Ann and Lassee to do up the morning's work. Lassee was quick and eager to be of service.

# CHAPTER XIII

THERE were excitement and hurry and bustle in the fourteen-by-sixteen-foot cabin. Spinning went on every waking moment. With Rose Ann at school the work in the wool would necessarily lapse somewhat, and there must be yarn enough ahead so that the knitting would not be interrupted. Rose Ann and Esther Amelia would, of course, knit steadily on the way to and from school, but the evening must be given over to lessons.

As Martha spun she exulted in the joy that had been hers as John's wife and the mother of his children. Life was mild and sweet with her joy in work and her simple philosophy that enabled her to minimize the hard things in her daily living and to wring the last drop of pure joy out of the blessings that came her way.

She looked forward happily to the day when there would be a substantial frame house instead of the crowded little cabin, floorless and with taut buckskin doing duty for windowpanes. The men were now splitting trees for putting down the promised puncheon floor, and last night she had heard John and Uncle Adzi debating whether to build a lean-to on at the back of the cabin, now that their family had increased by two. She did not really think it was worth while to add it to the cabin, but still it would make present living much easier.

221

The frame house would be possible in another year. The Island Milling Company at Oregon City was already turning out real finished lumber and they did say that James Athey, who had come in with the emigration, had managed to secure a turning lathe somehow and was making wonderful tables and chairs and lovely bedsteads with fluted posts. If they all kept well and could work hard for a few years life would be full and rich beyond their wildest dreams.

They had a start of cattle; the heifer calf would be a cow before they knew it, and Doctor McLoughlin had promised Siah-hen that he would give them all a good start of poultry in the spring. She looked forward eagerly to the soft spring days when she could set hens and run about in the awakening outdoors looking after little chickens. How she gloried in her inborn knack with hens. There would be geese, and that meant feather beds and plump pillows, and when the ships came in, oh, when the ships came in from Boston next summer, there would be snowy sheets and in time the wonderful pieced coverlids such as she had tried in vain to bring across, but had discarded a few at a time on the journey.

She hoped to live long enough to find time to make one of those beautiful counterpanes of muslin with a pattern of pink poppies and green leaves set on with matched bits of calico. She could see herself in the joyous spending of happy afternoons quilting after she had put in hours of exquisite stitching on her set-on pattern. Perhaps Aunt Morning Ann would come down and help her quilt, or better still, there would be merry quilting bees about the neighborhood.  To-day her feet hurt her cruelly because her shoes were so worn, and she had been pacing back and forth, back and forth, for long hours at a stretch the last few weeks at her spinning.  But in spite of the dull pain she laughed softly to herself.  Next year at this time the pain would have been entirely obliterated from her memory.

Weaving the woof of her dream into the rude circumstances that she knew was the warp (warp is commonplace and never lovely like woof, but it must be set in place with firmness and precision, for it supports the woof and comes first in the making of any fabric, whether it be the fabric of life or merely of perishable cloth), she spun and spun all the long rainy morning on feet that ached and burned.  Spinning gives one such a sense of isolation and time for beautiful dreams.  At times she forgot everything that troubled, and for sheer joy in living lifted up her voice and sang, in a sweet treble, snatches of the hymns of her girlhood.

"Jerusalem, the golden, with milk and honey blest,
  Beneath thy contemplation sink heart and voice oppressed.
  I know not, oh, I know not what joys await me there;
  What radiancy of glory, what bliss beyond compare!"

Buoyancy of spirit had carried Martha Bainbridge through many a dark, hard day.  She had learned to allow her spirit to float like a cork upborne on the troubled waves of her existence, knowing always in the innermost recesses of her being that the wave that bore her out seemingly beyond her depth would with the inflowing tide bring her back in safety to the shore.

Little Sintwa had not been quite so well the last few days, notwithstanding the regular and generous anointings with bear's grease and turpentine. He seemed, in spite of their vigilance, to have somehow taken a fresh cold. It was tight on his lungs; his breath came in short painful rasps and he had for the last day or so shown an alarming rise of fever about two in the afternoon. He was playing about listlessly, often coming with a little whimper for his mother to hold him.

Martha eased the anxiety in the back of her mind with the thought that most likely he would soon cut the troublesome eye and stomach teeth; he was nearly a year old and a teething baby may show alarming symptoms. But she could not dispel her uneasiness. She had heard that the young Indians at the Jason Lee mission many of them developed lung trouble as soon as they began to live steadily indoors. Many had died with consumption, so that the Indians feared to send their children there.

Of course Sintwa was a half-breed, with rugged Scotch blood on the father's side, and he had always been tenderly nurtured in a warm cabin. Whenever she thought of the situation a wave of fiery indignation swept her fairly off her feet. A white father who could turn his own flesh and blood out in the middle of winter to subsist in a filthy vermin-infested Indian village! Her thoughts were not flattering to the male of the species, but, no use in harboring malice and spite. One knew that there

were unprincipled men in the world just as there
were honorable, high-minded ones, and, after all,
clean honest men were greatly in the majority.

Anyway, her duty was plainly mapped out for her.
She would shelter and comfort Lassee and see that
Sintwa was cured of his cold and that he cut his eye
and stomach teeth without too much acute discom-
fort.   She lifted the protesting baby to her knee,
and with the thumb and forefinger of her left hand
deftly shut off his breath by holding his nose to
force him to open his mouth, then exploring for teeth
or swellings indicating their near approach with a
right forefinger.

Sintwa was a forward baby; he had eight strong
white teeth and four generous swellings where the
eye and stomach teeth would shortly erupt.   Martha
carried him to the light of the doorway to determine whether the dark line indicating that the teeth
were nearly through were visible.   If it showed, it
would be safe to rub the teeth through with her
thimble and the baby would recover immediately,
but she decided that it might be three weeks before
he cut those teeth.

Lassee hovered about in the background, very
much interested in watching Martha care for her
papoose, but with a worry that she made an effort
to conceal.   "He walked so soon, Mrs. Bainbridge,"
she announced with pride.   "Indian babies seldom
walk before they are two years old; the squaws
keep them strapped in the cradle-boards all the time,
but little Sintwa rolled around on the floor all summer.   He's quick in teething and talking just like

white babies. Say kitty, Sintwa," she coaxed the
papoose. But Sintwa sullenly hid his face in her
lap, refusing even to notice the string of oak galls
that Esther Amelia had made for him. The little
girl brought a much-battered doll with one arm missing to appease him.

Lassee picked up the doll and turned it over and
over in her hands. Evidently she recognized the
dilapidated little toy; a faint shadow of pain crossed
her face, to be instantly concealed behind the ex-
pressionless mask. She had never spoken to Martha
of McDermott or of her life before she reached the
Indian village, and Martha, who would as soon force
a safe as a confidence, respected and admired her reticence. The whole family had followed Martha's
strict injunction of complete silence, simply accepting Lassee and whole-heartedly making her one of
them.

After the first day or so of gentle kindliness Lassee
resumed her natural manner of talking and acting.
She was cheerful company for Martha, but especially companionable to Rose Ann, as she flew about
the cabin performing the heavy routine duties with
a neatness that proved her early teachings in housewifery to have been thorough. One day it was
making a huge kettle of wheat hominy; she showed
them how this was done in Oregon. The method was
similar to that of making hominy of corn in Illinois, though wheat is a little more tedious to clean
and requires a longer time for boiling. "We need
half a cup of good strong lye from the leach, Mrs.
Bainbridge," she explained. "Wheat has to boil

slowly in it all day to soften the kernels and loosen the hulls."

It was a full morning's work next day after the boiling to carry the kettle to the spring above the cabin and, after draining off the lye water in which it had been boiled, wash the kernels in change after change of cold water, stirring all the time with a wooden paddle. Lye water will take the skin off the hands. After soaking over another night, Lassee said it was safe to rub the kernels between the hands to remove the hulls or at least loosen them and then there must be another day of slow boiling, finally adding salt. Lassee and Rose Ann made close to ten gallons of hominy, which during the cool winter days could be covered up and hung on the limb of a tree out of reach of the dogs.

Each day they took out the portion needed. Of course, every woman knows that to be properly served wheat hominy should be reheated in a skillet of sizzling bacon fat, and given a generous dressing of cream at times to vary it. But bacon was not to be had in the country in any quantity, and, anyway, it sold quickly at ten cents a pound, which, of course, was clear out of their reach.

Pop Simmons had killed a bear and Aunt Morning Ann promptly sent them a haunch of the meat and a generous quantity of the fat, and, tried out, this served very nicely for seasoning. Bear grease is so good for doctoring colds; she had used it constantly on little Sintwa. Lassee told them how to make pie crust with it, and dried-huckleberry pie is the very last word in pie, especially with cream for it;

but Martha shook her head dubiously, promising that perhaps later they might have a pie, but that she must save the flour they had left for thickening. It is desperately hard to manage the food for a large family with hearty outdoor appetites without a tablespoonful of flour for making milk gravy. Every little while Uncle Adzi killed a pheasant or a squirrel or two, and milk gravy is absolutely necessary to piece out the meat and make it go clear around the table.

As soon as there was flour ground, Martha conciliated them with promises of the fluffy saleratus cream biscuits when they had pheasant and cream gravy. It takes an expert cook with a sure eye for measuring the saleratus, and an accuracy in gauging the sourness of the cream that amounts almost to a sixth sense. Then there must be deftness in handling the soft dough and just the right heat in the Dutch oven to turn out creditable cream biscuits—no task for a simple, inexperienced girl or a poor, slack housewife to attempt.

The baby was now better and now worse until toward the last of the week, when one morning he flatly refused to take the wheat gruel and thin cream that Martha was giving him to piece out his breast feedings. It was high time the child was weaned. According to Lassee, Indian women have the silly habit of nursing their papooses until they were three or four years old. Martha had been carefully schooling the eager Lassee in the white mother's methods of caring for babies, telling her all about catnip tea, that panacea and cure-all for the ills that juveniles fall heir to, just how to prepare it and when to give it. She showed her how to induce vomiting in a baby or even a grown person by binding a piece of moist leaf tobacco over the pit of the stomach. Martha, like every other woman in pioneer communities, was skilled in first aid. Doctors were seldom at hand and oftentimes a life depended upon knowing just exactly what to do in an emergency. Bear oil was for rubbing on the chest, if skunk oil was not to be obtained, but Lassee knew all about distilling and using skunk oil; it is a time-honored Indian remedy.

After declining to eat, little Sintwa sat miserably on the floor for a time, refusing even to notice Esther Amelia, though she vainly shook his red beads before his eyes and tried in every way a resourceful little girl could devise to gain his attention.

He stiffened, and Martha caught his rigid little form in her arms as a convulsion seized him. Instantly she began removing his clothing, and under her instructions Lassee and Rose Ann prepared a hot bath, with cold water standing beside it. She bared her elbow to test the heat of the water, and immersed the baby, then placed him swiftly in the cold bath, repeating hot and cold alternately until the little form relaxed and drowsiness indicated that the convulsion was over. Lassee crouched beside the baby, though she instantly obeyed Martha's slightest command with a presence of mind that did not permit of a single waste motion.

Martha placed the limp baby on the bed and stood looking down at him a moment; then she called Rose Ann: "Go for Aunt Morning Ann, and tell her to bring her simples if she has any. Replenish the fire and fill all the kettles so as to keep plenty of hot water," she told Lassee. She began rubbing little Sintwa, then rolled him in a blanket and sat with him across her knees, watching and praying silently that he would not have a second convulsion.

Aunt Morning Ann was one of those "mothers in Israel" who welcomed the newly-arrived as they were ushered into the world and ministered to the dying, folding tired work-twisted hands to rest with a resignation that amounted to spiritual exultation at their release, yet comforting the sorrowful ones left behind in the tedious journey of life. The title "Aunt" in a frontier community is one of great distinction, to be earned only with years of patient self-sacrificing devotion. It means doctor, nurse, father confessor, friend to the poor and the needy. In its spiritual significance, aunt-to-a-community means "universal motherhood," giving itself freely to every human being in need without thought of reward.

Aunt Morning Ann shook her head ruefully as she gathered her scant supply of simples together. "I wisht we had boneset," she mourned. "Thar's a pinch o' catnip, an' thet'll help, but a good strong brew o' hot boneset tea'll make a body sweat when nothin' else will." Rose Ann shuddered involuntarily at the mere mention of boneset tea—strong and hot and terrible, one of the horrors of childhood.

She glanced at Lassee as they came into the cabin, but said nothing, for which Martha was thankful; she was in doubt as to whether the Indian girl was known to the settlers, but decided that her story had not gotten about generally yet. But Aunt Morning Ann had no time or thought for anything but the sick baby. She scrutinized him carefully as he lay in a stupor on Martha's lap, searching with her forefinger for the pulse in the tiny wrist, then laid a cool hand on his forehead to note with an astounding accuracy the degree of his fever.

Martha sent Lassee and the girls out of the cabin on a pretext and turned her anxious face to Aunt Morning Ann. "What do you think it is?" she asked.

"Acts mighty lak lung fever," Aunt Morning Ann admitted reluctantly. "Hez thet thar baby bin outerdoors in the wet, er how in time did he git thet thar lingerin' cold onter his lungs?" But she did not wait for Martha's answer. The baby's case occupied her whole mind; any gossip could wait. "Lucky Pop got thet li'l' pinch o' catnip down to Vancouver," she philosophized. "Thar hain't no physics nor simples ter speak of in the hull country; we done used up all we had a-crossin' the plains, an' in course they hain't none down ter Vancouver."

"I had the bear grease that you gave me and a bottle of turpentine. I've been putting that on his chest for nearly a week," explained Martha.

"Thet's jest erbout as good's anything," consoled Aunt Morning Ann. "Natur must take its course; we-all kin only help out a little by keepin' a baby warm an' fed. Lung fever's mighty tricky in a teethin' baby. I reckon I'd best plan ter stay an' help ye a spell, Marthie. Pop an' the younguns kin git along. No light task nussin' a baby night an' day through a spell o' lung fever." She shook her head dubiously to herself.

The men came in to dinner and Rose Ann and Lassee served them as best they could, with Martha and Aunt Morning Ann never giving so much as a thought to the household economy. After dinner Manuel and Asa tiptoed about and John and Uncle Adzi hung helplessly about the cabin, full of wordless sympathy, until Martha drove all four of them off to the timber to work.

"We cain't have a passel o' men folks underfoot when they's a baby ez sick ez this un," said Aunt Morning Ann. "In one o' these fourteen-by-sixteen-foot cabins their room's a hull sight better'n their company, not castin' airy reflections onto 'em, Marthie." She smiled whimsically, but the faces of both women were strained and anxious.

The afternoon wore slowly to evening, with no perceptible change in little Sintwa, who lay by turns in a heavy stupor or tossed restlessly. The men came in at dusk and hovered anxiously about until Rose Ann and Lassee gave them their supper. Lassee worked bravely, but with eyes and ears strained to catch the slightest movement or sound from the baby. After supper John and Uncle Adzi did the chores methodically, and then sent the boys to the stable to bed to get them from underfoot.

They went about outside for a time on futile, aimless errands, neither speaking, but finally came in and sat by the door with hands on knees, waiting, fearing to go out. They might be needed. It is difficult to sit quietly, and just as difficult to carry on routine duties when anxiety fills a cabin with its terrible brooding presence. John and Uncle Adzi had watched just like this through an interminable night when their baby, darling little Clarissa May, had slipped so quietly away from them in the early morning, and through other nights when Esther Amelia had gone almost to the gates of death and won her way back. Lung fever reduced them both to a pitiable helplessness, a numb agony of anxiety.

A short time after candle-lighting there was the sound of a horse's hoofs on the trail and a familiar whistle as the rider neared the cabin. John and Uncle Adzi exchanged grim glances. McDermott had come to spend the evening. A suave, complacent McDermott, who had not left the farm since he sent Lassee and the papoose away, and so was thanking his lucky stars that the problem of Lassee and the papoose was solved with the Bainbridges none the wiser.

Much as he longed for news, he had not gone to Oregon City, and Lassee had left so quietly that he was in high spirits, though he had mooned about his desolate fireside until he felt an acute need for the society of cheerful human beings.

John and Uncle Adzi did not stir, nor so much as look at each other, though both were listening to the muffled sound of dismounting. Lassee, too, was listening; she left her work and cowered in the farthest corner near the baby's bed. Martha and Aunt Morning Ann heard nothing; they were absorbed in replacing the cooling poultice on Sintwa's chest with a hot one.

With his jaw set like a vise, and the huge muscles of his arms working convulsively, John Bainbridge, without a word, took down the ox-goad that he had carried always on his right arm when he crossed the plains. He opened the cabin door as the first knock was impatiently repeated, and went out, closing it quietly behind him.

# CHAPTER XIV

THE smile of greeting froze on McDermott's face at the first glimpse of John Bainbridge. He moved aside involuntarily as John came out, closing the door with a finality whose meaning was unmistakable.

"Come with me." The note of command in John Bainbridge's quiet voice compelled obedience in the nonplused McDermott. The two men walked beyond the stable to an open spot that was to be the garden patch. The rails to inclose it had already been stacked in orderly piles ready to lay the Virginia worm fence.

"Sit down," John said in the same voice. Uneasily, McDermott sat on a stack of rails and John took a seat close to him, deliberately taking his own time before opening the subject on his mind. McDermott shifted restlessly two or three times before John spoke.

"I have brought you out here to demand an explanation, McDermott," John's low steady voice broke a taut silence. "I understand that you are a squawman, that you have been living with an Indian girl since your wife died, and that you are the father of a year-old baby. We are not folks to mind other people's affairs, McDermott, but this concerns us. You have been a welcome guest in our house, and a short time ago it reached our ears that your name has been coupled with my daughter, Rose Ann. What have you to say for yourself?" This was a long speech for John Bainbridge. When he had finished he waited expectantly for McDermott's answer.

McDermott managed a laugh with a hint of a sneer in it. "So that's the trouble, is it?" he asked with fine scorn. "Bainbridge, you don't understand the situation here at all." His voice changed perceptibly, taking a conciliatory note, such as one speaking out of a vast wisdom used in explaining the perfectly obvious to a stubborn, ignorant person.

"I understand. I'm listening to your explanation." John was patient.

"There were no white women here, except the missionaries' wives, until last fall."

"Yes, I know all that. Go on," commanded John, still in a deadly, unemotional tone.

"Most of the men hereabouts lived with Indian women before white women came into the country; they thought nothing of it until the meddlesome missionaries came and began to dictate."

John cut him short impatiently. "Where is the Indian girl and her papoose? I'll not judge any man until he has a chance to defend himself, but, by the living God, things look black, McDermott!"

He waited for McDermott's answer, but none came. "When did that Indian girl and her papoose leave your home?" His tone demanded a reply.

"A week or ten days ago. I don't just remember," McDermott answered evasively.

"What provision did you make for her when you

cast her off? Do you even know where she went?" John asked.

"I suppose she went to the lodge. She belonged to me; I bought her at the slave mart. I gave her her freedom and told her to take what she wanted," he said virtuously.

"She went to the lodge because the papoose could not stand the exposure of the timber in the dead of winter," John said with a searing scorn in his quiet voice. "Perhaps you do not know that the Indians tried to bury her alive with Chief Cleek-a-tuck."

"Oh, my God!" ejaculated McDermott, jumping to his feet.

"Sit down," commanded John, and McDermott sank to his seat again.

"What became of her?" faltered McDermott. "I cannot believe that. It's ten years or more since they buried a slave alive."

"She's in our cabin now. There's a long cut on her head that one of the Indians made with the stock of a gun when she broke away from them. My wife stood off a whole party of Indians who wanted to take her out of the cabin."

Again McDermott rose to his feet, and again John commanded: "Sit down! The papoose is dying to-night, I am afraid. The women are working to save him, but he has lung fever. It's exposure and neglect; his blood is on your head, McDermott." John Bainbridge's voice struck terror to McDermott's heart with its calmness—the calmness of the terrible meek, of the man given to few words and slow wrath.

"And to think that you wanted our innocent little

girl, and everybody in the whole settlement knew it but us!" It was as if the low voice were the accusing voice of his own soul.

But John was speaking again. "I was minded to kill you when you knocked on my door. You deserve it when you think that you turned a girl, who had lived with you so long that she had your ways and was just like a white girl—that you turned her out with your own child at her breast in the middle of winter without caring what became of her or the baby. And you did that dastardly thing so you could marry Rose Ann."

For the moment remorse gnawed McDermott's heart. He was shocked at the turn of affairs. Chaotic emotions surged through him. He had missed Lassee more than he was willing even to himself admit, and little John William was dying. In the space before John spoke again he saw himself, a naked soul warped and shriveled by selfishness.

"For the girl's sake I'm going to give you a chance. You must marry her; the white men in the settlement will be expecting you to do that when they know about this affair. Agree and I'll never mention the matter to anyone. Remember, McDermott, we aim to have honest marrying in this country, if we have to enforce law in our own way. We're not adventurers or gunmen; we're husbands and fathers. We'll not shoot or stab in the back, but *we'll* enforce *our* law." John waited for McDermott's answer, but none came.

Two powerful natures were struggling for mastery in McDermott. Like a drowning person, his whole life flashed before him as he sat there reaching his decision before making ready to speak. He knew that he had taken "the left-hand road" all his life, that his real fight was self against what he recognized in that brief space as the rights of others, and that law stood for human justice, which in its essence is the protection of the weak against the strong. He recognized that always since he took his first misstep back in the States, the misstep that had made him a fugitive from justice, that he had unconsciously arrayed himself against human law, declaring that he was a law unto himself.

The same course had driven him from wild, reckless California, where for the last year of his life there he had never dared turn his back on anyone for fear of the treacherous dirk of men whose rights he had trampled, because for a time he had gained power over them. Until that moment he had not realized that Lassee was a human being, or that he owed any debt to little John William who lay dying in the cabin. He softened as he sensed the agony that gentle little Lassee had endured, and the scale was for an instant very near balancing in favor of right and justice. But pride and stubborn arrogance turned the quivering balance. A squaw-man he would not be in a respectable community of white men and women; to recognize half-breed children was more than any man need endure. McDermott had reached his decision, the decision that John Bainbridge was so patiently giving him time to make.

He rose, this time defiantly. John said nothing but rose also, and they stood facing each other. The night had been dark and overclouded, but the moon suddenly broke through a rift, bathing both tense faces in its light. McDermott drew himself up insolently.

"Who are you, John Bainbridge, to tell me what I shall or shall not do? I've lived in Oregon nine years, and I'll take no orders from a penniless emigrant with a half-naked family and scarcely enough to eat. Law or no law, you'll not tell *me* when to marry. I'll marry no Indian squaw when there are plenty of white women to choose from." He laughed sneeringly in John Bainbridge's face.

John drew himself up straight and spoke slowly. "You did not notice, McDermott, that I am carrying my ox-goad over my arm; you've so seldom seen me without it. I'll not kill you," he said simply, "but I'm going to whip you within an inch of your life."

Before McDermott realized what John intended to do, he had uncoiled the heavy black ox-goad from his arm and brought it down with all his might about McDermott's shoulders. The force of the blow almost felled him, but with a mighty oath John Bainbridge dragged him to his unsteady feet and applied the lash again and again, keeping his powerful grip on the back of the neck, a grip which McDermott, soft from easy living, was as powerless as a child to break.

John finished his gruesome task at last, and flung McDermott from him. His face worked with emotion as he coiled his ox-goad with precision and pulled the culprit roughly to his feet.

"I am a peaceful man," he said at length. "I

never expected to use an ox-goad on my nearest neighbor, but low-lifed varmints like you must feel the lash and know the scorn of decent white men." He had finished and made to let McDermott go, but turned with an afterthought. "If I ever hear of your mentioning my daughter's name or speaking to her, I'll kill you."

When McDermott would have fallen he took him roughly by the collar again and led him to his horse. Seeing that he was unable to mount, he threw the bridle rein over the pony's neck and helped him onto the restless animal's back.

"We'll rid Oregon of your kind, without gun-play," was his parting shot as he handed him the bridle rein and stood watching him as the pony made his surefooted way down the trail.

He stood for a few minutes in the dark (the moon had suddenly disappeared behind scudding clouds), lifted the latch of the cabin door, and went in, hanging the ox-goad on its accustomed peg, before he seated himself again by Uncle Adzi. There was comprehension in Uncle Adzi's eyes as John looked up, but neither spoke.

Aunt Morning Ann came with a wooden pail and asked John to bring water, and as he rose quickly, Uncle Adzi rose with him and went to carry in a huge armload of split oak wood which he deposited soundlessly near the fireplace and began raking out the coals in front of the half-burned backlog so as to replenish the fire to make it hold well the rest of the night. He put the kettle of water where it would heat, as John set his pail of cold water on its bench by the door, and the two men renewed their helpless vigil out of the way of the women, but instantly ready to do the slightest possible service.

The long night wore itself slowly away. Martha sent Rose Ann and Esther Amelia to bed, and Lassee sat quietly hour after hour on the floor near the head of the baby's bed. Martha and Aunt Morning Ann kept up their fight with death, glancing at each other in full understanding. The overburdened heart was giving way under the terrific strain put upon it.

The tide of human life reaches its ebb with the turn of the night. "If we can hold him past three o'clock, we may pull him through yet," Martha whispered hopefully to Aunt Morning Ann, as she heated fresh bear's grease and turpentine for a poultice.

But wise Aunt Morning Ann shook her head sadly. She had sat all too often through long nights by the bedside of sick babies and she knew that little Sintwa's appointed time for slipping out of the chrysalis of mortality was near at hand.

He died an hour later. Lassee had scarcely moved from the floor near the head of the bed the whole night through. She arose and stood looking down at the little form until Martha led her away, returning to place her one whole linen sheet over the dead baby.

"Martha and Aunt Morning Ann, you had best lie down a spell," said John. "There's nothing more you can do until morning. Uncle Adzi and I will sit up the rest of the night."

The exhausted women climbed over the trundle-bed

where the two girls lay, and slept until daylight strained through the buckskin of the cabin windows.

Unobserved, Lassee had slipped from the cabin to be alone in her grief. She picked up the trail leading around the face of the bluff, though the darkness was the dense black of the hours before dawn. She went to the same place on the face of the bluff with its overhanging rock that offered shelter. It was a good three miles from a cabin, and no one would hear. This time she did not build a fire, but sat for a long time with her elbows on her knees and her bowed head in her hands. At length there sounded through the hush just before daylight the same heart-rending wail of the Indian woman for her dead. Until it was fully light she wailed, rocking back and forth in her agony, then she ceased and rose dry-eyed, but bearing in her drawn copper-tinted face the stamp of the Gethsemane through which she was passing. She made her way down the trail and entered the cabin just as she had left it. Breakfast was being put on the table and she began to help with the serving, as quietly and efficiently as on any other morning.

Martha and Aunt Morning Ann wept and tried simply to offer Lassee words of comfort, but she took no notice. Lassee's was the heritage of the Indian women, stony and dry-eyed grief.

Martha led her tenderly to the bed and turned down the sheet, and she stood quietly looking down on her sleeping baby's face, until John brought a block of wood and placed it near the bed; she sat down then and remained through the day with her hands lying supinely in her lap, scarcely a muscle of her body moving.

After breakfast, which no one could eat, Uncle Adzi prepared to go to Oregon City after planed boards for the coffin.  Martha took down the linen sheet from which she had cut the bandage for Lassee's head and began measuring it very carefully.

"Go to the stable and take down the wagon cover," she told Rose Ann.  "It's hanging on two pegs back of the ox-stalls.  Have the boys help you and be careful not to tear it in taking it off the pegs.  Asa, you help Rose Ann carry it into the house so as not to trail the ends in the mud."  She turned again to her measuring.

"How fortunate I could bring those sheets through," she said to Aunt Morning Ann.  "I expected to make white ruffled curtains for our windows as soon as we could get glass."

Aunt Morning Ann gazed admiringly at the linen, fingering it lovingly as she spoke.  "Ruffled curtings air homey," she said with a hint of longing in her voice.  "In Novelty, Missouri, whar we-all come from, ther wuz fine frame houses—thet is, one er two," she corrected herself in strict honesty.  "I allus loved ter walk down the street and see the wind rustlin' the curtings at the windows, er the candle-light a-shinin' through at night.  I'm hopin' Oregon City'll soon be a town lak Novelty."

Rose Ann and Asa came in, carrying the wagon cover between them.  Martha took one side and Aunt Morning Ann the other, and they spread it out carefully on the floor.

"I reckon thisahar's the wust worn part," Aunt Morning Ann pointed to the tatters with her forefinger.

Martha nodded. Taking her scissors, she cut off the tatters very carefully, and turned to the fireplace to pour out hot water to wash the scraps in her hands.

"You cut the shroud, Marthie," said Aunt Morning Ann. "I'll wash the sail-cloth and dry hit right quick by the fire, an' then the gals kin ravel out the thread. We cain't sew, anyway, ontil ye git hit cut out."

Martha laid the sheet carefully on the table and secured Sintwa's little buckskin dress for a pattern, carefully calculating so that not an inch of her precious linen should be wasted. She was obliged to stop a moment to take Esther Amelia on her lap and comfort her. She had wept all the morning. To have a baby to play with and then see him snatched right out of her heart was more than she could bear.

"We'll make short puffed sleeves and a low neck and put narrow ruffles around them and on the bottom," Martha planned as she cut, turning one corner back and truing it up to make the bias ruffles. Yards and yards of the inch strips she allowed for ruffling. "The best we have is for laying away the dead," she said, and Aunt Morning Ann nodded assent.

By this time the wagon cover was dry, and, though a little gray from its long traveling in alkali dust, was clean. Aunt Morning Ann showed Rose Ann how to ravel it to the best advantage, cautioning her to wind it smoothly on a stick so that there would be

no kinks or knots and to break the threads at the
weak points.

"Hit's slow work a-sewin' with raveled-out thread,
but I've done hit mor'n oncet. Glad ter have rave-
lin's ter use. You-all is lucky ter hav a wagon
kiver. Like ez not we-all'll never see our'n ag'in.
The Injuns has probably toted hit off long afore
this. This here kiver'll keep ye in thread fer a long
time. There wun't be no spool thread in the settlement ontil the ships come in."

"We have three needles." Martha was taking
down her cherished box of little things that she kept
high out of the reach of the children, though no one
of them dared to so much as touch it without her
permission. The contents were so valuable that they
stood in awe of it. Thimbles and needles and pins
must be cherished and hoarded. There was no replacing them.

Martha handed Rose Ann a brass thimble without
an end, and adjusted her own. Aunt Morning Ann
had already taken hers from the cavernous pocket
in the gathered folds of her skirt, and the three of
them drew their blocks of wood up near the door
where the light was good and sat down to hem the
ruffling for the little shroud.

The hush that the death angel brings was over the
cabin. All work but the necessary chores had ceased
outside. A family pauses reverently in the presence
of death. John sat on the puncheon bench outside
the door, or went uneasily about the stable or over
the garden patch, and Asa and Manuel tiptoed awkwardly through the cabin or followed the men.

Uncle Adzi returned before noon with smooth boards cut just the right length and John helped him all the afternoon with the coffin, fastening it together with the pegs that the boys whittled. Dinner was somehow gotten onto the table, but appetites had gone. Esther Amelia sobbed herself to sleep. The three hemmed and hemmed and hemmed on the ruffles as the little garment grew under their swift fingers.

Siah-hen and Dick came down in the early afternoon. They had been busy on Dick's claim and had not even known of the papoose's illness. Siah-hen went to the motionless Lassee and spoke soft words to her in their native Klamath tongue, and she answered with an occasional monosyllable. He sat for a long time with one of her listless hands in both of his, then in silence rose and went outdoors.

Aunt Morning Ann left off her hemming to put beautiful smocking in the gathers to hold the fullness of the dress about the high yoke and the puffed sleeves. Rose Ann finished her ruffle and could do no more, so her mother told her to find Dick and her brothers and go up the hill and dig the grave. "Dick and Manuel can easily dig it before dark and you and Asa gather all of those long green ferns that you can carry and bring them down when you come," she told her. "A plain board coffin is so bare and cold and hard."

Rose Ann called to Dick and he hurried to get the shovel as she went on up the path. She began to cry again as she realized that little Sintwa was dead and

a grave must be dug. She had seen so many graves
dug in the last year.

Dick overtook her, his heart full of the bitterness
of youth at the cruelty of men. It unnerved him
terribly to see Rose Ann cry. He ached with longing to comfort her, but could think of nothing to say
or do. He was thinking angrily that life was too
hard, too hard for all of them. He was a young man
just beginning, with his prospects bright and glowing
before him, but hard and bitter his childhood had
been for him, before he reached Oregon City and became, as he felt, overnight, a man.

Bitter life was for Siah-hen, his one loyal friend
among men. He strongly suspected that Siah-hen
loved Lassee, and it was excruciating agony for him
to see her suffer as she had at the hands of an unscrupulous white man. Hard and bitter life would
have been for little Sintwa. He was strangely
grateful that the innocent little half-breed baby had
been taken out of it all.

He walked along in silence beside Rose Ann. At
least she would know he was there and feeling her
sorrow keenly. Somehow he must spare Rose Ann
from the stern realities of life. He wished he dared
to put his hand on her head and smooth back the soft
yellow hair, but Rose Ann was a being sacred and
apart, never to be defiled by the rude touch of men.
He could only hover anxiously above her bowed head
in mute sympathy.

But Rose Ann, nearly blinded by her tears,
stretched out a timid hand in search of his. The
gesture was simple—anyone grasps a friendly hand

in sorrow—but Dick knew when he covered her hand awkwardly with his that shielding Rose Ann from the realities of a too hard world would henceforth be his main object in life. Rose Ann gently withdrew her hand to wipe her eyes, and pointed out a spot under a large fir tree standing a little apart from its fellows where the little grave had best be dug.

Dick and Manuel dug the grave—they knew exactly how to go about it—everyone had helped in digging graves in crossing the plains. Rose Ann and Asa gathered huge armloads of the luxuriant sword ferns growing in the timber. She found the broad, glossy, everygreen leaves of the salal berry and the finer-cut red huckleberry, with here and there the pungent heart-shaped foliage of the wild ginger or some delicate trailing vine that still survived in sheltered hollows.

They reached home at dusk. The coffin was finished, and Aunt Morning Ann was just putting the last of the smocking on the shroud. Martha looked at the plain little box that Uncle Adzi carried in, and shook her head sadly, "Let's line it with this linen," she said. "I think I can piece it so there will be enough; there's still a whole sheet left and some of that can be used if we have to. Windows are small, anyway. One sheet will be plenty to make ruffled curtains. The best we have must be for laying away the dead," she said again.

At last Martha led Lassee to see little Sintwa. She fingered the little dress lovingly. Indian women are strangely touched and pleased to have their dead given burial after the white man's custom.

"Be ye goin' ter call the Elder?" Aunt Morning Ann inquired. "Brother Waller'd come if you-all asked him. Seems on-Christian ter lay even a Injun baby away without a-offerin' prayer," she told Martha in an undertone.

"Uncle Adzi spoke to Elder Waller yesterday," said Martha. "He'll hold a service here at ten in the morning. We didn't say anything to anyone in Oregon City, for Lassee is an Indian and lots of folks don't care much for Indians, and no use to spread gossip." She had told Aunt Morning Ann Lassee's story and both agreed that it was not to be discussed outside.

"Pore little gal!" Aunt Morning Ann had said in pity. "But she'll have it to remember that we done all we could fer her."

Brother Waller came in the morning with the Methodist ritual under his arm and a worn Bible carried carefully in his hand. Mrs. Waller, quick and energetic and capable as a circuit rider's wife must be, came, too.

Pop Simmons was there with the six barefooted Simmons children, all carefully washed and combed and with their buckskins thoroughly cleaned by vigorous rubbing between the hands in clean dry sand from the river bank. Pop had found it no small task to renovate six buckskin suits, but each must appear at his simple best.

The cabin could not hold them all, so the sorrowful little procession wended its way up the hill in a drizzling rain to the open grave, and there under the kindly shelter of the big fir tree Elder Waller read a Psalm, the ninety-first, beginning: "He that dwelleth in the secret place of the Most High shall abide under the shadow of the Almighty." The Methodist burial service, a short sermon and a prayer, was followed by Mrs. Waller leading the hallowed old funeral hymn, "Far-away Home of the Soul," and little Sintwa rested in Mother Earth.

# CHAPTER XV

THROUGH the weeks that followed his illy-
timed visit to the Bainbridges' cabin McDermott sat moodily nursing black and blue
stripes across his broad back. But worse than physical wounds, far worse than raw lacerations in quivering flesh, were the black and blue discolorations his
pride was suffering. Wounds that festered and
ached, refusing to heal, under which his spirit
writhed and twisted in agony, had been brought
about by the well-directed blows of John Bainbridge's
ox-goad.

McDermott ordinarily was not averse to being
alone. Before he had had no special reason for solitude, but this remoteness was the crawling away to
hide a searing shame. He had suffered at the hands
of his neighbor the worst humiliation that one man
can inflict on another. Stabbing or gun-play he
had no taste for, still he could have borne this sort
of strife, but to be beaten like an inferior, like a
nigger on a plantation, he told himself, was an indig-
nity from which he could never recover. He would
carry the spiritual scars of that flogging to the end
of his days.

For days the one end of his existence seemed to
him to devise a fitting revenge on John Bainbridge.
He had before known the urge to kill, but this time
he did not thirst for blood; his one burning desire

was to cause suffering, poignant and terrible, and yet to inflict it in such a subtle way that his poisoned barb would turn and rankle for years.

He meant to take that lovely bit of girlhood, Rose Ann. He assured himself that he had gone about the matter in a perfectly honorable way, and if he were not allowed to declare his intentions like a gentleman, well, then other means must be found.

He planned diabolically, as he sat by the fire through long days with his gun always within reach of his hand, starting uneasily at the usual noises, then laughing to himself at the absurdity of his nervousness. Oregon was peaceful and he had done nothing of late years to bring about swift frontier justice. He was too much alone. There was nothing to fear, unless it be Quimmo's treachery, and that was remote, just a possibility mirroring in the back of his mind. Quimmo had his own good reasons for keeping out of sight. He would likely disappear into the Klamath country with the breaking up of the winter.

He had kept closely within the cabin, at first through sheer inability to move about until his bruises healed, and later from a sort of shamed reluctance, though necessity compelled him to mend fences to keep his longhorns from straying off into the mountains. He wondered if the Indians had any inkling of what had happened. He fancied they were especially unfriendly of late.

They must be held on the place, somehow, to keep up the chores, and if they could be induced to dawdle away a few hours on wood-cutting or some other

simple task he would be so much to the good when
the spring work began. He resolved to question them
when a favorable opportunity presented, but the Indians were adroit at preventing opportunities, taking a sinister pleasure in reticence. He could not
manage an opening, though they had exasperating
spells of volubility in which they freely discussed
this and that and what not.

But something must shortly be done. The cabin
bore terrible evidence of the absence of capable
womankind.    McDermott,    when    circumstances
forced, could manage to prepare his indifferent food,
but the hearth had not been swept for weeks. The
fireplace was choked with ashes. Dirt and disorder
prevailed in the kitchen. A messy table held un-
washed unsavory dishes. Domestic chaos had spread
from the kitchen through his large living-room to
his bedroom with its tumbled bed and a near-by litter
of wrinkled garments, boots and leather chaps.

The bridle he had been mending was thrown down
in a corner and forgotten. He brought in a wet
saddle-blanket to dry and then neglected to hang it
before the fire. It lay a sodden evil-smelling mass
on the floor. The acrid odor of the stable mingled
with the sundry smells of an unaired house.

Hang it all, something must be done. He recalled
trappers' cabins in the mountains where woman's
presence was never known. His house was taking on
the same desolation. Regretfully he recalled the
gentle ministrations of Lassee; her presence had
meant far more to his physical comfort than he had
realized. Strange that in sending her back to the

tribe the lack of creature comforts that would follow her prolonged absence had never entered his head. Always moving swiftly but never hurried, the work that unobtrusive girl had done was simply past belief.

There was little hope of finding another squaw to take her place. There were Indian girls about the villages who had attended Jason Lee's mission and understood the rudiments of housewivery, but on returning to the lodge they reverted to savagery. Evangeline, now, was rather a bright forward squaw, though she was getting old. She had lived with a notorious white trapper until he cast her off. Since she had occupied rather a unique position in the tribe. She was a "washer," one of those squaws familiar with white ways whose duty it was to coach the fortunate young girls chosen as brides to the French-Canadian trappers and farmers. Before the bride left the lodge she was divested of her bear grease and red clay and salmon-oil paint and scrubbed within an inch of her life. White men would not tolerate Indian filth, and in so far as they could learn what was expected of them they endeavored to live up to white standards.

McDermott finally sent one of the Indians down to the lodge to bring Evangeline to clean the house and wash and cook for him. Squaws are always glad of the chance to secure old clothing, beads, or trinkets, for a few hours' work. He had a bright-red blanket and sundry strings of beads that he kept for trading. These properly dealt out should secure domestic tranquillity and comfort for the rest of the winter.

Klanic, the more forward of his two aides, went willingly on the errand, grinning in a manner that made McDermott seethe with rage, but in a few hours he returned, declaring that Evangeline *wake chah-co* (no come). Questioning him did no good; he declined to state the reason for her refusal, though he carried the air of one who could divulge vast information should he choose to do so. A shrug and *"Wake chah-co"* was all the satisfaction McDermott could get.

Evangeline's curt refusal disturbed McDermott far more than he dared show the Indians. He sat far into the night before his choked fire, listening to the beat of the rain, melancholy because it seemed that the coyotes howled worse than common, cursing the steady rain, cursing the harmless coyote for calling to his mate or holding conversation with his friends a few miles away.

Matters might be worse than he realized. He wished he could find out exactly what had happened, and wondered if sending Lassee back to the tribe had insulted the Indians. For all he knew, Evangeline might be engaged elsewhere, but still, in view of past events her refusal and Klanic's noncommittal attitude boded no good.

If he had completely lost power over the Indians, to remain in Oregon was hazardous. He had set Indians against those who stood in his way times enough to know what to expect at their hands. Taken altogether, he had inadvertently gotten himself into a nasty mess, especially since that old issue, slave burial, had revived. If news of this piece of mischief reached the ears of Doctor McLoughlin—and in all likelihood it would—his name would be mentioned in connection with the affair. The Doctor was sure to bring the guilty Indians to book, and he did not stand any too well with the Hudson Bay Company, anyway.

Here was a terrible three-corned dilemma, dangerous from all three angles. The settlers, the Hudson Bay Company, and the Indians, all might strike at him in concert or severally. He must go into retirement as soon as possible. He wondered if he had best risk a trip to the settlement to find an emigrant to live on the farm while he was away, but thought better of it. He would hide and wait until the tide of feeling that he felt sure must be running high against him had ebbed somewhat.

He was sure that the papoose was dead. The Indians had enlarged on the fact that they had seen Elder and Sister Waller going up the trail to the Bainbridges' cabin on the third day after his encounter with John Bainbridge, and this could mean but one thing. With an altogether disproportionate sense of his own importance, due to too much solitude, he felt sure that his story, probably with the most elaborate embroideries, was being bandied about in every cabin in the country. He lived in daily fear of a delegation of settlers visiting him and demanding that he leave the country or dealing out rude justice as they saw it, but days had worn slowly away and he was apparently forgotten.

He would seek a still more remote frontier. There were plenty of places to go if one had money, and if

things went as he hoped they would there was no need
to fear on that score. Australia was wild and new;
he could go there and perhaps develop a farm and
start all over again, this time going perfectly straight
and in time becoming a pillar of society. He told
himself he had had enough of living in constant fear
and dread.

But speculation as to what to do availed very little.
He could only wait and wait and wait, fretting his
heart out. Even his revenge must depend upon that
fickle jade, Opportunity. He must keep out of sight
until the middle of summer or well into the fall.
There were so many problems to solve and so much
that rankled and hurt. Leaving the farm was his
only regret at taking himself out of the country.
How was he to realize a good profit on its sale? No
one had money, and land was there for the taking.
The improvements would more than likely go for
nothing, but his cattle, a hundred longhorns, were
readily saleable and could be disposed of a few at a
time to eager buyers.

Whom could he trust to carry out his commissions?
He must leave very shortly; he knew a certain cabin
about twenty miles back in the mountains to the east
where he would be safe and could superintend his
affairs after a fashion. But the greatest problem
was how to manipulate a good-sized cargo of a certain contraband article so as to realize its full value
without risk. That alone was enough to keep a man
fully occupied with his planning far into the night
and after toss him about restlessly until the early
morning hours.

The silence was ominous. Better an issue forced to settlement than the breaking of a strong man's nerve waiting, waiting, waiting in a disordered cabin for a blow, whose nature he had no way of discovering, to fall. He knew that his disappearance would cause but little comment. No one would look for his return, and that gave him security to direct his affairs so long as he found some one he could trust. Men who have been humiliated often slink out of sight on one frontier to appear on another where no questions are asked.

He did not take decisive action for nearly six weeks. One morning he called Klanic into the cabin, motioning to his companion to go on about his wood-cutting when he would have followed out of curiosity.

"Klanic," he said when he had shut and barred the door and looked furtively out of the window to be sure that Cartoosh was fully occupied, "you like to have a good drink of *lum* [whisky]?" Klanic's eyes brightened and his sullen mien changed instantly to one of extreme affability. He was all respectful attention at the mere mention of the charmed word.

"*Mit-lite*" ("Wait"), said McDermott, entering his bedroom and closing and barring the door carefully behind him. He returned with a small demijohn from which he thoughtfully poured a fair-sized draught of amber wheat whiskey and gave it to the eagerly waiting Klanic, shaking a stern head when the glass was handed back after the liquor had been tossed off in one gulp.

"You do what I want, more *lum*, plenty *lum*," McDermott promised.

"*No-wit-ka*" ("Yes"), smiled Klanic.

"You do errand for me to-night. *Wake wa-wa* [Do not tell]" McDermott cautioned.

"*No-wit-ka klat-a-wa*" ("Yes, I'll go"), Klanic was a very deferential Indian. McDermott now had a faithful henchman. *Lum* was a *potlatch* not to be compared with red blankets or jack-knives or even muskets or ammunition, and the dispenser was to be served to the death and venerated far above other men.

"*Hy-ah klat-a-wa mamook*" ("hurry back to work"), McDermott ordered with a show of his old authority, which the delighted Indian acknowledged tacitly. With a secretiveness that gave McDermott great assurance he sauntered out with a carefully assumed air of indifference, but with an important swagger that had not been present before. His companion, Cartoosh, wonderingly curious, would evidently be none the wiser, unless his employer should decide to take him into his confidence also.

McDermott stood by the window, watching Klanic as, with an energy altogether foreign to his former manner, he joined his companion, who was leisurely piling limbs from a tree that had been cut for firewood. He had made a momentous decision that morning, had "crossed the Rubicon," so to speak. There could be no faltering or turning to look back now, and his course would be precarious. Had he intended to remain in Oregon, it would have been the height of folly to control an Indian with liquor. Perhaps there would be disaster as it was, but this was the last resort. There was no foreseeing the

train of events that whisky might start, but there was
no other way to accomplish his purpose, and, anyway
(he shrugged his broad shoulders contemptuously),
he would be out of the country before the source of
the wheat whisky was discovered.

McDermott, always a patient man, bided his time
for his various and sundry enterprises to mature.
His most perplexing problem was to dispose of a
large quantity of wheat whisky that had been mellow-
ing in casks safely hidden away since 1836. Selling
liquor had been a pet scheme that he had secretly
nursed ever since coming to Oregon in 1834.

When Ewing Young, coming up from Lower California, had been coolly received by Doctor McLoughlin on account of advance information from the Governor of Lower California that the party were horse
thieves, some little resentment had been engendered
in his mind. He was innocent of the charge, having
been joined by the band on the trail up from California. The horse thieves had never come to Oregon.

Seeing the opportunity to recoup his fortunes, he
secured the vat that Nathaniel Wyeth of the Columbia River Fishing and Trading Company discarded
when he abandoned his trading project. Wyeth was
an enterprising American who had great visions of
packing salmon on the Columbia and shipping it to
the Atlantic coast and selling American goods to the
Indians. He established himself on Wappato Island
at the mouth of the Willamette River, but his venture failed ingloriously.

Ewing Young began distilling wheat whisky, but
had promised to destroy his distillery when a petition

signed by thirty settlers and missionaries protesting against his business had been presented to him. Young told the petitioners that necessity had forced him into liquor manufacturing, since he had been denied the right to trade or engage in business by the Hudson Bay Company. He was a man of his word; the still was dismembered and he supposed the liquor had been poured out.

Doctor McLoughlin had sternly decreed that no more wheat should be used in distilling liquor in the territory over which he had absolute jurisdiction. The Hudson Bay Company's policy was against selling liquor to Indians, though the matter was largely in the hands of the factors of the one hundred and fifty posts in America. Doctor McLoughlin never allowed spirits to reach the Indians if he could prevent it, but the trade was lucrative and ships plying back and forth frequently brought in cargoes and disposed of it *sub rosa*. Once the good Doctor, knowing that a cargo of whisky was in port and having no way to prevent its distribution, resorted to the expedient of buying up the whole consignment and putting it under lock and key. His policy in keeping liquor out of the Oregon country was not so much one of morals as it was good business, just as encouraging hunters and trappers to take Indian wives in order to cement friendly relations with the Indians was good .business.

Firewater had been one of the principal factors in debauching and degrading the native population since the coming of the white man. The Indians are simple and child-like, accepting everything the white

man tells them, until they learn to the contrary. At
first they rebelled against firewater, but with American free traders and trappers continually forcing it
upon them they developed on inherent taste for it in
time, so that in a generation or two the desire for
liquor was a consuming passion with them. The Indians of the Pacific coast were not constitutionally so
vigorous as those of the territory east of the Rocky
Mountains and the effect of the debaucheries taught
them by licentious white men had a great deal to do
with their rapid decimation.

With the coming of settlers there was all the more
reason for suppressing the liquor traffic. The Indians felt a natural resentment toward the American
settlers who would so shortly by means of the plough
take their lands from them, and liquor flowing freely
meant that life would not be safe for whites in
Oregon.

The worst crime against society of which a man
could be guilty in Oregon was giving liquor to an
Indian. If caught, he was sure to have justice
speedily dealt him. McDermott was certain that no
one so much as suspected the presence of his cache
of whisky. There were often vague rumors of liquor
in the country, and of late Indians had sometimes
obtained firewater from sources that could not be
determined, but this was attributed justly enough to
leakage from ships.

So far McDermott had never allowed a drop of
whisky on his premises, as anyone knew. He was not
a drinking man himself, was supposed to be against
the practice. His policy had been to give this im-

pression. Time enough to dispose of his holdings secretly when coastwise trade was well established. Whisky would be whisky still in California when that time came.

Klanic, all eagerness, came in the evening to do any errand that McDermott might indicate, and was sent to bring back an emigrant named Calkins who was barely keeping his large family alive in an improvised shelter down on the river bank.

Calkins came immediately, and readily agreed to McDermott's demand for secrecy in return for the privilege of living in the commodious cabin and running the farm and tending the longhorns on shares. Calkins was a man known in the settlement as "close-mouthed"; that was McDermott's reason for choosing him, and after talking with him he felt sure that there would be no leaking of information.

Thanks to judicious fingers of firewater dealt with a niggardly hand, Klanic and his former companion in indolence, Cartoosh, suddenly developed a passion for work amounting almost to frenzy.

McDermott lost no time repining after his course was fully determined. He destroyed letters, and packed necessities for his journey. He took down his most cherished books and did them up in two compact parcels for carrying on a pack-horse. There was much that he must do before he made his departure. With a great wondering joy at their good fortune, the Calkins family was installed and everything seemed to be going well. McDermott was freer from worry than he had been for a long time, but he reasoned that perhaps it was partly because he was so busy.

His greatest pang was leaving his orchard. Like parting with dearly loved children. Grafted trees were scarce in Oregon, but he had wonderful varieties of fruit trees growing thriftily. Nathaniel Wyeth had traded him a few trees when he abandoned his project on Wappato Island. There were varieties of apples and pears and plums that had come from the islands of the Pacific. He had carefully grafted seedlings, and right here was a fortune in a few years' time if only he might stay to realize on his years of work. If stock broke into the orchard his beloved trees would be destroyed.

He decided to prune all the trees before he left, and spent long days when he felt almost happy. The grapes he left to the last, deciding that the sap was up too much to make their cutting safe. Grapes should not be pruned until along the last of February and this winter had been so mild that the sap had scarcely gone down at all. But the last day before his departure he went to examine his vines. As he started down the long carefully trellised row with a sharp jack-knife in his hand, he noticed that here and there a twig had been broken off and lay on the ground. First he looked to be sure that the fence was not down, but it was intact; no stray longhorn had broken in. His face wore a puzzled frown as he stopped to examine the first vine. He recoiled in horror; it was like stumbling onto the body of a murdered friend. The grape vine had been skillfully cut so that it had bled to death. "Quimmo," he muttered involuntarily, his florid face growing pale. He turned to the other vines. The work had been thoroughly done by some one who knew just how to go about it. The vines were cut with a sharp knife so that the slashes did not show. He remembered taking Quimmo through his orchard once in the years when they were fast friends, and explaining to him how carefully grapes must be cut, allowing three eyes on the laterals that were to bear the clusters of fruit. In those days Quimmo had often helped him. No one but Quimmo could be guilty; he alone knew how dear these grapes were to his heart.

He went down the row, hoping against hope that a few had been overlooked, but the destroyer had been thorough, even making slashes next to the earth so that there could be no possibility of growing from the root. With grief at his loss mingling with the fear of unseen hands shaping his destiny, McDermott went in and sat moodily by the fire; but the cabin was fairly over-run by the Calkins children, so he finished his packing and made ready to leave in the middle of the night.

There was no moon when he left, with his two faithful Indians leading pack-horses and anticipating his wants in a most gratifying manner. Now that he had gained the upper hand again, he felt perfectly safe with them. They would do as they were told and keep his secrets; their exaggerated importance was amusing.

Calkins caused it to be noised about that McDermott had left the settlement. Where he had gone he did not know, which was all perfectly true. Some one, possibly Elder Waller, had told the story of the papoose's death. His sending Lassee back to the tribe had been common knowledge before. Had McDermott only known, it attracted but little notice. No one was particularly interested in the up-risings and down-sittings of lousy Indians in a filthy lodge, so the attempted slave burial escaped notice and John Bainbridge had kept his own council in regard to his part in the affair. The settlers were more than busy providing food and clothing and shelter for their families. McDermott's fears for his safety had been unfounded where they were concerned.

# CHAPTER XVI

SCHOOL was to start soon. Martha had been very busy making the children presentable with the scant means at hand. She made a shawl for each of the girls by hemming the best parts of two frayed blankets, and the boys were very brave indeed in serviceable coats made out of the canvas wagon cover.

Dick Skelton made a pair of shoes for Esther Amelia so that the child could be kept dry and warm. Manuel and Asa had been barefooted all winter and did not seem to mind at all.

It was a memorable Monday when the little expedition fared forth in quest of knowledge. Dick came to the Bainbridge cabin fully an hour before time for the children to start, for fear of being late. He had a pair of strong new shoes, a new pair of buckskin pantaloons, and a blue flannel shirt that Siahhen had secured for him in Vancouver. His coonskin cap was a relic of the days in Missouri, rather battered and moth-eaten, but it served well enough. He wore the leather coat with which Siah-hen had outfitted him when he first became his protégé. He was comfortably dressed, much better than most of the boys who would attend school.

Dick was eager to attend school. He was anxious to mingle with young people of his own age, and especially to learn all he could from the new teacher.

He admitted to himself that Siah-hen had done well by him in the short time he had been under his tutelage, but, after all, Siah-hen was only an Indian, and surely a white man could teach him faster and better.

Then there was the chance to walk to and from school every day with Rose Ann. Perhaps she would allow him to carry her books and help her across the foot-log. Independent Rose Ann was capable of walking unassisted across any foot-log that had yet been put up, still he fully intended to help her across. He had his cherished books, Webster's Speller—he could spell nearly every word in it—and McGuffey's Fourth Reader that some one had cast aside on the trail and he had retrieved and cherished. Siah-hen had promised later to allow him to take that highly entertaining and instructive history, Peter Parley's Tales, which began with Adam and Eve, so to speak, and covered all events down to the present time.

Siah-hen also owned Comstock's Philosophy, a wonderful treatise. The preface modestly announced that it was "a system of Natural Philosophy in which the principles of Mathematics, Hydraulics, Pneumatics, Acoustics, Optics, Astronomy, Electricity, and Magnetism are fully explained, and illustrated by more than two hundred engravings." Dick had always stood a little in awe of this profound book, though he had pored over its pages almost from his first attempt at reading. Siah-hen cherished his few books tenderly, but regarded no sacrifice too great to further Dick's education. He intended to allow the books to go to school, that they might serve as reading books for the more advanced "scholars." Printed matter was so scarce that one with a taste for reading and studying simply absorbed the contents of anything that came to hand. Ambercrombie's Intellectual Philosophy had drawn Dick like a magnet, though it was abstract philosophy. This, too, would serve admirably for reading exercises.

There were excitement and commotion in the cabin of the Bainbridges when Dick arrived. Martha with a basin of hot water was relentlessly scouring the neck and ears of the protesting Asa and Manuel. When she finished to her satisfaction she placed the basin on the floor, insisting that they wash their feet, a rite which both considered wholly unnecessary. They declared they *had* washed them the night before and had muddied them up doing the chores that morning, and would just get dirty again going down the trail, but Martha was sternly unrelenting—wash they must, or remain at home.

Rose Ann, immaculate, with her hair smoothly braided, was doing the squirming Esther Amelia's hair. Esther Amelia could not stand still. She had never been to school and was fairly beside herself with excitement. There was the luncheon to "put up," a jug of sweet milk with a tin cup to drink from, and a small pail of wheat hominy, and the ever-present salmon.

With knowing looks and aggravating giggles the boys and Esther Amelia went ahead, taking good care to keep within earshot of the self-conscious Dick and Rose Ann. Here was just the opportunity Dick had longed for and planned over and over. But, he was suffocated with embarrassment, now that he was walking along beside Rose Ann. "How far have you gone in arithmetic, Rose Ann?" he stammered finally in a frantic effort to make conversation.

"I know the multiplication table and fractions and the rule of three," Rose Ann answered from some place way off in the fog. Silas Simmons, with his two smaller brothers in tow, overtook them just as they neared the foot-log, and Asa and Manuel, with sly nods and nudges and winks, appraised them of the fact that Rose Ann had a beau. With burning cheeks Rose Ann allowed Dick to help her across the foot-log over the rushing little torrent that tore down the hill just before they reached Oregon City. She resolved to tell mother the minute she got home how Asa and Manuel were snickering and tormenting.

Silas Simmons had news to impart. The Simmons children had taken a short-cut that led past the McDermott place, and he told Dick importantly that they had seen five Indians lying in the fence row above the orchard, watching the cabin. "One o' em' war Quimmo, too," Silas had insisted. "I kin allus tell him 'cause he's pock-marked. We ran," he admitted. "We-all air powerful 'fraid o' Quimmo."

Dick laughed. "You think every Indian you see is Quimmo. They were probably out hunting and sat down to rest. The Indians are short of provisions at the lodge. They let white folks have nearly everything they had gathered for the winter." But the children had reached the school and the subject was dropped.

There were nearly fifty children assembled. A number were nearly grown boys and girls—young ladies and gentlemen, they were called. They were a motley group in various stages of disrepair as to wearing apparel, though an honest effort had been made to hold the garments together with patches. Some were barefooted, others had on Indian moccasins, but most of them were frankly innocent of stockings. A few of the girls had knitting with them. All would have had knitting to do to and from school had it been possible to secure wool for spinning.

Sidney Moss had a good-sized frame house that he had built the year before with lumber from the Island Milling Company. To the citizens of Oregon City it was the last word in the way of an elegant home. There was a real upstairs with ample space for bedchambers, though no partitions had as yet been put in, and the floor above still answered for the ceiling below. The large room across the front had been given over to the school. There were two rows of wooden benches, made of planed lumber, with long desks in front of them. The boys shambled awkwardly in when the young schoolmaster, John Brooks, beat a stick on the side of the house to "call school." They took their places on one side of the room and the girls on the other, with the children nicely graduated as to size.

John Brooks was a slight, gentle young man. Dick was instantly drawn to him. He read the chapter from the Bible and tried out the children carefully to see where they belonged. It was late afternoon before he reached Dick. He smiled when he saw

Comstock's Philosophy and reached eagerly for Ambercrombie's Intellectual Philosophy. Here was a
treasure that any studious person might pore over
through long evenings.

John Brooks questioned Dick closely, and outlined
his studies so that he might forge ahead as rapidly
as possible. As he left him, he said meditatively,
"There's one law book in Oregon City, the Iowa code
of laws; the Organic Law of Oregon has just been
drafted from it. Mr. Nesmith is studying it nights,
but I'll get it for you to read while you are in school.
We'll need lawyers later. You may as well bend your
studies in that direction. There'll be law books on
the ships next summer, or perhaps a few will come
in with next year's emigration."

Dick was suddenly lifted above the earth. He bent
eagerly to his work, oblivious of the giggling girls
who were trying to attract his attention from across
the room. He was not even conscious of the presence
of Rose Ann. To make the most of a wonderful and
entirely unexpected opportunity completely en-
grossed his attention.

John Brooks was a born teacher. The lack of facilities troubled him not at all. Few of the children
had books. It was a sort of catch-as-catch-can form
of teaching by writing on a space on the wall, painted
black, with a lump of chalk. Every pupil who could
muster them brought scraps of blank paper, and
there was a very limited supply of goose-quill pens.
The only plentiful commodity was black ink, manufactured from oak galls steeped in vinegar in an iron
pot. Good ink it was, too, black and free flowing.

Dick resolved to tell Siah-hen about the five Indians, one of whom might have been Quimmo, that Silas Simmons had seen spying on the McDermott place, but it was not necessary. When he reached the teepee he found them there in solemn council with Siah-hen. Quimmo was the spokesman of the party. Since the death of old Clcck-a-tuck and the falling into disgrace of his son, Kil-a-poos, the Indians had tacitly chosen him to lead them out of their difficulties, and were resolved to hide him from the Sniapus at all costs.

As Dick came up he heard Quimmo say in Chinook, "*Nika til-a-cum wake muck-a-muck*" ("my people have no food"); "*ne-si-ka hi-yu o-lo*" ("we are much hungry"). They fell silent after greetings were exchanged, and Dick, feeling that the conversation was not for his ears, went on up to split rails for a fence that they were making.

He was angry with the Indians and perplexed at the situation. Here, like five-year-olds, they had traded and given away a large portion of their winter supplies to the settlers, who had greedily taken all they could get without a thought as to what the Indians would do for food through the winter. He knew that the whites would hoard what they had, and in all truth it was little enough, and leave the Indians to shift for themselves.

Darkness and supper-time finally forced Dick back to the teepee. The Indians were reluctantly leaving after having partaken largely of the food Siah-hen provided. He heard Siah-hen promise to secure *po-lal-ly* (gunpowder) for them at Vancouver on some condition whose provisions he did not catch, but their agreement was not so certain. Their mood was sullen; they scowled and shook angry heads, muttering something about "McDermott *hi-yu sap-o-lil*" ("McDermott has much wheat"), to which Siah-hen said something, evidently a warning in his strange unintelligible tongue, as he saw Dick coming up to the teepee.

Dick recounted the happenings of his first day at school to a delighted Indian, who seemingly forgot his perplexities in Dick's bubbling enthusiasm over his opportunity to study law. After supper both were occupied in fashioning a pair of shoes for Martha Bainbridge, working by the fitful light of a small candle inside the teepee. They intended to make a pair for Aunt Morning Ann Simmons also, in anticipation of a great event.

The winter before, "The Pioneer Lyceum and Debating Society" had been organized to while away the tedium of winter evenings with nothing to read, and this society had really been the cradle of government. It was through debates and arguments between the citizens that the Organic Law had been drafted and a government established in the meeting at Champoeg the last May.

During the activities of receiving the new emigration and the settling in their cabins the meetings had suspended, but now the Lyceum was to be a regular social feature in Oregon City. Every man, woman, and child who could possibly come would be there to listen to the discussion and the debates. Dick knew that Martha Bainbridge had never left the cabin,

much as she longed to see Oregon City.  She had
said but little about it; she was a proud woman, and
her lack of shoes had kept her out of sight as much
as possible.  Aunt Morning Ann, used to life in
Missouri, had not allowed notions of pride to stop her
going.  She went barefooted or with moccasins minus
stockings to church or wherever duty or inclination
led her.

The whole Bainbridge family was anxiously awaiting the eventful Friday night.  Dick and Siah-hen
were going.  Martha had urged Lassee to learn white
ways by mingling with the settlers and listening to
their discussions.  The Lyceum, sometimes called the
"Falls Association," so its sponsors stated, was "to
discuss the whole round of literature and scientific
pursuits."  No one living the starved intellectual life
of semi-isolation could afford to miss a single session.

Dick had, with fear and trepidation, mustered up
courage to ask Rose Ann if he might "see her home"
from the Lyceum, and his request had been granted
so graciously that he was put to it to conceal his surprise and delight.  This was at least a tacit acknowl-
edgment on Rose Ann's part that she recognized him
in the possible light of a suitor; but since starting
to school Rose Ann had many admirers, and distributed her smiles impartially.  Many a young swain,
as well as older ones, was hoping and guessing.

Rose Ann was independent, and inclined to be
quick and spunky in spite of her mother's constant
admonition.  On one occasion, during a visit of her
mother's to Aunt Morning Ann, she had threatened
to untie the dogs and set them on a persistent elderly

suitor who chanced to call at the cabin. Her father had rebuked her sternly, but she intended to make her own choice. The concensus of opinion was that Rose Ann, being seventeen in the spring, should be thinking seriously of marriage. Aunt Morning Ann constantly deplored the fact that the girl would be an old maid unless she married before she was eighteen, but Martha had always laughingly turned the subject. There was little danger of spinsterhood in a country where there were ten men, anxious to marry, to one single woman.

Dick, like all young lovers, hung between doubt and certainty. One day he was sure Rose Ann felt more than a sisterly interest in him, and the next day he was certain that she favored lanky Charlie Summers. The effort to determine whether to come out and settle the matter one way or the other, or to wait until he could be more certain of a favorable answer, reduced him to a pulp of helpless misery.

In the meantime Rose Ann was "all things to all men"; even her mother could not determine where Dick stood. Secretly Martha hoped Dick would be successful, but she wisely refrained from mentioning the matter to Rose Ann. She watched Dick closely. His secret was no secret to all. She felt helpless and sorry for him, while Rose Ann, exasperatingly noncommittal, showered smiles on Charlie Summers in poor Dick's presence.

Uncle Adzi's interest in the Lyceum was as great as that of the young folks. He confided to Martha that he intended to ask the sponsors of the society to make sure that "waterways to the sea and trade with ports of Chiny" be discussed at an early meeting. He had ingeniously contrived a lantern to light them to and from the meetings by piercing holes in a piece of tin and bending it into a sort of can with a socket for holding a candle and a hooded top to prevent the wind blowing out the flame. With a handle for carrying at the side this contrivance made it delightfully easy to cover the mile and a half of trail.

Martha had contrived to wash her linsey-woolsey dress and to apply patches so that she was clean and whole, and with her new shoes she fared forth as joyfully as the children. Pop Simmons and Aunt Morning Ann, with their restive brood of boys, were waiting where their path joined the main trail, and they proceeded to the huge granary of the Methodist mission, the largest building in Oregon City. The trustees had cleared almost the entire lower floor. The legislature would meet there the next time, and as this was only a few months away, the building might as well be used for public gatherings too large for the half-completed Methodist Church.

The upper floor was full of wheat, and some salmon and a few peltries had been piled compactly at one end, but there was abundant space. A puncheon table was arranged to hold the papers of the debaters, and there were puncheon benches for seating the audience. Joyful workers had put evergreen boughs up on the bare walls, giving the whole place a festive air. Families fortunate enough to have candles had brought one along to provide light. Most of these were placed at intervals along a narrow ledge behind the speaker's table. By allowing the melted tallow to drop in a little pool and then placing the candle in it they were held firmly in place. The cavernous room itself was engulfed in a huge twilight in which lovers surreptitiously held hands. Courting was in full swing among the callow youths of eighteen and nineteen and the fifteen to seventeen year old girls. It was rumored that some of the young folks were already "promised," but this was only conjecture. It was not considered modest or becoming in girls to discuss their matrimonial intentions until the wedding day; decorous women kept their love affairs strictly secret.

Sidney Moss was master of ceremonies. He reported with pardonable pride the progress of the pupils in his school, and, noticing many of the older pupils as well as a number of newcomers in the audience who were not thoroughly conversant with the political situation in Oregon, said that since this was the first government formed west of the Rocky Mountains, and would go down in history as a notable achievement, he proposed that the most salient portions of the Organic Law as drawn up and approved by the people July 5, 1843, should be read. He asked Elder Waller to read portions of the newly drawn Articles of Compact, explaining that when the legislature convened it would be expanded and perfected.

Elder Waller drew himself up to his full height and solemnly read the document, beginning:

"We, the people of Oregon Territory, for purposes of mutual protection, and to secure peace and prosperity among ourselves, agree to adopt the following laws and regulations, until such time as the United States of America shall extend their jurisdiction over us."

He went on, reading of judicial proceedings according to the course of common law as outlined in the Iowa code.

At Section Three he paused impressively and looked at the audience over his square horn-rimmed glasses. "This, brothers and sisters," he said, "is the most important article in the whole Organic Law. It determines the character of the great commonwealth we are forming from this small nucleus." There was breathless expectancy as he resumed his reading:

"Religion, morality, and knowledge being necessary to good government and the happiness of mankind, schools and means of education shall be forever encouraged."

There was loud applause as the Elder concluded. He waited for it to subside, then went on to the next provision:

"The utmost good faith shall always be observed toward the Indians. Their land and property shall never be taken away from them without their consent, and, in their property rights and liberty, they shall never be invaded or disturbed, unless in just and lawful wars, authorized by the representatives of the people, but, laws, founded in justice and humanity, shall, from time to time, be made, for preventing injustice being done to them, and for preserving peace and friendship with them."

A peculiar uneasiness ran over the audience. There was stirring and muttered conversation. Siah-hen, a little apart with Lassee, reached for her hand under

cover of the gloom and said something in the Klamath tongue. Lassee returned the pressure of his
hand and nodded gently; in her sore heart she understood Siah-hen's bitter despair. The grandiose dec-
larations of the Sniapus in regard to their treatment
of the Indians in settling on their lands did not agree
in any detail with their actual practice. They were
taking the land as fast as they came into the country, with no regard to the prior claims of the
Indian.

"*Kultus wa-wa*" ("Idle talk"), muttered Siah-
hen. "What the Sniapus wants he takes; he's strong
and wise. Our people are weak and child-like."

The droning voice of Elder Waller went on
through section after section. There were shouts of
enthusiastic approval and he concluded with the
promise to read more of the Organic Law at the next
meeting, adding that the people should be thoroughly
informed in regard to their government, so that suit-
able laws could be enacted when the legislature convened on the 18th of June.

All was then in readiness for the big feature of
the evening's program, the debate. The subject was
one of breathless interest: "Resolved, that it is expedient for the settlers of the Pacific coast to form
an independent government."

There were perspiring flights of oratory between
the speakers chosen to argue the momentous question. The argument for the affirmative was clear
and convincing, though the sentiment of the meeting
was always with the negative speakers who wished

to see the settlers come speedily under the wing of the government of the United States.

The affirmative speaker quoted from a speech of Senator Dickerson of New Jersey on the floor of the Senate in regard to the settlement of the Oregon country:

"The distance from the mouth of the Columbia to the mouth of the Missouri is 3,555 miles; from Washington to the mouth of the Columbia River 4,703 miles, but say 4,650 miles. The distance, therefore, that a member of Congress from the state of Oregon would be obliged to travel in coming to the seat of government and returning home would be 9,300 miles; this, at a rate of $8 per every twenty miles, would make his traveling expenses amount to $3,720. At the rate which members of Congress travel according to law—that is, twenty miles per day—it would require to come to the seat of government from Oregon and return, 465 days, and if he should lie by for Sundays, it would require 531 days. But if he should travel at the rate of thirty miles per day, it would require 306 days. Allow for Sundays, 44, it would amount to 350 days. This would allow a member a fortnight to rest himself at Washington before he should commence his journey home. This rate of traveling would be a hard duty, as the greater part of the way is exceedingly bad, and a portion of it over rugged mountains, where Lewis and Clarke found several feet of snow the latter part of June. Yet a young able-bodied Senator might travel from Oregon to Washington once a year, but he could do nothing else. It would be more expedient, however, to come by water round Cape Horn or to pass through Bering Straits round the north coast of this continent to Baffin's Bay, thence through the Davis Straits to the Atlantic, and so on to Washington. It is true this passage is not yet discovered except on the maps, but it will be as soon as Oregon shall be a state."

This scored heavily for the affirmative. Rather reluctantly the audience applauded the truth of the statement of the famous Senator. The speaker clinched his argument with an excerpt from another distinguished Senator from New Jersey, W. L. Dayton, in regard to the possibility of a railroad ever being built to connect the Pacific coast with the Atlantic seaboard.

"The power of steam has been suggested. Talk of steam communications, a railroad across 2,500 miles of prairie, of desert, and of mountains. The mines of Mexico and Peru disemboweled would scarcely pay a penny on the pound of cost. Nothing short of the lamp of Aladdin would suffice for such an expenditure."

The affirmative side won the debate on the sheer weight of evidence, the judges declared. It was against reason to hope that Oregon would ever be a state, but just the same, every loyal American hoped and fully expected that Oregon would one day come into the Union, and in the meantime, until the question as to whom the country would ultimately belong was settled, the people would govern themselves with order and democracy.

At the conclusion Sidney Moss promised that at the next meeting he would read from a novel he had recently written, called *Leni Leoti, or The Prairie Flower*, a story of crossing the plains and life in the Oregon country. He announced that plans were on foot to establish a circulating library, that one hundred shares were to be sold at five dollars a share. One hundred dollars had been sent to New York for books which would arrive within the year. Three hundred volumes had already been collected. The public library was to be known as the Multnomah Circulating Library.

"It is the intention of the promoters of this enterprise to keep out a certain type of light literature and to confine the books to serious subjects almost entirely. No books harmful to the young shall ever appear on its shelves," he stated emphatically. Everyone present declared that the meeting had been a great success.

There was the lighting of the candle lantern and a lingering outside by the young people to allow their elders to advance well upon the road home so that they might loiter a little along the trail as lovers have always done.

Dick was in the seventh heaven. He had at least made a public appearance with Rose Ann and thus tacitly announced his serious intentions to the world. In the accepted etiquette of courting he was now recognized as Rose Ann's beau. He hoped hard that he might maintain his precarious foothold that led to her favor.

Siah-hen and Lassee passed them on the way home, speaking together in their own tongue.

"What do you suppose they are saying, Dick?" Rose Ann asked.

Dick hesitated before he answered. "I think Siah-hen means to marry Lassee and take a 'tomahawk claim' on the land above mine. Lassee and he must live with white people; they can't be Indians any longer. They'll marry just as we will, Rose Ann."

"Why, how you talk, Dick Skelton!" Rose Ann exclaimed indignantly. Poor Dick realized, too late, that his tongue had slipped. The walk home was a miserable adventure, completed in a silence so dense and thick as to almost prevent breathing. Tortured young love is miserable in trying to find itself!

Aunt Morning Ann and Martha were joyful over the evening's entertainment. "Just to think," exulted Martha, "that in the newest frontier in all America we have a chance to spend an evening like this! We'll never miss a session of the Lyceum." To which Aunt Morning Ann whole-heartedly agreed.

"But," doubted Aunt Morning Ann, "I cain't think hit's rightful for Sidney Moss ter read no novel books afore all them young folks. Novel books air jest a pack o' lies, an' I'm fer truth in readin', but"— she laughed at her own inconsistency— "I kin hardly wait ter hear about this here Leny Leoty's adventures a-crossin' the plains."

As the party ascended the trail the sky suddenly lit up to the south. "Fire," the men shouted, and everyone stopped in terror.

"It's not a timber fire," said John Bainbridge, surveying the sky.

"No," said Pop Simmons. "Hit 'pears lak hit mout be McDermott's cabin."

"He war 'lowin' ter have me build a new chimney fer him, but I didn't git round ter hit," mourned Uncle Adzi. "I'd hate ter see my dearest enemy

lose his cabin when shelters air ez scarce ez they be
here. Let's go see if we-all kin put hit out er save
some o' the things." And they all hurried through
the timber.

When they came in sight of the building they
paused. "Hit's not the cabin; hit's the granary, an'
thet granary war plumb full o' wheat and salmon an'
all kinds of pervisions. He had a power o' fine
seed taters inter one o' them thar bins." Uncle Adzi
was inconsolable at the loss, when food was so scarce
and hard to get.

By this time most of the attendance of the Lyceum
had seen the fire and were arriving in groups, but
there was nothing to be done. The building was a
mass of flames before anyone had noticed the glow
in the sky. The Calkins family had been at the
Lyceum, too.

"I told him last fall when I war a-helpin' him harvest 'twar dangersome ter store wheat ontil hit was
clean dry an' hard. Hit'll combust o' itself sometimes
an' burn down a buildin'," one ganky Missourian
affirmed.

As Dick and Siah-hen left the party to go on up
the trail, Dick observed thoughtfully: "That granary didn't burn like it was full of wheat; it looked to
me like an empty building. It was over so soon.

Siah-hen shrugged his shoulders and grunted, refusing to talk any more that night. Dick felt that
in some way he had offended his friend, but for the
life of him he could not tell what he had said.

# CHAPTER XVII

THE spring of 1844 was exceptionally early. An unusually mild spell along about the last of January had permitted working the light well-drained soil on the south slope. Martha Bainbridge was incredulous when the older settlers began putting in their early gardens. She was almost afraid to risk her scant stock of seeds, but finally planted a portion of the pea, lettuce, turnip, beet, and onion seeds that Siah-hen had brought her from Vancouver.

By early April, when the real farm work began, John and Uncle Adzi had finished their rail-splitting, and nearly all the clear land was under fence, awaiting the plough. The buildings were roofed with water-tight shakes. The winter had been one of driving hard work for the whole family, but they were more than satisfied with the results.

"I 'low we got more right now than ever we had back hum," Uncle Adzi gloated to John as they looked out over their holdings while they rested by the cabin door in the soft April twilight.

Siah-hen had given them a dozen of the fruit trees he had secured from Doctor McLoughlin's orchard at Vancouver. Fruit trees were treasures indeed. The little orchard was tightly fenced with shake pickets to keep the deer from destroying the tender little trees that were now unfurling soft green leaves.

The only grafted trees in the whole country were

those McDermott had so tenderly cherished, but his long rows of seedlings had been destroyed by the longhorns. His renter, Calkins, had had a round of trouble with the Indians since McDermott's disappearance. The fences that held heretofore had often been mysteriously lowered in the night.

"No wonder McDermott thought best ter leave the kentry," Calkins had complained to John and Uncle Adzi one day. "The Injuns air a-takin' their spite out on his farm. Fust his granary goes up in flames, then they keep his fences down so's the cattle's purty nigh destroyed his orchard that he'd depended on stockin' the whole kentry with grafts fer fruit trees. Them thar trees 's a loss to all of us."

But the fruit trees from Vancouver were good of their kind. The apples and pears were just seedlings, but the peaches were good and the plums and sour cherries threw out suckers from the roots, making good-sized trees that came true to variety in no time. William Bruce, Doctor McLoughlin's Scotch gardener, had a wonderful flair for breeding up trees and plants. He had given Siah-hen a number of thrifty grape roots and a quantity of fine strawberry plants that by intensive cultivation and natural selection he had developed from the wild strawberries that covered the sunny slopes. Siah-hen had been so delighted to divide with the Bainbridges that his gift brought an added pleasure to them.

"This here's a healthy climate," Uncle Adzi went on as he whittled pegs. "My rheumatiz hain't pestered me none ter speak of, an' me a-workin' all day in the rain in wet buckskins. Oregon sure is healthy

fer folks as well as fer fruit trees an' sech.  Pop
Simmons 'lows we'll have ter kill a man when we git
ready ter start our graveyard."

"No chills and fever here.  I'm glad to get out of
having the ague every year," supplemented John.

"John, we'd better go to Oregon City airly to-
morrer ter git the plough stocked.  I'm fair eitchin'
ter turn over this black sile with a plough," said
Uncle Adzi.

"We'll raise wheat for our bread, and have some
to sell; we must plan on plenty of oats and cut enough
wild hay to last next winter.  We'll buy or trade for
cattle if we can manage it next fall," said John.

"There's be a big demand fer all sorts o' garden
sass when the next emigration comes in.  Us ez is
here a'ready must raise all we kin, er the kentry
cain't support the settlers ontil they kin git a crap
outen the sile.  Seed taters air mighty scarce.  It's
a cryin' shame McDermott's granary burned with
that bin o' seed taters," Uncle Adzi said.

"There'll be seed potatoes enough," comforted
John.

"We cain't ship ter the ports in Chiny yet awhile,"
he admitted regretfully.  "We gotter supply hum
consumption, but we'll be a-exportin' afore many
years, or my name hain't Adzi Clarke."

"Oh yes, in time, perhaps."  John was musing on
other things.

"I was plannin' on making Marthie some cheers an'
a-puttin' a mantel over the fireplace with a planed
board from the mill, but about all I'm going ter git
done this spring is a home-made cookin'-stove lak

Sister Waller invented." Uncle Adzi talked on as much to himself as to the silent John.

Sister Waller's home-made cooking-stove was the envy and admiration of every woman in the settlement. They all planned to make them as soon as circumstances permitted; they saved the heavy lifting and would be such a convenience when there was flour for baking bread. Sister Waller had made a frame of oakwood with a firebox and a compartment for an oven at the back, then covered it all over with wet clay. When the clay dried hard enough to prevent cracking, she built a low fire, and finally succeeded in burning out the oak framework, leaving the clay intact. Brother Parrish, the mission blacksmith, had fitted an iron top and contrived doors for the firebox and the oven, and Sister Waller had been cooking and baking with this stove for seven or eight years.

Martha came up from the hen-house with a dozen eggs in an Indian basket. John had made a special trip to French Prairie early in January with six pairs of Martha's wool socks and had had no difficulty in trading them for a dozen hens and a rooster. With the warming up of the weather every hen was laying right up to capacity.

"We'll have eggs to eat from now on," Martha told them proudly. "I'll lay by the best for hatching, and set every broody hen we have. I just came through the garden; the lettuce and onions and radishes will be large enough to eat in another ten days, and the peas we planted in January are showing the buds; the beets and turnips are nearly large

enough to thin out for greens. I never expected to
live in a country where garden stuff came along in
April. We'll never be short on our table again.
Boiled wheat and salmon will be just memories from
this on."

But this was the enchanted season of the year—
spring in Oregon. The air was drowsy with the
drone of insects and sweet with bird-song. The
near-by hills were masses of pink flowering currant.
Esther Amelia wandered happily, bringing in great
bunches of wake-robin and gracefully nodding
lamb's-tongue, or dog-toothed violets.

Lassee made excursions to the woods almost daily
to bring in delicious wild things for food. She gathered thick, succulent shoots of the wild raspberry to
boil with a few shreds of bacon rind, or cooked the
tender new curled fronds of the white fern. ' She
found wild cresses by the streams and miner's lettuce in the deep shade. She caught trout by a method
all her own.

Lassee was a joy to the Bainbridges. She adjusted herself to the simple ways of the household,
becoming one of them, going about with Martha to
church or to the women's gatherings, helping with
the spinning and knitting as Martha taught her.
She read aloud in her turn by the evening candle-
light. Except for her copper-tinted skin, Lassee
was in no way different from the white women. She
still wore her buckskin dress; so did Rose Ann and
Esther Amelia; but Martha had enough credit at the
trading-post to buy them all everyday dresses of blue

drilling, and sprigged calico for Sundays, when the ships brought in yardage.

Martha attended every meeting of the Lyceum and took the family to church on Sundays. They came to know their neighbors and joined in the spelling-bees and cabin-raisings all over the settlement. Life in Oregon City did not differ in the least from other frontier settlements with its simple joys and numerous vexations.

The way Dick Skelton had prospered was the talk of the whole country. The first cabin-raising had been for him. His cabin stood complete even to puncheon floors and two pegs behind the door. One for the pink calico sunbonnet and the other for the wedding dress of the same luxurious material. All was in readiness for his bringing home a bride. Dick had done remarkably well with his cobbling. He had worm fences in place, and a good orchard set out and inclosed. The neighbors freely admitted that Siah-hen had really set him on his feet. Siah-hen came to be called "that white Injun."

There was lively curiosity as to whom Dick's bride would be. It was agreed all over the country that he was "a good match" for any girl. He had studied clear through the blue Iowa code of laws and was waiting for law books to come in so that he could be admitted to the bar, and he had a good claim and made money cobbling shoes. Dick Skelton was a rising young man.

There were numerous worries and vexations over difficulties with the Indians. Supplies had run low in the villages and they were pilfering. Calkins declared that McDermott's cattle were being driven off by them, that there had been eighty-eight head when he came to live on the farm, and that now there were less than fifty, but there was no proof that they had been stolen. Cattle were often lost in the timber for months.

In February, feeling had run very high over the liquor question, particularly as the Indians had given Oregon City a good scare, when Cockstock and a few followers, painted for war and brandishing tomahawks, galloped into town. During the skirmish that followed two white men were killed. The fight was due to a misunderstanding. Cockstock was merely seeking an interpreter to adjust a difficulty over his failure to secure pay for work he had done, but the timid ones lived in daily dread of an Indian uprising and especially when the Indians were securing liquor from sources that could not be determined.

A man named Conover had started to operate a distillery. Joe Meek, the jovial mountain man who had been elected marshal at the founding of the new government, had gone in the name of the new commonwealth and confiscated the still. In a facetious mood he had made a trumpet out of the worm and shouted the fact that liquor should not be manufactured in Oregon; but until the legislature met in June there was no law to be enforced, and nothing but the vigilance of the citizens could protect the country from uprisings of drunken Indians as well as degenerate whites.

The Sons and Daughters of Temperance was quickly organized. The women of the settlement joined the "Sons and Daughters" *en masse*. Martha, Lassee, and Aunt Morning Ann had not missed one of the fortnightly meetings, so determined were they that the curse of liquor should never gain a foothold in Oregon.

Spring passed delightfully with its round of outside duties. One very warm day about the middle of May Lassee came into the cabin with a basket of wild strawberries and sat down to hull them. "Aunt Martha," she said slowly, after working awhile in silence, "our buckskins are too warm and your linsey-woolsey will hardly hold together." She averted her face, finding it difficult to speak. She had never before referred to her grief. "I hid my clothes when I left McDermott. I knew the squaws at the lodge would take them away and I couldn't bear to see them wearing them. There are two woollen dresses and four blue cotton ones. I'm going after them to-morrow morning. We can each have a summer dress. You and Rose Ann are small enough to wear them and one can be cut down for Esther Amelia."

Martha laid a tender hand on Lassee's head. "Don't get them unless you want to, honey," she admonished. "The ships'll be coming in any time soon now, with cloth. When the hurt is all gone from your heart you can wear your dresses."

Lassee looked shyly up at Martha. "The hurt is gone now," she said simply. "And we need the dresses. Siah-hen says I must not be an Indian any more. We love our people, but he is like a white man, and for his sake I must never go back to Indian ways. He and Dick are building a cabin up above Dick's place. He has set out a little orchard and will have a farm," she went on proudly. She turned shy again. "Siah-hen has made a 'marriage tree' near his cabin. He showed it to me. He means that I am to marry him." She resumed work.

Lassee rose before daylight and went after her clothing. It was a good three miles from the Bainbridge cabin. She paused as she picked her way up the narrow trail and looked down to where the Clackamas shimmered in the early morning light. She could see the deserted lodge on the high promontory where the two rivers joined. An involuntary shiver ran through her as she recalled the terrible days when she was a captive there. But the place was quiet enough now; the Indians had scattered on their food-gathering missions, some fishing, the squaws to the camas-beds and to their root-gathering. Soon they would be gathering berries in the mountains. Dumbly she prayed to keep from going back to the customs of her people as Indian women almost invariably did as age crept upon them. She would cling to white ways for Siah-hen's sake, and keep his cabin clean and be a companion to him. She felt no bitterness toward McDermott, only a fierce unreasoning anger, wholly without jealousy, that he should want Rose Ann.

She looked around as she reached the overhanging rock where she had spent the night after leaving McDermott's cabin. Some one had been there lately; there were footprints in the dry dust under the rock. She went anxiously around, fearing they had discovered her hiding-place and taken her clothing.

She went to the narrow entrance hidden behind the
rock and stooped to enter the mouth of the cave.
Lifting a fair-sized rock, she uncovered the recess
where she had hidden her bundle.  It was still there,
dry and intact, but as she became accustomed to the
semi-gloom of the cave mouth, she saw the fresh footprints.  Curiously she looked carefully about the
walls of the outside entrance, that, like a vestibule,
had its inner recesses.  She knew the cave went back
into the bowels of the bluff, but had never explored
farther than the entrance.  Her quick eye noted a
flint and tinder-box on a small ledge and a small pile
of pitch knots that were evidently placed there to
be used for torches.  She lit one and felt of the rocks
in the wall until she found a large one that had been
carefully placed before the entrance of an inner
chamber.  She pushed it aside with all her strength
and crawled into the recess.

She was in a good-sized room, holding the torch
to see what the chamber was like.  It was filled with
five-gallon kegs, and on a ledge stood jugs and dark
brown bottles.  She cautiously opened one and smelled
its contents.  Wheat whisky!

She came out swiftly and extinguished the torch,
putting the tinder-box exactly in place, and, taking
her bundle in its bright blanket on her back, hurried
home.  Martha was just finishing breakfast as she
came; there were two good hours of chores to be done
before the men were ready to eat.

When breakfast was over and the roll of clothing
had been examined and exulted over, and tears had
fallen over little Sintwa's bits of finery, Lassee made

an opportunity to call Martha aside. Schooled as she had been all her life to patience and self-control, she could hardly wait in her eagerness to impart her news.

"Aunt Martha," she whispered when the two had reached the picketed garden behind the barn, "I have found a big cache of liquor in the cave overlooking the Clackamas. I hid my bundle there behind a rock, because I knew the Indians wouldn't take it from there. They say the cave is full of evil spirits. When I went back this morning I saw a man's tracks in the dust and found a flint and tinderbox. The casks are there in a recess hidden behind a big rock."

Martha was immediately business-like. "Could I climb up there?" she asked.

"Yes, you could, or I know a little longer way to come in from above, up past Aunt Morning Ann's house. It's not so steep and rocky that way," answered Lassee.

Martha was hurrying to the cabin, attending to a few necessary duties before setting out. "Rose Ann and Esther Amelia must see to dinner to-day. Esther Amelia, be sure to feed the little chickens twice while I'm gone and give them fresh water at noon," she directed.

"We'll just keep this to ourselves and let the children guess where we are going," she whispered to Lassee. "We'll stop and get Aunt Morning Ann on the way up." She was putting a piece of jerky and a dish of wheat hominy in her basket as she spoke,

"We'll find strawberries at noon. This is going to be a busy day for us and we'll need plenty to eat."

Aunt Morning Ann was just finishing up her morning work about the cabin as her visitors knocked. She was all eagerness to hear their story, sending her two reluctant boys back to their weeding at a knowing look from Martha.

"You younguns weed two rows o' carrots while mammy's gone," she told the children sternly after she had heard about the liquor and had given directions for warming up the dinner for Pop and the boys who were busy in the timber.

"We have a basket of luncheon," said Martha.

"I 'low I'll cut one o' my cheeses. I done made four. Them two cows Doctor McLoughlin loaned us picked up right smart in their milk when the grass come on. Pop's been urgin' me to cut one fer the las' few days." She led them to her spring-house with its crocks of milk set in the trough of water that ran through the house and out into the little stream below. Proudly she displayed her four five-pound cheeses ripening on the puncheon shelf. She carefully turned each one, thumping them to see which was cured the most, and finally cut a generous slice to put in Martha's basket.

"Mebbe you think I warn't glad ter make cheese ag'in. Pop got rennet from a farmer up on French Prairie. He kills a calf every year jest ter make rennet. I'll give ye some, Marthie, when ye git ready ter make cheese."

She tied her sunbonnet under her double chin and they started through the woods. Lassee led the way, pausing at steep places to help Aunt Morning Ann. Martha needed no assistance; she was as quick and nimble as a girl. The climb to the cave was a long, hard one. Aunt Morning Ann was panting when they reached the rock at the entrance, but all three were in high spirits. Here was high adventure with the delightful spice of secrecy.

"Wal, I swan!" ejaculated Aunt Morning Ann, after Lassee and Martha had moved the rock from the inner recess and the three had stooped nearly double to enter. "I got a li'l' secret, too. I bin a-puzzlin' over hit quite a spell, but this here find o' Lassee's cl'ars things up in my mind. Ye know, McDermott hain't lef' the kentry at all. I seed him a-ridin' roun' the rim o' the hill one day las' week when I war a-gatherin' strawberries. He never let on lak he seed me, an' I never, neither, but hit sot me ter thinkin'."

Martha made a startled exclamation. "He'll never dare to show his face in the settlement again," she said with a puzzled frown between her eyebrows. "Mrs. Calkins told me just a few days ago that she thought he had gone out on one of the boats."

"Them Calkinses sure is a-featherin' o' their nest. They'll say jest what McDermott tells 'em ter say. I reckon this here cache belongs ter him. What say? Thet's whut brung him past our place."

Martha shook a puzzled head, but Lassee nodded and smiled. "I think so," she said, fingering the flint and tinder-box. "I thought this morning I'd seen this box before. McDermott knows the Indians; hardly any of them will come near this place.

Quimmo told him about it years ago, and laughed at the superstitions of his people. Quimmo's not afraid of anything."

"But McDermott's never been a drinking man," protested Martha.

"Thet hain't a-sayin' he's above sellin' the cussed stuff," retorted Aunt Morning Ann. "He's a sly, ornery varmint allus a-gittin' some one ter do his dirty work fer him. I heared the other day thet thet thar Klanic war drunk an' had a fight 'ith t'other Injun—whut's his name?"

"Cartoosh," Lassee said smilingly. "They don't need to be drunk to have a fight."

But Martha had risen. "We'll just take care of the cache and find out who it belongs to afterward," she laughed.

The three women tugged the casks slowly to the mouth of the cave. Like children in mischief, they laughed as each cask rolled into place.

"Hit's gonna be a hard chore, but wuth the work," Aunt Morning Ann chuckled.

"But an enjoyable one for three Daughters of Temperance," said Martha, tugging at her cask.

There was a sheer drop of a hundred feet to the river below. As they pulled the bungs from cask after cask the gurgle of five gallons of mellow old wheat whisky was sweet music in the ears of the three perspiring women. It took them nearly all day. Just before the last one was opened Aunt Morning Ann wiped the beads of perspiration from her forehead and paused thoughtfully.

"His mout be a good idear to make a li'l' cache o'

this one our own selves, Marthie," she counciled. "Ye know thar's boun' ter be sickness in the settlement an' sometimes a li'l' good liquor'll save a life. We'll never let airy man know whar we're a-gettin' hit. Cain't afford ter have a passel o' sick men on our han's." The three of them laughed hilariously.

"I know where to hide it," said Lassee. "We can roll it back in the farthest recess and cover it up with stones; they'll never think of looking there for it."

"Hit's lucky these bottles an' jugs is all brown glass," exulted Aunt Morning Ann. "They cain't tell they're empty ontil they heft 'em. We'll save us a bottle, too. We still got all those jugs an' bottles ter empty, an' hit's not a hour ontil sundown."

"Let's put the casks and bottles back just as we found them," said Martha with a sudden inspiration. "We'll have our little joke on them when they come to lower them to take them down the river in canoes. I think that's the way they plan to get them out of here."

"I can't remember when I've had such a good time in one day before," smiled Lassee, as they finished their task with whole-souled enjoyment and made their way home, leaving the cave exactly as they found it, with not so much as a footprint to betray their presence there.

# CHAPTER XVIII

SIAH-HEN'S marriage tree was growing. He told Lassee one day in late August that the tree would shelter them in their old age. From the time of the plighting the troth when the marriage tree is made until there is certainty of its survival is an anxious period for Indian lovers. Should the tree languish and finally die the omens for a happy marriage are not suspicious. The more superstitious wait until another season for forming a marriage alliance, or do not marry at all.

A marriage tree cut at the right time and under favorable conditions does not die. The whole countryside bore mute testimony to the love of young braves and squaws for each other, for generations uncounted. A young Indian having fallen desperately in love selects a straight, promising young yellow fir tree and carefully splits it from the top down to within a foot or so of the ground, holding the sections apart by a wedge of wood. If the tree survives, the bark quickly heals over the cut surface, making two trees springing from one root.

Siah-hen's cabin was in readiness. He had selected a claim just above Dick's and hoped that he would be able to hold it without molestation. Uncle Adzi had taken special pains with the fireplace and John Bainbridge and Pop Simmons had helped to raise the cabin, taking fully as much interest in Siah-hen as they had in Dick Skelton. His orchard had flourished from the first, and by changing work with his friends his little farm differed in no way from those of the other settlers.

Elder Waller married Lassee and Siah-hen. Both had held aloof from the Indians since Lassee's unfortunate experience at the lodge, though Siah-hen had carried their differences to Doctor McLoughlin at Vancouver and counciled them in their difficulties. The good Doctor had taken no steps to discipline anyone over the attempted slave burial, holding that they had punished the guilty medicine-men according to their tribal custom.

He had refused the request of a delegation of citizens of Oregon City to turn Quimmo over to them, after hearing Quimmo's story of the capsizing of the canoe in coming down the Columbia. The evidence against him had been flimsy. Quimmo had been unable to handle the boat when one of the occupants lost his cap and stood up in the effort to regain it. Doctor McLoughlin believed he told the truth and said so in emphatic terms to the men who insisted that for the safety of the whites they would hold their price on the Indian's head.

The Indians were returning from their various excursions at the time of Siah-hen and Lassee's marriage, and Quimmo headed the party who visited them on the evening of their wedding day to beg them to allow the tribe to give them a marriage feast and to perform the ancient ceremonies celebrating their union. Neither was willing at first, but Quimmo pointed out that they wished to make what amends they could for their treatment of Lassee and to cement friendship by showing their good will, so consent was rather reluctantly given and the delegation departed at once to make preparations for the feast, which would last three days.

"They just want you to make them presents for me," said Lassee, when their guests had gone. "And I do not belong to any of their households. I am free. McDermott gave me my freedom when he cast me off."

But Siah-hen soothed her. "They're just sorry, little one," he said. "You and I will keep to the ways of the whites, but we must not estrange ourselves from our people, or we cannot help them when they need us." To which Lassee finally agreed.

Early next morning Siah-hen and Lassee presented themselves at the lodge where the elaborate preparations were under way. A splendid new blanket was placed under the spreading pow-wow maple. Lassee was taken in charge by the squaws in the main lodge, and Siah-hen went to a smaller lodge a little apart. At the appointed time Lassee was borne to the outspread blanket on the back of a squaw and Siah-hen on the back of a brave. Each was completely covered with a blanket and great care was taken that their feet did not touch the ground. The blankets were then removed, disclosing the rather sheepish Siah-hen and Lassee, who had somehow lost taste for Indian ceremony. The pipe was smoked all around and speeches made declaring eternal friendship and lauding the brave deeds of Siah-hen and the gentleness and docility of Lassee, and then an old squaw who had second sight, so everyone believed, performed the feather dance about the bride and groom, to drive away evil spirits forever.

The feather dance must be performed three times for as many days while the dancing and feasting go on. It was a fantastic dance watched with breathless interest by all the Indians. The old squaw circled widely about the pow-wow tree, throwing feathers in the air and making a peculiar gurgling cry as the circling narrowed until it included only the pair on the blanket.

Taken altogether, the marriage feast of Siah-hen and Lassee was gay and happy, every Indian making a child-like effort to please, thus tacitly admitting their sorrow for the wrong done Lassee and their wish to be forgiven. There were the most elaborate presents that the lodge afforded—heaps of bright new blankets, new cooking-pots, splendid strings of beads, finely woven mats and baskets, and elaborately beaded and stitched buckskins. Quimmo presented seven ponies, and of course there were any number of dogs. Provisions were not overlooked. There were ammunition and stores of dried salmon, a sack of fish pemmican, besides generous quantities of dried blackberries, camas, and wappatoes. Siah-hen was a rich man according to their standards, and they were joyful for him; he had interceded for them with the great "White-headed Eagle" many times when they were in difficulty and had counciled with them and arbitrated in their differences. Even as late as the early spring he had gone to Vancouver and gotten supplies and ammunition on credit to be

paid when the salmon catch was in. All of the virtues
of Siah-hen were extolled over and over in speeches
during the three wearing days of the feast.

Siah-hen and Lassee endured the ceremonies politely, Siah-hen making a speech expressing his gratitude and his friendship for his people and above all
his desire to help them and keep them out of difficulties with the Sniapus. He cautioned them against
pilfering and told them what it would lead to, and
they hung their heads rather shamefacedly, though
he mentioned no names or no specific instances.

As they left the lodge the third night, Lassee,
cradled in the bend of Siah-hen's arm, spoke softly:
"We must turn from the ways of our people. While
we were among them I longed to wrap a blanket
around me and sit by the lodge fire again. Wild
ways are in our blood. It's harder for a woman to
break away than for a man. We must not go back
to the lodge for feasts or ceremonies. We must cling
to our white friends. The feel of the new buckskin,
smelling of smoke, brings back my old longing for
the teepee. We must forget our language; never let
it be spoken between us. I loathe the life, and yet
I will always long for it."

Siah-hen assented, and there was a long silence between them, a silence that needed no words. He
understood Lassee's inward struggle, knowing that
his would be a struggle, too, and that each must
support the other.

"The Indian must learn the way of the plough,"
he said at last. "The advance guard of this year's
emigration is already in Oregon City, and they re-

port a thousand on the way. 'Twill increase from
year to year. There will soon be no hunting-ground,
and if our people are to survive they must follow
white ways."

"Yes," agreed Lassee. "We must try to teach
them, but they do not want to learn."

"No, they are stubborn," said Siah-hen, "but the
wiser among them see that within a few years their
lodges will be gone. The game goes when the plough
comes, and the ruthless white man kills for pleasure.
We will have our last *battue* this fall; after that each
man must hunt for himself. Fire cannot be used to
keep the forest floor clean; 'twould destroy the settlers' homesteads."

But the little cabin that was home to them stood
clear cut in the bright summer moonlight and the
melancholy mood changed to one of hopefulness as
they approached their home with its promise of
security and peace and plenty through the years to
come.

Siah-hen assumed his round of duties with the joy
that comes with any form of creation; he was building a home, and Lassee moved about the cabin with
happiness in her heart. Life, after all, was good.
Routine duties, while they irked at times, were necessary to keep the mind balanced.

He was extending his fences so that more land
would be ready for fall ploughing after the first
rains when McDermott came through the timber on
his calico pony. He was not the complacent, well-
fed McDermott who had disappeared so mysteriously
from the settlement, but a hunted, haggard man,

careless in his clothing and unkempt as to beard.
He was driving three longhorn cows with young
calves by their sides. He rounded them up carefully
and drove them inside the fence Siah-hen was laying,
to prevent their running away, before he stopped to
talk.

Siah-hen paused, seeing that McDermott wished
to talk to him, waiting politely for him to open the
subject on his mind. He cleared his throat a time
or two before he found words to make a beginning.
His errand was by no means a pleasant one.

Siah-hen's silence was discomfiting. McDermott
pointed to the three cows running around the fence
seeking an outlet to the inclosure, and said at length:
"I'm bringing you a *potlatch*, Siah-hen. Did Lassee
tell you that I promised to make her rich when she
married?"

Siah-hen shook a noncommittal head, but made
no answer.

"These three cows with their calves are for you,
sort of a marriage portion," he tried to laugh, but
Siah-hen's face was grave and the laugh suddenly
died in his threat. He looked furtively about to be
sure that there was no one within earshot, then sat
down on the end of a log, motioning to Siah-hen to
take a seat beside him. Siah-hen did not notice the
gesture and remained standing, waiting for McDermott to speak.

"I want to make a bargain with you, Siah-hen,"
he said slowly. "I'll make you rich if you do as I
ask you. You have influence with your people, es-

pecially with Quimmo, and you must exert it or it will go hard with the whole tribe."

"How?" asked Siah-hen shortly.

"They're hounding me, and Quimmo means to kill me," he said.

"Why should Quimmo kill you?" Siah-hen questioned sharply.

"You know well enough," McDermott answered angrily.

Siah-hen shrugged his shoulders.

"I went to a cabin way back in the mountains. No one knew where it was but Klanic and Cartoosh, and they would not tell."

"Unless they were drunk," Siah-hen interrupted.

McDermott started involuntarily, but went on. "Quimmo found the cabin in less than a week. He left a bundle of peach twigs on the table, so that I would know he had been there."

Siah-hen shrugged his shoulders again.

"Quimmo stood in my doorway one evening at dusk. Before I could get my gun he was gone, but twice after that I caught a glimpse of him and once I heard him laugh under my window in the middle of the night. I'll kill him if I ever get within range of him," McDermott concluded heatedly.

"You'll never get within range of Quimmo," Siah-hen laughed derisively. "The Indians'll give you no peace. I'd advise you to leave the country," Siah-hen warned, sobering.

MccDermott took no notice, but went on pouring out his harassed soul. "And that's not all. The cabin burned one day while I was away for an hour or so, and I had to come back and live with Calkins."

"Yes, I know," said Siah-hen.

"How did you know?" demanded McDermott.

"Indians know everything," declared Siah-hen. "Did you think you could hide from them any place in the country?"

McDermott paled as he continued: "Calkins is threatening to leave, the Indians have made him so much trouble. He can't keep a fence on the place. The stock was in the grain fields so much that he hardly got a crop. The cattle have been driven off. I have only about twenty head left."

"Why do you lay all this to the Indians?" Siah-hen asked patiently.

"You know why well enough," McDermott began angrily, but checked himself. "You know that my granary was empty when it burned. My grape vines were ruined. The trees in my orchard are all dying. They were girdled just below the ground in June."

Siah-hen shook his head, but made no answer.

"It's got to stop. I'll not be driven out of the country by a few greasy Injuns. Last night my milk cows were fed blue larkspur. They were shut up in the barnyard. Three of them were dead this morning. Larkspur grows in only one place in this locality—way up back of the third bench on that south slope, but we found an armload of it in the barnyard this morning."

"There's a price on Quimmo's head," said Siah-hen irrelevantly. "Two hundred dollars, I think. You put up that money, didn't you? Hadn't you better withdraw it? White-headed Eagle refuses to turn Quimmo over to the Sniapus for trial. Do you think he capsized that canoe on purpose?"

"He's dangerous to the settlers," McDermott insisted virtuously. "I merely took that step as a measure of safety."

"Yes, safety for yourself," Siah-hen sneered, drawing himself up angrily. "You'd better leave the country, McDermott. Take my warning."

"You could stop this if you saw fit," said McDermott.

"I use my influence to keep peace between my people and the Sniapus, but they are unruly. They killed a *keel-al-ly* and his five helpers along in the winter because he had deceived them. You're a false *keel-al-ly*; you've always lied to them and duped them and they know it now. But you know what happened at the lodge this last winter without my telling you." Siah-hen closed the subject abruptly and turned to his work.

McDermott lingered in spite of Siah-hen's dismissal. "You call off the Indians for a month or so and I promise you I'll leave the country," he pleaded. "I'll make you rich. I'll give you all the cattle I have left."

"Withdraw your money and let Quimmo go and come as he likes, and you'll not be molested," promised Siah-hen, poising a rail that he was preparing to place on the fence.

"Quimmo is only to be brought up for trial," argued McDermott. "If he's not guilty he won't be harmed."

"Indians have but little faith in American justice. Cockstock only rode into Oregon City to find an interpreter this summer, to have his troubles adjusted fairly, and he was killed in the fight. No one took the trouble to find out what it was about. Sniapus shoot first and investigate afterward. Take the price off Quimmo's head and the matter will soon be forgotten. You know Quimmo, McDermott; he's not guilty of capsizing that boat." Siah-hen paused hopefully for McDermott's answer.

"No!" shouted McDermott angrily. "And I'll shoot him if I can ever draw a bead on him." He fingered the gun at his belt threateningly, as if he might shoot any Indian who displeased him.

But Siah-hen paid no attention to his veiled threat, going nonchalantly on laying his rails, while McDermott, pale with anger, mounted his calico pony and started off through the timber.

As if struck by a sudden though, Siah-hen called after him. "Thank you kindly for the *potlatch*, Mr. McDermott. Three cows and calves will stock the farm in a short time." He grinned with whole-souled enjoyment as McDermott made no answer but struck the pony viciously to hurry him along.

Siah-hen hastened to finish his fence to keep the cows inside the inclosure. He had worked only a few minutes when a large stooped Indian emerged from a clump of underbrush.

"Kla-how-yam [good day], squaw-man," he grunted derisively, his pock-marked face hard and sullen, though his eyes lit up with his greeting.

"Quimmo, you heard what McDermott said just now?" Siah-hen inquired.

"*A-ha* [yes]," said Quimmo scornfully. "Mamook memaloose [make dead]. He no let *ni-ka ty-ee bat-tue* [me master of the battue]. *Yah-ka mamook ni-ka sol-lex* [he make me angry]."

"Only make matters worse," Siah-hen said decisively. "You kill McDermott, then the Sniapus hunt you out and hang you. You keep out of sight now, they soon forget."

But Quimmo shook a perplexed head. Always since he was old enough he had been master of the great fall hunt, a position requiring great skill. Being deprived of this privilege was a far worse grievance than anything he had yet suffered at McDermott's hands.

"*Sawnik chah-co tyee battue. Yah-ka wa-ke kum-tux* [Sawnik will be chief of the battue. He does not understand]. *Is-kum wake itl-wil-lee* [Get no meat]."

For a long time Siah-hen argued with him, lapsing into their strange tongue. Quimmo understood very little English and seldom attempted to use an English word.

But at last he rose to go in to dinner with Siah-hen, leaving the matter still unsettled. Quimmo would make no attempt to be master of the hunt unless he could in some way be cleared, and both agreed that this seemed hopeless.

# CHAPTER XIX

SUMMER was over. The first rains would shortly set in. The Indian roads were thronged with the returning tribes laden with their winter stores of food. The Indian is a natural engineer in his road-building. Nearly always these ancient highways climbed the points of the hills and coursed along the sharp backbones of the mountains to avoid fallen timber, as well as to reach the natural passes leading to the waterways in the valleys. These roads, unmarked by blazed trees or sign-posts, were often wide enough to allow three horses to walk abreast and were many times worn down to three feet below the surface of the ground by the tread of countless generations of moccasined feet.

From the Clatsop beaches they came with loads of clams. The patient squaws had straps of buckskin fitted about their heads to hold their heavy loads in place on their bent backs, and perhaps atop the load blinked a black-eyed papoose riding sedately in his *te-cash*. Troops of laughing children, half naked, each girl with her little burden on her back, capered about, while walking leisurely behind, with arms folded at ease, came the lordly braves.

From the berry patches on the west slopes of Mount Hood they came with ponies loaded with baskets of *shot o-lil-lee* (blue huckleberries). The berry harvest had been a bountiful one. When baskets

were exhausted, buckskin pantaloons with the legs
tied at the bottom had been pressed into service as
carriers. A horse could carry four or even five of
these filled to the brim with *o-lil-lees* astride his back.

The *le-mo-lo sap-o-lil* (wild wheat, or tar weed)
had all been gathered and winnowed and the whole
countryside could now be baptized in fire. It was in
this way that they had kept the forest floors clean and
free from the tangled underbrush that grew up so
rapidly after the settlers' advent. The Indian in his
hunting must be able to see his game as well as keep
the space open to provide pasture for the deer.

The Indians looked eagerly forward to the great
fall hunt, or *battue*, when they took their supply of
winter meat. There was a certain sadness about the
*battue* this year; in all probability it would be the
final one. The settlers were fearful for their cabins,
but for this last once, preparations were being made
on an elaborate scale. Every boy old enough to
manage a bow, and all the decrepit old men, would
take part. The settlers, all who could be spared,
were planning to participate, leaving men enough at
homes scattered through the country to keep down
fires should the flames escape with a sudden shifting
of the wind.

Five or six hundred men were required to conduct
the great game round-up that would occupy two or
three weeks' time. The Indian's way of stalking
game and driving it into the valley seemed pure
magic to the incredulous white men, but the Indian
himself thought but little of his prowess. He knew
the runways and the habits of the animal life of the

country and haughtily disclaimed making use of an extraordinary sense of smell or intuition. The gun had not changed the habit of centuries of bow-and-arrow tactics; the Indian stalked his game and shot always from close range so that no ammunition need be wasted.

The east side of the Willamette Valley from the Molalla to the Santiam River was the site chosen for the *battue*. This was a section of the country running well back into the foothills, with the river guarding it on the west side. The program was an elaborate one, requiring great skill and obedience to signals in those taking part. A stretch of country almost fifty miles square was surrounded by a cordon of men placed about a quarter of a mile apart, with stations closer together and the most capable men placed in the most dangerous places. The best hunter was master of ceremonies. Until this time Quimmo had filled this important position, but now Sawnik, a sub-chief, had been most carefully drilled by him. The signals had to be rehearsed by the participants until each knew his part. A *battue* managed badly meant no meat in the wigwams and lodges in the winter. It was disastrous to allow the game to break through the line of fire and escape to the mountains. Each hunter took his post the evening before. With the first streaks of daylight the signal was given. A circle of flame inclosed the valley. By skillful firing and backfiring the battle went on, narrowing all the time until the cordon of hunters were often within easy speaking distance, with a solid wall of fire shutting off the escape of the game.

It was a rather hazardous undertaking, especially for the untrained settlers. It took the greatest skill and attention to detail to keep the fire burning yet not allow it to escape control. Sometimes a high wind wrought disaster and even loss of life, but an Indian places very little value on anything that has cost him nothing. Life was his commonest possession, to be gambled at any time.

When the circle of fire became small enough to make hunting a very simple matter, the best hunters went inside and selected the game needed. They were careful not to injure the animals to be left for breeding purposes. With the same attention that a breeder of fine stock would give his herd, the best males, the youngest and most vigorous females, were carefully cut out before the rest were taken. In a sense the Indians had bred up the game until their source of meat was assured. One of their bitterest grievances against the settlers was the wantonness with which they destroyed wild life. Deer, bear, and elk were plentiful and easily taken before the coming of the white men.

The *battue* was to begin the second week in September; the country was as dry as tinder, but the fall rains were due shortly, so that the fire was not likely to get beyond control. Uncle Adzi was all eager impatience to participate in this great hunt. He had heard fabulous stories about the *battue* ever since he started across the plains. John Bainbridge was a little dubious. In his estimation there was too much danger of fire reaching the homesteads, but finally he decided rather reluctantly to go when Dick Skel-

ton told him that he was so overwhelmed with cobbling that he must stay at home, and Siah-hen, for
reasons he did not state, had declared his intention
of remaining home. Of course the mighty hunter,
Pop Simmons, was going. The boys would be home
and, after all, there was slight danger of fire to the
north of Oregon City. The Molalla River, where
the firing was to begin, is fully fifteen miles south
and the prevailing summer winds are from the north-
east.

McDermott had been eagerly awaiting the *battue*.
His plans had slowly matured as he sat through days
of enforced isolation and idleness, with nothing to
divert him but watching the Calkins baby whiling
away his time chewing on a piece of salt pork which
his mother had thoughtfully tied to the hewed-out log
that served him for a cradle. A perfectly safe
amusement—chewing on salt pork tied so he could
not swallow it. But watching the baby's enjoyment
palled on McDermott terribly.

From his tenant he gathered that sentiment against
him was adverse in the settlement. Calkins could
not be blamed for enlarging on the gossip that he had
heard in regard to McDermott. In truth, after the
first burst of indignation at his casting off Lassee,
very little had been said, though most of the men
discussing him when they met agreed that his sort
were not wanted in the country. But Calkins hoped
to keep his position on a good farm by frightening
his landlord into leaving the country altogether. He
had helped him to keep under cover when the cabin
in the mountains had burned, taking elaborate pre-

cautions to keep the fact that he was domiciled in the cabin on the farm from everyone.

McDermott had been unable to gather anything from the two Indians, Klanic and Cartoosh, though they were his most faithful henchmen, promising for a generous consideration to enlist four of their friends in his prospective enterprise.

McDermott's plan was a diabolical one, requiring the most careful plotting, but with the men away on the *battue* he could see very little danger. His anger at John Bainbridge amounted to an obsession through his nursing it for eight long months. His revenge was to be swift and complete, giving into his hands the thing he desired more than anything else, Rose Ann. He had formed the habit of skirting the timber above the Bainbridge cabin to a certain point of vantage where he could watch the comings and goings of the family without the least danger of detection. The woods were almost impenetrable in their wild ruggedness, and a large fir tree crowning the rocky point had a hollow large enough to conceal him perfectly.

The ship that was to take his cargo of liquor lay at anchor in the lower river. Circumstances could not have been more auspicious. Simple enough to have the Indians capture Rose Ann and carry her to the cave where Indians in canoes waited in the river below. With the help of Klanic he would lower the precious cargo by means of a carefully contrived block and tackle, swinging Rose Ann in a rope cradle free of the straight side of the bluff into the canoe waiting below; then he would make his way down to the river on horseback and reach the ship in a canoe under cover of the night. By morning they would have set sail for Australia with all his possessions aboard. Life was wild and free there. He would have a chance to begin all over again, and this time, he swore by all that was good and holy, he would walk the straight and narrow path the rest of his days.

Just how he would win the love of Rose Ann he left for another time. He hoped to win her love. He told himself over and over that his intentions were honorable. He would marry her in the first port they touched, and in the meantime he had arranged for a woman aboard the ship to take her in charge. In fact, he had driven a sharp bargain with Madam Chillicote.

Madam Chillicote was a curious and withal a most interesting woman. She had purchased the cargo of liquor from him at a good price. Her business in life was touching out-of-the-way ports with illicit cargoes on which she was reputed to make enormous profits. McDermott had wondered greatly about Madam Chillicote. She said she was English, but had the look and manner of a Frenchwoman. She was undeniably educated and in spite of her mode of life adhered to the little refinements acquired in an earlier, more gentle day.

Madame had been much amused at what she termed McDermott's "forty-year madness," but had promised to take the girl in charge. She could be very charming when she chose to, and could be depended upon to take excellent care of an innocent young girl. Though her ways might be deep and dark, she maintained rigorous standards for the young. She told him of a lovely young daughter who had been most tenderly nurtured. Her education was now being completed in a French convent. Rose Ann would take on polish and learn the ways of the world by association with Madame Chillicote. McDermott at times even persuaded himself that he was doing the girl a great kindness in taking her out of her uncouth environment and giving her a chance to develop into a real lady.

He would be able to lavish money on his wife. Perhaps, after a time, he would return to the States, where Rose Ann might have the advantages that money would provide there. He thought of her mother, poised and calm and sweet in her maturity, fearless in danger, soft-voiced and gentle, yet firm in her decisions. Rose Ann had the same firm chin and the determined carriage of the head, though in maturity she would far exceed her mother in beauty.

He admitted misgivings about gaining Rose Ann's love at times, but always assured himself. After all, what did a sixteen-year-old girl know of love? She could be swayed to the will of a determined man. He would marry her with her consent or without. She would find herself away from her people, with no other alternative. And, after all, forty was not so old. He would cross bridges when he reached them.

The *battue* began. McDermott arranged the smoke signals with Klanic, who was to manage the abduction. Each day he took his place at the fir tree above the cabin where he could watch. The opportunity to take Rose Ann alone was practically all that stood in the way. Three days dragged away with the Bainbridges remaining close at home.

A dense pall of smoke hung over the whole country; it seemed to Martha that nothing would be left standing, and yet the fire was not close. It rather irked the children to stay in their own dooryard, but Martha was obdurate. She was afraid of fire breaking out in the timber. Lassee came down one day to go nutting. The hazelnuts were just right for picking and there had been a full crop. If not gathered soon the squirrels would have them all. The gently reassured Martha, telling her that it was like this every fall. The Indians had the fire under their control.

There had been a wonderful berry season. Plentiful supplies of blackberries were gathered, some dried on the roof and quantities of preserves stored away in stone jars for the winter, but fruit was scarce and Lassee promised to help gather elderberries. They grew luxuriantly along the streams and made the most delectable pies. There was plenty of flour now that the grist mill had caught up, and pies were a delicacy not to be slighted in a season when fruit was available.

The boys had dallied over their work and must finish their wood-chopping before their father came home. They could not go, but finally Martha decided, rather against her better judgment, to allow the girls to go with Lassee for the afternoon. After all, it was foolish to be so full of fears when there was food that might be gathered for the winter.

With a smile of satisfaction McDermott from his point of vantage watched the three set out. His field glasses followed them until they were lost in the timber. He moved quickly to the open spot that had been agreed upon for signaling and immediately kindled his little fire, covering it with his coat to keep the smoke confined, then releasing it quickly, allowing the tiny column to ascend. At ten-minute intervals he sent up his smoke signal, and in less than half an hour was rewarded by the appearance of Klanic astride his pony.

McDermott quickly gave him directions to follow the nutting party with his companion, and to take the girl as quietly as possible, but to take her in some way; there was no time to lose. He promised to make his preparations by dusk and to meet them a quarter of a mile below the cave. Neither Klanic nor Cartoosh could be prevailed upon to venture nearer than that to what they firmly believed to be the abode of evil spirits.

There were numerous last details demanding attention. He must see that the Indians were waiting below with their canoes. He had taken his block and tackle and the improvised swing for lowering Rose Ann, and hidden them in the woods near by a week before. Klanic and Cartoosh would join their companions in the river below as soon as they had done the little piece of abducting. So far things could not be working out better.

He must go at once to the cabin to get the few things he meant to take with him; they were already tied up in shape to be seized at a moment's notice.

This time he was not furtive about going through the timber.  He went boldly, knowing that there was no danger of detection, or if he was seen it would make no difference.  He would have left the country forever in a few hours.

The cabin was empty.  Calkins had gone on the *battue*, and Mrs. Calkins had spoken in the morning of walking down to the settlement to trade.  He featured her going, the baby on her hip, with the smaller children hanging to her bedraggled skirts.  The cabin, when he entered, was disgustingly untidy.  The baby's well-chewed piece of salt pork still hung by its string to the log cradle.  Mrs. Calkins was what is known as a slack housekeeper.  He hadn't blamed her so much (her clamoring brood of children absorbed her), but he felt a sharp regret at leaving a place that harbored so many tender memories to the mercy of a dirty family with a devastatingly rapid increasing brood of children.

He looked out over what had a few months before been his well-developed farm; it was taking on the same down-at-the-heel look as the cabin.  Not a fruit tree living, scarcely a fence in place.  The desolation smote him like a cruel hand.  He turned back into the cabin and deliberately heaped pitch wood near the walls, setting his fires carefully before he closed the door and mounted his pony. He reasoned that setting fire to the cabin was a happy thought; it would divert the settlers until he made his escape.  In all probability the fire would spread through the stubble of the grain fields and burn wildly in the timber, but his mood suddenly turned savage.  He did not care:

he would leave no trace of his farm behind him. If
the settlers had to fight fire to save their homesteads,
still he did not care. The Bainbridge cabin might
burn; 'twould be part of his revenge.

Klanic rather relished the task in hand, especially
as he was to have a full five gallons of *lum* (whisky)
if he succeeded in his enterprise. He trailed the girls
noiselessly all the afternoon, waiting until they separated a little before making his attack. Carrying
off a small white squaw did not trouble him in the
least. Toward the middle of the afternoon the hazelnuts were harder to find. Unconsciously Rose Ann
had worked her way farther up the hill, while Lassee
and Esther Amelia had gone down. It lacked an
hour of sundown before Rose Ann realized that she
was out of earshot of her companions. She started to
cup her hands to give the Indian call that reverber-
ated through the timber, carrying for a long distance, but she was seized by a horridly grinning
Indian and before she could make an outcry a gag
of buckskin was securely in place over her mouth
and her arms pinioned to her sides with leather
thongs. Klanic unceremoniously carried her a short
distance to where his horse stood with his bridle rein
hanging.

A protesting squaw meant nothing to Klanic. He
tied the terrified girl securely to the horse with her
head on his flanks and her feet drawn down under
his belly and tied together with thongs, an entirely
safe way to convey a squaw who might prove unruly.
His packing finished to his satisfaction, he drew the
bridle rein over his arm and started off through the

timber at a brisk trot, grinning widely in anticipation of the promised reward.

He skirted the hill, making a wide détour around the Simmons cabin—it would not do to risk being seen with such a burden—and at last reached the spot McDermott had agreed upon. McDermott, watching, could scarcely conceal his elation as they came up the hill. He hastily cut the thongs and lifted Rose Ann off the horse, chafing her wrist where harsh red lines showed. Rose Ann, when her arms were free, fought like an incensed tigress, until, half regretfully, he bound her again and carried her to the mouth of the cave. He tied her securely to a stick of timber while he busied himself in fastening his block and tackle and making his improvised cradle secure. There was no daylight to lose, and as soon as darkness settled in the boats would be ready below.

Lassee filled her basket with nuts and another with great panicles of blue elderberries and had helped Esther Amelia with her little basket before she noticed the absence of Rose Ann. She gave the shrill Indian call, repeating it time after time. When she received no answer she made her way in no great haste up to the spot where they had left their other baskets. They had not been disturbed. She called again and again. Startled to hear no answering halloo, she looked about in the grass until she found Rose Ann's trail up the hill marked by trodden grass and bent-down hazel and elderberry bushes. Once she paused and sniffed the air—the fire was closer, the smoke was lower and smelled fresher. There was fire in the timber not more than a mile or two away.

Consternation struck her as she noticed fresh flakes of smut floating in the sultry air. Esther Amelia felt something amiss and began to cry as she trudged along behind Lassee.

She came to the spot where Rose Ann's overturned basket of hazelnuts and trampled dry grass showed evidence of some sort of a struggle. Her slatted sunbonnet, on the ground, confirmed her suspicions. Rose Ann had met with disaster. Rose Ann was gone and some one had carried her off by force.

She got down on her knees and looked for the trail. It was an Indian who had done the work; a white man would have left a clearer trail. Moccasined feet were difficult to track. She found the general direction by the bent grasses, and came to the edge of the timber where a horse had stood. Here were fresh evidences of a struggle. The soft earth bore plain evidence of hurrying feet incased in moccasins. She followed the horse's tracks up through the timber until she was certain of their destination. Suddenly it dawned on her who the Indian was. Klanic, of course. This was his reason for not attending the *battue*. She had wondered mildly when Siah-hen had spoken of seeing him as he passed near the McDermott place the day before.

They were only half a mile above the Simmons cabin. She told the trembling Esther Amelia to go down there and tell Aunt Morning Ann to take her home and to tell her mother what had happened, and that there was fire not so very far away and if it came closer to set the stubble around the cabin afire and beat it out near the buildings with wet sacks, to make a back fire.

She turned then and ran through the dusk to her cabin. It was fully dark when she fell over the threshold. She was out of breath from running; her face was scratched and bleeding from her headlong flight over the rocks and through the underbrush. Her blue cotton dress was torn.

"Rose Ann!" she panted. "McDermott has taken Rose Ann! I'm sure she's in the buzzard's cave!"

Dick sprang to take the gun off the deer antlers over the fireplace, and Siah-hen, without a word, seized his hunting-knife and fastened it in the sheath in his belt as he ran. Lassee followed, too breathless to explain even if there had been time. All Dick needed to know was that Rose Ann was in danger. Siah-hen had been on the lookout for developments for some time. He knew that McDermott was planning to leave. Quimmo, outraged at being obliged to remain away from the *battue*, was watching his every move and had told him so.

The three stumbled through the darkness of the timber. Lassee fell and Siah-hen pulled her quickly to her feet, steadying her with a protecting arm. Lassee, strong and agile, was almost ready to drop with fatigue. Not a ray of light penetrated the timber, so that traveling was entirely by unerring Indian instinct. To Dick it seemed an interminable journey with the very life of Rose Ann at stake and every moment precious.

McDermott worked desperately securing the ropes to the limb of a large overhanging maple so that they

could swing free from the bluff. He paused and listened intently, thinking sure he heard a burst of derisive laughter somewhere above, then cursed himself
for his nervousness. This living with Quimmo always
at his elbow, yet never being able to lay hands upon
him, would break any man's nerve, he told himself.
As the evening became chilly he stopped to speak reassuringly to Rose Ann, debating whether he dared
take the gag from her mouth; but, fearing an outcry, decided against it. He wrapped his coat about
her and carried her inside the cave, partly for her
comfort, but more to keep her angry accusing eyes
from boring into his back as he worked.

His task finished, he sat in the darkness, chafing at
the delay of the Indians with his canoes. He esti-
mated that it would take a good three hours of hard
work to lower the casks. He wished he had induced
Klanic or Cartoosh to come to the cave to help him,
but knew that that would have been futile. No
Indian in his right mind would go near the cave,
especially after dark.

At last his straining ears caught the sound of oars
in the river below and he dimly made out the canoes.
He called to them softly and lighted a candle to go
inside the pitch darkness of the cave. He had a
dozen candles in his pockets ready to set in place
inside, so that he could see to work. With a frenzied
eagerness he began dropping candle grease on the
ledges of rock to set his lights to the best advantage.

He looked pityingly at Rose Ann, telling her that
nothing would harm her. The girl's face was ashy
pale in the candle-light. He ventured to loosen the

gag a little, but again she fought and struggled to
loose her arms from the stick of timber to which he
had bound her. There was no use reasoning with
her. He turned quickly to work, rolling away the
rock from the inner recess where the cache of liquor
was stored. He held the candle aloft. Yes, it was all
there, just as he had left it early in the spring. No
one could possibly discover such a hiding-place.

He set a candle inside where it would give him the
best light, and put his weight against the first cask
to roll it out. The response almost threw him off
his feet. The cask was empty. A look of blank surprise overspread his face, changing to consternation
as he hastily lifted cask after cask. They were all
empty. He made sure of it, then went to the ledge,
holding the brown bottles. He jerked a candle from
its mooring of grease and held it up to inspect them.
They, too, were empty!

He turned weakly away, but strength came in a
mighty surge of insane anger. "Quimmo!" he
shouted as, candle in hand, he turned to leave the
recess. A derisive peal of laughter answered him.
Quimmo had entered the recess when he turned his
back to inspect the bottles, and stood speculatively
hefting the casks while he shook with laughter at
McDermott's chagrin.

But McDermott, white with rage, made his way
out. "*Mi-ka mam-ook mam-a-loose,* [I'll kill you]!"
he shouted, making for the gun that he had left outside.

"*Kul-tus wa-wa, Wa-ke al-ta, Mi-ka tsee-pee po-
lak-ly* [Idle talk. Not now. You miss the mark in

the darkness]," laughed his tormentor, enjoying the situation immensely.

Candle in hand, its feeble flame blowing in the breeze, McDermott made for the ledge, to come face to face with Siah-hen, who had picked up the gun and was fingering it knowingly. All reason left McDermott when he saw he was trapped. At the voices of the three outside, Quimmo peered out of the entrance of the cave with a candle he had taken from the ledge in his hand. Dick dashed past him into the cave in agonized search for Rose Ann, as Quimmo, still grinning, emerged and stood facing McDermott nonchalantly, his coolness prodding his ancient enemy's anger beyond endurance.

McDermott charged like an angry bull, but Quimmo stood his ground with his arms folded across his broad chest, the smile of contempt still on his pock-mark face. As McDermott struck wildly at him he tripped him with a dexterous foot. He gained his feet unevenly and Quimmo waited for him to charge again; but McDermott in the uncertain light missed his footing and fell outside the glow from the candle-lighted cave. The ledge narrowed perilously there, and a huge rock gave way with his weight. Too late McDermott grasped at the limb of a tree, but it broke with his impact. He followed the rock down the sheer hundred feet to the Clackamas below.

The three Indians peered over the edge in the darkness as his body struck the water.

"*Ni-ka me-sah-chee til-a-kum klat-a-wa whim. Hyah hi-yu hy-as keel-al-ly.* [My enemy fell. A

great medicine-man indeed]." Quimmo turned with
an indifferent shrug of his shoulders.

Dick saw Rose Ann and rushed to her. With his
jack-knife he cut the buckskin thongs that bound
her to the piece of timber and took the gag from her
mouth. Her inert head fell on his shoulder as he
lifted her in his arms. For the first time in her
healthy young life Rose Ann had fainted from fatigue and terror.

Dick groaned. He was sure she was dead. But
the Indians entered the cave just then and Siah-hen
felt cautiously for her heart.

"Take her out in the air," he commanded Dick,
and together they carried her through the narrow
aperture. Lassee took up a candle and hurried back
into the inner recess, emerging in a few minutes with
a pint bottle of whisky. She had unearthed the secret
store that was hoarded to save lives. They poured
the whisky, a few drops at a time, down Rose Ann's
throat, and rubbed her cold hands and feet. Quimmo
brought water in an empty bottle from the spring
close by. They bathed her head, and after a time
Rose Ann opened her eyes.

"It's Dick, Rose Ann. You're safe. McDermott's
gone. We've come to take you home." But Rose
Ann only buried her face in Dick's shoulder as he
swept her into his eager arms. He kissed her drawn,
tear-stained little face and she did not protest or
draw away, but her arms crept tightly around his
neck and she kissed him in return.

"Dick! Dick!" she sobbed. "I was so frightened.

I tried to call you, but I couldn't. The Indian tied something tight over my mouth."

But Dick had retaken the trembling Rose Ann to his heart. He felt a great shaken power. Rose Ann was his; after all the months of anxiety, he knew for a certainty that she loved him. Hadn't she tried to call him in her terror?" He kissed the tears from her eyes, and then through the mist of tears in his own caught sight of a little curl on her temple. He had always wanted to kiss that little curl when they had gone back and forth to school, but had never so much as dared lay a reverent finger on it; now he would. Awkwardly he smoothed back her tangled hair, muttering incoherent nothings, to soothe Rose Ann back to composure.

But Rose Ann only trembled and clung tightly to him, until at last Siah-hen warned him that they had better make their way down the trail. Rose Ann's mother would be frantic with anxiety, and the whole sky to the west was alight with fire in the timber.

They took the candles to light them through the timber. It was light as day in the open spaces. Dick waved Siah-hen and Lassee away and carried Rose Ann down the steepest part of the trail, putting her gently on her feet where the slope was easy.

Siah-hen scanned the heavens anxiously. "The fire is down near McDermott's place. If it gets into the underbrush along the creek it may take the Bainbridge cabin, or even make a clean sweep of everything clear back to the mountains. We'd better begin backfiring," he said to Quimmo, as the three, without a word, turned off down the trail leading to the McDermott place. Lassee, with lagging feet, insisted on helping with the fire-fighting. She could watch a backfire until Dick took Rose Ann to her mother.

Martha Bainbridge sat with her worn Bible on her knee, reading to Aunt Morning Ann and Esther Amelia. She had sent the boys out to watch the direction the fire was taking, so that if there was immediate danger they could burn off the stubble fields. The boys had filled barrels with water and placed sacks beside them so as to be in readiness to beat out fire should it leap into the stubble field, as timber fires have a treacherous way of doing.

She could only wait and hope and pray for Rose Ann until Lassee or Dick or Siah-hen came with news of her. Aunt Morning Ann tried to offer comfort, but there was nothing to say and nothing to do but wait.

"Read hit ag'in, Marthie, about the Lord a-rescuin' folks," she begged.

And Martha read slowly again the Thirty-seventh Psalm—"And the Lord helpeth them, and rescueth them from the wicked, and saveth them, because they have taken refuge in him."

Dick with a transfigured face put Rose Ann in her mother's arms. Not waiting for her expressions of gratitude, he strode off alone. He must hurry down to help fight the fire, but first he could be alone a few moments with his great joy. Rose Ann was safe and she loved him. What more could a mortal man ask?

# CHAPTER XX

INDIAN summer is the most delightful season of the year in Oregon. The first heavy fall rain comes early in September and clears the air of smoke and washes it sweet and clean of the dust of the dry season.

The growing season had been a strenuous one for the Bainbridge family. The crops had flourished almost beyond belief. Uncle Adzi had made crude harvesting implements. He fashioned a creditable pitchfork from a straight oak sapling by pegging on two gently curving tines to supplement the extension of the handle that served as the middle tine. John had bought a scythe in Vancouver and Uncle Adzi had made a cradle and a flail.

Uncle Adzi could hardly wait to harvest the first crop of wheat. He examined the heads every day from the time they began to show. "I allus 'lowed I could perdict the number o' bushels t' the acre when the wheat war in the milk, but this here stand o' wheat plumb beats my time." Every head bore its full number of plump kernels.

The first crop from the virgin land was like the fulfillment of a Divine promise. In awe the Bainbridges garnered in their first harvest, that neither drought nor pest had molested. The new granary of squared logs was filled to bursting.

"We'll git our grist to mill airly, and there'll be

flour fer bread this winter. We got ter hev light bread an' cream biscuits fer them parsarves Marthie's made. We got a bouncin' crap o' taters, too," he exulted. "There'll be wheat an' taters ter sell ter the emigrants—they be a comin' a'ready; we'll save plenty fer our own use, though. No more livin' on b'iled wheat an' salmon. The grist mill is done ketched up, an' flour ahead, an' another mill in buildin', so there'll allus be flour aplenty arter this." Uncle Adzi fairly glowed as he took stock during the Indian-summer days.

"By another year we'll have a frame house with bedchambers upstairs and a parlor for Martha and Esther Amelia," John paused thoughtfully. "Dick Skelton asked me for Rose Ann last week." He smiled to himself. "The boy's been two or three weeks screwing up his courage—seemed to be afraid I wouldn't let him have her."

Uncle Adzi waxed indignant. "I s'pose ye skeered him, John Bainbridge. I seen you when you didn't have sech a mighty amount o' courage. Hit seems lak jist a few weeks sence ye asked me fer Marthie. She warn't a day older'n Rose Ann, nuther, an' yore prospec's warn't so bright as Dick's, not by a long shot. Dick'll be a lawyer an' one thet we'll be proud of one o' these days. The schoolmaster tole me hisself that he had studied clear through thet blue Iowa law book, an' war a-waitin' fer a shipment o' law books this fall."

"I gave them my blessing," reassured John. "They're nothing but 'trundle-bed trash,' but a boy can't get along in a new country without a wife.

Dick's thrifty and forehanded. He's done well with his cobbling and he had a good crop. Of course," he added in strict justice, "Siah-hen really put the boy on his feet. Dick owes that Indian debts he'll never forget."

Uncle Adzi looked out over the blackened stubble just beginning to show a tinge of green from the fall rains. "Yes," he said meditatively, "we-all owe another Injun a debt we didn't ought ter fergit. Like as not we will, though. Ye mind you an' me traipsed off ter a *battue* this fall an' left our wimmen folks, an' if Quimmo hadn't been a master hand at managin' fire in the timber, our buildin's wouldn't be standin'. An' him savin' 'em on account o' Marthie a-being so kind ter his people, so Siah-hen says."

"Yes," agreed John. "He called her the *toke-tee ten-as klooch-man* [pretty little woman]."

"Wal," Uncle Adzi said fervently, "he kin come an' go as he pleases now. We seen ter thet, anyway. Us whites a-wantin' ter try a Injun because a man didn't have sense enough ter sit tight in a boat a-shootin' the rapids o' the Columbia!"

"McDermott was at the bottom of that, though. Never could find out who put up that money until after he died," said John. "They say at the settlement the money went into the state treasury."

"I won't speak ill o' the dead—that is, no more'n I kin help—but it's a good job the kentry's shet o' his kind." Uncle Adzi's anger choked him as it always did when McDermott's name was mentioned.

"Let's forget him," John said slowly, the red mounting to his temples.

But Uncle Adzi rambled on. "D'you know, John," he mused, "Injuns in their nateral state don't lie. White men taught 'em all they know o' hit. They steal some, I'll admit, but when one Injun has food no other Injun is hungry. I 'low God, a-lookin' down on all his children, thinks more o' the Injuns than he does o' most o' us whites. We measure Injuns by the smell o' 'em an' their savage ways, but God kin see underneath."

"I aim to treat them justly," said John. "They know their friends."

It seemed to the anxious women that the ships from Boston would never reach the Oregon ports. But late in August the glad tidings came that the *Chenamus* from Boston was in the lower river. But it was September before the cargo reached Oregon City. Captain Couch had anticipated women's needs in a manner much more thorough than they had dared hope. There was wonderful pink calico at one dollar a yard, an outrageous price, but well worth the money, the general conclusion was. There was plenty of heavy unbleached muslin for sheets and the various household uses, and drilling both blue and brown for summer clothing. Best of all, he had not forgotten needles and pins. No one but a woman knows how inconvenient it is to be obliged to take up a puncheon floor and search until a missing needle is found, or to break one of the two needles in the cushion when none can be bought for a year or so.

But the coming of the good ship *Chenamus* marked the new epoch in the annals of Oregon. The siege which remoteness had put upon womankind was lifted.

And joy of joys! There was a small consignment of glass windowpanes in the cargo. True to his promise that Martha should have the first glass that came in, John Bainbridge proudly bore home enough for four small windows, and secured them in real sashes that the Island Milling Company made. Martha polished hers until they sparkled in the fall sunlight, transforming the dark little cabin. She got out her one linen sheet and measured it carefully. By doing without the ruffles she had planned and piecing one a little—it would scarcely show—she could manage four curtains instead of two. Rose Ann should begin her life with Dick in a cabin graced with snowy curtains and the things that curtains stood for. And woe be to Rose Ann if those tiny windowpanes were not always sparkling and the curtains snowy clean and her puncheon floor scoured every other day with sand and cold water.

Rose Ann, shy and blushing, was swiftly hemming narrow ruffles of lovely pink calico with precise little stitches set with a fine needle and No. 60 thread. Pink calico is the very last word for wedding dresses; even in the States calico was not thought of lightly. It seemed as if Captain Couch must have had Oregon brides in mind when he stocked his ship. There were a few most beautiful little straw poke bonnets—straw woven in a lacy pattern-faced back with soft pink silk and adorned with a wreath of tiny pink rosebuds.

Martha caught her breath when she first saw those bonnets. How sweet Rose Ann would look in her

pink calico wedding dress and her little black slippers
from the *Chenamus* and one of those poke bonnets.
But the price fairly overwhelmed her—two dollars
and fifty cents.

John laughed and said he guessed they could manage this once. They didn't have a wedding every
day, and Rose Ann had no dower to speak of. Her
feather pillows and sheets and coverlids would come
to her by littles. By all means she should have the
bonnet.

Dick was all impatience. For the life of him he
couldn't see why it took so long to make a wedding
dress. It was October before the wedding day came,
but no bridegroom ever carried a more winsome bride
across his threshold than Dick Skelton. Dick knew
it, and all the neighbors said so. And of course pink
calico and little straw bonnets with wreathes of pink
roses around the crown set off the beauty of any
winsome bride.

In the last glowing days before rain would set in
for the winter John and Uncle Adzi sat on the
puncheon bench by the cabin door. It was the hour
of peace, the time for looking down lanes that led
into time to come. Uncle Adzi drove a stray chicken
that should have been on the roost—the sun was going down—out of Martha's flower bed with a just
anger at the perverse ways of chickens.

But his mood changed abruptly as he speculated.
"Marthie's sure a master hand with hens," he gloated.
"I counted fifty pullets an' nigh onter seventy-five
young roosters, from thet dozen hens you fotched,
John. We're plumb outer debt, with a fine crap ter

sell ter the newcomers. We sort o' blazed the trail for 'em. The settlement is purty nigh full o' kivered wagons thet came clar through. The way's open now. I 'low afore many years we'll be a thrivin' community, an' sellin' our craps ter the ports in Chiny, or mebbe Rhussia."

"Once women reach the frontier, it thrives and prospers," said John.

"Arter all's said an' done, with men a-braggin' an' sech, hit's Marthie an' her kind thet make a kentry. Men livin' alone air no better'n Injuns, but bring wimmen onto a frontier an' see whut happens. Wimmen air quare critters. Marthie'll work her fingers ter the bone an' do 'ithout the nedcessities o' life, but a scrubbed floor an' clean curtains an' a rockin'-cheer she must have. She'll scour the young-uns an' make 'em wash thar han's an' faces afore meals, an' l'arn 'em table manners an' verses o' Scripture, no matter whut happens ner how she situated." Uncle Adzi rambled on and on.

"Yes," said John, busy with his own thoughts.

"Yes, jist bring wimmen ter a frontier," concluded Uncle Adzi "an' in a few years hit hain't a frontier no more. Hit's a peaceful, law-abidin' community with schools an' churches, an' men a-actin' decent an' a-pervidin' fer their families. Men brag aroun' a power about subduin' o' a frontier, but, arter all, hit's the Marthies an' the Aunt Mornin' Anns an' the Sister Wallers thet actually do the subduin'."

### THE END

DATE D